Golden City on Fire

Golden City on Fire

prejudice as potent as a fire-storm
San Francisco 1906

by

Sherman Smith

Sherman Smith

Golden City on Fire

This is a work of fiction as are all of the characters whose lives are unraveled by the historical events that occurred on the first day of the great Earthquake that devastated the fabled golden city of San Francisco.

My work would not be complete without thanking my editor Randi Hilleso and my writing mentor Mr. Nibs.

CHAPTER 1

THE NIGHT, UNUSUALLY WARM FOR MID-APRIL, PROMISED A brilliant spring day once the sun rose. However, the night itself gave Cornelius cause for an uneasy sense of foreboding. The deep moan of a distant fog horn seemed out of place. The night sky, while laden with twinkling stars, did not stir his imagination. The darkness between each tiny distant light seemingly cold and impenetrable. The shadows around him seemed darker, deeper, and more troubling as foul insidious vapors drifted around his feet. The ground fog swirled no higher than his knees as it snaked out from the drains and grates that cover the cities sewers, and the darker secrets lost beneath its streets. He coughed, the fog affecting the taste of the night in an unsavory manner. It wasn't the eerie vapor that disturbed him. His nerves were on edge because his partner and best friend Sergeant Choice Pickens was down in the Shanghai tunnels. Cornelius knew that whatever was about to happen down there would, and there was nothing he can do to change it.

All he could do now was wait and see how it turned out. Regardless, he couldn't shake the feeling that trouble was close, whether it is down with Choice or trouble was stalking him through the streets and alleys of the Barbary Coast, where trouble is a permanent resident. One thing Cornelius does know is that the Barbary does not reveal its secrets readily - to uncover her many ugly truths is his job. No sixth sense, no cop's intuition can prepare him for what is about to happen . . . that the world is about to be turned upside-down in ways he could never imagine.

San Francisco Police Inspector Cornelius McCann chomps down on the end of his cigar as he walks away from the edge of a darkened alley to stand beneath the faintly reassuring flickering glow of a gas street light. His eyes take in the street, every movement, shadow, window, and darkened doorway. He doesn't look up, because he senses that she is there peering down at him from her second floor window. He first had caught a glance of her a week or so ago, during the day when the early morning light had been just right, and he had marveled, *What is a woman of her beauty, her gentility, doing living in this godforsaken neighborhood.* As he felt her looking down, he couldn't help but smile as the same question crossed his mind a second time.

Her window is open letting in a light breeze. Though it is a reasonably warm night, Lavinia Losekoor shivers as she feels a chill, a sudden unnatural deep winter hoarfrost touching her heart. The chill does not come from the night, but from somewhere beyond. Her breath catches with the certain realization that her life is about to change, her sanctuary is about to melt away as easily as the final stub of a bee's wax candle flickers out.

Her father, a Dutch brewmaster, had brought her to America just a year prior, and they had taken an apartment close to the brewery where he had been hired. The apartment was too close to the saloons, whorehouses, and beer halls dependent on his product. Lavinia rarely ventured out onto the streets without her father close at hand. The rest of their family had been taken by influenza and their home had become too sad a place for her father to remain. She loved her father and came to America leaving everything and everyone she knew behind. Now she had become a recluse, at age twenty-six, almost an old maid. He had promised with a father's love that they would move into a real home in a respectable neighborhood as soon as he could save the money. She dreamed of that day, and it was that dream that gave her strength and solace. That dream was bitterly dashed away the night her father had not come home. The night he had disappeared.

Now two months later, with little hope of ever seeing her father again, the money all but gone, without a friend to help her, she is waiting for the sun to rise on the morning when she is to be cast out into the wicked streets of San Francisco - homeless. It is not this terrifying future that chills her; it is something larger, more imminent, a dark massive storm just off the horizon.

Lavinia's fingers dig tight into the curtain as she watches Inspector Cornelius McCann from her window. She senses that it is this man, this stranger, who stands in the street light just below her window that has somehow been sent to save her. She wants to open the window a little wider and cry out a warning, but she cannot find the words to describe what her heart knows to be true, that something wicked and ugly is waiting just this side of dawn's early morning light. She watches as he stands motionless in the night, listening to the sounds of the city, guarding her from harm. They have never met, but she knows who he is, his name and pictures often in the papers. Inspector Cornelius McCann is a police officer, her sentry, who many nights stands exactly where he stands now, seemingly fearless, always aware of the dark forces that shape the infamy of the Barbary Coast - where Old Scamp, the Prince of Darkness, has a vacation home in one of the most beautiful and eclectic cities in the world.

She sees Cornelius as a handsome man of medium height, with short cropped sandy-blond hair, a face perhaps too weathered for a man in his early thirties. He has intense eyes and she wonders what color they might be. He carries with him an air of honest character, authority, and threat, depending on which side of the law one might be on. He makes her feel warm and safe in a world where otherwise she does not. So far, she has been afraid to speak with him, or to be seen, because he might turn away, dashing her dreams forever. A girl can't lose too many dreams and survive.

For a brief moment, Cornelius thought he heard a woman's voice, an angel whispering just to him. He stops, slowly takes the cigar from his mouth, checks his coat pocket for a match as he turns. The street is empty. He slowly brings his eyes up towards her window, only to see the curtain slide closed. He listens, wondering if it had been her. While the curtain is drawn, the window is open. No, it could not have been her, it had to have been his imagination - or had it? "Yes, you are pleasing to me," he said in a low voice. "But . . . who the hell are you?" This time he catches himself chuckling as he wonders if she's married. He chuckled because he has always considered himself to not be the marrying kind.

The street appeared to be empty, unusual for this time of the night. The music and drunken noises from the saloons is white noise to his ears as a distant fog horn's moan snakes its way through the night, a beautiful, if not haughty siren found in legends seemingly inviting him to a dance. The fog swirls low to the ground, afraid to venture any closer to the gas street light that flickers above. The whiskers of a rat probes its edge then scurries away as Cornelius glances one last time at her window and then moves on.

CHAPTER 2

THE TUNNELS BENEATH THE BARBARY AND CHINATOWN ARE tight and too small for most men to walk upright. Choice Pickens, who would never admit to suffer from minor claustrophobia, found it hard to breathe as he crouched behind Johansen, the big Swede, whose shoulder width pressed up against both sides of the tunnel. In all, there are seven police officers in the cramped narrow tunnels.

The weak light from their candles intensifies the closeness within the tunnels. Choice holds his short stub of a candle which momentarily lights up his face. One turquoise, the other copper, it is his eyes that distinguish him from most other men. There are scars on his left cheek and neck from when he had pimples as a teen, otherwise there is nothing remarkable about the man other than the eyes - the turquoise iris has unusual brilliance.

The ooze beneath their shoes is slippery, making it hard to stay on their feet. Gag reflexes are close in each man's throat as the noxious cloying fog that drifts around them seems to thicken with each long minute. The air is cloying, hot, and stale. Pickens had been in the tunnels eight times before, three with these same men from the Chinatown Squad. This is the first time he felt the stomach churning apprehension that he does now. The tunnels stink of dank earth, rancid Chinese cabbage, wet rats . . . which scurry about seemingly unafraid of their human presence . . . rotting seaweed, pier mussels, alcoholic sweat, fear and corruption. The Shanghai tunnels are, under the best of circumstances, black forbidding conduits to either hell on earth or that bleaker purgatory feared below. Each time Choice had come down he had sworn that he would never do it again. It is only the greater fear of being branded a coward that keeps him from turning tail and running towards fresh air and the brighter night outside.

Frank Darcy, the lead man, holds up his right hand signaling that it is almost time.

Choice shifts his weight in the slippery mud and wonders if he should pull seniority and take command. Darcy is known as "Half- Ass Darcy" for a reason. He is irresponsible, untrustworthy, and lazy. Choice has never liked Darcy and felt uncomfortable playing second to him down here. Men's lives are at stake and he does not respect Darcy as a human being nor as a cop. In the sewers and tunnels, or up on the streets, Frank Darcy is a crooked cop, and a bungling fool, not to be trusted with a simple bowl of chicken soup. That Darcy is the lead man down here in the tunnels only shows how close to the rats he truly has come.

Experience had taught them that torches give off too much smoke and so now each officer holds a single small candle. The air is bad, rats unusually aggressive, the dark bleaker than anything they have experienced before. The place they have chosen to set their trap for the shanghaiers, known as crimps, is the spot where multiple tunnels come together, three leading off to the waterfront.

Sergeant Pickens smells the sour sweat of the officer closest to him. "Easy Lads," he whispers barely loud enough to be heard, "surprise is on our side. We'll take out these bastards, save a few fools from fates they don't deserve, and be home to mama before she can pull the pies out of the oven." A flicker of light can now be seen down one of the tunnels. "Easy." Each man puts out his candle, stilling his breath, as they listen and wait. Now they can hear voices, quick, high pitched, and sing-song.

Caught in their own candle's flickering they can see that they are Chinese.

"Damn it." One of the officers swears. "Anyone got a match," asks another. "Damn it's dark."

A match is struck.

"Oh shit!"

What came from behind the officer's backs was sudden, violent, and unexpected. The crimps had set their own trap, turning the tables on the cops with their own surprise. A stunning blow to the back of his head dropped Sergeant Pickens wordlessly into the mud and into a spinning darkness that far surpasses the gloom of the stinking passages. Nearby an officer cries out, his voice a sudden death gurgle, the last sound Pickens hears. None of the officer's had seen Frank Darcy step deftly into a side tunnel the moment they were hit.

As far as Darcy was concerned, his fellow officers were now whale bait and he was going to leave San Francisco on his own two feet with a pile of money in his pocket. Boss Ruef paid well when he needed to, and Darcy had asked for a bundle. He had been told that Scout would pay him then and there, when the deed was done. "Scout?" he didn't bother to whisper as he held out his hand to a shadowy figure who waited for him in the murky tunnel. "Scout?"

It wasn't Scout he realized as the dim light went black.

CHAPTER 3

UNAWARE OF THE TRAP CHOICE PICKENS AND THE OTHER officers had fallen for Cornelius continued to walk. He needed to be seen, to draw attention to himself. His gut tells him that something is very wrong . . . but what? This is the Barbary, one of the wickedest neighborhoods in the civilized world, and it is not civilized. He walked past *The Living Flea*, a notorious Barbary Coast bar, for the second time, its music and raucous laughter blasting out onto the street. At five foot six, slender build, age 35, Cornelius is not on first impression intimidating, which sometimes gives cause for someone to underestimate him. His eyes, sky blue, are quick and curious, hinting of an underlying sense of humor. Outside of a slight well-manicured mustache, his face is clean shaven, making him appear much younger than his years.

He walks past three blocks of dance halls and whorehouses that extend from the foot of Telegraph Hill to the shoreline along Pacific Street and Broadway. The Barbary Coast, Sodom and Gomorra, where anything, any body, can be had for a price. He knows each of these sin palaces as well as he knows his own shortcomings. Cornelius is a San Francisco cop, Inspector First Grade, Vice and Corruption, and perhaps the only ranking officer on the force who isn't on the take.

He reached into a pocket searching for a match, and found none. He looks around seeing numerous men smoking but opts not to ask anyone for a light, at least not in this neighborhood. The cigar he clinches tight, unlit, between his teeth as he eyes each doorway and alleyway he passes looking for anyone to look back the wrong way. Tonight he is looking for trouble. His partner, Sergeant Choice Pickens, working with the Chinatown Squad, had gone into the shanghai tunnels just south of the waterfront looking to bust a few crimps' heads and free a few involuntary deck hands before they are rowed out to the awaiting ships - shanghaied. It hadn't seemed right from the get-go. The precinct captain had appointed half-ass Darcy as the squad leader. That was mistake number one. What would be mistake number two? The saloon, gambling hall, bordello, and long-shoremen hotel owners who work with the crimps all know Cornelius, so his being seen prowling around the streets might just make the sin merchants nervous and draw attention away from Choice Pickens and the others.

Cornelius passed the Dew Drop Inn, Opera Comique, and Canterbury Hall, which specializes in erotica of the highest order. Through the open doors and smoke stained windows he can see the working class men and the fancy dans in their evening coats and bowler hats. He watched as they staggered from one door to another, all this glorious sin provided for their personal enter-tainment. *There's one,* he thought, as he spotted a dandy stumble out of a bar with that look they all have when they had been given some laudanum and directions to a place where they could delve into their greatest perverted desires.

He observed a crimp rise from a window table at the Ye Olde Whore House across the street. A bartender had given the crimp a nod, letting him know that this dandy was about to become a deckhand on a fowl smelling whaler. A moment later the crimp followed the dandy out into the street.

The music from the steam pianos, gramophones, and orchestras drowned out Cornelius's thoughts as he followed the crimp from a respectful distance. Fog horns moaned as the now thick ground fog swirled low against the street. Near Chinatown, the dandy, fool that he is, turns down Dead Man's Alley where a secret network of tunnels run to Murder Point and Bull Run, through which people as well as booty are smuggled. This is where the dandy has been told by a friendly bartender that he could find the debauchery or drug that he is seeking. The crimp stops at the edge of the alley and gives a short three note whistle which is answered with a low single note reply. Cornelius could almost hear the thump as the dandy is dropped by a sharp blow to the back of the head. A second crimp steps out into the darkened alley to lend a hand as the now unconscious dandy is dropped into one of the tunnels, shanghaied, to replace some other poor wretch on a scurvy crew of a whaling or cargo ship. There was little hope that he will ever return to the golden shores of San Francisco.

Cornelius put the cigar, chewed end up, in his breast coat pocket, pulls out his service revolver, cocks it, as he prepares to step into the alley.

A hand touches his shoulder.

Cornelius's eyes narrow, highlighting his well-defined crows feet that add character to his face, as he pivots a quick step to the side, turns, prepared to defend himself from a sudden knife attack, and if necessary shoot to kill without warning.

The officer that had come up behind him should have known better. Cornelius' gun is now pointed an inch from his heart causing it to skip more than a beat.

"Jesus . . . August! I just about blew a hole through your heart. If you had any . . ." Cornelius eased the pressure off the trigger as he lowered the .38 Long Colt service revolver. August Freeman is an experienced beat cop. If Cornelius ever needed to replace

Pickens as his partner, his first choice would be Freeman. Cornelius kept the gun in hand and to his side as he looked past Freeman to see if they had any other unwanted company. "Stupid mistakes like that usually don't get a second chance, August. You of all people ought to know that."

August nodded. Coming up behind Cornelius like that had been stupid, and he knew that he was lucky to still be alive.

August was a stocky character with legs too short that made him comical to watch when he walked. He had a personable smile which came out warm and friendly beneath his coal black hair with mutton-chops that were a poor choice in hairstyle. "As long as you are here August, I wouldn't mind a little company." He nodded towards a dark shadow down the alley where a trap door to a tunnel was known to exist as he holstered his gun. "Odds are that we'll find nothing more than a few wharf rats down there. Choice and a few of the Chinatown boys are down there right now working the tunnels - we won't be going in there tonight, so you can relax." He took the cigar out of his pocket and held it up. "Match?"

August searched his shirt pocket then shakes his head that he had none.

"Figures."

The look in August's blood-shot eyes caused Cornelius' blood to suddenly run cold. "What, bad news?"

"The Captain sent me down to find you"

That alone was bad news. The Precinct Captain and Inspector McCann could not stand to be in the same room together. "Go on."

"Captain Palmer said that you are wanted at the District

Attorney's Office soon as you can get there . . . if not sooner." A metal trash can lid clanged and rattled as a cat raged at something back in the darkness of Dead Man's Alley. August showed little curiosity, though the hair on the back of his neck tingled. "The Captain didn't say why, just to get your ass over there." The low ground fog wrapped around their feet, slowly rising, bringing with it an unpleasant whiff of corrupt earth and clogged sewers. "Are you and the D.A. on speaking terms these days?" August asked as he nervously eyed the shadows around them, the alleys and dark entryways around them seeming more threatening the longer they stand there. "It's not a good night Cornelius. I've got a bad feeling that some serious trouble is headed our way." He scratched the back of his neck. "I can feel it right back here, and I don't like it. No Sir. I don't like it at all."

Cornelius nodded. "It's just a night like any other." He answered nonchalantly. Somehow his words did not seem very reassuring.

ALSO BY MATT SPENCER:

THE DESCHEMBINE TRILOGY

The Trail of the Beast
The Blazing Chief

TALES OF OLD DESCHEMB

Changing of the Guards
The Renegade God

OTHERS

Story Time with Crazy Uncle Matt
Cult of the Stars
Chapel of the Falcon
Summer Reaping on the Fields of Nowhere
The Drifting Soul

For Mike Dabney
'Cause you know what I'm sayin', brother

Much thanks to Christopher Walsh, Kay Croto and Sydney Isle, for their early editorial assistance and encouragement.

This novel happened because I wanted to read it, and no one else seemed to have written it. And because life is strange, and it put me in a state of mind such that the story and characters emerged onto the page as they have.

I'd like to thank some folks who shared the crazy times with me, the ones who still put up with my crazy ass afterwards, and those who helped me find the assurance that I'd told a tale worth taking somewhere: Aaron Ryan, Adam Broderson, Alley Ryan, Amanda Fish, Andrew Michaud, Bill Hilburn, Cyndal Ellis, Dan Seitz, David Pierce (in loving memory), Ian Bigelow, Jacqueline Soniat, Jason Isle, Jay Craven, Jesse Cross-Nickerson, John Sheehy, Joslyn Haineswood, Kurt Amaker, Laura Janisieski, Luke Burke, Mike Dabney, Roy Wright, Stephanie McCray, Sydney Isle, Steve Seitz, and Tahir Chaudhri.

Author's Note

Much of this book's depiction of Brattleboro, Vermont was initially written from memory. Many local businesses that figure into the narrative no longer exist. Readers familiar with the area may notice some liberties taken with local geography and infrastructure. If you're not sure whether or not certain out-of-the-way spots actually exist, the author takes no responsibility for what happens if you go looking for them.

Between this book's original publication and this re-release, I wound up writing a great deal more material set in the universe/mythos introduced herein. So while preparing the book for fresh publication, I took the liberty of making a few adjustments to the mythos/world-building details, for the sake of continuity. This story is still set in a Brattleboro of a less-distant-than-it-feels past, but I sprinkled in a few fresh expository details to account for things like the lack of technologies that hadn't proliferated society quite so heavily at the time I originally wrote it, in the interest of introducing it to a new audience, as though publishing it for the first time. I also took the opportunity to give the prose a fresh spit an' polish, thanks in no small way to the fact that my girlfriend is a better proofreader/editor than most professional in-house editors I've worked with. On that note, I also removed a few of the original publisher's house-style editorial impositions, which never sat right with me. Beyond that, the essence of the book remains unchanged. I still think it's a damn good yarn that I'm damn proud of, so I didn't try to fix what wasn't broke. Enjoy the ride, folks. As always, we take no responsibility for your safety here.

THE NIGHT AND THE LAND

PROLOGUE

That Jeep has something to do with those Richmond murders.

Nah, that was stupid. Why would it? Rob wasn't one of those pansy kids, who heard about bad things happening somewhere else and got nightmares about the bogeymen or crap like that. Since they'd seen it on the news, though, Dad had made a point of not bringing it up.

Yeah, 'cause it had been the weekend, so Dad had let him stay up late. They'd watched TV together, and that's what came on the news. Since then, a week of school had passed. Rob had heard teachers and a few other kids chatter about it, but no one at home in the Coscan household. Now here it was, Saturday again. The news lady had read whatever the news-writers had given her to tell people while the cameras scanned the bloody walls on an alley somewhere in Richmond. Rob guessed he'd seen about half of the report. Then Dad's face went a new shade of grim and he told Rob to leave the room. That was weird, because the stepmom hadn't been there, and Dad hardly ever made a big deal about what Rob saw on TV or whatever—hadn't at all really, for a couple years now—unless the stepmom threw a tantrum and made him.

The screen hadn't even shown anything really nasty, and before long, Rob didn't remember too much of what he'd seen or heard. Still, he remembered that look on Dad's face...the kind someone gets when a bad memory comes back to haunt them, or they see someone they hoped they'd never see again. All Rob could figure was that he'd been kept in the dark about a lot of things in life.

Now here came the gray Jeep, kicking a dust cloud back across the driveway, dented and scraped like it should be shaking to pieces on the sharp gravel. Yet it ran and purred like a sports car on a smooth strip.

Rob found Dad striding up through the back pasture. "Dad, I think someone's here to see you."

"Yeah. I was just on my way up to 'em."

"You were expecting someone?"

"Nope. Just the birds and the wind said I had a visitor." Dad used that tone when he wanted you to think he was joking. "Didn't say who, though."

When they reached the yard, a hulking black man stood by the Jeep, obviously not one of Dad's farmer buddies. All those guys drove pickups, for one thing. Also, Dad wasn't prejudiced, but most of his farmer buddies were. Black or white, Rob had never seen anyone like this, not in Bedford, Virginia—almost tall enough to be a giant, bald as a turtle shell, carrying his gnarled bulk with a rugged dignity Rob hadn't thought real-life people had, just Samurai or Indians in movies. His dark clothes were ripped in places, rumpled like he'd slept in them. If you looked close, strange stain patterns speckled them. It was hard to tell the scars from the craggy lines in his face. Rob tried to peer up through the windows. What kind of cool stuff did the Jeep carry?

The big man stepped in the way, meeting Dad's eyes. "How've you been, Metaiew?" Wow, when had anyone last called Dad by all three syllables?

"Okay. Rob, go inside." Dad's face looked like it had when he'd seen the news report of the murders. "Barb'll yell if that living room ain't picked up."

Dad was *shooing him away*, because there was *adult stuff* to talk about. Dad hadn't talked to him like that in years. *First he's all sensitive about what I can see on TV, and now I can't stay and hang out with him and his cool new friend. If this is a new thing with Dad, life's really gonna suck from now on.* Rob thought the big man grimaced. Why would a guy like that care? *He thinks I should hear whatever he has to say...because somehow, I'm part of it.*

"Aw, that never takes me long anyway," said Rob. "I—"

"*Rob!*"

Rob neither sulked nor hurried. Dad's yell jangled his nerves, but he wouldn't let the visitor see that. At the porch step, he glanced back. Talking to the giant, Dad didn't look like himself, at all. Dad wasn't a big guy—almost as tall as his guest but far thinner. Side by side, you'd never spot the difference. Right then, Dad held himself like as big a hero as the black giant must be. They'd both look this at home anywhere, no matter what was going on.

Rob swore one of them said *Richmond*. Then the guy said something about *neutral status being threatened*, and Dad yelled. When Rob looked again, his father had crouched, teeth bared like a wolf, tense hands curling and twitching...his whole frame moving like his joints were built differently. The black giant leaned back, his big arms draped across his Jeep, waiting for whatever Dad did.

Rob stood still, drifting in and out of a trance, coming out the other side in a changed world. A minute ago, he'd been pissed at being sent to finish folding laundry. Now something hot and paralyzing rattled under his skin, throbbed in his temples. The world might explode, if one guy decided to take a swing at his old friend, and it wasn't just something on a TV you could switch off. The black man met Rob's eyes across the yard and nodded, once. Dad didn't seem to notice.

Instantly, Rob's paralysis broke, and he walked inside. He made short work of the living room, because life's irritations and distractions had switched places. Folding clothes and straightening up the coffee table reminded him he was in the same world as always. It was scarier now—a new *kind* of scary—but it hadn't gone off the rails into out-of-control violence like some places did all the time. Dad's old friend knew those places, and he knew how easily even the quiet farmhouse yard could turn into something just as ugly. He'd make sure it didn't, though…no matter how much he'd like to see if Dad still had it in him. Somehow, he'd told Rob all of this, with one nod.

Dad or his friend had mentioned Richmond. *Talk about a place where people are used to their world going off the rails.* Even folks in those ghettos weren't used to things like that alleyway, though. Rob called to mind what he remembered about the news report. He wasn't sure the news lady had said so, but he remembered getting the idea that it had been a *fight*. Gangs didn't brawl like that, though it had been in the right part of town for it. It sounded like wild animals had torn those guys apart, except forensics investigators said the perps had used *knives*.

When Dad and his friend came in, they laughed and joked as though the earlier outburst had never occurred. Dad had lots of scars like the black giant's, but Rob had never wondered about them 'til now. Dad was eager to talk about how great life in Bedford was. Usually, once he got going, you couldn't shut him up about all the ignorance and hatred poisoning the region.

No, Rob wanted to shout. *He's lying. Our life here sucks. Take us away with you in your Jeep. Dad doesn't need Barbara. He can find another woman out there on the road—a real woman, strong and brave and smart like I'll bet my real mom was. So what if it's scary? It's gotta be better than this slow, dying crawl. I never noticed 'til now, but that's all life here is, and I can't pretend otherwise anymore.*

Whenever the man tried talking about old times, Dad steered things someplace else. When the man did invite Rob into the conversation, Rob wanted to tell him everything and ask questions. Before he could, though, Dad always interrupted him and changed the subject again.

When the stepmom came home, Dad introduced her politely to his old friend. She shook hands with the guy, put on a sour face, then slunk into the kitchen and strode back and forth, making as much clatter as possible, just so no one forgot her disapproval—at what? Of Dad having a life beyond his end of the household? Maybe it was 'cause the giant was black—Barbara pretended not to be like that, but she was actually worse than Dad's farming buddies. Except why did her hands shake like that, making the clatter worse?

She's scared, Rob realized. *So is Dad.* Dad spoke stiffly so he wouldn't stammer, and his eyes darted pensively between his family and his old friend.

Later, out on the porch, the stranger said one last thing about *neutral territory*. Rob had already been chased back inside by then, so he was pretty sure he wasn't meant to have heard that. He fell asleep that night to a shouting match between his dad and stepmom, which had become a pretty regular occurrence. For a while, it had hurt to hear what Dad was going through. Hopefully he'd leave Barbara soon, or throw her out, or whack her on the head with a shovel and use her to fertilize the garden. Usually by now, Rob would have pulled on his headphones and fallen asleep to music. This fight sounded different, though…closer to violent.

"I told you everything you had a right to know from the start. Hell, I *would've told you more*, but you made Goddamn clear you didn't wanna know me that well, even though I was just fine for someplace to sleep, eat and get laid."

"Oh, do *not* start on who's living off who these days."

"You're just desperate to cut my balls the rest of the way off, aren't you? Then you'd just have to get by with that slimy little lawyer pansy at the office."

"You're right, I still don't want to know. Or maybe you're the one who's afraid I'll stop being so stupid."

"No, actually, that'd be nice."

"Oh really. Do you *want* me to bring up what I heard around Gladstone, why they told me I should stay the hell away from you? I can name *three people* who said you were in on—" She cut herself off with an ugly gasp.

"You know what, *maybe I should just let you know everything.*" Dad's voice changed, like his body earlier, out in the yard. The night outside filled the house between his words. Every chirp and howl, every distant car crunching on gravel, or windy gust through the pines…"Yeah, why don't I take you along on it, *give you the show of your life!*"

No, not her…Take me *along, Dad.*

Maybe Rob should have been scared of such a sound coming out of Dad's mouth. He couldn't fool himself like that, though, not anymore. He wanted to hear it in his own voice too much. He wanted everyone else to hear and feel it, wherever he went. People like the stepmom wouldn't even matter anymore. Nothing would but the life being lived, at the other end of all those night noises.

That weekend, Dad left on a little trip, leaving Rob at home with the stepmom. He never said where. If anyone else got hacked up in Richmond, it didn't make the news. Rob guessed the *territory* had stayed *neutral*, whatever that meant.

PART ONE:

THE CALLS

THE FIRST CALL

ONE

Sally found her way into Harmony Parking Lot, through a short tunnel off High Street. She'd held out hope for an all-night diner, someplace where they wouldn't bother her if she sat for a while. Local businesses and apartments encased all the cracked concrete on three sides, with a rocky, weed-choked rise on the fourth. Everything looked closed.

So why had she picked this town? So far, it was like a winding, hilly maze of overgrown foliage and jutting old-time architecture. Roads and sidewalks stretched and twisted in odd shapes over the mountain-shrouded terrain. Well, it was as good as anywhere on the map, not that she carried one. Vermont had been the closest neutral territory. New England in general had always been fairly safe for civilians from either surviving line, a small miracle considering what fine camouflage its deep forests, granite mountain ranges and rolling terrain provided whenever the feuds heated up. Hopefully she wouldn't have to run or fight for a while.

Her duffel bag was strapped to her shoulders like a regular backpack, biting at the circulation, pulling her neck muscles taut. It was a good kind of ache, more stabbing and quickening than this cold air. Her narrow hand slipped into the pocket of the denim jean jacket at least two sizes too big, fingers curling around the money she'd taken from the dead man three days ago in Pittsburgh. When the pocketknife fell against her knuckles, she felt crusted blood on the grip, like caked, dried syrup built up on the rim of a plastic container. The dead man had provided food from his flesh and organs, a night's shelter in that dirty apartment, and money from his pockets. The money would buy better food, hopefully nicer lodgings.

She wouldn't have ended up in Pittsburgh if the kids she'd hitched a ride with hadn't kicked her out. They'd been fighting amongst themselves, and somewhere the fight had become about her. The driver should have asked before stopping for hitchhikers, someone said. So next thing Sally knew, she'd been dumped off. When she realized where she was, she'd panicked. From there, she'd been out for any sanctuary she could find.

Sure, the man had said, he had food at his place, and sure she could stay with him. Even on the street, she must have known it was a bad idea, but she'd been so hungry and tired…

As she'd walked towards his kitchen, he stepped into the doorway, blocking the path. She laughed it off and tried to push past him, but he shoved her against the doorframe so her shoulders strained back. Years ago, a man called Talino had pressed her from behind, breathing like that…except they'd been in a dining room bigger than this man's whole apartment. Talino had been the one holding the knife, while others watched. This time it was Sally who pulled a knife, along with those old reflexes that had been ingrained in her since childhood. When she stabbed the man, he gasped and folded like anyone, holding on like she might rescue him from drowning, like he forgot she was the one who'd stuck the blade in him or why. Once he was dead, the first thing she remembered was the money in his pockets. She fished it out hurriedly, before the blood seeped out of his shirt, then down through his jeans 'til it looked like he'd wet himself pissing blood. She really thought that would be the end of their involvement. Then her hunger made it harder to think.

She remembered turning away from the refrigerator, closing the door fast, wrinkling her nose against the grease smell of leftover fried chicken and moldy pizza. She had to clean up, get out of those stained clothes, decide what to do next. She shook so bad that she could barely wash her hands. The bloody smell wouldn't stay out of her nose, kept invading her brain thicker, like even in death he'd found a way to violate her. Not the blood drying on her clothes, but what still seeped out of his dead trunk in the doorway. The blood and the flesh…

Then came Talino's regal voice again: *Ah, but we almost forgot. We have a recovering Spirelight's daughter in our midst, and she didn't get to eat before she sat down.* The edge trailed her throat, before Talino pressed the handle to her palm and guided it towards the table. *Go ahead, little Spirelight girl. Cut off a piece to eat. You start cutting, or I do.*

In the dead man's kitchen, Sally squeezed her eyes shut and saw Talino's dining room. As she tasted the first bite, the others chanted their malignant incantations. Had she been thirteen or fourteen back then? She still carried the same pocketknife, and she'd just used it. What did it mean— how was it different—to kill one of the Earth-line people?

With a sob, she remembered cutting from the body on Talino's table. She smelled the one in the doorway, and she imagined tasting it like Talino had made her taste the runaway girl.

Except—no, wait—she wasn't *remembering* or *imagining* anymore, because she was *kneeling in the doorway, cutting.* No matter how nasty it smelled, the chanting told her brain it was the sweetest scent ever. So she tasted…and kept tasting.

Sally had slept on the dead man's couch. He said she could, after all. The next morning, she hauled ass to the bus station, and now the bus had dropped her off in this town.

At the far end of Harmony Lot stood a crumbling vine-covered brick building. Up the rickety back stairs, three shapes sat watching. By their casual murmur, she knew they didn't mean to spy on her. Still, she felt more and more attention coming her way. She ambled closer and peered up into darkness. The shapes leaned forward, probably to see if they knew her. Two girls, one guy…Just kids, probably around her age.

"Hello." The melodious female voice was young and spacey. "We help you?"

"Uh, yeah," Sally said. "Is there any place open that sells food?"

"Um, well, you know the town at all?" The guy didn't pause for an answer. "'Cause if you go down to the end of Main Street, then about…a mile up Canal Street, there's Price Chopper—they're open twenty-four-seven. Oh, and I think an all-night diner just opened up that way, too, but I'm not sure. I hear it's pretty sketchy, though. You old enough to drink?"

Sally shook her head. The guy was cartoonishly thin

and long-limbed, his boyish face lightly bearded, with dark hair that was almost long and shaggy enough to camouflage his unusually long neck. He wore an army jacket, fingerless gloves, and loose jeans cut off below the knees.

"Well, I was gonna say, I think the two bars down that way serve food sometimes." He pointed up the street. "If you order food but no beer, maybe they won't give you shit."

Sally leaned on the railing, considering it.

One of the girls bent forward so some light fell on her. She was plump and moon-faced with short, ratty hair that might be red. "Are you from around here? You know anyone in town?"

Sally shook her head again. "I never even heard of this place 'til a few days ago."

"So…you don't got anywhere to stay?"

"Nope. I was just now sorta trying to figure that out."

The girl who might have red hair stood up and hugged herself. "Hey, you know what? Let's go inside. It's freezing out here."

Funny thing was, Sally hadn't noticed any of them reacting to the cold 'til now. She agreed, though, now that someone mentioned it.

The second girl still hadn't spoken. She looked up, small and curvy with a great black bush of dreadlocks. She had a broad nose and full lips, with skin pale enough to stand out in the night… the closest Sally had ever seen Earth-line skin come to *glowing*. Above her ragged skirt, a torn sweater tumbled dangerously low off one smooth, bare shoulder. "Jake won't mind?"

"Jake won't be in 'til like noon tomorrow," said the

short-haired girl. "If he bitches, I'll kick his butt."

Sally climbed the narrow metal steps. "Thanks. My name's Sally."

"Hi, I'm Liam," said the guy. "This is Clover…" He indicated the short-haired girl. "And this is Bethany." He pointed to the pale African-featured girl.

Sally followed them through the back door, then through a cramped, musty storeroom. By the street lamps through narrow windows, she made out some kind of restaurant, all rustic wooden surfaces and quaint homespun adornments. Liam and Clover lit candles and oil lamps. Sally looked around for signs of electricity, saw none. Heat pumped from somewhere, though it was still chilly. Was that a faint gas odor? The straps of her duffel bag slid from her shoulders, and the descending weight almost pulled her over backwards.

Bethany trudged around a great oak table to a stuffed shopping bag. "We'd give you something to eat, but all we really have right now is bread. And some oranges, somewhere around here. Is bread okay?"

Sally was already on her way around the table. Bethany handed her a long loaf of French bread. The outside was a hard, flour-dusted crust, the inside all soft doughy goodness. "Thanks," Sally said, her mouth partly full. "That's wonderful."

Bethany giggled. "What was the last thing you ate?"

"A really nasty ham sandwich."

"So, what's your story, anyway?" Liam drifted back over. "You, like, homeless, or what?"

"Yeah."

"Hey, that's cool." Clover came over and tore herself a

chunk of bread. Bethany added, "Yeah, it's pretty standard around here, actually."

"So, are you guys homeless too?"

Clover and Liam looked at each other, then shook their heads. "Well, I am, sort of," said Bethany. "I've been mostly just sleeping here, or on rooftops along the other side of Main Street—I can show you how to get up there with no one seeing sometime if you like—then working during the days. I think I'll be moving in with some people soon. C'mon, have a seat. You look ready to fall over."

"Thanks." Sally hadn't guessed how grateful she'd feel, just to flop her bony ass on the long high-backed bench. "So what's the story with this place?"

"The Common Ground?" said Liam. "That's a good question lately."

It turned out the place was a kind of non-profit all-organic diner, the oldest community-owned restaurant in Vermont, no less. They'd run into money problems and hadn't had electricity since spring. So the place wasn't officially up and running, but the local hippies still had the doors open most days, whipping up dishes on the fly, serving them to whomever came in, taking donations. At least they had a gas stove, so they could still cook, just a matter of getting fresh ingredients daily. Would the situation be fixed soon? Again, good question.

"Do you have to get home any time soon, Liam?" Bethany scooted closer to Sally.

"Nah, I'm good for, like, another few hours. I don't have to work for another two days, which, like, never happens to me, so I'm chillin' while I can." He packed and sparked a glass pipe, caught a deep drag and passed it to

Clover, who'd set to tuning an old acoustic guitar.

Sally caught the musty, piney aroma. It had been months since she could relax enough to accept cheap beer, let alone weed. Then Bethany leaned against her and held the pipe in front of her face. Sally reached, paused…Look where she'd ended up last time she got too comfortable too quickly with a group of kids. Still, the scent smelled like green wafting relaxation, of a depth that's hard to resist when you've forgotten how it felt. As she took a deep drag, she noticed Bethany hadn't leaned away. The cold was tolerable, but it was nice to absorb someone else's body heat.

After another hit, Clover retrieved her guitar and strummed the first soothing chords of some gentle old tune. By and by, she started singing, too low and soft for Sally to catch most of the words, though the sound was too soothing for that to matter.

"So where you come from originally?" Bethany asked.

"Virginia." When Bethany asked more questions, Sally named some towns and cities she'd stayed in, odd jobs she'd worked, and dodged everything else. Nice and stoned, she decided Bethany by candlelight was the most beautiful sight on earth. Not that she'd mind cuddling up with Liam or Clover, either, except she wouldn't interrupt the latter's music for the world. Instead, she put her arm around Bethany and saw her smile. *The closest Sally had ever seen to an Earth-liner who glowed*…Was that why Sally already liked this girl so much? Maybe that was part of it, to feel warmth and acceptance, if just for a moment, from someone who felt even a little closer to that world Sally hadn't been part of for years. That, or she just couldn't remember the last time she got laid. That business in Pittsburgh had probably put her off guys for a while, and hell, Bethany was hot.

How old did Bethany think she was? Glancing over the full, soft face, Sally guessed Bethany was about her own age. Except how old did she, Sally, look? She'd be eighteen in a month if she figured right—or was it seventeen? Nineteen?—but people often took her for much younger. Of course the Earth-line date was there every time you looked at the news—on TV, or a stray free paper, even the internet, which she barely knew how to use, whenever she randomly found herself in front of someone's computer— but she'd long ago lost track of the Spirelight Refugee calendar. The oversized coat made her look even smaller, the way her skinny neck and wrists stuck out with so much space around them.

Bethany's hand slid inside Sally's coat, sending tickling shivers through her. The hand was cold, so Sally placed her own over it, felt warmth set in. Before she knew it, Bethany's other hand found hers.

"Yeah, I know, my fingers are so stubby and silly-looking…"

Without answering, Sally gazed at the round fingertips in the candle glint, running her own over them like a child playing at the petals of the first flower she'd ever picked. When she looked up, Bethany's wide smile was a cartoon caricature of lusty sweetness. Sally peered closer, made sure she read the girl's mood correctly, and wondered how she'd been so dense 'til now.

Across from them, Liam stood up. "Well, I think it's time to go home, head to bed. Clover, you wanna help me find some blankets for Sally?"

Clover smirked and set her guitar aside. "Sure, I'll get 'em."

"And…Bethany. You sleeping here again tonight, too?"

Bethany nodded and smiled sweeter.

"If Sally's still here when Jake comes in, you'll make sure he doesn't throw a fit?" He looked at Sally. "Jake's one of the people 'round here who's sort of a manager. He's technically in charge of getting this place running in the mornings, or as, like, close to technical as anything gets around here. I sorta help run things too, so I have a right to say it's okay for you to sleep here. Just sometimes he gets twitchy."

Clover slapped Liam's arm. "I told you, don't worry." She turned to Sally. "I'll talk to him before he comes in, let him know what's going on, so he doesn't throw a hissy-fit."

Once Clover and Liam drifted off, Bethany leaned over and kissed Sally. As Sally reclined against the bench, Bethany kissed a little harder and a tongue flicked across Sally's teeth. Bethany's mouth tasted sour-sweet and she smelled musty and earthy. To Sally's stoned senses, they painted the air with the girl's life— something wild, but in a playful, wonderful, gentle way, the essence of a warm, good, safe place with well-meaning, unaffected people. The loose folds of Bethany's sweater seemed to catch of their own will on Sally's thumbs, fingertips gliding blindly up tough-soft skin.

Bethany righted herself coyly as Liam and Clover came back with the blankets. What the hell was Sally jumping into here? *Just a little precious relaxation.* Even if she stayed in Brattleboro a while, Bethany didn't exactly seem like she was out to tie anyone down. Besides, it was too late and cold to go exploring this strange new town.

Two

Edging towards three in the morning, and Rob felt like a Goddamn Jack-in-the-box. It was too late for the bars, and he wasn't in much of a people mood anyway. He rubbed at his jaw and still felt last week's brawl. At least his front teeth had stopped hurting. He still couldn't sleep, though. After cycling through the little CD booklet he'd carried through the road days, he grabbed a Bud from the fridge and went downstairs for a smoke.

One of those old Vermont winters was headed in. Through the chill, an odd smell reached him. Later, he'd realize it hadn't been a smell at all. It wasn't anything he could attribute to his basic five senses. That's still how his brain made sense of it right then, though, making him more restless, more pissed off than he'd felt all night. At the same time, he felt more grounded and focused than ever…but on what? How the hell could you be focused on something, with no idea what or where? For a moment, he had a mind to take off walking—no, running, barefoot—and chase down the source. Not so long ago, he might have expected to find something.

Might expect to catch *something*—

Rob blinked, felt like he'd gone somewhere else for an instant that had taken forever. For a weird moment, he had to remind himself where he was and how he'd gotten here. The hardest part was remembering *why*. Where had the road gone? Where had this boarding house come from, full of people even crazier than he felt lately?

After everything he'd seen and done out there, how could they—or anything—still seem strange? The landlady was a short, waddling, twitchy, paranoid-schizophrenic butterball who communicated by screeching like a demonically possessed moron. She liked to brag how she'd renovated the house herself from an unwired wreck. Near as Rob could figure, she'd done it with spare parts past their sell dates.

The outside was a gruesome blend of Christmas and Halloween colors, the inside full of epileptic plumbing, the wiring frayed and exposed everywhere, with sockets and light switches in the damnedest places. Rob's room held— no shit—an electrical outlet in the corner of the ceiling. Before he moved out, he'd have to find some practical use for it, just for shits and giggles. Hey, it was cheap lodgings, in a quiet neighborhood where you didn't have to be ready for a fistfight every time you stepped outside.

Suddenly, there was that New Orleans stripper on his mind, the one he'd lived with for a while. She'd done Tarot readings in Jackson Square when she wasn't shimmying down to her glittery panties and pasties in various French Quarter dives. He'd gotten a free reading once at the kitchen table, decided he liked it better when she practiced her other job at home.

Same night as that reading, she'd had friends over, and she brought up what an empath she was, how she could *read auras*. "Oh yeah," she'd told someone, "there's a little monster somewhere in that boy, for sure."

That first soothing-harsh drag of American Spirit

distracted him from the cold stone porch under his bare feet. A few more puffs helped him forget the strange smell, almost. Maybe he should have put on an extra layer. Then something in the grass got his attention, the spot where the street glow gave way to the blackness of the front yard. Vague silhouettes continued onward through the gloom, revealing new aspects as the eyes adjusted.

"Oh yeah…" Rob smiled, not sure why he was thinking of the stripper. "Little monster, right here."

Within the shadow's edge sat something he first mistook for a smooth rock. When he stepped down, it looked more like an oversized pinecone. Then it scuttled further into the gloom. When he stepped closer, it hopped again, spread outward on either side, flattening slightly. A tiny head bobbed on a narrow neck, facing away. Must be some bird, born wrong in the head. Why else would it nest on the ground, near the sidewalk? So now it played maimed, trying to lure the predator away from its young.

"Don't worry, birdie." Rob smirked. "You ain't on this predator's menu."

Except there was no nest in sight. The thing kept flopping, wings spread, seeming to make for the corner of the front step. Its neck looked too long for a pigeon, and its floundering wings seemed thicker but not feathery, more like a pair of twin flattened funnels, wrapped in smooth leather. Rob leaned closer. The thing flopped and scuttled so violently that he jerked back. By now, he made out a head that was too thin and a back that was too narrow and defined for a bird. That twitching stubby tail was odd, too.

Rob glanced up, past the trees that led downhill to a huge cemetery, past mountains that loomed from across the

Connecticut River, to where he looked the fattening moon in the eye. Its sloppy toothless Jack-o'-lantern face gazed back like a wasting crackhead, but it didn't light the yard any better. When Rob looked again, the scuttling thing was gone. Weird…He hadn't heard it move. A low breeze whistled across the center of the walkway, sending two thin parades of stray dry leaves skittering and pinwheeling up the front steps, passing him on either side. Once he was sure those steps were clear, he chucked his cigarette butt and walked swiftly back inside.

BRATTLEBORO

ONE

Rob found the Lucca Bistro locked, so he got in through the basement the place shared with the Latchis Hotel along Flat Street. The sight of the dishwasher station almost depressed him. It wound up pissing him off instead. These days, any kind of contentment felt like a drunken stupor that was wearing off.

Milano came out of the office. "You can go, dude. It gon' be slow tonight. Salad guy can handle the dishes."

Okay, so there went another shift cut, as usual without a phone call. Granted, Rob hadn't bothered to replace his cell. It got broken last week. He hadn't bothered replacing it because he didn't like cell phones and had only gotten the shitty little pay-as-you-go thing because a girl he'd dated for two weeks had hounded him into getting one. He'd given the bosses the landline number at the boarding house, not that they'd ever bothered calling him about things like sudden schedule changes in the first place.

He felt cold relief at not having to put up with the place tonight, a relief that extended to everything but his next paycheck. He left through the side door, which he unlocked for the waiters and bartender who'd show up soon. Outside, he thought kinder of his job, though business was obviously circling the drain. Before his shifts started vanishing, he'd even been managing to save up for a change. Inertia and anger feeding each other, squeezing more painfully the harder he fought it…Hey, it was like being a kid all over again.

Rob headed up Main Street and stepped into Mocha Joe's. Fresh ground java scent tickled his nose. He inhaled, held it, and felt his brain unknot. He bought a Red Eye, left it dark and bitter, and headed towards the empty couch against the back wall. He flopped down, propped his feet on the coffee table, and fished his notebook from his backpack. After jotting a few tangential musings, he flipped back, read a few lines, and recognized the first hand-written draft of that short story he'd written about New Orleans. Lately he'd thought of typing it up, maybe look for someplace to get it published. His housemate Darren, quite the aspiring author, was always telling him what a natural storyteller he was. Just sitting around over some beers, Darren claimed, Rob could tell some story about someplace he'd been, something crazy he'd seen or done there, and something about his voice just…took you straight there. He ought to learn to write it all down the way he told it out loud. Darren even offered to show him how to look for markets and submit pieces professionally.

What a natural storyteller he was…Funny, that's what Louis always used to tell him.

Looking this piece over now, Rob missed the street days. Nice as it was having a roof over his head, part of him hated being a rent-paying wage slave again, hated himself as a wage slave as opposed to the self he'd discovered on the road. Especially whenever he woke sluggishly in the afternoon—instead of snapping instantly alert, from light but sufficient sleep on cold concrete, knotted bark, or damp moss—when his reflexes lapsed in ways that would have gotten him killed or thrown in jail in that world.

Not for the first time, he wondered what Miss Morrow would say about the sights he'd seen out here, in the world at large in general…Miss Morrow had lived on the same winding weedy gravel road as the Coscans, somewhere on the mile stretch between Rob's home and the nearest civilization, back in Virginia. He'd spotted her now and then, on summer walks or treks home from the bus stop, but he'd never had a reason to talk to her 'til she'd been looking after some dogs for out-of-town friends. One was a Doberman, the other a mix of Pit Bull and German Shepherd. Rob had been eleven, on his way home from the bus stop, the first time they'd come running at him from Miss Morrow's yard, snapping and snarling.

He'd been halfway up a thin tree that should barely have held his weight when the old black woman came out and called them off. After checking the time, she promised to keep them leashed or inside at that time of day from now on. A week later, he again found himself facing onrushing howls and growls and barks and snaps. This time, though, it was days after that weird visit from Dad's old friend, and Rob came fresh from a fight at school, his first real one in a while. He'd gotten in a lot of trouble for that 'til he was eight, when his dad yelled and slung him around enough that he decided he'd better curb it. Maybe he'd been thinking of Dad's strange visitor when those punks started messing with him. No way would the black giant take shit like that from schoolyard punks. Either way, Rob remembered how good it felt to throw real punches, to do more than scuffle impotently while redneck bullies manhandled him. He'd knocked the wind out of one kid and bloodied the nose of another. He hadn't known if the school had gotten ahold of his dad or stepmom at work, and he didn't care. When the dogs charged snarling and snapping, he hadn't cared about that, either. Holding his ground, he stared straight at them. The rush wasn't unlike the exhilaration of a good fight…only higher, purer.

No one told him 'til years later how you weren't supposed to look an angry dog in the eye, how dogs took that as a signal to fight. Maybe that's the message Rob meant to send. Then out came Miss Morrow, apologizing all over again about time sneaking up on her. Rob shrugged and almost walked on, but for some reason, he stayed to listen to her. She dressed and acted like an old hippie, except she looked too old to have been a sixties flower child. Also, she was sharper than any old hippies he'd met, most of them burnt out or rehabilitated into corporate hypocrites like the stepmom. He ended up making friends with those dogs, so the next time he walked home from the bus stop, they ran barking to him in friendly joy.

Next time winter rolled around, Miss Morrow taught him how to split firewood. While he chopped, she told stories. That's what he remembered most…Tales of ancient beasts and spirits, living in the earth and air, hidden from human eyes since before the time of the Indians, of magic conjure-men, of the little people whose song you could hear in the night if you knew how to listen. Listening at night for the song of the little people, Rob's strange awareness had really set in…

Just the birds and the wind told me I had a visitor. Yeah, one more thing he and Dad had never talked about.

One afternoon, Miss Morrow was telling Rob about one of those conjure-men, draped in magical animal furs, with heads that rose and snapped and spoke with otherworldly animation. Then the stepmom drove by in her little red sports car, the one she'd nagged Dad into buying her when her mid-life crisis set in. Rob ignored it 'til it ground to a halt. The stepmom's tall, broad, mannish form rose from within, her chubby face scrunched with anxiety, eyes narrowed to neurotic slits. Rob didn't think she looked at Miss Morrow for more than two seconds, just came straight at him, demanding he get in the car right now.

At first, Rob looked pleadingly at Miss Morrow, as if she could get the bitch to see sense. Miss Morrow just said he better do what his momma told him. Rob shot back, that wasn't his mom, and he didn't have to do a damn thing she said. So the stepmom grabbed his arm and dragged him towards the car, and he'd fought her. He'd never know what really caused his arm to pull from the socket—one of the stepmom's heaving pulls or his jerking against her— but he knew he kept fighting even after he noticed the screaming pain.

On the rumbling drive home, the stepmom glanced over and realized he was really hurt. Maybe the fact that he was seething and champing and sweating like a horse with a broken leg had something to do with it. So of course she was *so scared, so sorry, so desperate to find out what was wrong,* to get him to a doctor. He'd have hated her less if she'd skipped the act. There might be fewer dreams, of returning to that afternoon as his strong, twenty-two-year-old self, grabbing a log and splattering her prim metropolitan businesswoman's brains all over the yard.

As Rob's mind found its way back to the coffee shop, it snagged on the night before, on that bulbous shape in the grass, unfolding into something that might have been a pigeon or a bat. Except no, it hadn't really looked like anything. There'd been the strange smell, then the even stranger, more alien feelings it had kindled within him. For the first time, Rob realized that it hadn't been a smell at all. Whatever it was, the memory was very powerful right now.

A girl he didn't recognize had just walked in, her movements alone catching the corner of his eye. At the counter, she dug change from her pocket. She was slight, medium height, maybe his age, with long, dirty, caramel hair tied back at the nape of her slim, tense neck. The oversized jean jacket hid the shape of her body, but he could tell she was undernourished. Her hands shook from cold 'til her long fingers slid around the coffee cup. Even trembling, the grace in those hands was apparent. She lifted the coffee and inhaled deeply, so the tremble fled from her lips and nose.

When her eyes closed contentedly, Rob heard his soul screaming, *Oh God, no, don't close your eyes. Your face is pretty, might be beautiful if you got more food in you…and your hands…but… God, girl, those eyes…* Yeah, reddish copper…Deep and hard like strange jewels. *Please don't close your eyes, 'cause I never wanna stop staring into them.*

Then she opened them and walked past him, on her way to a seat in the back. No, her eyes weren't as hard as he'd thought. The coffee warmed the rest of her body, but the chill behind those eyes had set in long before touching this late Vermont Autumn. Haunted, that's what they were, holding themselves together so stubbornly against whatever troubled the soul that dwelt within. Horrifying in a way, eyes like that, yet too few of them in the world. Rob had only seen one other pair quite like them, and never expected to again. For all he knew, this girl might have the only set of eyes left like that anywhere. What haunted her?

So what, his brain fired back. *Brattleboro's got one more freak. If you got up close, you'd find out you've imagined it about her eyes, find they're just hard and bled out like a million others. Great, now she's noticed you checking her out.*

Maybe, but she's the most beautiful freak I've ever seen.

That's not all you see when you look at her, though, is it?

I...I don't know what I see. Well, stud, one way to find out, ain't there?

"Very true." He closed the notebook, got up, and walked towards her.

TWO

Sally woke up alone, swaddled in the blankets she'd shared with Bethany. Footsteps sounded, along with a groggy male voice. She sat up as the guy came around the corner. They looked at each other in surprise, then his face settled sullenly. He seemed a few years older than Liam, same dress style and similar features, only harder and darker.

"You Bethany's friend?" he said.

Sally nodded, pretending to still be half-asleep. This must be Jake.

"Well, get a broom. They're by the stove. C'mon, time to clean." Bethany was already sweeping. Sally got an extra broom and started on the next room. In the morning light, the place looked more like an eighteenth-century tavern than a modern restaurant. Except those places hadn't been decorated in psychedelic artwork, Oriental tapestries, or fliers screaming radical political propaganda, she was pretty sure. Weed smell lingered like morning mist.

Jake set a large pot heating on the stove, whispered with Bethany, then approached Sally. Once he saw her sweeping job, his face wasn't any nicer, but his tone was more polite. "Look, it's okay if you sleep here sometimes, long as you ain't just making this place your crash pad, y'know? Try not to bring anyone else up here after hours like that. I mean, bring 'em up if they want food, just…Look, we can't have this place turning into a homeless shelter."

"Yeah, cool. I'll try not to abuse it."

"Hey, just as long as you help out." He took another glance at the swift, neat, thorough job she'd done. "You could maybe volunteer for a couple of shifts, if you're gonna be around town a while. On a lucky day, it's a good way to score cash in tips. We like to help out people who help us."

Not long after, Jake pulled the cooking pot from the stove and served up a strange concoction of black beans, rice, and eggplant. Sally picked out the eggplant and ate it separately. All in all, it was pretty tasty. Bethany told Sally to meet her back at the Common Ground at three that afternoon. After work, she'd come back and show Sally around town. Sally said she'd like that, kissed Bethany quickly and clumsily.

Bethany giggled, hugged Sally, and pecked her cheek. It felt weirdly chaste. Maybe the girl felt put off at not getting any further than a little make-out time? Oh well, one more reason to avoid sex. Social interaction was screwy enough without it.

After exploring the town for a few hours, Sally returned to the Common Ground and chewed all this over while she waited. Then she realized Bethany was an hour and a half late. Hell, after recent treatment elsewhere, getting stood up didn't offend her much. Avoiding the pocketknife as much as possible, she dug out her cash stash. Seventy bucks, better than she'd thought. Yeah, might as well explore a bit more. When she saw the sign for the coffee shop—a smiling stencil of a man in a fedora that might be James Cagney, smelling fumes off a fresh cup of java—she realized it had been a while since she'd treated herself to anything. A cappuccino, as Sally saw it, wasn't such a shabby thing to treat yourself to. It wasn't 'til she had her drink that she noticed the young man eyeing her.

Young man…*for lack of a better word.*

To anyone else, that must be what he looked like. Not so hard on the eyes, his long body stretched out, feet on the coffee table, shoulders broad and straight, features sharp, eyes sharper, scruffy blond hair. That Mead notebook suggested someone more studious than the black leather jacket, faded jeans, cowboy boots, or ratty shirt let on. Sally spotted dark, dried spatters around his collar, too small for most people to see at a glance. Blood stains? She looked away and sat at a small table on the opposite side of the room. There was no way she could be sure, except— Damnit, she'd known the instant she spotted him. Of course, she wouldn't know for sure unless he approached, and then only if he acted more or less instantly.

Hold it together. Vermont's neutral territory, remember? Even if he's one of them, he's not allowed to do anything, and he knows it. Even if he does, you know how to handle yourself, remember? It can't have been that long since the last one.

Her hand slipped into her coat pocket, around the knife handle. Even if he tried something, at least it was one of them, not one of her family…or one of the others of the Secret Police. At least with his kind, the answer was simple, if not easily achieved.

When she looked again, he'd stood up. *Oh shit, he's headed my way!*

Crimbone was the word for what Sally saw. She hated the word, one she kept from her thoughts as much as possible. The name of those the Crimbone belonged to, she could stand even less, because that's what Talino had been. This young man moved with the same animal grace as both of Talino's three servants and the few she'd faced since…like they didn't quite have the same skeletal structure as everyone else, which Sally happened to know was the case. You wouldn't spot it unless you knew what to look for. Her mother had shown her once on the dissection table, when she was eight or nine, mostly to do with the joint and ligament structure. Except there was nothing lazy about this guy, like there'd been with those creeps. Sally's hand tightened on the knife in her pocket. Then his smile caught her off guard…because it was *almost* enough to make her doubt the obvious.

"Oh, hi, sorry," he said. "Thought that was a different book you had there."

She looked at the Faulkner novel someone had left lying around. "Oh, that's not mine."

He picked it up. "I think I read this back in high school."

Yeah, that's right, the Crimbone kids were sent to Earth-line schools. "Any good?"

"Couldn't say. I've blocked most of high school out. So you go to Marlboro?"

What's he trying to play? Nothing about him makes sense. "Huh?"

"Marlboro College. You a student there?"

Unless, somehow…"Oh, uh, no. I'm not from around here."

"Friends? Family?" His voice was kind, soft and young with a faint gravel grind…hard to imagine it *changing*, like theirs could.

"Nope. Just passing through." For a panicked moment she thought, *Is Vermont still even neutral?* She'd been out of the loop for so long, she couldn't be sure. Grinding her teeth, an icy jolt ran through her. She should have lied, said she was from the college named after cigarettes.

"You okay?" Wow, he really looked concerned.

"Yeah," she said hurriedly, forcing a smile. Could he be just a very unusual Earth-line kid…who'd maybe taken some *extremely* strenuous gymnastic training, giving his body that hard to pinpoint, abnormally limber quality? That was a stretch, so to speak. Still, there was something else, like maybe…

"Well then," he said, "mind if I sit?"

She shrugged. "Sure." If he was playing cat-and-mouse, she'd play dumb 'til he tried to spring his trap. That's when he'd notice a blade slitting him groin to sternum. If he wasn't…She had no idea.

As he sat, she spotted no scars except a small, faint one on his left ear. His face's sharp edges were slightly uneven, like he'd taken more than his share of beatings. High on his left cheek were the fading remnants of a black eye.

"So you don't have friends or family here, but you're *just visiting?*"

"Yep. So you go to this…what's it called, Camel?"

When he laughed, she found herself *wanting* the sound to ease her. "Marlboro College. Nah, I used to go there, a couple years ago."

"You graduate?"

"Nah, not yet. At some point, I got stupid and decided I wanted to take some time off, travel, get some perspective on life. Thought I'd save up money, get my shit together…you know." His tone was weary, like he'd gotten sick of recycling this story out of habit. "Except I suck at saving money, and it seems like I'm even worse about getting my shit together."

"Right…well…uh…I guess I'm kinda here to get away from shit. 'Cept, well, it's been a long time since I had anything to get away from, if you know what I mean." Bullshit, that. She'd never gotten away from a damn thing. Wasn't he living proof of that?

"Yeah," he sighed.

She tried to hide how much it got to her, that offhand exclamation of understanding. People who faked understanding were easy to spot. He didn't sound at all like them. "Yeah, um…well, yeah."

"Hey, it's cool. Good times, right? Except…I don't

know, part of me's never stopped feeling like I went crazy from it."

"Being homeless, you mean."

"Among other things."

"So you've been one of those crazy homeless people you always see on the street, mumbling off-the-wall shit?"

They both laughed, and he said, "Yeah, probably."

"So you gonna put your tinfoil hat back on when you go outside?"

"You're the one who's still a crazy homeless person."

"Hey!" She tossed a rolled-up bit of napkin at him.

"Look, lady, you said it like that first." His hands went up in mock defensiveness. "It's cool. Just means I've found the right company."

For a moment, they just chuckled mischievously at each other. She really hoped he wasn't one of *them*, and not just because she wouldn't have to fight for her life. God, though, even the patterns and rhythms of his speech…Except his tone should have been laced with spite, not only for her, but anyone watching who might glimpse what would soon happen. She tried to see him the way anyone passing on the street would, just a cute kid of a man… Except no, he wasn't quite that, not even on the surface. All the Earth-line people had to see it, too, even if they had no idea what they were looking at, just shook their heads and told themselves it was nothing.

They talked more. He said, "So they took you in at the Common Ground. Jeez."

"Why? What's up with that place?"

"Nothing, it's a great spot. Just, well, I've had to stay there, too."

"Oh." They laughed together again. "When you showed up in town…most recently or the first time?"

"Huh?"

"You said you used to go to college around here."

"Oh right. The second time."

She told him about making friends with Liam, Clover and Bethany. She didn't mention her stoned make-out session with Bethany, though maybe she let on enough without meaning to. His smile broadened a bit when she mentioned the girl's name. When she scratched at her nose or brushed absently at a wisp of hair in her face, she still caught a trace of Bethany's scent. Did he notice? Damn, the thought must be turning Sally beet-red.

"So, where you from originally?" he asked.

"Virginia."

"Hey, me too. Where in Virginia?"

"Hampton. You?"

"Ever heard of Bedford?"

"There's a Bedford in Virginia?"

"Okay, guess you haven't. Good for you."

"What's your name?" It was weird, realizing they hadn't exchanged those things yet.

"I'm Rob Coscan. You?"

Oh well, lying wouldn't help much now either way. "Sally Wildfire."

"Pretty name."

Periodically, her hand drifted into her coat to touch the knife, reminding herself she had it, just in case. Suppose yeah, he was one of them, recognized her for what she was…but didn't care? Yeah, while she was entertaining that pretty notion, maybe she should think of training honey badgers. Either way, before they realized it, they'd talked for two hours.

Finally, he said, "Say, you wanna get out of here, grab a drink or something?"

"I'm…not old enough to drink."

"Oh." He looked crestfallen. Then his smile returned. "Okay, lemme think. What else is there to do in this damn town?"

"I think there's sleep to do in this damn town." The decision wasn't painless.

"You wanna go to sleep this early?"

"Before last night, I hadn't gotten to really sleep for three days."

"Okay, look. My place isn't exactly hospitable; otherwise I'd let you crash there…Ah hell, you can have my bed tonight. I'll sleep on the floor if you want."

Now that sounded like the Pittsburgh man's offer. Except Rob wasn't at all like that…even if he did hold out hopes of renegotiating those sleeping arrangements. Crimbone or not, he was a guy, after all. If not for her other suspicions, it might be tempting.

A new sexual encounter two nights in a row…Just the idea freaked her out. "Nah…that's okay."

"Yeah, I understand, but…Well, sleeping at the Common Ground's a pain in the ass. You got money for a motel room? I can ask around, see if any of my friends have a spare couch."

He wasn't bullshitting about that either, even though it left him out of covert motives. Even if he wasn't one of them, just what kind of guy was he? "That's okay," she said. "I've got some money. I think I'll sleep a while at the

Common Ground, if there's not too many people there. If that gets so I can't stand it, I'll find…something."

"You want me to walk you back there?" His eyes looked brighter than ever, their sharpness almost gone.

"You can if you want…Yeah, I'd like that."

The whole way, her hand stayed curled around the knife in her pocket. God, to know for sure she didn't have to…

"How long you think you'll stay?" he said. "In town, I mean?"

"I have no idea. Why?"

"Well, if you don't plan to fly off into the Wild Blue Yonder right away, I'd like to see you again."

"Sure!" The enthusiasm in her voice startled her, but not as much as when he hugged her goodbye. Still, she let go of the knife long enough to wrap both arms around his neck. For a split instant, oh God, they might melt into each other naturally, thoughtlessly… as if one another's arms should be like a million daily comforts they were both used to. Then again, she wasn't used to daily comforts in general.

As he drew away, his lips brushed her cheek. Spontaneously, quickly, she felt herself kiss him right above the jaw line. Then they said good night.

THREE

Rob climbed to the floor where all the crazies lived. In the kitchen, an emaciated, stringy-haired man labored painfully at fixing a salad, the human facsimile of a broken old mule that just won't die, even with two broken legs, even after you'd tried shooting it in the head, two or three times. Rob hadn't tried breaking Gus's legs, or shooting him in the head, yet.

"Heeey, Rob," Gus muttered in his sheepish monotone.

Rob grunted civilly and grabbed some bread and sandwich fixings, along with his last beer. Gus asked how his day had been. Rob said fine, so Gus mumbled for five minutes about how Julia, the landlady, had been harassing him over some petty household matter. Rob tried not to look at him. Gus had one of those mouths that always drooped, often drooled when he was wasted, which was most of the time. Julia never stopped talking and wouldn't leave you alone, Gus often mentioned.

"Oooh, Roooob, this nozzle thing here in the siiiink…Could you make suuure you leave, like, the tube out? I mean, it's no big thing, juuuust drape it behind the taaaaps…'cause, like, it's hard for me to puuuulll it out…"

While Rob fixed his sandwich, Gus kept mumbling, somehow working in rhapsodies on the sprouts he grew in jars on the kitchen table, and some conspiracy theory involving a secret blood brotherhood between Elvis Presley and Richard Nixon. When Rob took his sandwich and beer to his room, Gus mumbled louder, even after the door closed and locked, asking something about New Orleans. Rob should never have mentioned hailing from the place. He thought about throwing Gus down the stairs, then zoned him out and put on Tom Waits' *Heart Attack and Vine*. When the song *Jersey Girl* came on, he thought about Sally Wildfire. For all he knew, she'd lied about where she was from and actually was a Jersey Girl. It didn't matter. She could be his incarnation of Tom's myth, at least for tonight, in his head.

"*Nothing else matters in this whole wide world,*" he sang softly, "*when you're in love with Sally Wildfire…*Who are you gonna turn out to be, Sally, once I get to know you too well to keep up the fantasy?"

Ah, who was he kidding? How many guys, all over the country, had looked up as she wandered in from the cold, got one look at those crazy reddish copper eyes of hers, and fell head over heels for her instantly?

He could think of at least one. For right now, that was just fine.

FOUR

Sally helped Jake and Clover close up. All evening, Clover seemed pretty bright and talkative. When Jake left in a hurry without saying much, she grew sullen and quiet.

Something on the silent air made Sally fidgety, so she asked, "Where'd Jake take off to?"

"To fuck some bitch on the other side of town."

"Huh? So…Okay, but I thought you two were sorta…"

"It's an *open relationship.*"

"Oh." Sally guessed that arrangement hadn't been Clover's idea.

"Shit, I'd better get home, do some laundry. Wanna come, drink a few beers? You can do your laundry, too, if you like."

"Thanks. Does Bethany have a key to get in, whenever the hell she turns back up?"

"Yeah, but—Oh, that's right, she took off to Keene today, with that old guy of hers who showed back up in town. She probably won't be back tonight."

Sally had no idea where Keene was. "Oh. Then she's bisexual?"

"Yeah, pretty much. That and she's just a slut. You?"

"Yeah, I guess. Bisexual, I mean. Not a slut."

Clover, for her part, showed no sexual interest in Sally, even when they drove out to the house. Maybe that's part of what Sally liked about her, though she mostly talked about sports, cooking, movies, music and other stuff Sally didn't know much about. Her place was way out in the boonies, about half an hour from town. It was a spacious one-story with a basement barely big enough for the washer and dryer. She had a couple roommates, but they were out of town this week. Jake lived there too, she said, theoretically. After heaving her laundry bag down the stairs, she fetched the beer. Sally sat down there while Clover got the first load of laundry going. After that, they lounged around drinking.

The basement was as muggy as mid-summer. Somehow, though, Sally was halfway through her second beer when she realized she still had her coat on. Without thinking, she peeled it off.

"Say, which way to the bathroom?" she said.

"Right up the stairs, next door down on the left," said Clover

On her way upstairs, Sally noticed the beer had already gone to her head. What all had she eaten today? A bowl of

Jake's beans-rice-eggplant mix for breakfast, two more for dinner, with a few crack-snacks and that coffee in between. *Starting to get silly, girl. You know what happens when you do that, right?*

Maybe this time she'd covered her tracks as well as she thought, and it was safe to stay in Brattleboro a while, get to know the people she'd met at the Common Ground. Maybe she'd get to know Rob Coscan, too. If she'd been wrong about her first impression of him…then yeah, definitely.

When Sally got back downstairs, Clover glanced up, then quickly set her eyes forward, on the wall. How much beer had she polished off? Sally's jacket lay pressed and crinkled against the wall like a squashed bug. As she sat back down on it, she found herself right in the line of Clover's dull gaze. On the stone floor by her butt, the closed pocketknife lay three fourths exposed…including some of the dried spatter. Clover's face stayed dull and buzzed, but it might be hovering around alarm.

Sally's tiny palm covered the knife. "What are the good local newspapers around here?" she asked.

Clover gave her a weird look, then said, "Well, there's the free rag, the Advocate. That's pretty good, 'specially if you wanna know about up-coming art events, live music and stuff. Here, have another beer."

"Thanks, I'd like that." With a motion that might have been an idle brush, Sally passed the knife back into her coat. Clover's suspicion seemed deflected, if there'd been any.

Sally went for another beer, trying to hide her relieved sigh. She hadn't felt guilty over the man in Pittsburgh. It had been about survival, with no more ill will than towards a rabid dog that needed putting down. What happened afterwards still bothered her, though. Having to kill Clover, or anyone in this town, just because they picked up on the wrong things…She'd rather not think about that, even if she'd been seconds away from doing it.

Just another survival reflex, she told herself. She drank her next beer very fast.

PITTSBURGH

ONE

The terminal was mostly empty this late, so the information office was locked and dark. A few caffeine-fueled patrons sat around, waiting on late night connections. Cops strolled through and woke a sleeping man to see his ticket, making sure he wasn't a vagrant. Near a connector gate, a soldier on his way back to duty stretched out and dozed, using his duffel bag as a pillow. A massive Mennonite woman in full regalia, fanning bonnet and all, changed her baby's diaper on a table in the café. Everyone must have assumed the ticket clerk had gone home.

Had anyone peered closely through the office blinds, they'd have noticed the faint bluish glow still flickering. Had they pressed their ear to the glass, they'd have heard two soft eleven-year-old voices, one boy and one girl, interspersed with faint mutterings.

Tonight's ticket clerk had worked the afternoon shift two days ago. Both kids wore plain clothes made from a chemically treated hemp that rarely left stray fibers behind, but from which DNA traces slid like water off a duck just in case. The soles of their leather sandals were similarly coated. You could tell they were twins by their faces, though their hair threw some people off—the boy's fair blond, scruffy, getting longish so it hung in his eyes; the girl's reddish brown, neatly combed, hanging midway to her waist. Tonight, she'd tied it back, out of the way of the delicate work before her. They'd exhausted their last lead—another clerk who worked here—in a gas station bathroom on his way home.

"You're doing it all wrong." The girl shoved the boy back, so his fingertips slid out of the slick, softening brain matter. The clerk stopped singing the Tom Petty song. Hopefully the sudden jostle hadn't damaged the brain, screwing up the interrogation.

"Is that a one-way or round-trip ticket to Baltimore, sir?" The clerk drooled. The top of his skull had been cleanly removed, exposing his brain, which the twins now explored.

"Hear that?" asked the boy. "I'm on the right track. Let me try and…"

"You just got lucky," said the girl, "found the right *pathways*. We gotta follow all the steps Grandpa taught us."

"I was!"

"No, you weren't. Here, I'll show you."

With that, her fingertips pressed the same area. The clerk muttered what sounded like some kind of drill…the office's opening procedure.

She massaged the brain some more, then leaned forward and whispered. Her fingers trailed around rhythmically, pressed harder, pressed softer, moving fast then slow. Into the clerk's ear she described aspects of her older sister's most basic movements, voice patterns and aura. This clerk probably couldn't see auras, but he'd make the connection once she tapped into the right pathways. She described her sister's present appearance, as close as she knew for sure, from a security camera still her father had tracked down half a year ago in a Detroit train station. Hopefully it was close enough to register, assuming the clerk had even seen Sally.

"It's not working," groaned the boy. "C'mon, Sissy; she must've left town some other way. We'll talk with Mom and Dad, and we'll figure something else out."

Ignoring him, she spoke in a nearly perfect imitation of her older sister's voice. "Hey, how much is a ticket to—"

She cut herself off. The man stayed silent. She repeated the same phrase several times with different inflections, then rephrased the question.

"Excuse me, I'd like to buy a one-way bus ticket to—"

"Can I get a ticket to—"

"Say, when does the next bus leave for—"

Sheldon stood by fidgeting. "It ain't working, Sissy."

Sissy huffed. "So when's the next bus leave headed—"

The boy's eyes trailed to a glass-framed U.S. map. "What about the neutral states?"

Sissy winced, then paused. However she might shift or shrug the rest of her body, her fingers froze stone still in brain goo. "Didn't you already try that?"

"Not the current ones. What was the nearest one *before* she ran off?"

Sissy, who prided herself as a geography and history student, bent back over the clerk. "So, will this get me to Vermont?"

When the clerk didn't answer, she almost moved on. Then she tried other inflections.

"Where in Vermont you wanna go to, miss?"

Her fingers shifted, pressed again, and the clerk said in a rough facsimile of Sally's voice, "Well, how far'll it get me?"

When Sissy pressed again, he answered.

TWO

Blocks away, a black Buick sat parked in deep shadow. Within were two adults dressed identically to the children who'd just interviewed the clerk. Both were stout and stoic, the man short with white hair, the woman tall and dark-haired. Her hands stayed folded, ready to spring to the glove box for the Magnum. Since leaving the van full of dead punk kids on the roadside an hour north of here, they'd done nothing to raise any profile. From the moment that driver blubbered where he and his friends had kicked out the hitchhiker, the family knew the mindset they'd need for this. Death might have already scented out this car, might be circling slowly inward.

As the twins came ghostlike up the street, their mother's eyes peered hard into the shadows around them. The spires of a cubic tower gashed the skyline like black glass slivers, barely passing for a simple office block to Earth-line eyes. The children's silent poise held 'til they opened the door, then they scrambled in.

"She's headed for some place called Brat-o'-boro," blurted Sheldon. "In Vermont."

The parents exchanged looks. Vermont had been

neutral territory 'til about a year ago, when a cluster of wandering Schomite kids broke truce. By the end of the skirmishes, the Crimbone had established control, and it had proved profitable for them. Of course the Schomite Cabinet insisted the original aggressors were Spirelights, and it had been the Schomites who'd managed to move in and set up their base of peace-keeping. Factoring in manpower and threat of exposure against Vermont's loss, the Secret Police Tribunal decided to cut their losses for the foreseeable future.

"Not Brat-*O*, Sheldon," said Sissy. "Brat-*OL*. Yeah, he's right, though, it's in Vermont."

"You covered your tracks like we went over, right?" asked their dad.

"Yes," they practically sang in harmony.

Sheldon passed Dad the plastic bottle of the eroding fluid with which they'd sprayed down the body, along with anywhere else in the office where they might have left fingerprints.

"No one saw us, either," added Sissy. "We slipped into the office in the afternoon when the guy left on his lunch break, stayed real quiet and still and out of sight, then waited 'til he locked up. Once we were done with him, we left through a side door, so no one in the lobby saw us."

"Good going," said Dad.

"We should get on the road," said Mom.

Everyone nodded. Sissy and Sheldon's work wouldn't be discovered 'til morning, but it wasn't the cops they were racing in this city.

"True," said Dad, "but it shouldn't be a problem. The only connections the Earth-line police could make any time soon would be to Indiana or Tennessee. Unless Sally's gotten very sloppy, they won't. Even if they do, I don't much see how they could trace her to this…Brattleboro place."

"They have security cameras in bus stations," Mom noted.

"I disabled the cameras," Sheldon said. "Then I traced the wire to where they keep the tapes, and I sprayed 'em down."

Dad answered Mom, "Like I said, unless she's gotten very sloppy, they won't have an accurate facial description to match those tapes. Still, good thinking, Sheldon."

In the back seat, Sheldon grinned.

The family drove off, silent because there was nothing to speak about—at least nothing the parents would discuss around their children, or vice versa. Sheldon saw Sissy's scorn, like he didn't have the right to seek Mom and Dad's favor when he thought of something she hadn't. Instead of punching her in the ribs, he turned and looked out the window for a while. When he glanced back, she still stared off sullenly, so he gave her a playful jab. She winced, so he persisted 'til she giggled and jabbed back at him. By and by, she got sleepy, so he gathered her ponytail and spent the next fifteen minutes weaving it into a single whip-like braid. She grew drowsier and settled back against him. Before long, they were both asleep, holding each other the way the Earth-line children hugged their teddy bears.

Soon the Buick was on the interstate, headed for Vermont.

ANOTHER DAY IN BRATTLEBORO

ONE

Rob struggled, first to wake up, then to remember the dream. That red, wet room…Had the walls always been painted, or was that the color of the moisture? Either way, Louis had been there, happy the way Rob liked to remember him, not like when they'd last spoken. The far wall had been stripped away so the room stood open to the festival outside. Randall had come into the restaurant weeks ago, telling Rob how Louis had stabbed himself in the chest the night before, after a violent tequila-fueled outburst.

So he's not actually dead, Rob thought.

Nope, the crazy bastard had just told everyone at the party he was, after downing all that booze. So they'd spread the rumor for him, and the campus rumor mill canonized it far and wide as fact. Now Rob noticed Louis holding his knife, the one he liked to twirl between his fingers expertly, like a practicing ninja. Had Louis stabbed himself with that particular knife? No one would tell Rob. Obviously, 'cause Louis hadn't stabbed himself at all. He still would, though, in a few weeks.

Out across the festival, strangely dressed men and women danced and played carnival games. Beneath their feet grew the greenest grass Rob had ever seen, sprouting thickly from the cracks. Soon you wouldn't be able to spot the scorched stone. Before the flames, it had shimmered like ivory, almost crystalline, never letting grass sprout between its seams.

"C'mon, man," said Rob, "we should be out there enjoying ourselves."

"So, why aren't you?"

"'Cause I gotta figure out what's got you so down, then get *you* out there."

"It's not a celebration for us."

"It's able to happen *because* of us. C'mon, we just fought a war. There are bloodlines to replenish." Rob picked up the champagne bottle, corked with Gus's shrunken head. The label bore one of those funny symbols that always showed up in Louis's drawings…a pair of vertical curved slash marks, almost like parentheses, serrated on the outer edges with three thin upward-pointing teeth. Teeth, sure, or flames maybe. Another crescent slash crossed the center. Had it been in only one of Louis's drawings, or a lot of them?

If Louis drinks this champagne, dream logic insisted, *he won't stab himself.*

"Anyone got a camera out there?" Louis shouted into the festival. "I wanna get a picture with Rob here." At least he sounded happier. Except wait, wasn't everyone supposed to think he was dead? Oh, right, none of those folks would be here.

Rob still asked, "Will they…see and hear you?"

Louis shrugged. "Oh, to them we just look like wolves. So they won't think it's weird if they see you talking to me."

Gus's shrunken head mumbled something about Elvis and Nixon. Why the hell had they brought him along?

"Gus," Rob said, "if you keep babbling, I'm gonna knock your fucking brains out."

Louis chuckled, then smiled sadly—guiltily?

"Roooob, could you, like, turn the booootttle some? 'Cause, like, I can't see the crrrooowwd, maaannnn…I hear Elvis is supposed to be playing today…Y'know, Elvis and Nixon were secretly brothers? Elvis met with Nixon at the White House, and he, like, wanted to be a DEA agent, even though he was, like, addicted to all these prescription drrrrruuuuuugggs…"

Rob pressed Gus' shriveled chin, so the neck slid out like a sopping wound-up dishrag. Then—*pop*—the head flew and hit the corner of the ceiling, opposite the missing wall. It was no longer shrunken when it splattered like a rotten melon, brains flying everywhere. The bubbling foam was red and pulpy, so when Rob filled the glasses, flecks floated. Louis was still calling for a camera. Had those things even been invented here?

"Relax and have some champagne first, dude."

"Nah, I'm not in much of a drinking mood, man."

They had a while, so Rob shrugged. He could talk Louis into it. When he sipped, the pulp had the texture of thin strings of chicken fat, except so sweet…Rob felt it dissolve in the liquor as it went down his throat, warming his veins. Again, he looked at the bottle label. Louis's symbol looked as out of place and time as a camera. Both belonged somewhere far ahead, Rob sensed vaguely.

Somehow, though, Louis had found someone with a camera and pulled them up into the red room. He threw an arm around Rob, hoisting him to his feet, and they grinned at the lens together. Rob realized he didn't have any photos of him and Louis together. Anyway, the pulp had dissolved, in both the glass and his veins, kicking the change into motion…

Once the camera flashed, there rose a huge mirror where the knocked-out wall had been, where a photographer had stood. As Rob's reflection started to change, Louis took the glass.

Oh, to them, we just look like wolves. Louis had to drink before Rob's change went too far. If Louis saw too much of it, he might decide not to drink.

There'd been more, but Rob couldn't remember it, so he opened his eyes. Either way, here he was, back in this reality where Louis was actually dead. The only picture of them together was still stuck in dreamland. Did he still have any of Louis's drawings? Back at the start of the friendship, Rob had spent a lot of time sitting and watching Louis draw, the way his pencil hand would start edging along the paper, so unsure. Louis only drew when he was at his most lost, most convinced of his own utter misplacement in this world, incapable of seeing any good in his decisions. That's when his golden-brown eyes shone with that hard, cold glow, like ice catching the morning sun. Like he'd been keeping himself frozen, not really against the world, but to hold himself together, to keep whatever haunted him from ripping him apart from the inside. Then he'd start drawing, and the lines on the page would slowly take shape. The ice would melt out of his eyes as the fluidity spread up his arm through his being. After a good drawing kick, Louis would be at his best for hours.

Rob dragged himself out of bed and put on a Hank Williams CD—Hank *Senior*, thank you kindly—to help the waking world feel more real. When he remembered his reflection in the dream, changing into a wolf or something, his waking body felt too soft. He dropped onto his front two knuckles, straightened his back, kept his eyes up and on his door, and pushed himself up forty times. When he stood, his limbs felt hot and tight and throbbing. He cranked the CD player before heading to the kitchen, where he fixed coffee to wash the last champagne and human pulp taste from his mouth. He didn't find it strange that the dream's taste lingered, but it worried him that it might mean something. So where was the sensation it had loosed in his veins, not to mention his new reflection? The weird symbol on the champagne bottle… He'd seen it in one of Louis's drawings.

Most of those drawings had been fantasy art, creatures and knights and exotic women straight out of all those fantasy novels covering Louis' bookshelf. Except Rob had read plenty of those books too, and he'd never pictured anything in them quite like Louis' drawings. Likely you could only trace the difference back to the finest subtleties of line work, shading, the engravings on ancient walls, and embroidery of the otherworldly clothing. Only later, when Louis hadn't drawn anything in months—at least nothing Rob knew of—would it start to make sense. The artistic act didn't just nourish Louis' better spirits. It was one of the only things that breathed at all. It was the ice in his eyes he gave to the page.

With another gulp of coffee, Rob closed his eyes and breathed to the rhythm of Hank's twanging guitar and voice. Something Louis drew must be around here, somewhere. Goddamnit, he knew Louis had given him at least one to keep. So, had he lost it in the shuffle while getting out of New Orleans? No way he'd let that happen, not when he remembered first seeing it…

He must have flipped through a third of Louis's art when he'd come across that shaggy-headed form, eyes blazing from within a shadowed face. The long dark coat billowed, and a dripping black blade curved outward from either fist. The figure stood on the rocky bank of a mist-drowned valley. In the foreground, there rose the silhouettes of those who looked on his coming in awe. Behind him, the mists parted to reveal what he'd left in his wake, though his looming form obscured most of it…

"So, who's this guy supposed to be?" Rob had asked.

Louis had leaned over from whatever he'd been doing. "That's *Magur Sevi.*"

"Weird name."

"Hell, I was just fuckin' around with lines and shapes, and he's what came out." Louis was a terrible liar. Rob was used to that, but it was strange to catch him doing it about a piece of fantasy art.

As Rob saw more details etched in the shadows of the face, a thrilling chill tickled him…as if the shadows wavered, threatening to recede. "All those lines on his face, neck and hands, are those supposed to be scars?"

"Yep. You really like that one, don't you?"

"Hey, you've got talent, man. Ought'a come up with a story behind this guy."

"You're the natural storyteller. What do you think it is? You can have that drawing if you want."

So, had the symbol from the dream been in there, emblazoned somewhere on Magur Sevi? Where the hell had that drawing ended up? *C'mon, Rob, drink more coffee and think!*

Out of the bathroom came Darren, groggy and scruffy. "Hey, man. How's the face?" Darren, the only housemate Rob got along with, had been in last week's bar brawl with him.

"Fine. How you doing?"

Darren held out his hand. The backs of his fingers had almost healed. "Better. They're calling me *Knuckles* at work now."

Rob grinned. "So, how's that detox process going?"

"Well, I've got a pretty nice hangover right now. Got a cigarette?"

They climbed through the kitchen window onto the wooden fire escape for a smoke—a *wooden* fire escape being yet another of the landlady's ingenious contributions. At least it made a fine hangout space on a gently brisk Vermont morning. Summer's last musky tang floated up from the grass, tickling the clean woodsy smell of red leaves ready to fall.

"You work today?" Darren asked.

"In theory. They keep cutting my fucking hours, then not telling me 'til I show up."

"Wow. Business that bad, huh? Wanna go get breakfast?"

"Your treat?"

"Hell, why not?"

"Linda's?"

CHAPTER 4

CORNELIUS ENTERED DISTRICT ATTORNEY WILLIAM LANGDON'S office without knocking. It was late, it had been a long walk, he hadn't eaten, and he was worried because his men had gone into the tunnels without him. Of course, that had been Captain Palmer's decision. Cornelius came into the room pissed, having no time or desire to play word games with crooked politicians. Langdon was different, elected to the office for less than a year, he was standing up to the Ruef - Schmitz political machine, and in this town that took some brass balls as well as character.

"Apple?" Langdon asked as he studied Cornelius's expression to measure his mood. He held a green skinned apple out for inspection, then with slow intent set it down on the edge of his desk closest to the vacant seat he motioned Cornelius towards. "Sorry to ask you to visit my humble office at such a late hour but as you know, it is sometimes best to conduct business when there are fewer prying eyes and ears about."

Cornelius knew that there were quite a few individuals on the District Attorney's staff that were also on the Ruef - Schmitz payroll. Now he knew why he was here, something to do with Abe Ruef and Mayor Schmitz.

"Inspector Cornelius McCann, I'd like you to meet the Senior Special Federal Prosecutor, Jacob Rhodes. He comes to us at the request of the President of the United States on this matter."

Cornelius gave the man an appraising eye before extending his hand. Rhodes looked fit for a man who might be in his mid-forties. His dark hair is well trimmed, dusted with just enough salt to be distinguishing. Dressed in a dark brown three-piece suit, too rich for San Francisco, gave him the appearance of being from head to toe a Washington man, one who is used to playing cards with the powerful and mighty. "Pleased to meet you, Mr. Rhodes. I take it you are not here to investigate our latest rounds of shanghaiing."

Langdon gave Cornelius an eye that suggested that he wanted to cut the small talk and get to the point of why they were all there.

Rhodes chuckled. "No, the maritime crime of shanghaiing and kidnapping is a little below my pay grade. I am here to dig deeper into police graft, rate graft, and franchise graft within the governing agencies of San Francisco. I understand that you might know a thing or two about that. Mr. Langdon here tells me that you have been quite helpful over the last few months in helping him build a case against Abe Ruef, Mayor Schmitz, most of the city supervisors, as well as your boss, the Chief of Police."

Cornelius almost smiled. "Well, I am a police officer and sworn to uphold the law when it comes to graft and corruption even when it includes my boss." *No mention of Captain Palmer, the poor bastard must be too low on the totem pool,* Cornelius thought as he glanced at Langdon and pulled the mangled remains of his cigar from his pocket. "Do you mind?"

Seeing the cigar's mangled condition Langdon slid open a desk drawer, pulled out a box of cigars, and slid it across the desk. Cornelius took two, pocketed one, rolling the other between his fingers before he bit off the tip, spitting the small tobacco plug on the floor. Langdon finger tapped a large file marked confidential that sat on his desk. "I was about to share our discoveries to date with Mr. Rhodes and thought it might be helpful if he could hear it straight from the investigating officer. Everything is in the file so there is no need to go over the day to day details."

Cornelius looked at the file. He knew what was in it, that there was enough evidence to bring the entire Ruef - Schmitz machine down with solid indictments, if the D.A. could get it tried in an honest court. *Looks like this time we might actually get somewhere*, he thought as he mulled over where to begin. He lit his cigar, savoring its aroma. The cigar cost as much as a half dozen of his regulars. "Mr. Rhodes," he began, "are there any decent French restaurants in Washington."

"A few." Rhodes looked a little confused as to the topic of conversation.

"That is good to hear. I'm sure it does a lot for our international relations." Cornelius paused. "I'm not sure if we have any French restaurants here that are owned and managed by any Frenchmen. I've never cared for their food, but as a duly sworn officer of the law I am interested in what is being served upstairs or behind closed doors. Here, the term *French Restaurant* has a meaning which conveys much more than the implication that a given restaurant has a French proprietor. The term has been loosely adopted to mean that a restaurant is selling much more than what is recommended on their menu. In short, it implies that the business is a peculiar kind of transient house of assignation, obviously arranged for immoral purposes, sometimes having a conventional restaurant dining room on the ground flood, and often a banquet room and a few private dining rooms upstairs. The real money does not come from the restaurant but from the business conducted upstairs. Good French restaurants in San Francisco are in reality upper scale houses of prostitution." *He loved using the highfaluting words, he hadn't mangled a single one.* "The building is often five or six stories in height. The presence of the restaurant on the ground floor gives it a certain air of legitimacy. They are immensely profitable, the sale of food and liquor to persons using the upper stories, and for the rental of the rooms above, bring in a remarkable amount of cash. I might add that the profits from upstairs keep the prices in the restaurant low. Considering the skill of the cooks and the quality of the food served it is a bargain in anybody's book. As strict conduct is required in the public dining room, many respectable people patronizing the place have no idea what else is going on. Why, you could bring your mother there and she would be pleased with the experience."

There are a surprising number of socially prominent people who accept a portion of the profits of these so called French restaurants as a normal matter of doing business. Because of the the extremely liberal rentals paid, the system is received with easy toleration."

"Last year I began to pay special attention to one particular restaurant which was located on a prominent corner in the downtown shopping district, where hundreds of women daily passed its doors, many dining there. The building, five stories in height, had four stories devoted to the private supper bedrooms. The land was owned in trust by one of the largest, if not the largest, trust company in the West. A lease was obtained by a man notorious in the French restaurant business. The officer of the trust company which held the lease of this particular establishment was and still is a regent of the State University. That the French restaurant burned to the ground at the time of his appointment was, in the least, convenient.

"I think you will find that the file on the Municipal Crib is a good illustration of the tolerance which permits a corrupt Mayor to deal in illicit privileges and to take profits from vice. The case in point arose with a raid we made on a famous house of prostitution during an earlier and unsuccessful investigation of the Ruef-Schmitz regime. They had one of the best steak dinners in town, if I do say so myself. The immunity from police interference which this place was accorded had earned it the name of the "Municipal Crib." Many of our highest ranking police officers were quite perturbed with me when we closed it down. My own Precinct Captain threatened me with a reduction in rank, but he being a married man chose not to push it too far. In the raid, one hundred and sixty prostitutes were arrested and released on bail money exceeding sixteen thousand dollars. The money was furnished by a prominent liquor wholesaler who, at the time was the president of one of the most powerful, and the richest of the merchant associations in the city. That their president, a wholesale liquor man, might also be a wholesale backer of prostitution did not arouse the merchants to the extent of anyone making an investigation. The fact that his company was selling liquors to a large number of resorts whose licenses were dependent upon the Schmitz Board of Police Commissioners, was accepted by many as a sufficient excuse for his supplying the bail.

The Ruef-Schmitz organization, recognizing how easily such illicit enterprises could be made to pay tribute, devised a plan to obtain a share of their profits. They included the trust company's restaurant I already described. Their plan was made the easier when one of the members of the Board of Police Commissioners began to oppose the granting of licenses to these places, as soon as he had become aware of their extremely vicious character with some prodding from his civic minded wife. The Mayor inspired another member of the Board of Commissioners, who had absolute power to grant or withhold liquor licenses, to begin an attack on the entire association and to threaten refusal to renew the licenses. The restaurant keepers soon discovered it was necessary to employ Abe Ruef as their attorney to defend them before the Board. Ruef was paid large fees by the restaurant proprietors, and the licenses were renewed at their expiration."

"Five indictments were brought against Schmitz and Ruef based on these extortions. Ruef later pleaded guilty to the charge on one of them. Schmitz was convicted by a jury, but the conviction was set aside by a decision of the District Court of Appeal, on the ground of a technical defect in the indictment, which also released Ruef."

"Go on." Rhodes was interested but so far there wasn't enough for the President to call for a special investigation.

Due to the late hour Langdon cut Cornelius short. "Abe Ruef, Mayor Schmitz, all the City Supervisors, control and have their hands into just about everything the city of San Francisco needs to function. Utility rates are fixed, you can't get a phone without a special permit. Public transportation is hamstrung because both of the railroads who want to put in more street cars and trolleys are tied up in court because they can't get their permits approved. They can't get any satisfaction in court unless they hire Abe Ruef as their legal council. Building permits are dead upon arrival at city hall, unless large and often discrete fees are paid. Unions, the same. A working man can't join a union, and that includes the Longshoremen's, Carpenter's, Plumber's, Butcher's, and Music Unions, unless he is willing to pay a fee which many of them can't afford."

"Who is the kingpin here Schmitz or Ruef ?" Rhodes asked as he fingered the file for thickness as if its sheer weight mattered.

"Abe Ruef," Langdon answered. "Schmitz was the President of the Musician's Union before Ruef put him in the mayor's office. Mostly, he is nothing more than a rubber stamp lining his own pockets as long as he does as Ruef says."

"Well, gentlemen, if everything you say is documented here, and I have no reason to doubt that it isn't, I think the President will be interested. I've got a train leaving for Sacramento at ten in the morning where I'll share what I can with the State Attorney General. I should caution you that nothing will happen with this unless it has the President's approval. Once asked by the President, the Attorney General of the United States will take the lead. It sounds like we may need one or two newly appointed Federal Judges out here before it can go to a Grand Jury." Eyes locked, while hands were shaken, each looking in his own way for confirmation that this time they would be able to bring the Ruef-Schmitz corrupt government down.

"Oh, and one more thing," Rhodes said as he prepared to leave. "Inspector McCann, I can't thank you enough for all you've done. In time, the good people of San Francisco, and California for that matter, will owe you a large bill of thanks. On that note, watch your back, and those of the officers closest to you. There are some powerful people out there with a lot to lose when this all comes out. Without our primary witness to everything here," he patted the file, "it will be much more difficult to bring them to justice. I suppose the funeral parlor union is also subservient to Ruef?"

The laughter was a shared chuckle, the truth being too close to home.

"William Langdon," Rhodes continued, "you are a good man. You have risen from School Superintendent to District Attorney; perhaps you can teach us all something. I couldn't help but notice that you came into office on the Ruef- Schmitz ticket and shortly thereafter began your investigation. Watch your back my friend, for as sure as the sun will come up tomorrow these people will be as unforgiving of your transgressions as they are the Inspectors." No further farewells or words were needed as Jacob Rhodes stepped out into the night air with evidence in hand.

"He's right you know," Langdon said as he retrieved a bottle of brandy from a desk drawer with two glasses. Cornelius took his neat, not by choice, because there was no ice. "I'm not worried that much about myself," Langdon continued, "it comes with the job. I guess it is the same for you."

Cornelius knew that he was a bigger target if Abe Ruef decided to play it rough. "Me, I can take care of myself. There are a couple of officers, good friends, who they might target to get my attention, though."

"Perhaps you should bring them in close, they can watch your back, you theirs."

"I'm considering that. Right now they are down in the shanghai tunnels with five other officers, all good men. Well, almost all. There is one I wouldn't trust at a school girl's bake sale. I wouldn't put anything past Ruef to cover his own ass. I've had an uneasy feeling about this detail all night."

Langdon finished his drink, grabbed his coat, with a quick glance at the phone. "You want me to send in a squad from the County Sheriff's Department just in case."

"Thanks, but no thanks. The fewer people involved the better. This isn't the first time Sergeant Pickens has been down in the tunnels. He knows every jack-man on the detail. Still, I . . ."

"You know where to find me if you need me," Langdon said as he locked the door behind them.

"You want me to walk with you?"

"No, I'll be fine." Langdon said, "I'm too public a figure, at least for now. Maybe I should walk with you," he grinned.

"Thanks, I've already got a shadow." Cornelius knew that Sergeant August Freeman would be out there somewhere in the shadows watching his back.

CHAPTER 5

IT WAS THAT TIME IN THE MORNING WHEN MOST DECENT people are safe at home in their own beds, the exception being the Barbary Coast where the saloons run all night. The prostitutes work until dawn, some to noon. It's the time of night when the cats, rats, and crimps own the streets. The feral cats keep the rats in check. The crimps own too many cops which means that no one is safe.

Inspector Cornelius McCann relit his cigar as he decided that a walk down to the waterfront might do him some good. If a crimp wanted to test his luck, it was okay by him. He hadn't gone but a block before he sensed that he was not alone; friend or foe, that remained to be seen. His gut told him that it was a foe, his hunch being that a few of the crimps might be working for Ruef this night. He reached into his coat and drew out his .38 Long Colt revolver from its shoulder holster, chambered a round, as he listened to the sounds of the night.

A fog horn moaned for no good reason at all. A dog barked in the distance, another answered. A cat hissed and yowled in a nearby alley. Music filtered through the streets and alleys followed by the drunken laughter of men too stupid to know that they were easy prey. The only footsteps he heard where his own. The ground fog thickened the closer he got to the waterfront. A tiny reflection, perhaps the white of an eye drew his attention to a shadow out of place in an all too dark alleyway.

Gun in hand, he relit one of the cigars he had helped himself to from the District Attorney's desk. He looked past the close brilliance of the flame into the dark recesses of the alley. In the light, he was making it perfectly clear that he knew they were there and whoever it was had best be the one who should be afraid.

Officer Freeman stepped out into the alley as Cornelius' match went out. "Fools and mangy curs is all this damned neighborhood is good for. August, you are a mangy fool. Another second and I just might have shot you just because I'm in a bad mood." Cornelius said as his eyes adjusted to the dark again.

August, a Sergeant on the Chinatown Squad, had worked with Cornelius on many occasions. He had served with the Marines in China, same as Cornelius, only in different companies. Once a Marine, always a Marine, brothers at arms. He knew Choice Pickings from the siege of the International Compound in Peking during the Boxer Rebellion. "I told you it was not going to be a good night," he said as he stepped to Cornelius's side. "Thought you might need some help. I had your back side all the while you were upstairs." August was curious but knew better than to ask. If Cornelius felt like sharing what had been said between him and the D.A., he would in his own good time. "You have an unwelcome shadow, Scout, and he may not be working alone tonight. He tried to slip in behind you as you entered the building the D.A.'s office is in. He missed the open door by this much." August showed him a knuckle's distance. "The front door locked, Scout stepped back into the shadows." August stared hard back into the alley where he had come from, then into the alley across the way.

"You sure it was Scout?"

August nodded that he was sure.

"Knowing Scout," Cornelius continued, his eyes continuing to search the night for the mystical Scout's whereabouts, "he could be standing right here between us and we might not see the bastard." They both knew Scout. He was a light footed crimp with the uncanny ability to move about with more stealth than a cat. He is good with a knife, and usually worked alone. He is smart, which is what makes him more dangerous than most crimps. He is loyal to no one and truths no one. The almighty dollar is what can buy his loyalty, but only for a given time, and there have been reliable rumors that on one or two occasions, Shadow had acted as a hit man for Ruef. "He's out there all right, I can smell him." Cornelius said. "Now that there are two of us, he'll keep his distance." His voice showed an edgy hesitancy. "If it makes you feel any better," Cornelius said," I've had an uneasy feeling most of the night too." He noted towards the brightening horizon. "Well, it won't be that long until the sun comes up. Thought I might walk down to the waterfront, care to come along?"

"Try to stop me," August answered, his voice saying all about loyalty and friendship that needed to be said.

"I thought you'd say that." said Cornelius.

The first light of dawn suggested the beginning of a magnificent day as they stopped for a moment across from the Market House where East Street ended at the Union Street Wharf. The Market House is where the Italian and a few Japanese fishermen brought their catch, where the city's restaurants and markets come to buy fresh fish and produce. It is loud, noisy, and smells of the sea: fish, tobacco, and men's sweat. The two police officers walked out to the end of the wharf and stared out across the bay at the long row of tall ships.

"There," Cornelius points. "You see those two tall ships anchored half way between here and the Oakland Long Pier?

They're Portuguese, and most likely the ones waiting for the crimps to deliver them their new crews. If they were already onboard, the captains would be making sail before any of the shanghaied crew wake up with a bad laudanum hangover." He laughed. "Nothing worse than paying good money for a crimped deckhand and have him swim ashore before you can get a day's work out of him. It doesn't look to me as if they're planning on going anywhere, at least not this morning."

The ground fog abruptly cleared.

Now don't that beat all, Cornelius thought as he tossed the well chewed cigar into the water. "Did I ever tell you the story of Shanghai Kelly's birthday?" Out of habit he checked his pocket for another cigar, cursing silently that he should have helped himself to a few more back at Langdon's office. He had one left and opted to wait. "One day - some sources say it was in 1854, others say the mid-1860s - Kelly found himself with an order for nearly 100 deck hands, and a dearth of sailors at his usually full boardinghouse for him to shanghai. Now, old Kelly was a fairly sharp rascal and he quickly came up with a plan. First he chartered an old paddlewheel steamer. Then he put the word out on the streets that it was his birthday and everyone was invited aboard to celebrate with free food and drink. Ninety men, maybe more, showed up and they put out to sea amid great merriment of drinking, eating, and song. Old Kelly knew how to throw one hell of a party. When all his guests had passed out from the drugged drinks Kelly sailed to the three ships waiting out by the Farallon Islands. The still unconscious "sailors" were handed over to their new captains, who paid, and quickly sailed away. With money in his pocket, Kelly now saw a slight problem. Everyone on the Barbary Coast knew he had sailed off with a shipload of merrymakers. How would he explain returning with the ship empty? He sailed on down the coast to mull it over. As the story goes, it was somewhere off Point Conception that he met with an incredible stroke of good fortune. He came upon the ship Yankee Blade that had run aground and it wouldn't be long until she sank. Kelly saved its entire crew and sailed them on up to San Francisco, plying them with as much booze as they wanted along the way. No tricks this time, just good clean booze and a good time for all. Hailing him as a hero, no one seemed to notice that his full ship carried not one of his original party guests." Cornelius paused after an empty chuckle died in his throat. "The shanghaiers we've got today are nothing like Shanghai Kelly. These crimps would just as soon slit your throat and sell your corpse to some unsuspecting Captain."

August looked long and hard out across the water. The sun was just beginning to rise, the early morning light making the tall ships appear closer than they were. He couldn't quite figure out which two were the Portuguese, but did not want to admit to his poor eyesight.

"What do you say to grabbing a cup of coffee and heading back to the station? Sergeant Pickens should have wrapped everything up down in the tunnels by now. No doubt he'll have a tall tale to tell and it won't be coffee he will be wanting." Cornelius suggested.

The seagulls that normally swooped and dove around the fishing wharf abruptly rose into a screaming wave and took flight towards the far shore while the sea lions bellowed in protest at being disturbed. Cornelius eyed the birds, then stared down into the water at the edge of the wharf where a bull sea lion had suddenly splashed before diving and swimming away.

CHAPTER 6

A T 5:13 A.M., OFF THE COAST OF CALIFORNIA A PLUME OF water lifted an old wooden hulled deep sea fishing boat completely out of the water. The ship landed in a chaotic swirling whirlpool that threatened to suck the ship and its entire crew beneath the surface as a mountain of water poured down upon them. The Captain, a superstitious man, fighting for the life of his ship, clung furiously to the wheel as he tries to steer his ship towards seemingly calmer waters just beyond the whirling madness. "Holy Mother Mary, protect me." At first he thought he saw a pod of whales, then as he rubbed his eyes while straining to hold the wheel, he is sure that he is seeing a great white shark like no man had ever seen before. He stared, searching for a fin, but only found a tail - this was no shark. The serpentine tail left a long white trail on top of the dark blue sea as a rip in the ocean floor opens and closes as it makes its way towards the coastal shores.

A hundred and fifty miles north of San Francisco the fissure strikes the shore nearly collapsing the lighthouse at Point Arena. The monster carved its way through land as easily as it had the sea, Mountainsides crumble, forests of ancient oak and stately redwoods fall as if they had been cleaved by a single swipe of Paul Bunyan's axe. The thundering cannonade caused by millions of trees snapping echoes throughout the canyons and countryside as the rip turns back towards the sea shattering sea cliffs for miles as it dives back beneath the sea only to reemerge at Bodega Bay shattering the sleepy coastal town. Just as dawn is breaking, the earthquake hits Santa Rosa with terrible ferocity. Before anyone can comprehend what has happened, the entire downtown district becomes a maze of shattered ruins, the fires quickly spread - elsewhere across the city not a single house survives without some damage.

The rip carves its way through Southern Marin County until finally it reaches San Francisco, where forty-thousand houses twist and groan in protest as the monster strikes the city.

The dance halls, barrooms, opium dives, slave-dens, parlor-houses, cribs, French restaurants, deadfalls, melodeons and concert saloons reel as the quake tears through their foundations. Brick walls crumble, windows shatter, wooden beams break as the Barbary Coast - Sodom and Gomorrah - is punished for her sins.

CHAPTER 7

THE FIRST FLOOR OF LAVINIA'S APARTMENT BUILDING IS suddenly lifted from its foundation then dropped four feet spilling the second and third floors into the street. Lavinia had just gotten into a hot bubble bath, when the outside wall is peeled away, the bathroom tilts as she finds herself naked wearing only a cloak of bubbles, her tub rides a wave of buckling bricks and debris down onto the street before coming to a rest near the gas street light that now spews a roaring flair of dancing, swirling flame, ominously close to the shattered wooden ribs of her fallen home. She is surrounded by hordes of screaming people trying their best to remain on their own feet as collapsing walls and falling masonry clatter around them. Her breath catches in her throat - she can't find the words that barely quiver on her lips. "Help me."

A drunken man, with lust in his eyes, staggers towards her, only to be stopped by the sudden collapse of the front of a building nearly burying him alive. Rising from the dust with a bleeding scalp and a limp arm he forgets the naked woman in the tub as he stumbles away. Crossing her arms over her exposed breasts, trying her best to not slip from the tub, she manages to squeak a breathless "Help me." Those near enough to hear are caught in their own overwhelming sense of helplessness. Her cry goes unheard. Who cares? The street, the city, everything has just been turned upside down and everyone is in mortal fear for their own lives.

CHAPTER 8

ALONG THE WATERFRONT, HUNDREDS OF SHIPS, MANY TWO and three masted masters of the seas, slammed against the docks, straining their anchors, tossing both men and cargo into the suddenly churning water. The bay rises two feet, its water sloshing back and forth from shore to shore, before dropping abruptly back down three feet.

At the Union Street Wharf, vast numbers of bubbles rise from the dark bottom of the bay, the water suddenly brownish-green and thick with mud.

Cornelius leaned forward to get a closer look as the bubbles as they appear all around the water beneath him. The wharf lurches, tilts sideways, then rises again, the water beneath belching thousands of gassy globes. Neptune himself seemed to reach out to pull Cornelius into the churning, muddy salt waters.

August fell, but managed to remain on the wharf as its wooden beams and deck planking creaked and groaned, somehow managing to hold together. As the ground heaved, the sand which the buildings near the waterfront had been built upon, liquefied. From where August clung to the wharf he saw the first buildings collapse in a thundering cloud of dust which soon obliterated his view. A cacophony of noise jarred his senses as more buildings collapsed, timber splintering, people screamed in terror. Horses panicked, spilling wagon loads of goods. Hundreds of ship's bells rang, their hulls banging against the wharfs and piers as the water rises and falls, seeming to surge in all directions at the same time. As the dust rose, he saw a horse and wagon sink from sight in what a moment before had been a solid street. A live electrical line whipped, lethally, where the horse and wagon had disappeared.

Cornelius sputtered to catch his breath as his head bobs back to the surface, only to be slammed back down by a brown pudding-like wave as an undercurrent drags him beneath the wharf. Spinning and fighting for each breath, he is slammed against a piling, sharp barnacles tear his shirt, peeling back the skin on his forearm as one might peel the skin from a tomato.

The sudden sharp pain warns him that if he doesn't get himself out of the undercurrent he could be skinned alive. Using all his strength, he kicks upward, breaching the surface as his breath exhausts itself, causing him to suck in both air and muddy salt water in the same gasp. The current forces him deeper into the gloom beneath the still quivering wharf. Struggling against the swirling surf, he barely misses another barnacle covered piling as he frantically searches for a ladder, a rope, anything that he can catch hold of.

Things go from mind-numbingly bad to worse as a stone seawall collapsed in the dark shadows where the wharf is anchored to land. He tried to back paddle, only to be drawn by the current towards the collapsing wall. With a thunderous report a huge beam supporting the wharf above cracks and splits apart, one part now hanging precariously close to the undulating surf with foot long splinters sticking out like so many sharks' teeth. The powerful current drags him straight towards the lethal spears.

In the dark, against the chaos, Cornelius's trained cop's eyes catch sight of something out of place in the shadows. A twelve foot dory skiff is drifting out of what appeared to be a dark tunnel near where the sea wall had collapsed. One man stood in the skiff trying to reach out with a fishing pike to another who had fallen overboard. The man in the water, frantic, unable to swim, is slammed by a wave against what remains of the sea wall, then slammed again. Cornelius knows that the man is as good as dead, or soon will be. "Hey, over here!" Cornelius screamed, his voice lost against the drum of the waves and the chaos around them.

A tremendous boom shakes everything above causing more of the sea wall to collapse. A wave lifts the skiff, the man onboard losing his balance, falls back and with a visual but silent scream, he is harpooned by the massive splinters of the fallen beam, his body suspended briefly, as the skiff passes beneath unharmed.

CHAPTER 9

A STRONG AFTER SHOCK STIRS THE CROWD INTO A HIGHER frenzy as what is left of Lavinia's apartment building leans further out over the street, the collapsed floors beneath groan with the stress of the shifting weight as the entire structure threatens to give way. Either from the heat, the aftershock, or both, the metal pole to the gas street light breaks, sending an explosive plume of flame up and into the brightening dawn sky. A shattered beam pushed out from the shifting ruin is close enough to catch the flame. The fire, hungry to expand, quickly spreads, leaving Lavinia with no choice other than to abandon her tub lest she be crushed. Naked, with no hope of retrieving anything from her home, she bolts from the tub towards a fallen curtain she had seen in the debris. The ground covered with glass, her feet bare, the building shifting ominously towards final collapse, the curtain is unreachable.

"Here," a neighborhood butcher said as he grabs hold of her wrapping her in his full length apron. She recognizes him as the German sausage maker who works down the street. His hands, large and rough, touch her where no man has touched her before as he tries to wrap her into the blood stained apron. His intent has no ill purpose; nevertheless, she panics as she feels his hands glide across her exposed breasts. She pulls away, turns and runs straight into the piano player from the Golden Spike, a popular dinner and dance hall around the corner. Terrified of being caught between these two men, she screams.

The piano player sees the cause of her panic and urges the

sausage maker to be on his way. On another day, the butcher might have chosen to shut the piano player's mouth with his fists. Today he just swears "To hell with you, Missy, I've got me own family to help."

The pianist takes off his tailed tuxedo coat and with concern for her modesty, gives it to Lavinia. All of five foot two, small and petite, the coat and apron cut for larger men, more than cover her feminine features. Her feet bare, he picks her up and carries her through the shattered glass and debris, setting her down a half block away in a spot where the street is mostly clear. As a pianist at a dance hall, he had seen it all and could tell that Lavinia was not a dance hall girl or one of the floozies that fill the dance halls nightly - nor is she a working girl from one of the many cribs or French restaurants in the Barbary. She is a young woman of quality, and he treats her as such.

Lavinia wants to cry. In a split second, she has been rendered homeless without so much as a cloth to cover herself with. She has no one to turn to, no one, and only this tall ill-shaven saloon man has offered a kind hand. At the moment, she does not remember that the butcher had only wanted to help.

A strong after shock rolled beneath the street, more bricks fall, buildings groan, hysterical screams sounded all around her, a thunderous boom compressed the air as something huge exploded or collapsed somewhere nearby. The man touched her on her shoulder telling her to stay where she is until she gets her wits about her again.

He walked, with a cautious eye for falling objects or fissures suddenly opening in the tortured street, towards a collapsed building where he saw two people who lay dead in the rubble, one a woman whose feet sadly stuck out from beneath a mountain of debris. The blood seeping through the shattered brickwork tells him that she would not be needing the shoes, The shoes are brown, almost new, American Beauty, very fashionable and hopefully not too small for the little woman wearing his tuxedo coat, who stood very much alive not twenty steps behind him. He brought back the shoes and gave them to her apologizing for leaving her alone in the chaos, then disappeared in search of his own family.

CHAPTER 10

THE BOOM THAT HAD ECHOED ACROSS THE CITY HAD BEEN a brick warehouse that had collapsed, covering part of the wharf with a mountain of brick, glass, and splintered timbers. A fire immediately rose from within the twisted debris.

Disoriented, August wasn't sure what had happened. He had been in an earthquake before, but this was too strong. Perhaps the gasworks had blown up or something. *Where is Cornelius?* he thought as he realized that his boss and partner had vanished. "Cornelius? Cornelius, wait up." That was when he remembered seeing Cornelius going over the side. He went to the edge of the wharf where Cornelius had last been standing. "Cornelius?"

It was useless, the current too strong, there was no way that Cornelius, or anyone else for that matter, could fight it. He knew that if the current took him beneath the wharf he'd be battered to death or drowned.

August couldn't swim, and fearing for his own life, as explosions and fires drew his attention back to that was happening in the city. In the Marines, he had learned that you never leave a man behind. Now he had to, Cornelius was dead and he needed to get off the wharf before it collapsed beneath him.

A mountain of debris from the collapsed warehouse blocked his escape, the only other way off was a boarding plank linking one wharf to another. He made his way towards it as another building collapsed nearby, dust and smoke making everything surreal, the blood orange morning sun foreign in its own sky.

CHAPTER 11

WITH ONE EYE ON THE BODY DANGLING FROM THE SHEARED beam, the other on the skiff, Cornelius recognized the face of the dead man as a crimp who normally worked out of Sacramento. *What the hell is he doing here,* Cornelius thought as he made for the skiff. He glanced one last time at the skewered crimp. *He was a mean bastard, no tears shed for that son-of-a-bitch.* Cornelius caught hold of the skiff, allowing a wave to lift him as he pulled himself aboard. One of the oars floated nearby -but not near enough to reach - making it damn difficult for one man alone to row his way out of this nightmare. The sounds coming from the city above, the turbulent surf, the groaning wharf, and a few unhappy sea lions were all magnified to a point where he could barely hear himself think.

A beam of light cast down through a crack in the wharf briefly illuminated the back of the skiff. There were five men, hog-tied, face down, banged-up and bruised. "What the hell?" he said as he caught a little seawater in his open mouth. *I'll be damned,* he almost said, as he coughed up some vile muddy salt water. There was no way he could miss Choice Pickens's bald patch with a small half-moon birthmark on the back of his head. Cornelius never stopped razzing Choice to keep his damn hat on, lest some jack-ass mistake that moon of yours for an outhouse. Sergeant Pickens, and all the officers, had all been shanghaied. Seven experienced cops beaten at their own game. "Choice?" He sputtered as he positioned himself to try to steady the craft with only one oar. Choice had not moved and he was gripped by the sudden fear that Choice and the others were all dead.

Wrestling with the oar, while trying to keep the skiff from being dragged back into the brooding gloom deeper beneath the wharf, it took him less than ten seconds to pull out his pocket knife, cutting Choice free from the ropes that bound his arms to his legs. The gag he left in place.

Choice Pickens moved.

It took everything Cornelius had to keep the boat from being slammed into a nearby piling. "Now that you've had a nice nap, I'm going to try to get us close to that oar before a wave takes it beyond our reach. You grab it, then we can row this thing out into the light of day," he said dryly, as he sunk the oar into the water pushing them away from the barnacle encrusted piling.

Two of the other officers struggled against their bindings, swearing roughly, beneath their gags. "First things first, gentleman." Cornelius said as he gave a stern look towards Choice. "There, can you reach it?"

Choice reached out for it just as a wave lifted the skiff up and away. A second wave, part of a returning tide caused by the quake, turned them back, tilting the skiff at a dangerous angle where it almost scooped up the oar along with a boatful of water. The weight of the hog-tied cops in the bow allowed the skiff to right itself with little flooding. Choice had the oar.

"Row," snapped Cornelius as another wave threatened them.

Choice ripped off his gag, spat, drove the oar deep into the water. Every muscle in his body screamed in protest as they were forced to straighten out after hours of being man handled and bound by rough rope. In the gloom, he could see that Cornelius's shirt was torn, with a nasty scrape that was bleeding profusely, the blood running down his forearm to his wrist making the handle of the oar slippery and hard to handle. "That must hurt."

Choice said as he reached deeper into his own gut to find the strength to pull the oar deep and hard.

"Row, you son-of-a-bitch, or I'll show you what *hurt* really means."

They did not have much choice but to row with the current which would take them beneath two adjoining wharfs - if they made it that far; that was a big "if". When they reached a bright patch of light that marked the gap between one wharf and the next, they slammed against a mussel covered piling.

"Easy," Cornelius muttered as he swung the skiff around to avoid a second battering. Looking up, having to squint as his eyes adjusted from the dark to the smoky light, he saw a man balanced precariously on a bowed boarding plank, his weight almost too great for the plank connecting the two wharfs. "August, god-damn it, if I had wanted to see a circus act, I'd have brought some peanuts." He swore as he reversed the oar to hold them in place. "Get off that damn thing, before you fall and put a hole in this nice new skiff I found. Go find a rope or something and get us out of here, August, and hurry."

Cornelius pulled his pocket knife out of his shirt pocket and tossed it to Choice Pickens, his best friend and partner. "Cut these guys loose. I'll be damned if I'm going to haul their lazy asses up a rope ladder." He looked at his bleeding arm, which wasn't as bad as it looked, although the blood made it look downright ugly. It strung like a son-of-a-bitch, but he could handle that. He suspected that it wouldn't be long until he got a bit lightheaded if he didn't find a way to staunch the bleeding.

The adjoining wharf was an old one that had seen better days, the center planking was broken with a few gaps here and there. How many planks were rotten through was anyone's guess. August tested his footing as he saw a rope tied off to a rusty metal eye hook on the far side.

Once there, he started to pull the line out of the water only to find it unbearably heavy. Looking over the side to see if it had hung up on something, he found that it had. A very hairy, large man clung to it unable to climb up by himself. "I've got you," he yelled down as he put all his weight behind the line and tried to pull. "But you are too damned heavy to haul up by myself."

The huge man, looking somewhat like a floundering sea lion, tried to climb the rope, hand over hand, only to spin haphazardly back and forth, as August anchored his feet, putting his back and full weight into what seemed like useless effort. "Jesus, this guy weighs more than a team of horses," he swore as he struggled to pull up the line. Finally, a ham-hock sized hand gripped the edge of the wharf, followed by a huge head matted with wet, dark hair, with a large thick walrus mustache twisted below a set of dark eyes almost hidden by a single eyebrow thick with the same coal black curly hair. Once on deck, August could see that the man was easily 6'5", and three hundred pounds or more, maybe thirty-two to thirty-four years of age. He wore the striped clothes commonly worn by Greek fishermen, though what was left of his were mostly rags.

The man remained on his hands and knees for a moment while he caught his breath, then he kissed the filthy warped wharf planking. "I am in America," he said in broken English, "God has been good to me."

He then rose, and before August could resist, the huge Greek sailor, wrapped him in a suffocating bear hug, the smell of the sea, unwashed clothes, and months at sea without a bath, dizzying. "Let me go, or I'll shoot," August protested, not that he could have reached his gun.

The huge, smelly giant, finally released him.

"I am Leonoudokis. Achilles Leonoudokis. You have saved my life. I am now indebted to you." He then looked around. "What has happened?"

The view from the old wharf was surreal. Two ships anchored just off shore were ablaze near the quay of ships. Inland, one of the most beautiful cities in the world, the great golden city of San Francisco lay broken, smoke rose from dozens of fires. The fires' reflections colored the plumes red, orange, black, blue, all the colors within the devil's rainbow. Across the bay, smoke rose from both Oakland and Berkeley.

"What has happened?" the big Greek asked again.

"I think it may be the end of the world." August said

"August, if I have to climb up there to find my own god-damned-rope, I'm going to hang you with it," Cornelius bellowed from below.

"Glad to meet you, Leanedou . . ." August said.

"Achilles, please. I am indebted to you now. We are like brothers. Yes?"

"Achilles. Okay. Now, help me with this line, we've got some police officers trapped down there." August stopped dead in his tracks, having realized for the first time that Cornelius was not alone. That in fact, Cornelius, who he had given up for dead, was very much alive and rowing a boat filled with hog-tied police officers - many of them his friends. *What the hell? Is that Choice Pickens next to him? I thought. . ."*

"Police." Achilles looked uncomfortable; the police in his village back in Greece were not to be trusted. Because of his size, he had been ordered to join the militia where they wanted him to become a prison guard. He had not the heart to beat men because they had different political opinions, or did not have enough money to pay a bribe. His only choice had been to serve as a guard or become a prisoner himself. Given that choice, he he had fled his family's small farm to become a fisherman. Now, if he returned to Greece, it would be he who would be beaten beyond reason or perhaps executed in a Greek prison. He was a man without a country. He spent two years, moving from one fishing boat to another as either a fisherman or ship's cook. He never sailed on a Greek ship, for it would most likely take him back to Greece. Often the ship's crew did not speak his language, or he theirs. His only dream was to one day reach America, where he would jump ship to find a job as a cook in the great land of the free. He had his dream, but little hope.

It took three men to tie the skiff off to a piling. The rope lowered, Cornelius was the first to be pulled up. Having been bound for so long none of the men were able to climb up on their own. From the skiff, Choice helped the others one by one, Frank Darcy first, followed by Al Smith. Ted Asbury, the smallest of the men was the last. Johansen, the big Swede, had taken a pretty good shot to the head when they had been caught by surprise in the tunnels. Whether it had been a concussion, or he had bled to death, it didn't matter, he was dead either way. Cornelius made the decision to leave his body in the skiff. Even with Achille's immense strength the big Swede was too much dead weight.

CHAPTER 12

WITH TEARS IN HER EYES, LAVINIA WATCHED AS THE PIANO man disappeared. She shivered, though the morning was not cold, she felt frozen inside. For the moment, she couldn't escape the sudden shock of the last few minutes, the sudden drop in her bath, her nakedness - vulnerable for all to see. Her eyes misted over as it all became a foggy blur, a distant nightmare - only the nightmare wasn't distant, it swirled around her in real time, in the real world. "Papa, why?" She whispered in Dutch. "Why have you forsaken me? Damn you." She pressed the first three fingers of her right hand to her lips to stifle the next words before they come out. She had never sworn before, at least not at her father. "Damn you! Why?" She screamed at the sky, though with so many lives disrupted, her plea was insignificant.

An elderly man, disoriented, mumbling in Italian, bumped into her. Jarred, she almost fell to the ground.

The sudden jolt snapped her back to her senses. She again heard the horrific noise around her. She looked at the shoes in her hand, the ones the piano man had given her. She laughed two short birdlike notes. The shoes were too big.

A building collapsed nearby.

A baby screamed.

A church bell clanged

A dog whimpered.

A multicolored parrot flew by.

She smelled smoke - and fear - then took a deep breath. She had to go, this place was not safe. But, where? She dropped the shoes, her hands touching the lapels of the piano man's coat, beneath the coat the blood stained apron, as she realized that she was still close to naked. She wanted to retreat back into her mind, to a place deep and faraway - a happy time when she had been just a girl on a picnic with her mama and sisters. Her eyes latched onto the parrot which squawked and flew in circles, disoriented, afraid to fly away, afraid to land anywhere. "Oh!" She, like the parrot, was caught unexpectedly in a wild and wicked world, and she, like the parrot had to fly somewhere to survive.

She heard a church bell which clamored chaotically rather than rang praise. Not sure of anything she picked up the shoes, looked at them, then her feet, broke off the heels, slipped her feet into them and began walking towards the center of the city, in the opposite direction from everyone else who was fleeing towards the water front as the fires spread. She followed the sound of the church bell where surely God would protect her. The only sound she seemed to hear as she walked through a hurricane of noise was the flip-flop of her shoes.

She was lost.

The church bell, now strangely silent, no longer guided her.

The farther she went, the more confused she became. She was swimming upstream against a storm surge which became a yellow tide as she entered Chinatown. She had never stepped foot in Chinatown before. Her father had always told her that it was no place for a proper Christian woman. He preached that the Chinese were not human, they were yellow devils, lower than the niggers that had come from Africa. If given a chance they would steal white babies and small children to make their Chop Suey.

She didn't believe that, of course. Her father had held a narrow and stern view of the world, and when it came to the church, he was an inflexible man. She had never met a Chinaman, seen them only at a distance; now she was amongst them. Like her, they were frightened, scared to death, small timid people who even in these harrowing circumstances would not look her in the eye.

Where is the church? Someone will help me there.

Three blocks away the brick bell tower had collapsed, the bell a dented metal boulder buried within.

In the smoke, the chaos, the tide of strange yellow people, she was completely lost. The faces of the Chinese women and children drew back in horror as she approached them. They screamed, quivered, and whimpered as if she, not them, were the devil afoot in what had become a flaming hell on earth. Ahead the wooden buildings of unusual color and shape burst into flame as explosions with powerful booms tossed flaming material up in to the air spreading the fires more quickly than they would normally burn. An old Chinaman, dressed in coolie faded blue, with a long ponytail, held up a butcher's knife defensively warning her off with a quickly chirped sing-song frightened curse. It was then that she realized that the bloody apron she wore was what terrified them. That, and she was a white woman traveling alone in their midst. It just wasn't done. She started to strip it off, but stopped short, the piano man's coat not enough to cover her. Perhaps it was better to frighten them than to give the Chinese devils a revealing look at a virgin white woman's naked breasts and more.

"Go!" She screamed in Dutch at the old Chinaman with the butcher knife.

With frightened eyes and a curse he quickly scurried away.

A powerful explosion tossed flaming debris above and onto the wooden buildings in front of her. The boom was followed by a shock wave that hurt her ears. Confused, she tried to run down the nearest alley only to stumble and fall, painfully twisting her left ankle. Because of the number of Chinese fleeing through the alley she crawled back into the relative safety of a recessed doorway.

A second explosion blew flaming debris onto the roof of a corner building. It did not take long for the flames to catch. She could not see how dangerously close the fire was spreading towards her.

CHAPTER 13

ONE BY ONE THE BEDRAGGLED COPS TOOK IN THEIR surroundings, their hearts sinking lower as each bore witness to the death throes of their city. They had been rescued only to report for duty in a hell on earth soon to be as hot as the hell below.

"Everyone okay?" Cornelius asked as he took in the size and the smell of the new arrival. "Who, or should I say, what is that?"

August knew exactly what Cornelius was thinking. The Greek had seaweed stuck in his hair, looking very much like something that crawled out of the sea that you'd want to throw back. "That," he answered with a knowing smirk, "is Achilles. It seems that the quake tossed him from one of those ships. He washed up my way, and I now have an ox for a man servant until he repays his debt for my saving his life."

Cornelius took in August's five foot four, stumpy legs, slightly portly frame, and compared it to Achille's girth. "Is that a fact?" He stared back into the depths of the city where multiple columns of smoke rose merging into a dense menacing monster that swirled and undulated above the hills and streets that defined San Francisco. "Taking events for what they are, I suggest you keep him around, he just might prove useful."

"Cornelius, you had best have your arm looked at by a doc. You've been bleeding for some time now." Choice knew that his partner preferred to have as little to do with a doctor as possible.

Cornelius looked at his forearm, wiped some of the blood

from his hand and wrist on his pants. He took out his pocket knife and began to cut the shirt sleeve from his uninjured arm. "It appears to me that the quacks are going to have their hands full with a whole bunch of folks who need more medical attention than me. This here is only a scratch." He grimaced as he tied the salt water soaked cloth around his injured arm, the make shift bandage barely covering the nasty looking scrape.

He looked the men over, sizing each on their own merits for duty. He had a lot of questions, but no time to do the asking. They could sort out the *could've* and *should've beens* after they got done with the rapidly growing list of urgent calls that were stacking up around the city. "So they got the better of you before you could get them. Now ain't that a sad state of affairs."

The men, still recovering from their ordeal, couldn't look him in the eye. They were ashamed, embarrassed, and frankly did not know how it had happened. Frank Darcy, not a man known for his courage, seemed to squirm the most under Cornelius' scowl.

"Do you at least know who did it?"

"I think they were beaver beaters," Ashbury said. "I thought I heard some French."

"They knew we were coming, Cornelius." Choice said in defense of his men. "They came at us from our rear and had us before we could get turned around in the tunnels. I didn't get a look at a single one of them."

Cornelius looked at the battered squad. "Same with you?"

They all nodded, none of them saw who had shanghaied them.

"Wait a minute, counting Johansen down in the skiff there are only five of you. Who's missing?"

They all looked around. Until that moment no one had realized that both Randell and Royce were unaccounted for.

"I think I saw Royce with a knife to his neck, then everything went black." Al said.

"Well, we can't change what's been done, and we can't go back down into the tunnels looking for them - at least not now." Cornelius looked at the burning city around them. "We may never know what the hell happened down there. Just bless your lucky rabbit's foot that you are alive and pray that you make it through the rest of this day. It looks nasty out there, and I've got a hunch we haven't seen anything yet."

The rumble of a collapsed building and the sudden silence of a church bell that had been chiming since they had all gotten out of the skiff brought their attention back to the reality of the moment.

"Al, why don't you, Darcy, and Ashbury work your way back to the station? Let the duty Sergeant know that the three of you are still alive, and find out where you are needed the most. I know you're tired, but you are going to be a lot more tired before this day is over. Choice, August, keep an eye on ox-man here and we'll see what we can do to help out over by the Ferry. The fire is pushing everyone towards the water front. Before long, there very well may be ten - twenty thousand, give or take a few, refugees who want to get on a ferry boat that can only handle a hundred or so." He stood, a little shaky from the blood loss, tested his legs, and grimaced when he moved his arm the wrong way.

August reached out, only to be pushed away.

"Nothing broken, and nothing that won't heal," he said with little conviction, then snatched a cigar that rode in August's shirt pocket. Cornelius' last cigar had been lost when he had taken his swim beneath the wharf. He bit off the tip, spat, then stuck it between tight lips. "Match?"

August searched his pockets. Nothing.

Cornelius queried the rest with his eyes and came up short. If they weren't soaked to the skin, their pockets had been cleaned out when they were shanghaied. "Figures, you useless bunch of bastards. I don't know why I bothered."

They left the wharf, entering East Street that ran parallel to the multiple wharfs that lined the waterfront. He knew where they were now. They had been on the Vallejo Street Wharf which is three - maybe four wharfs down from the ferry terminal.

While fighting for his life beneath the wharf there had been the sounds of the surf slamming against the pilings, the creaking of the wharf above, the sound of his own heart, the sound of his own gagged on filthy salt water. Now Cornelius stared at their view of the city. She was burning and he could hear her myriad screams. "She was a beautiful woman, wasn't she? A temptress if there ever was one. No man could refuse her, from the giants who paid respect to a lady of grace and charm, to the street beggars who suckled at a whore's tit. Listen to that fire take her from us and there isn't a damn thing we can do about it."

"What? You giving up being a cop to become a poet philosopher?" Choice said.

"Cornelius, that's not the fire, it's too far away." August interjected. "I don't know what it is, but I ain't never heard anything like it."

Cornelius paused taking a second to listen a little closer. "I think we have, it's the city speaking to us, only we couldn't understand her voice until now. It's the Tower of Babel. The city, she's made of people. People who have come here from faraway places like China, Japan, Russia, Italy, Germany, Greece, Poland, and Australia. What we're hearing is their voices as everything unravels around them. The Italians had their neighborhood, the Chinese theirs, the Pope worshipers, and the Jews - theirs. Most, for one reason or another, have stayed with their own kind, continuing to speak the languages they brought with them. Hell, better than half this city can't speak much American." His eyes took it all in. Thoughtfully, he continued. "San Francisco is burning and as it does the racial, religious, and ethnic barriers are all going to come down. The rich, the poor, they're all about to become equal, whether they like it or not. That noise is the Tower of Babel as it all crumbles to the ground."

"What?" Choice was transfixed by the dense smoke building over the city, the colors of the flames beneath reflecting against a black screen, and hadn't really heard a word Cornelius had said.

"Never-mind." Cornelius turned and gazed one last time at the dark shadows beneath the wharf where they had left Johansen's body. "Don't go nowhere, we'll send someone for you, soon as we can."

Biting down on the cigar, he set off.

As they left the sanctuary of the wharf behind them they found the waterfront to be in chaos and carnage. Trolley, electrical, and telephone lines hung in disarray, some sparking, few buildings stood, most shattered mountains of debris. Fires were breaking out everywhere. Trolley tracks were twisted and bent at odd angles. One trolley had fallen into what was now a quicksand trench. Parts of buildings continued to fall with thunderous explosions, followed sometimes by a scream as someone failed to duck in the right direction. Water mains were broken, making any attempt at firefighting all but useless. A dead horse was held upright within a mountain of bricks, its bulging white eyes no longer terrified. People ran, stumbled, walked blindly here - there, most towards the ferry terminal.

A noticeable aftershock brought everyone back to blind hysteria, which after a moment or two, settled back down to an amplified, slightly under control, panic as a dozen or more languages floated to their ears, mostly lost within the dreadful din of the dying city. The air tasted of char, smoke, garbage, vinegar, roasted vegetables, scorched hair, rotting fish, seaweed, raw earth, and corruption. The smoke rose from a dozen major fires across the city, each adding its weight to a huge plume above the city which was black as coal with splashes of purple, rose, orange, brown, dark and menacing, blotting out the sun.

Cornelius, suddenly found himself a little dizzy, the raw scrape on his arm finally beginning to hurt like hell. Everything around him screamed at his cop's mind to snap to attention, to take charge of a hundred issues, to be in command, to rise to the occasion. He just couldn't find enough energy to keep on going. What really nagged at him, was that he was beginning to think that one of his men was a traitor. That the shanghaiing had been a set up from the inside. Cornelius leaned against what remained of a brick wall, the rest of what had once been a rope warehouse, now the makings for a giant bonfire, its wooden frame window just beginning to burn, and lit his cigar. "Choice, it seems to me . . ."

The wall suddenly leaned precariously forward as a wild eyed steer, reared up kicking and snorting, its head pushing through the window, its snout breaking the cigar, startling the daylight out of him. "Jesus, Mary, and Joseph!" Cornelius swore as he stumbled back. The steer brought down the wall, the wooden window frame caught around its neck; a burning collar. Its left front leg snapped. Bellowing in pain and terror, it floundered in the bricks, unable to rise. Finally it laid back, breathing heavily, eyes bulging, as it awaited its fate.

"Where the hell did that come from?" Cornelius said as he studied the stub of his cigar. He turned to where he thought August to be. "You got one more of these?"

August, who had been but two feet away lay buried beneath a section of the brick wall, his out stretched arm and the back of his head the only things showing. One look is all it took, August Freeman was dead.

Cornelius stared for a long moment at August, then back at the steer, whose breathing had quieted, but still lived. He shook his head sadly as he looked each of the remaining men in the eye. "Damn. Damn fool luck . . . August was a good man, better than many men I've known." It's hard to compartmentalize death and move on as if nothing had happened. He has had to do that too many times since he joined the force. Losing August hurt, his death too close to home. August and Choice were more than cops, they were the younger brothers he never had - family. What energy he had seemed to flow out the soles of his feet as he grew cold and distant, wanting to shut down and take time to grieve.

Two more steers ran blindly by before anyone could say anything else.

"Cornelius," Choice said, "we've got to get moving. There is no telling how many crazed steers are running around like that. We've got to put a stop to them before any women or children get hurt."

Cornelius nodded, took a deep breath, and looked one last time at August Freeman.

CHAPTER 14

BRIGADIER-GENERAL FUNSTON TOOK A MOMENT TO STARE out over the city as he stood in front of his home on Washington Street near Jones Street. From there he had one of the most elevated views in the city. From where he stood, he could see the damage done to the city by the quake and could only assume that the worst was yet to come. He could see that several fires were already burning fiercely in the banking district, and he could see the columns of smoke rise one after another as fires broke out across the city. The integrity of the city's underground infrastructure had been a matter of public debate for some time and he knew that most of the water pipes were most likely broken throughout the city leaving the firemen all but helpless. This, in addition to the number of fires he could see, convinced him that disaster was already at hand. The city's police and firemen were not going to be able to handle the crisis by themselves. Human nature, being what it is, he knew that looters were already busy. How much time remained before the city became a lost cause? Perhaps it was already too late.

With no time to waste he turned and found himself surrounded by refugees. *Where are they all going? Where?* That would become one of the big questions of the day.

If an automobile could be had, it wouldn't be able to maneuver through the streets. In a few seconds, public and private transportation had been rendered nonexistent. The General hastily wrote a brief note addressed to the Commanding Officer, Presidio, directing him to turn out the entire garrison and report for duty to the Chief of Police at the Hall of Justice. His chauffeur was directed to deliver this as fast as he could run.

Having no other option the General set went on foot to the headquarters of the Department of California. Everywhere he turned buildings were down. He was stunned by the unimaginable damage the earthquake had done.

At about 7:45 a.m., the first troops reported to the Mayor and the Chief of Police, and were directed to guard the banking district with additional patrols sent out along Market Street to prevent looting.

At about 8 a.m. the garrison from the Presidio reported for duty. The Mayor ordered all bars, liquor stores, and saloons closed. The General stood by wondering how they were going to enforce that. He knew most of the politicians and power brokers who ran the city and how inept they were. Martial Law had not been declared by the civilian authorities. The troops sent out into the ethnic neighborhoods had no authority, which with poor to no communication made the situation worse.

By 9 a.m., the various fires were merging into one great conflagration threatening the Palace Hotel and other large buildings along Market Street. The waterfront itself was relatively undamaged, compared to the rest of the city, but as the fires approached the waterfront, it became more isolated with few firemen or police, except for a hand full of officers under the command of Cornelius McCann. No one at City Hall or the Department of Justice knew that.

The military forced thousands of refugees from the fires towards the waterfront. There were plenty of saloons and liquor stores ripe for looters along the way, which only added fuel to a tense situation. No one knew what to do or where to go, other than away from the fires. Many spoke little or poor English which made the din from their expanding Tower of Babel even more befuddling.

From the first moment of the earthquake, James Phelan took charge. As the former Mayor and Senator Elect, he was not afraid to make tough decisions. He also knew that the current Mayor was afraid to spit without Abe Ruef's approval.

Phelan's mansion at the southwest corner of Valencia and 17th Street survived the quake. The brick chimney had crashed down and many of the windows shattered. A gas chandelier swayed alarmingly overhead as the smell of gas alarmed him. In moments, he ordered his house staff to turn the gas off, that there were to be no fires lit. Doors and windows were to be opened to let out the fumes. Prepared to notify his neighbors of the same risk, he found that structures around him had not fared as well. Houses had been knocked off their foundations, some sitting at awkward angles, siding popped, windows broken, chimneys fallen. Two blocks away the Valencia Hotel had collapsed, killing most inside. He ran in an urgent frenzy to help as flames seized the hotel. It was no use. He was too late to save the dead. As the smoke plumes rose above the city, he called for his driver and carriage, sucked in his breath, and headed off to City Hall. He knew everyone there and how they would fare in this crisis - not well.

When Phelen reached City Hall, there was no longer any doubt about the magnitude of the calamity. There was no City Hall, much of the classic dome had fallen, leaving what remained of the cap hanging precariously, the brick structure on each side ruined, here and there a column standing. He then drove to the Phelan Building which housed the Department of California. The damage to buildings around him was so severe he barely made it through the cluttered streets.

Upon his arrival, he found General Funston supervising the removal of important records. While the General had ordered the Federal troops to report to civilian authorities, there so far was no one to report to. He suspected that many were dead in the ruins of City Hall. Mayor Schmitz had yet to be heard from, whether he was alive or dead, unknown. He was missing and someone needed to assume authority. With no power or communication, each ruined block isolated from the next, and no civilian authority in command, the military was hamstrung. All General Funston could do was wait for someone with recognizable authority to take command and tell him where and how his troops were to be used. James Phelen took charge, though he was no longer an elected official.

CHAPTER 15

ACHILLES WASTED NO TIME IN RECOVERING AUGUST'S BODY. He had made an oath to serve this man who had saved his life, and within a brief space of time had been helpless to save his. Greek Orthodox, he spoke a short meaningful prayer no one else understood.

With a sigh followed by a deep breath, Cornelius sucked in the adrenaline he needed to take the next step. With a slow turn he took in everything that was going on around them. There were small fires nearby, the dark plume of smoke over the financial district spoke for itself. The wind, though light, would sweep the conflagration into Chinatown which would go up like a barn full of dried hay. Farther away, the crown of Rincon Hill was visibly ablaze. It would burn downhill towards Market and Mission Streets forcing everyone fleeing before it towards the waterfront. Like it or not, everything was coming their way.

"Watch it!" Another steer ran by, which made him wonder about the stockyards which were located along the waterfront just below Rincon Hill. Caught up in the sudden death of August Freeman he had not heard Sergeant Pickens' voiced concern about the loose cattle. Several plumes of smoke rose from the Barbary, judging the ruins he could see, and the wind, he wrote the waterfront along the Barbary and the north side as lost. The thought crossed his mind that before this day was over the waterfront would be completely cut off by a huge firestorm, with tens of thousands of refugees with nowhere to go but the ferry, which can only hold a couple of hundred at a time.

The tall ships would pull up anchor soon as the wind started sending hot ash and sparks towards their vulnerable sails. From where they stood he could not see any of the ferries.

What he wanted to do was to see that August's remains were properly taken care of. How the hell they were going to do that, he hadn't a clue. What he needed to do was walk away his grief and his exhaustion, because the living needed his attention more. . . and the day was still young. *Well,* he thought, *I guess we'd better get over to the ferry terminal and see if it's still there.* Like it or not, he most likely was the senior police officer on the whole damned waterfront.

A block further on there was a liquor store its front caved in, its gaping hole easily accessible for looters who were already helping themselves to what bottles were unbroken. Damn *drunken fools, that's all I need - can't send them home to sleep it off either.* He reached down as Achilles laid August safely away from the fire and retrieved August's firearm and his badge. There was nothing to cover the body with. Cornelius commandeered a hat from a passing refugee using it to cover August's face.

Smith, Ashbury, and Darcy turned to leave, following their orders to report to the central police station. "Change of plans," Cornelius said, his voice clear in his meaning. "Darcy, you stay here with Choice and me. Al, you and Ashbury, take August back to the station, then report back here. . . and make it quick. The way I see it, I am now the senior officer representing the great San Francisco Police Department here on the waterfront. The spot where we stand I now declare the new Waterfront Police Station." *He did not want to keep Darcy. He wasn't worth much as a cop but at least here he could keep an eye on him.*

He turned towards the wharf where they had just come from. "The Broadway Wharf managed to hold up against all this, so

I'm banking that it will continue to do so. Achilles raise your right hand. That's good enough, no time to waste words, you are now a fully sworn police officer." He then pinned August's badge to Achille's filthy shirt, keeping the gun for himself. "When it's all said and done, I'll see that you get paid." He counted the bullets in the gun. "See if August has any dry bullets on him before you take him away."

A loud boom thundered from somewhere within the financial district followed by towering flames visible from where they stood. *Damn*, Cornelius thought, *we've got less time than I had hoped for.* "Darcy, you and Achilles clear this area of bricks." He walked over to the edge of the wharf and pointed at the ground. "Clear enough of the rubble away to open a pathway onto the wharf. Use the bricks to build a brick wall about two feet high from here to, say about ten feet that-away. He pointed towards a bent light pole, then back to the other side of the wharf. That, gentlemen, will stake out the new police station. The wharf will serve as a field hospital, resting place for the old, kids, families. No weapons or alcohol allowed. No drunks, and I mean no drunks. Find some rope and tie off a dozen, make that two dozen, hog-ties for prisoners, fix them right here near the entryway to the wharf where you can keep an eye on them. They'll serve as a reminder to those who might be inclined to misbehave that we don't have time or patience for games." He looked hard at all the men. "You see a doctor or a nurse, you keep them right here. You see a fellow cop, he's now assigned to this station."

"Darcy, you are now a Sergeant. That is most likely the biggest mistake I'll ever make. You think you're up to it, half-ass? If anyone gives you a problem, looters, drunks, anyone that does not snap to it when you give them an order, you shoot them in the foot, then hog-tie them right over there."

Pleased with his promotion, Darcy puffed out his chest. "Cornelius, how can I shoot someone if I don't got no gun?"

Cornelius gave him a steely-eyed look. They only had one gun between them - that had been August's. He had lost his beneath the wharf, the shanghaiers had gotten everyone else's. He sure as hell wasn't going to give the one and only sidearm to Darcy. "There is enough dying here today, and I suspect there will be a lot more." Cornelius picked up a broken two-by-four. "Here, you smack them with this, then you whack them on their foot so they won't try to get away." He paused with a wry smile. "If that don't work, whack them on their other foot - that rarely fails to get their attention." He then pointed with his eyes. "Choice and me are going to wander over to the ferry terminal then down towards the stock yards to see what type of shape they're in."

Darcy was eying the rubble and the mountain of bricks that had to be moved. "Cornelius I can't . . ."

"Here, on my waterfront, the word *can't* is hereby abolished. If you don't like it, find a way to make it happen. There will be no half-assed excuses from here on out. Is that understood? Or, would you rather I shoot you in the ass - which I must admit would give me just a little bit of pleasure."

Cornelius turned back towards the liquor store as a couple of looters came out with their arms full of bottles. "First things first," he said as he took the dry bullets Achilles had collected from August's pockets. Without looking back, he added. "Sergeant Darcy, you are authorized to recruit as many volunteers as you need to help with those bricks. There should be quite a crowd here within an hour or two, so don't be too humble in the asking."

Inspector Cornelius McCann walked purposefully towards the liquor store, mindful of the downed electric lines and rubble in his path. At a chosen distance he drew out his firearm and carefully aimed at one of the looters. No warning given, he fired. The man fell, his loot shattering. The second ran, the bottles he carried shattering in his panicked flight.

Choice Pickens approached the wounded looter fully aware that Cornelius had the only gun between them. The man writhed on the ground as he held his leg where he had been shot just above the ankle. Choice waved back at Darcy to come and take custody, then double-timed best he could to catch up with Cornelius who was about to enter the liquor store.

Inspector McCann held his gun ready as he scanned the liquor store before entering. The store was empty, except for the manager who now lay dead where a wall of shelving and bottles had come crashing down. Most of the bottles were broken but there were still enough whole to liquor up a whole lot of problems.

Cornelius reached down and picked up a box of cigars, pocketing as many as one pocket could hold. He searched for and found a box of stick matches and turned as Choice Pickens arrived at the store front. "Like I said, we just need to get their attention," he said as he looked back towards the injured looter. He lit a cigar then dropped the still burning match into a pool of liquor which burst into flame. Looking past the ferry terminal towards the stockyards he stepped away. "Shall we?"

CHAPTER 16

SAN FRANCISCO HAD SEEN ITS SHARE OF QUAKES. AT FIRST Mayor Schmitz did not think the earthquake was that serious. This one nearly threw him from his bed. Having been up late the night before, sufficient alcohol his usual routine, it took a moment for him to grasp that this time it was different. By the time he was dressed, a car pulled up with two men from the District Attorney's Office who told him of the damage they had already seen. He could not comprehend the magnitude of what they were saying. He stood for a moment, jaw open, head still pounding from a hangover, and stared out over the city, their words going unheard. From where he stood, the smoke rising from the multitude of fires told him all he needed to know. "God damn," he muttered, "tell me this isn't true." That being said, as the smoke bellowed into a brooding cloud, an aftershock caused him to lurch. He sobered up quickly, hopped in the car, ordering his driver to find a way through the rubble to get him to the Hall of Justice. He could see the collapsed dome of City Hall. It didn't make any sense to go there; he needed a center of operations. Along the way he ran across the troops from the Presidio. He ordered them to be spread out across the city, in particular the financial district, and the U.S. Mint, where the fire seemed to be out of control. "Keep the people back away from the fires," he ordered. "Let the news be widely spread that anyone caught looting will be shot. I'm declaring martial law."

"Will you take responsibility for that order?" Colonel Morris, their commanding officer asked.

"I will. We have no time or manpower to coddle looters. I doubt there is a jail cell still standing. The order stands, looters are to be shot dead." With that potent declaration, he then ordered Morris to send troops to the ruins of City Hall.

The men from the District Attorney's Office remained silent as Mayor Schmitz gave what they knew to be an illegal order; Martial Law could not be declared at the whim of the mayor. Arriving at the Hall of Justice the same order was given to General Funston and all ranking police officers on site.

CHAPTER 17

CAPTAIN RALPH LAFFERTY OF THE SAN FRANCISCO FIRE Department, stood frozen, mouth agape, near the ferry terminal. He could see evidence of upwards of fifty fires, the worst being the conflagration burning the financial district; the fire that was devastating Rincon Hill, the worst. He had not gotten any sleep the night before, neither had the rest of his Engine Company, who had been called out to fight a cannery fire just before eleven the night before. While the company had retired back to their station around 4:00 a.m., he had come down to the waterfront to pick up some produce and bacon and eggs, for the men's breakfast. Now the produce was spread out on the street, trampled by panicked civilians, his wagon, axle broken, overturned, his horse had been gored by a longhorn steer, lay on its side suffering; he had nothing to put it out of its misery. The steer had come out of nowhere. He had to count his blessings because the steer had come within a hair's length of goring him when he had been thrown from the wagon.

His fire station was on the far side of the fire raging in the financial district. With the wind, it looked like it might connect with the Rincon blaze which would split the city in half. As far as he could see, he was cut off, unless he followed the waterfront out past the edges of the Barbary Coast and Little Italy where the shore line curved in to where he could connect with Van Ness Avenue. It was a long way around and there was no guarantee that his engine company had survived. If they had, they'd be out fighting the fires - but which one - and how could he find them? He surveyed the immediate area noting that the water mains were all broken, and if it was the same everywhere in the city there was no way they could fight the fires. The city was lost.

"Ain't it a bitch!"

He turned to find Inspector McCann and Sergeant Choice Pickens behind him, both officers he knew.

"Ain't it a bitch," Cornelius repeated as he looked past his cigar at Lafferty's exhausted face, his low morale showing in his bloodshot eyes. "And on my birthday of all days."

Cornelius' eyes slowly dropped down to the injured horse. Without another word he walked the five steps to where the horse lay, brought out his revolver, pointed it four inches from the animal's forehead and fired one shot. The animal jerked once, then fell silent. His gun still in hand, he eyed a looter coming out of a damaged store with what appeared to be a cash box. "Fire horses are mighty proud steeds," he said as he took aim and shot the looter in his left leg. "You okay?' He asked the fire Captain as he holstered the revolver.

The thundering shot jolted some reality back to the normally calm and decisive Fire Captain. "Happy birthday," were the only words that seemed to form for the moment.

Cornelius nodded, keeping niceties to a minimum. "Officer Pickens, why don't you mosey on over and see that fool isn't bleeding too bad." The liquor store that had been robbed, was now fully ablaze. "Consider whatever is in that cash box as our first contribution to the widows and orphan's fund for the new waterfront precinct." He turned back towards Lafferty. "I grew up an orphan so I don't rightly know my actual birthday. Come to think of it, give or take a year or two, I don't know how old I am." Eyes squinted against a sudden burst of bright sunshine that blazed through an abbreviated gap in the smoke, he looked back down at the horse. "Each year I pick a day to celebrate my day of birth. Since no one gives a damn, I figured that today is as good as any, there's not much else to celebrate."

Lafferty chuckled.

Cornelius nodded towards the burning liquor store. "You going to do anything about that?"

"Nope." Lafferty answered as he showed his hands to be empty. He knew that Cornelius' reputation for being a hard-ass was a bit overblown, one tough son-of-a-bitch against the world, who when put under duress, was probably one of the best cops in the city. The slight quiver below Cornelius' right eye spoke of his mounting duress. No one was going to get off easy this day. He took in the burning panorama around them. He was going to be needed right here, and there was no better person to partner up with under the circumstances than Inspector Cornelius McCann. "You've got a point there, Cornelius, sorry I didn't bring a cake."

"I appreciate the sentiment," Cornelius said as he watched Choice Pickens approach the wounded looter. "I've never been much of a fan of cake, don't cotton to sweets much, and the candles might have proved to be a fire hazard."

Lafferty laughed. "Did I hear you say something about a new Waterfront Precinct?"

"Two wharves back," he nodded, "near where the fish market used to be. Sergeant Darcy is in charge. It ain't much to look at, but under the circumstances it will have to make do. We've got the beginnings for a jail, hospital, refugee center, and who knows - perhaps a fire department."

That's smart, Lafferty thought as he eyed the two major fires that were starting to merge. *Firestorm, with our backs to the water.* "I think I'll wander over and see for myself. Are you offering me the job?"

"Captain Lafferty, when it comes down to it, you outrank me. You are in Command of everything to do with fire, and I'm the law. What do you say we do what the bureaucrats in this city have never been able to do - collaborate. Maybe we can get something done."

They shook hands.

Captain Lafferty scooped up an apple from his overturned wagon as he started off towards the new Waterfront Police and Fire Station."

"Captain," Cornelius called after him, "would you mind taking that fellow with you?" He nodded towards the looter, whose foot was being wrapped by Sergeant Pickens. "Just turn him over to half-ass Darcy, he'll know what to do. Come to think of it, it might be more humane to let the stupid idiot bleed to death here"

"You there, halt!" Captain Lafferty ordered as a delivery wagon slowed, trying to pass the dead horse and overturned carriage. The wagon was filled with hides straight from the butcher yards, ready for the tannery. Lafferty, seized the horse's harness, stilled the animal, whose frothed muzzle told him that it had been pulling too much weight for too long. The cow hides were fresh, wet, and ripe. "Where the hell are you going with this thing?" He barked at the driver who stared at him with an idiot's expression. The man just shook his head. "The tannery is back that-away." Lafferty pointed back in the direction the man had come from.

McCann moved to the side of the wagon, his eyes taking measure of the driver, his nose assaulted by the stench of the hides.

"Not . . . not . . . not anymore," the driver stuttered with a heavy uneducated cockney accent, "everything back there has done sunk half way into the ground. E'y, never seen anything like it. One minute the ground is sol . . . solid, the next thing yah know, it's done turned to swamp, mud sucking down most of the buildings and half the livestock before a bloke could bat an eye."

Another lone steer ambled by, less panicky, weary of humans. A heard of six goats followed in the steer's path.

"Don't that beat all." Cornelius said as he listened to the driver's story. "Now, why don't you be a good fellow and get down off that wagon and unload those hides."

The man didn't move. "Unload 'em?" The man clicked his tongue at the horse, which was quite content to stay where it was with Lafferty petted its mussel while still holding its harness. It had taken a moment for the driver to recognize Cornelius' uniform.

"Meet Inspector Cornelius McCann, San Francisco Police Department, perhaps you have heard of him." Captain Lafferty said.

See that fellow over there?" McCann continued. 'He was a looter, and I shot him in the leg for thievery and stupidity. You can keep those hides where they are. We'll just load him on top, then you and the Fire Captain here can take him down to our new police and fire precinct where I can lock him up before he does something stupid again." Cornelius paused. "You aren't thinking of doing anything stupid now, are you?"

"Ahh . . . no Sir, pleased to help."

CHAPTER 18

Frank Darcy, hands on his hips, watched as Achilles stacked the bricks exactly as he had been told, without question or reservation. Achilles looked up and grinned as he carried eight bricks in the crook of his massive arm. The weight of the bricks didn't even seem to bother him.

Darcy scratched the back of his neck not sure what to do or say to the big Greek. "You keep up the good work. I'm going to recruit us some more help." Truth was that Officer Darcy was lazy, rarely the first man to volunteer for much of anything. His pappy had nicknamed him *half-ass,* because that was the kind of effort he usually put into things. He was a Sergeant now, and damned if he was going to split a gut stacking bricks. McCann had ordered him to recruit some help, and that was just what he was going to do. He saw a woman with three boys dragging an old steamer trunk headed his way. The grating sound of the trunk repeated a thousand times over across the city as folks fled the fires with only what they could carry in an old trunk. The first two boys were young'uns, the third a strapping lad, perhaps sixteen, looked strong enough to lend Achilles a hand. He approached the woman with a wry smile, one hand offering shelter, the other hard labor. The waterfront was filling with refugees, easy pickings, this time he wasn't going to do a half-assed job.

The woman and the two boys were glad to get off their feet. For the moment, they were the only ones on the pier, which gave her time to sort out what they had just been through.

She and her family had come from Sweden the year before. She was now a widow, having lost her husband less than three months prior. She had been working two jobs to keep a roof over their heads. That roof had collapsed in the quake. The younger boys, Nils and Patrik, had watched their home burst into flame as the fires swept Rincon Hill. The trunk was the only thing she had managed to save when everything came crashing down. It did not contain anything useful or of value except for her grandmother's china, which she suspected was by now mostly broken. It had not even crossed her mind what she would do with it.

Where they would go from here, how they would live? She hadn't had time to think that far. Sven, her eldest, had gone to work building something with bricks. She could only hope that someone might pay him for his labor. Her younger sons were hungry, and as she looked around she felt more than hollow herself.

Sven introduced himself to Achilles and went to work moving and stacking the bricks. When he asked about being paid, Achilles raised his hands in a positive gesture. "The boss said I get paid, so why not you." He stacked his last armful of bricks showing the younger man how it was to be done. "No higher than this, yes." That was when he heard an almost human-like braying behind him. Turning in astonishment, he found six goats braying to be fed. "This is good," he said, "I have not eaten since yesterday, and the food we had on the ship I sailed with was not fit for an Albanian."

More men arrived and were put to work, their families finding sanctuary on the pier. Sven, was left in charge of building the brick wall as Achilles herded the goats into a makeshift corral.

CHAPTER 19

NEITHER CORNELIUS NOR CHOICE PICKENS COULD FATHOM how the ferry terminal managed to withstand the destructive power of the quake. All around it the streets in places had sunk three or four feet, in others great humps had appeared four or five feet high. The street car tracks were bent and twisted out of shape. Electric wires lay in every direction. Market Street and all of the grand avenues leading up to the financial district were filled with brick and mortar, buildings either completely collapsed or brick fronts had just dropped completely off. The ruins of the trolley barns that blocked the road behind the new Waterfront Police Station were evidence the ferry building's survival was a fluke.

At first glance the terminal building's massive brick walls with sandstone facing appeared to have suffered little damage compared to the surrounding buildings. The glass in many of the multitude of windows, mostly intact. There were cracks in the brickwork that suggested that the damage internally might at any moment bring the building down. Some bricks and sandstone face work had fallen from the clock tower, the four clocks all stopped at 5:18 the moment the quake ripped through the waterfront. The tower still stood straight, the lightening rod on top twisted oddly as it had moved with the violent rhythm of the quake. Further inspection showed that the entire south wall of the ferry building had crashed through a driveway down into the bay. The waves lapped at the crumbled brickwork as if it were a natural sea wall.

The farther Cornelius and Choice went the worse the damage. In places the ground was soft and spongy, large cracks filled with water crossed their paths, Market Street itself seemed surreal, a canyon of tall ruined buildings, backed by towering flames which were beginning to produce their own ominous winds, the sky black with swirling smoke, as thousands of people pouring out of the canyon of ruins onto the waterfront with what few possessions they had managed to salvage. The first wharf at Butcher Town, located at the base of Potrero Hill, had held a saloon which now floated half submerged, the tannery building next to it had slipped completely off its foundation into the water; what remained of its roof, afire. For as far as they could see, not one building, not one wharf, not one structure of any kind stood intact, a massive maze of timber waiting for the flames - nothing was left of Butcher Town.

Time was short. Cornelius pondered the value of going any further. Half-ass Darcy was going to have his hands full, which worried Cornelius because he could see that many of the people pouring out onto the waterfront were just shy of panic.

Shots fired! Nerve-jarring reports thunderously loud against the cacophony of noise that already assaulted their senses. Cornelius and Choice Pickens, lacking cover, stood where they were, with one gun between them.

There were four shots all told, from the sounds, possibly three guns, long rifles, their first guess. The shots had come from just beyond where a warehouse had collapsed partially blocking their way. They edged forward, cautious of the soft ground beneath, a wall of debris that threatened to further collapse, and the unknown threat of men with guns just out of view.

On the far side of the ruined warehouse they were confronted by a jagged trench, in some places better than three feet wide, filled with what looked at first like blood. An underground gas pipe uncovered by the trench sent up four separate geysers of flame, blue at their base, bright orange, with blue-white points, flickering serpents, taller than the men as they stepped back from their roiling hiss. On the far side of the heat's mirage, three men sat on an overturned barrel laughing, drinking cups in hand. *Jesus, what a God Almighty waste,* Cornelius thought. The trench was filled with wine, which ran from underneath a heap of bricks, to a collapsed wharf across the way, then into the bay. The California Wine Association's bottling facility had been only a few blocks inland. Cornelius knew of the place and estimated that close to four million gallons of wine had and still was flowing before them.

A small after shock further jarred their nerves.

Gauging their timing, and the erratic dances of the fire genies, they jumped the trench. What was left of the street sucked at their feet, the soil softening to mud just beneath what pretended to be a firm surface. As they passed the shattered tannery, they found the next wharf in the same, if not worse condition. The wharf had been the loading dock for the slaughter houses and the stockyards. The quake had liquefied the ground and the slaughter houses and stables had been sucked down into the mud. Hundreds of carcasses, sides of beef, body parts floated in the surf.

Another shot resounded.

It had come from a wrangler on horseback who was aiming his rifle at a horse whose neck and head remained above the mud. His first shot missed. The horse, buried in quicksand was only ten yards out, but it might as well have been a hundred, for the rider could not get any closer. Horses, cattle, sheep, goats, chickens, had all been trapped in the muck, most were dead, the rest being dispatched by five riders. Three had rifles, the other two trying their best to pull a terrified mare out of the muck with lassos.

Cornelius' and Choice could go no further. At least now they knew where the stampeding cattle had come from, and the shots.

The closest rider rode up, reigning in his brown and white spotted palomino just short of knocking them down. Wiping his brow with a bandana, his steel hazel eyes looked straight into Cornelius' - neither blinked. "I wouldn't recommend going any farther, partner, unless you want to wind up like those poor critters."

That was not something Cornelius was planning on doing. He held up his badge. "Inspector McCann, San Francisco Police. I won't mince words, this city is fucked. I can use your help."

The rider still had not blinked. "I'm listening."

Cornelius turned his gaze back towards Market Street. "The fires are driving everyone down to the waterfront, most are headed towards the Ferry Terminal. That is where they are going to be stopped, there are very few boats operating, and not one has come in yet. If they were, they couldn't move twenty or thirty thousand people across the bay to Oakland. I've got a wharf being set up back that away as a makeshift hospital and refugee center for kids and the elderly." He nodded towards the men drinking the wine. I haven't enough men to keep order. You interested in being deputized?"

"Not much else we can do here, can't get close enough to help what's left of the herd. We've managed to save only six out of seventy head. Folks call me J.T." He leaned forward, touching his hat. "Marshal McCann, you said?"

"Cornelius will be fine."

J.T. glanced and waved back towards the two riders trying unsuccessfully to pull the mare free from the muck. "Sidney, let that one go, it ain't no use. You and Henry come on over, the Marshal here has some work for us."

The two men let their ropes fall loose, one aimed his rifle, killing the animal in one clean shot. As they rode toward him, Cornelius could see that both men were somewhere in their twenties, one tall and thin as a corn stock, the other almost too short to climb on his own horse. J.T. introduced the tall man as Henry, the shorter one Sidney. "Sidney is the best man I've ever seen with a rope. Marshal, he can rope and hogtie just about anything that moves. He can handle a bullwhip just fine too."

Cornelius explained the situation, quick and simple.

Sidney nodded that he was on board.

Henry said he had family he needed to see to, surrendering his horse to Cornelius. They gathered as much extra rope as could be found, tied it to their saddles, and turned away from the carnage of what had been Butcher Town.

Horseless, Choice Pickens was the last man left standing as Henry headed home. Cornelius gave Choice his hand gun, having taken Henry's rifle along with the horse. "Choice, I want you to go up Market Street as far as you think it's safe. I know there are a number of doctor's offices up that way. Find me one or two, a nurse if you can, and get them over to the precinct. If they don't want to come, put them under arrest."

"On what charges?" Choice asked.

"Lacking community spirit."

Choice nodded that he understood. Not that he was happy. This was a fool's errand. The quake had happened before office hours. Doctors were smart people, they wouldn't have gone towards the fire's glow - they'd had gone to the hospitals were they were needed the most. He belonged at Cornelius' side. The waterfront was a rough place on a good day with plenty of criminals with a death vendetta against him. Now his best friend and partner had chosen some yahoo cowboys over him.

CHAPTER 20

CORNELIUS DIDN'T MUCH CARE FOR THE RIDE BACK. HE WAS a city cop and his buttocks had rarely met the backside of a horse. The crowd pouring out onto the waterfront was worse than he had predicted. It wouldn't be long until there were upwards of forty - thousand people, most homeless, hungry, and scared to death, not to mention those few who would take advantage of their fellow human beings when things went from bad to worse. Riding through the throng wasn't easy. No one wanted to get out of the way, each intent in occupying their own space, one step at a time, going nowhere - adamant in getting there.

"Jesus Christ, " he swore beneath is breath, "don't none of these folks speak English?" All these years on the beat it had not dawned on him that San Francisco wasn't part of America. It was a member of the Union of States but it acted more like a foreign country, but which one. The city had many personalities and today they were all going nuts. He shook his head in bewilderment as he sat atop his horse taking it all in. He looked at J.T. and Sidney, city cowboys, and had to laugh.

"What's got your chuckle bone going, Marshal?" J.T. asked.

"Not one damn thing," Cornelius mused, "not one damn thing." The world is burning and all the wretched masses and poor are being dropped right at my front door. Who says God doesn't have a sense of humor, he thought as he swallowed his smile, painting back on his don't mess with me face. "And don't call me Marshal."

Cornelius spotted two rough looking characters who were trying to hijack a wagon a family was pulling, loaded with their life's possessions on board. They did not seem to care that there was an old blind woman riding on top. Seizing control of the wagon they tossed the old woman onto the street. No one in the crowd lifted a hand. Cornelius fired a shot, which missed, he being better with a handgun then a rifle. Sidney took care of the other one with a lasso. The man Cornelius missed scampered up a fire swept street to whatever fate awaited him there. The one Sidney had lassoed swore in some obscure language before falling silent after a persuasive rap to his head from T.J.'s rifle.

After arresting one of the two hijackers, and helping the old woman back onto the cart, they arrested two more for attempted theft. There no longer remained any doubt in Cornelius' mind that they were going to have to become more proactive regarding who they arrested. They had gone less than a city block and now had three looters in tow. Leg shooting began to make more sense, depending on how many bullets they had.

As the three riders approached the Ferry Terminal they found bedlam, a lawless holy mess. There must have been ten thousand people all queuing for a seat on a boat that might, or might not come. Suitcases and trunks bobbed in the surf below, one bobbing trunk had a birdcage on top holding a parrot, flapping and squawking in mortal fear. Men, women, and children all bobbing and splashing in the water, having been pushed over the side by the turbulent crowd. The three men sat high on their horses, feeling somewhat aloof, if not knightly, as they tried to edge their way through the chaotic throng.

"Marshal?" J.T. asked.

God, I'd wish he'd stop calling me that, makes us sound like we're characters in one of those Wild West dime storybooks, Cornelius thought as he kicked his horse, trying one more time, to part the crowd. As they approached the ferry wharf a baby carriage splashed into the water, followed by a middle aged woman. The carriage, filled with pots and pans, and what appeared to be a framed picture of some kind, went straight to the bottom. The picture frame, bobbed back to the surface appearing briefly, before it too disappeared. The woman grabbed ahold of the half submerged steamer truck to keep from drowning herself, sending the caged bird with one final squawk beneath the waves.

Cornelius fired two shots from his rifle into the air, thinking it might be able to calm the crowd down before someone did get killed.

"That did a heap of good," Sidney groused as he spit some chewing tobacco, which landed on some poor woman's bonnet. Few people paid any attention to the shots, and those that did, seemed to care less five seconds later.

"How do you back this thing up?" Cornelius asked, meaning his horse. He thought of cutting loose the looters he had in tow, but opted to move them up front, where, with a rifle for motivation, they proved to be handy at moving folks out of their path. Riding on the fringes of the pandemonium, they worked their way towards the precinct wharf where he hoped Sergeant half-assed Darcy might have gotten something done. He shook his head, wondering why he had been dumb enough to have given Darcy the job.

"Hold it." Cornelius said as they approached the wharf. It had been less than two hours, he expected little to have changed, but found just the opposite. *I'll be damned!* Blocking their path were half a dozen tough longshoremen armed with pikes. No one was getting beyond them without Sergeant Darcy's approval. Darcy held court from a seat on an old barrel a few feet behind the longshoremen. On the far side of South Street, Captain Lafferty had a dozen men pushing back a fire line, clearing away anything burnable for a good twenty yards inland. The brick wall was almost complete with eight men laying bricks, while a hundred or so women and children rested on the wharf. At the water's edge, Achilles had built a makeshift kitchen where he was grilling two goats over a brick-lined fireplace. A mound of potatoes roasting on the sides. Despite the stench of a burning city, the roasted goat smelled like heaven.

"Let'em through," Darcy barked as he took off his hat, and held it over his heart as he bowed, one hand beckoning for the horsemen to pass - finishing with a big grin.

"Now that is what I call a half-ass job, Sergeant" Cornelius said as he dismounted. "Take these three looters and tie them off with the others." *Others, there are no others.* "Half-ass where the hell are the other prisoners?"

"The ones you shot in their legs are out at the end of the wharf. They're still tied up but at least the women folk can look after them. The others I granted parole, they're over with Captain Lafferty building a fire line."

CHAPTER 21

CHOICE PICKENS WAS NONE TOO HAPPY ABOUT HIS DETAIL to recruit some doctors. It had not exactly been a banner day, starting with the lights going out when he was knocked over the head by some shanghaiers. He suspected that he had been betrayed by one of his own team, but hadn't had time to suggest to Cornelius his thoughts about being shanghaied, the lump on his head still hurt, and having been hog-tied in an unseaworthy boat had hurt his back. Rescued, he was now operating alone in a sea of refugees in search of a doctor. The possibility that the fire might cut him off was foremost on his mind. God, he was tired, hungry, and needed a drink. No Sir, he was not a happy-camper. That and there was something else nagging at his gut. *The cowboys, especially the short one with the stupid sombrero hat. Sidney, what kind of name is that for a god-damned cowboy?* Choice thought. *I've had Cornelius' back for God knows how many years and saved his ass on more than a few occasion. Now, I'm out here running missions of little importance while he's playing Sheriff of Dodge City with a god-damned dwarfed cowboy.*

Scavenger wagons, drays, hay-wagons, milk carts, loaded with every sort of furniture and valuables someone might seek to save, or just plain junk, depending the state of an irrational mind under stress, seemed to block Choice's path as he tried to work his way up Market Street.

It snowed gray and white ash with little jewels of glowing sparks fluttering about as the fire storm on Rincon Hill became ominously real. He could feel its heat as a dry hot wind being generated by the fire that seemed to blow stronger the farther he went. There were thousands of people, some wearing three or four layers of clothing, some in their night clothes, a few babies crying, otherwise most passed him with an uncommon silence. Silence? The noise was stunning. Dogs barked, steamer trucks scraped along the street, buildings collapsed, explosions resounded across the city. Bells rang as fire engines hurried to fight fires they couldn't get to before they merged into one thunderous bonfire. Everywhere there was the sound of glass falling as windows shattered. Here and there a person screamed, parrots squawked, and what voices stood out against the din were Irish, Italian, German, Spanish, Russian, Chinese - a Tower of Babel he could not understand. Even the earth beneath his feet was not silent.

The bedlam was suddenly punctured by a rifle shot, followed quickly by a second and a third. The shots seemed to come from the direction of the Financial District, far enough away to not be an immediate threat, but close enough to raise the hair on the back of his neck. Forgetting his assignment to recruit some doctors, the cop in him told him that he had to investigate the gun shots.

Damn you, McCann, this ain't no time for a cop to be working alone.

He had not gone but two blocks when he set sight on a platoon of soldiers. They had come to a halt in the middle of the next intersection. Four of the soldiers dropped to firing positions on their knees with rifles aimed at a crowd of civilians packed in front of a collapsed store front. *Looters!* No sooner than he had thought the word the soldiers fired, followed by four more soldiers who fired from a standing position as the first rank reloaded. In a panic the looters dispersed, swallowed up by the crowd, leaving six or seven of their number dead or mortally wounded in front of the collapsed store. The soldiers didn't wait to see if any needed medical attention. An officer barked an order, the soldiers marched, bayonets ready, through the throng, before executing a sharp right turn headed deeper into the Financial District.

That did it. They've declared Marshal Law, Choice thought as he turned and beat a fast retreat back towards the waterfront. He wasn't about to get any deeper into this shit, looking for a doc who probably had his hands full anyway. Cornelius needed to know that Marshal Law had been declared and federal troops were shooting looters and god knows who else - and they were shooting to kill!

A thunderous explosion coming from the direction of Chinatown tossed wooden building parts visibly into the air. A second blast started fires where previously there had been none. Choice's jaw nearly dropped when he realized the dangerous ramifications. When the Rincon Hill fire and the conflagration devastating the Financial District connected with a burning Chinatown the waterfront would be cut off. Choice Pickens was not the only one who could not swim.

CHAPTER 22

"WHAT THE HELL WAS THAT?" CORNELIUS SWORE.

Achilles had just offered him a hot slice of roasted goat when two explosions interrupted his meal, followed by a bright flash which lit up a debris cloud that rose immediately after the jarring thump of the explosions.

Captain Lafferty stood next to him, a mouthful of roasted goat holding back his words. *Dynamite,* his first thought. He knew the sound, and didn't have to make a second guess as he watched the debris cloud rise and fall.

"Chinatown?" Cornelius asked, although he already knew the answer. "Your department?"

"Nope. No fireman would use dynamite that way. Either the fire set off someone's supply, or some idiot just tried to create a fire break in the middle of Chinatown. My guess would be politics." He gave a short knowing laugh.

"Politics? Cornelius mulled as he gathered his thoughts around what Lafferty had just said.

"Look there." Lafferty pointed. "The wind is blowing the Financial District blaze straight towards us. It's possible that it just might have bypassed Chinatown.

They watched the fires, hoping there would be no more explosions, while they finished their last bites of goat meat. The huge blaze on Rincon Hill was sucking in enough oxygen to draw the fire in the Financial District towards it, by-passing

Chinatown for the time being.

"There are some politicians in this town that would sure like to get their hands on certain real estate, if you know what I mean." Lafferty commented.

"Do tell," Cornelius acknowledged as a third explosion sent flaming debris high in the sky above Chinatown spreading the fires further. "Just my luck. All I need is a thousand or so

Chinamen mixing with these good Christian white folks down here."

Lafferty tore off a large bite of the goat as if he didn't know where his next meal would be coming from. "Cornelius," he said, after swallowing a mouthful, barely chewed, "we just lost the fucking city, not that we weren't going to anyway." Flames quickly rose above Chinatown, burning towards Little Italy, and the Barbary Coast. "Whatever idiot gave the order to dynamite coolie town ought to be horse-whipped." He nodded towards the huge firestorm that consumed the Financial District. "When those fires converge they will become one mother of a firestorm. And there is not one damn thing we can do about it. I'd say that within an hour, most likely less, our little corner of paradise will be cut off."

"At least our backsides are pointed towards the water." Cornelius eyed the Broadway Wharf which was rapidly filling with women, children, the elderly, all refugees, many of whom might not be able to swim. He looked thoughtful for a moment, then spoke softly as if thinking aloud. "Can you make a fire break strong enough to hold back this size a blaze?"

"Not a chance," Lafferty answered grimly. "By the time it gets here, it will be driven by some mighty powerful winds. You ever been in a tornado?"

"Can't say that I have," answered Cornelius as he accepted a hot baked potato, juggled it in his palm, it being too hot to hold. He gave the big Greek cook a well-earned smile. He turned back to Captain Lafferty. "So, the only way out will be by water, you say?"

"That's about it." Captain Lafferty made a conciliatory gesture with a hand full of goat meat. "You know what is left beyond the Ferry Terminal, and the Rincon fire is barreling down on everything south of there. To our right is the fish market, or at least what's left of it. Beyond that, the street car barns have come down in a quick sink field that makes any escape that-a-way impossible, at least for numbers like this."

"Well, that is something to ponder." Cornelius chewed, swallowed, took another bite, looked at his potato, not sure how to consume it, then bit into it like an apple, burning his mouth. Finally he said. "What to do? That is a troublesome question. That kind of question tends to be the best kind, the kind that takes a measure of a man."

"They do . . . indeed," Lafferty said. "I guess I'll go back to doing what I do - the best I can - and leave you to sort things out here." They watched as one of the tall masted ships raised her sails, readying to get away from the shoreline and hot sparks blowing on the wind."

I suppose they'll all be pulling out soon, Cornelius thought, assuming the fire captain was thinking the same. "Which reminds me," he spoke aloud, "I've got a big dead Swede tucked down beneath the pier in a tied off skiff. Any ideas?"

"Your man Darcy told me about him. Since we have no morgue, nor ice, we have a slight problem dealing with the dead. Can't bury them anywhere on the waterfront, and every foot of land is soon going to be needed by the living. There are now five bodies in the skiff. It's relatively cool beneath the pier, and for the time being out of sight." Captain Lafferty gave his departmental *glad to be of service* smile.

"Is August Freeman one of the five?" Cornelius asked, wondering how many bodies the skiff could hold before she capsized. He took a bite of the potato, which was still too hot, spat the bite out, tossed the remainder back towards the fire, then licked his fingers, dirty or not.

"August Freeman, he's there. Sorry I couldn't do better by him, but as you can see, we have our limitations. The other three we found in the ruins of the fish market. I figure the skiff can hold two more, as long as they're not as big as the Swede. After that someone will have to row them out to Alcatraz Island. The tunnels beneath the prison go back to the days of the Spanish. I've been down there and it's plenty cold and damp. There's an old ammunition dump left over from the Civil War days that might hold three or four hundred bodies"

"Alcatraz? The hell you say. We're not going to bury a good cop like August Freeman in a prison cemetery. It just ain't right."

"I wouldn't fret much. I doubt the Warden will go for it.

He watched the flames rise above Chinatown as one last dynamite blast spread the fire. "Before this day, or the next, is over, we may be needing more space than that." Captain Lafferty wiped some grease from the corner of his mouth with the back of his hand. "You need me, I'll be right over there. By the way, I'm going to need another twenty-five men to push back this fire break."

"Darcy, you hear that?" Cornelius bellowed.

"Twenty-five, why the hell not fifty? I ain't got nothing better to do." He bellyached.

"While you are at it, half-ass, we are going to need another dozen or so for crowd control." Cornelius said. He did a double-take on his surroundings and it looked like the crowd milling around just outside the precinct's boundaries had doubled in just the few minutes since he rode in. This gave him a knot in his gut. He looked out towards the tall ships, seeing two more raise their sails.

"Oh no, I ain't going to do it," Darcy whined as he read Cornelius' mind. "I ain't going to do it, I say."

Ignoring Darcy's protests, Cornelius mounted his horse.

So this is the difference between telling a story and being in one, he thought grimly as his stomach grumbled, *the fear.* He took a cigar from his pocket and clinched it between his teeth. "T.J., Sidney, you fellas ready for a cattle drive?"

They nodded, ready to do what needed to be done, but not sure what the hell he wanted of them. Without a word exchanged they watched Cornelius as he rode over to Captain Lafferty, spoke with him for a moment, then turned back.

With the cigar firmly entrenched between his teeth Cornelius made his pronouncement, short and sweet. "We're going to push this crowd back, all the way to the far side of the Ferry Terminal. While we're doing that we're going to recruit one hundred, tough, mean looking sons-of-bitches, to help with crowd control and Lafferty's fire break."

The cowboys nodded. Sidney checked his bullwhip.

Following Lafferty's command two dozen men broke off of the fire break detail, grabbed pikes, two-by-four's, or other possible weapons, then broadened the line of longshoremen already policing the precinct's boundaries, and waited for Cornelius' next directive.

"That is a tall order, Marshal, but we'll ride with yah." T.J. said. "I got me one question, if you wouldn't mind mulling it over. If we push folks south of the Ferry Terminal aren't we pushing them into harm's way? Shouldn't we be herding them this a-way?"

Cornelius winched at the word *Marshal,* but didn't have time to concern himself anymore with it. "T.J., you've got a good point. Yes, we will be moving people closer to the Rincon Hill fire. There are going to be so many people down here soon we won't have anywhere else to put them. If push came to shove and our only route to safety is through the ruins of the fish market, we can't afford to have that blocked by people who we can't move. If things get really tight, we have got to get the women and children out." It was then that he saw Choice Pickens pushing his way through the mob. Cornelius sidestepped his horse, looking as if he might actually know how to ride, as he cleared a path for Choice Pickens to get through. T.J and Sidney rode along-side.

"You trying to set some sort of a record?" Cornelius said having noted that Choice was out of breath. He looked past Choice and then back. "No docs? How about one little old nurse?"

"I couldn't get past the crowd," Choice lied. His mouth watered as much from the lie as from the aroma coming from the roasted goats. He really had not looked. "Federal Troops," he blurted out loud enough for many in the nearby crowd to hear, "are pushing everyone this way, and they ain't being polite about it. They're shooting looters and anyone else that gets in their way. And Cornelius, they are shooting to kill."

Cornelius caught the look of fear in people's eyes as he gazed out over the heads of the thousands of refugees who were already on the waterfront. "You don't say," he said slow and deliberately as he took a cigar from his pocket, realized that he already had one, pocketed the first, and struck a match. After blowing out a blue cloud of smoke he nodded towards Officer Pickens. "Well, with a little luck maybe one will drop by and offer his services. Why don't you stay here with Darcy and grab yourself a bite, while you've got a chance."

Choice gave the cowboys a hard look. He had expected to be at Cornelius' side, not sidelined with half-ass Darcy. Another thunderous explosion resounded from Chinatown. "Cornelius, I almost forgot, the army is blowing the hell out of Chinatown. The fires are spreading like nobody's business."

"Cornelius nodded. "You three," he said to the closest long-shoreman, "stay here with Officers Pickens and Darcy. If anyone gets past you, you throw them in the god-damned bay." He looked out towards the blazes that were consuming the city. "I don't know anything about Marshal Law being declared. I doubt there has been a legal declaration." The word declaration was drawn out in three long distinct syllables. In this Precinct, if federal troops are needed, they will report to the highest civilian legal authority. Right now, that's me." He looked long and hard at the longshoremen around him. "Darcy, Choice, T.J., Sidney, some of these men I've noticed are carrying side arms. Pikes, bats, and timber comfortable to the hand is allowed. No one, I repeat no one, will be armed with a gun or a rifle into this Precinct unless I say they can." He did not mean his chosen crew, it was the longshoremen and civilians he was speaking of. "Gentlemen," the word rolled like low thunder, "surrender your weapons right now. I will be the one to disarm anyone of you who thinks differently. Be quick about it, that fire and a heap of trouble is headed our way."

Cornelius watched as the weapons were surrendered. Better

than a third walked away preferring to keep their arms. He knew there were a few hold outs, but things being the way they were, maybe that was okay.

Satisfied, and unwilling to waste any more valuable time, Cornelius gave them their marching orders. "Once we've got this area cleared, no one will be allowed in who's carrying a weapon. As of now, you are all deputized. We will push this crowd back until the Precinct's boundaries are on the far side of the Ferry Terminal. Gentlemen, no hitting women and little kids, just move everyone back. No one gets in unless they agree to our terms of hospitality." He paused for affect. "If someone don't like it, they can go somewhere else. If they want to make a point of it, throw them in the bay. Gentlemen, the army has no authority here, and if they don't like it, we'll disarm them and throw them in the bay as well." His cigar had gone out and he relit it again allowing for a respectful pause. In less than an hour I want order here, those who need shelter and safety taken care of, and every able-bodied man put to work. You see any more goats, sheep, or cattle, shoo them back to that big Greek over there. He's a fair cook." He held his rifle barrel up just enough to show that he meant business. "Am I clear?"

The men answered, their replies not all in English.

"Then quit your lollygagging and let's get to work." He paused as if chewing on the thought. "Choice, soon as your belly is full, go back up Market Street and cut over to Chinatown. See if you can determine who, if anyone, is in charge, and how fast that fire is going to burn in our direction. Then, hustle on back here and report to Captain Lafferty with that information."

The three horsemen led the way as they formed a reverse 'V' formation. The people immediately in front of them did not put up much of a fight moving out of the way. It was the hundred or so packed in behind them that didn't want to give way. A few minutes into their ride, a group of belligerent men formed, determined to stop the deputies in their tracks.

"This here is public right of way, and no goddamned cowboy is gonna tell us where we can be or not be." A tall, wiry man, with arms flapping like some kind of a crazed bird, squawked. As a self-appointed leader he stood his ground, immediately in front of Cornelius. His flapping arms annoyed Cornelius's horse, causing it to rear, almost toppling him.

Reigning in his horse, Cornelius answered back gruffly. "Sorry you feel that way, Mister. Why don't you take it up with the city council the next time they meet." He nodded at Sidney, who brought out a long whip, which when snapped and wrapped neatly around one of the man's wrists.

It stung, drawing a light ring of red, making his point.

"People," Cornelius commanded with an authoritative voice, "unless you want to take a swim, you will move back."

The self-appointed loudmouth was rolled in by Sidney's whip, then quickly manhandled head over head to the edge of the wharf before being tossed two feet out, where he dropping a good six feet down into the roiling surf. It did not matter if he could or could not swim. There was enough debris floating to keep his head above water until he found a lifeline.

A few cheered, making it obvious that the loudmouth had not been speaking for them. "Now, move back." Cornelius pointed the tip of his rifle at the foot of a man who seemed to want to argue. "You got something to say?" Cornelius said as he took a deep draw on his cigar.

Sidney rolled up his whip into a ready position.

"To hell with you," the man muttered as he turned away, his exit helping to push the crowd back.

CHAPTER 23

"MARSHAL, WE'VE GOT PROBLEMS." SIDNEY WARNED AS HE pointed over the crowd towards where Market Street converged with the waterfront and the mass of people who were running out of somewhere to go.

"Cornelius, you are not going to like this," T.J. hollered as he rode up behind Cornelius' line of deputized volunteers as they pressed through. The longshoremen's line held, preventing T.J. from breaking through. He tried to yell to Cornelius, who couldn't understand much of what he was saying as a shrill whistle announced the arrival of a fire tug as it approached the Ferry Terminal.

Now what? Inspector Cornelius McCann needed to be right where he was, and three other places at the same moment. He bit down on his cigar, its tip glowing red, as he drew the smoke through the tightly wrapped tobacco leaves. What Sidney had just said had his strict attention. A platoon of soldiers from the 22nd U.S. Army Regiment from the Presidio had marched down Market Street to find their way blocked by the mass of refugees he and his deputies were herding. A saloon just to their right was attracting thirsty refugees, mostly men, who needed to take the edge off of what was already a bad day.

From where Cornelius sat, the saloon appeared to be open for business. Industrious son-of-a-bitch, he thought as he sized up the situation. The soldiers were forming a picket line with long bayonets pointed toward the crowd gathered around the saloon, some with liquor bottles clearly in hand. From all appearances it looked to Cornelius as if the officer in charge was about to order his troops to open fire. To add to the problem some drunken fool who stood between the soldiers and the rest, appeared to be baiting the soldiers. "Damn fool doesn't know any better than to mess with blue-bellies when they've got their rifles cocked. Let's see if I can at least keep you alive long enough to make a fool of yourself another day." Cornelius muttered as he raised his rifle. "Steady," he whispered to his nervous mount as he closed one eye, squinted the other, drawing his site out the length of his cigar, through the blue haze, to the site at the far end of his rifle barrel.

CRACK!

The drunk fell, shot just above his right knee; lucky to be alive.

The crowd around Cornelius fell silent, stunned by the sudden violence, not sure who, or where he was shooting.

The silence fell across the throng like a wave, as every muzzle the Army had swung towards Cornelius with deadly intent.

The fire tug whistled, demanding its own priority.

Cornelius raised his rifle high over his head. "T.J.," he said without looking back; the crowd, now quiet enough for T.J. to hear. "I'm a little busy right now. Why don't you do me a favor and ride on over and tell Captain Lafferty that a fire tug is inviting him to high tea." He kicked his horse. The crowd parted as Cornelius rode towards the soldiers, rifle held high and non-threatening. What Choice Pickens hollered after him, he didn't quite catch . . . something about trouble coming through their back door. The last word he thought he heard was crimps.

Crimps. Red warning flares went off in his brain. The most dangerous and unpredictable rogues that had ever haunted the waterfront. Tough, dangerous bastards he did not want to have to deal with now. As a cop he needed to respond to the greater danger. He also knew that he could use some serious help if the crimps wanted to pick a fight.

Second Lieutenant Reaves Charter, hard jawed and tightlipped, was well beyond his pay grade experience level. He watched, grimly, as a cowboy rode through this sea of humanity, rifle raised, as if he owned the goddamned place. He wanted to shoot the son-of-a-bitch. Marshal Law had been declared and he had the authority to kill the bastard, no questions asked. He looked back at the wounded looter he had first set his sights on. The man was down, squealing, as blood pumped from his wound. He was no longer much of a threat, nor someone to make any further example of. "Easy," he spoke low to his troops, their fingers ready on their triggers. "Easy . . . easy . . . let the bastard make the first move. On my command . . ." He could feel it in his gut, he wanted to shoot someone, that cowboy would do just fine. It had been the cowboy who had denied him the pleasure of executing the loudmouth by taking him out with a difficult leg shot made to look easy. The only thing keeping him from giving the order to shoot the cowboy was twenty-thousand watchful, if not curious eyes.

CHAPTER 24

CHOICE PICKENS LICKED THE GREASE FROM HIS FINGERS. The goat was better than good. He hadn't realized how hungry he had been. He was tempted to have a third helping but knew that too much would slow him down.

He eyed the fires burning in the Financial District and Chinatown. He wasn't comfortable going back out into the fires alone; a dangerous place to be. If he stayed put he'd be playing second fiddle to half-ass Darcy. Technically, Pickens was senior to Darcy. That being said, McCann had appointed Darcy to be in charge of the precinct in his absence, which left Pickens to put out fires while Darcy sat on his ass directing traffic.

Choice Pickens weighed his problems over in his mind. Achilles needed more goats, there were many hungry people and the aroma of the roasting goats he had only wetted their appetites. The collapsed fish market was beginning to stink. Buried beneath were an unknown number of fish mongers, and a ton of ripe fish, all going bad on an unusually warm April day, not to mention the hot wind from the fires around them. Four more bodies had been found so the skiff had now reached capacity. Someone needed to sail it out to Alcatraz and Choice had enough of small boats loaded down with bodies, dead or alive, to last a life time. Every able bodied man was occupied with either helping Captain Lafferty clear a fire line, or with McCann pushing back the overwhelming wave of refugees that were descending upon them. Shit happens, Choice Pickens thought, but why did it have to rain down on him all at the same time.

That, and his neck was stiff. When he got hit on the head while being shanghaied, it had given him a neck that refused to turn to the left without some degree of pain. He sighed. A hot bath, accompanied by a tall whiskey, followed by a good night's rest were not in the cards.

"Hey, Pickens, you want to check this out?" He tried to turn towards the sound of Captain Lafferty's voice, but his neck failed him. His slow turn, and pained expression made him look less than cooperative.

Lafferty had no qualms about the pecking order when it came to Darcy. McCann may have left him in charge, but as far as Lafferty was concerned, he was a goldbricking half-ass excuse for a cop. "Darcy, over here, right now," he bellowed, not wanting to get into an argument with Pickens. "You've got a problem, so handle it."

Choice Pickens rubbed his neck, preferring to sit this one out. He was still peeved that Cornelius had chosen the dwarf cowboy over him.

"All right, hold your britches, I'm coming." Darcy's thoughts were far from polite, but he did not want to get Captain Lafferty on his bad side. Darcy set the bottle of whiskey he had confiscated down by Achilles for safe keeping - with a guarded nonverbal warning that he had better not touch it. "Hold your water, I'm coming, what in hell's fire is so damn urgent?"

No sooner than Darcy had stepped away than Achilles grabbed the bottle, took a deep draw, belched, then poured the rest over the goat he had just turned over the fire.

Lafferty didn't mince words, preferring to point, as Darcy drew near. "There." He pointed at the west end of the collapsed fish market where several men had climbed over the debris, soon to be followed by others, all armed with clubs or pikes. They were coming from the ravaged Barbary Coast section of town, were most likely drunk, and looking for a fight.

Darcy stopped dead in his tracks, hoping that what he saw wasn't true.

Choice Pickens eyes followed Darcy. He immediately recognized Archibald Pipe, followed by the Walrus, both crimps. No telling how many Barbary Coast thugs they were bringing with them. This was trouble, no two ways about it, and stiff neck or not, he wasted no time in heading off to find Cornelius.

Darcy had other intentions.

CHAPTER 25

CORNELIUS STOPPED ABOUT TEN YARDS OUT FROM THE soldiers, their rifles still aimed directly at him. He slowly lowered his rifle letting it drop to the ground with an ominous clank. Not a soul dared to take a breath as he dismounted. The fires, not that far behind on Market Street blew hot, while a rumbling boom reminded them all of their limited mortality, as part of the massive dome over what was left of City Hall gave way. His horse snorted, breathing heavily, as if it understood the threat of all those guns pointed in its direction. Cornelius never took his eye off the army officer as he reached into his pocket, took out two cigars and a match, bit the tip off one before locking the cigar between his teeth. He considered himself a good judge of men and the man he faced wasn't that far away from being a shave-tailed boy. He has a pimple on his nose, since when do officers of the United States Army, have pimples? He stood as if he had a broom stick stuck up his ass, and not quite sure if he liked it there or not. A leader of men - not yet.

Cornelius walked slowly, confidently, to the officer, lit the cigar clamped between his teeth, while holding out the unlit one for the officer, while the single wooden match burned closer to his fingertips.

The closest soldier's bayonet quivered less than a foot away.

The officer's gaze dropped to the match, which highlighted the man's badge. He was the law; that changed things.

The crowd was stone quiet, while the horse made an impatient neigh. "Inspector Cornelius McCann, San Francisco Police Department, welcome to my Precinct." The match dropped to the ground. "You don't smoke," he added matter-of-factly, returning the unlit cigar to his pocket.

"Nice shooting. Marshal McCann is it?"

Cornelius was beginning to hate that word. "Lucky shot? Maybe. If I had missed I might have killed the poor son-of-a-bitch, and that wasn't my intent. I don't recognize a shoot to kill order down here."

The officer remained tight lipped.

"We've got some fresh roasted goat just off the grill, if you're hungry, but you'll have to check your guns here. No one . . . I repeat, no one is allowed on my waterfront with a weapon unless he is a dually sworn police officer of the City of San Francisco.

The two men stared at each other.

"I can see that you have a problem with that." Cornelius continued as he motioned to a spot of ground a few yards away, and out of the direct range of the rifles. "Why don't we step over there and we'll see if we can't come to an understanding." Cornelius walked to the spot leaving the officer to stew in his own pomposity.

Twenty-thousand eyes watched to see if the officer would blink.

"First rank, remain in firing positions, pending my order. Second rank," it was an odd order, but he needed to cut the tension, "stand easy."

Once the officer had stepped over the line and onto Cornelius's turf, Cornelius offered him the cigar again. Both had their backs to the throng. This time the officer accepted the cigar.

"Inspector McCann, you are aware that the City of San Francisco has been placed under Marshal Law. Under army regulations I am . . ."

"Going to do nothing."

The officer bristled.

"It would help, Lieutenant, if I could see your orders. Short of that, you will take your orders from the highest ranking civilian law officer in your immediate vicinity." He smiled to relax the tension. "If you kiss my ass just right, I might - might - just let you call me Cornelius, or do you prefer Inspector McCann, Sir?"

The officer took all that in. He did not have written orders. His troops were green, scared, and wound too tight; as was he. He looked back at the crowd for just a moment, turned back, lit his cigar against the hot coal of Cornelius', intercepting McCann's penetrating gaze. After blowing out an imperfect smoke ring into his antagonist's face he snapped, "Second Lieutenant Reaves Charter, 22nd U.S. Army Regiment, at your service, Sir. You may address me as Lieutenant, Inspector. We'll keep it at that, for the time being. And may I say, Sir, you are one son-of-a-bitch. That being said, what are your orders, Sir?"

"First, you can cut the "Sir" crap. Second, you can ask your troops to stop pointing their damn rifles at women and children." He nodded towards the crowd behind him. "My horse has never taken kindly to having rifles pointed at it either. Third, take care of that wounded man over there. I only shot him to keep you from killing the poor bastard." He blew a playful smoke ring back. "You've got what, thirty men. Fine, I need ten men here, another ten at the ferry terminal, and the rest to follow me. I've got some trouble coming in our back door."

"Trouble, Sir?" The 'Sir' punctuated loud and crisp.

Cornelius gave him a cocked eye on that. "If I knew,

I wouldn't be worried about it, Lew . . . ten . . ant."

The Lieutenant barked his orders, mindful of his image as twenty-thousand assorted eyes took measure of him. He had given ground to the Inspector, did not like it, but had quickly learned that Inspector Cornelius McCann was someone to be respected. He planned on finding a way to put the self-righteous son-of-a bitch in his god-damned place, when the time was right.

McCann knew that look. "Oh, I almost forgot. Lew. . .ten . . . ant," he said as he turned and walked back to his horse. "Your boys can keep their guns. If circumstances develop where lethal force becomes necessary, you will not shoot to kill. You are to shoot for the leg. If that don't work, shoot them in the other leg. I've got enough problems dealing with bodies around here." He stopped but did not turn. "Am I clear?"

"You heard the man?" The Lieutenant ordered. "The order stands."

The soldiers mumbled back a half answer.

"It's good to know that you are in solid command of your troops, Lew . . .ten . . .Ant."

Second Lieutenant Reaves Charter blistered. What authority had been his, had just been taken away. Without respect or fear, how was he to remain in charge of his command?

Cornelius gently stroked his horse's muzzle as he wrapped his own thoughts around the bigger picture. A raging fire storm growing around them would soon to cut them off with their backs to the sea. He had no link with higher command and all around him a sea of people waited for him to make decisions. He slowly turned back towards the burning city to find an even larger mass of people wanting to pour out onto the waterfront.

The soldiers were letting no one through. Behind them the flames flared high, dancing in their own winds as they devoured everything, including the air. These soldiers were not the best to have at your back when in harm's way. With the Indian wars over, the peace time army was poorly trained, lazy, and uneducated. Still, he might need them, that is, if they could take and follow orders. The Lieutenant, he should not have treated so harshly.

The fire tug whistled.

Lafferty, that one is yours, he thought as he pondered what Choice Pickens had been trying to convey. Choice was a good officer, not one to shirk his duties, or back away when things got tough. He had a bug up his ass and it had something to do with the crimps. That could only mean that whatever he was facing was beyond his ability to respond. He patted his horse one last time, then turned back to review the resources he had.

"Lieutenant, gather your Sergeants and Platoon Leaders over here for a little command and control conference." He walked back to the sacred spot where he and Lieutenant Reaves Charter had powwowed, turned back and said, "Please." This was not a word that came easily to him.

"You heard the man, Sergeants and Platoon Leaders, front and center. On the double time," The Lieutenant shrieked.

Cornelius grimaced at the sound.

Four Sergeants and a Corporal formed a circle. Cornelius gave each of them a tight smile, then addressed his remarks to the Lieutenant. "Gentlemen, we are caught in a shit storm, and nothing about it smells right. I reckon the best we can do is damage control. We've got god knows how many people on the waterfront right now, and that number is going to triple faster than you can spit. I want a picket line set up, right here, from that point over there to the front of that saloon which as of this moment is officially closed." He looked back at his longshoremen and volunteers, and did a rough count. "I'll detail forty deputies to work with you." He waved over two men, didn't know item one about either, asked their names - Mumm and Jeffers they said - jotting each name on a piece of paper he stuffed back in his pocket, promoted each to the rank of Sergeant, to even things out. "No one gets on the water front with a weapon who is drunk, or disagrees with our terms of hospitality. Lieutenant, push comes to shove, you are authorized to shoot." He took a moment to relight his cigar. "You are authorized to shoot them in the leg only." His eyes conveyed that this was not negotiable. "Lieutenant, we're going to need a second squad detailed to the Ferry Wharf. The building stands but I'll be damned if I can guess for how long. If, and when, she comes down any refugees squatting inside will be squashed like June bugs. The interior ferry landings are just as useless. Rope off the building so it's clear that folks are to stay clear. The berth on the North side is the only one left that can take a ferry, the South now filled with rubble. If or when a boat actually shows, we will need some serious command and control there to keep a thousand people from trying to board a boat that can carry just a couple of hundred. Lieutenant, you and the rest of your men come with me and we'll see what kind of trouble is headed our way from what's left of the Barbary Coast. I do expect trouble, and there will be some shooting."

"Does that mean, shoot to kill, Sir?" The Lieutenant asked, still highlighting the Sir.

"Only if one's own life is threatened," he thought about the type of men who made up the crimps, "otherwise you are authorized to shoot a little higher, and if you blow a few of their balls off, I can't think of a more deserving bunch."

"You heard the Marshal," the Lieutenant bellowed, liking the last command. "Sergeant Wilcox, you are here. Cambridge, detail your men to the Ferry Wharf. Sergeant Schmidt and Corporal Blaine, you are with me. Marshall McCann, at your command."

"Lew . . .ten . . . ant, I'm only going to say this once. I am an Inspector with the San Francisco Police Department, not some dumb-assed Marshal. Now, do we have an understanding?"

"Sir, yes Sir, snapped the Lieutenant. He turned back to his men. "You heard the Marshal, now let's double-time."

Inspector McCann shook his head. It was going to be one long day.

CHAPTER 26

UNUSUAL FOR A THIEF AND A MURDERER ARCHIBALD PIPE was an educated man. He stood just under five foot nine, lean, with a long angular face, whiskers that always seemed to be a perpetual five o'clock shadow on a double cleft chin, a slightly hooked nose, with small beady eyes that threaten an internal violence always close to the surface. He often wore a black tarnished evening jacket, worn more like a vest, and a top hat that Abe Lincoln would be proud of. He usually carried a cane, though he didn't have a limp.

Pipe had attended a Catholic Jesuit School, and had come close to becoming a priest himself. He had taught mathematics in Omaha until he discovered opium as an alternative to his boring teacher's life. The salary of a teacher was not sufficient to support his habit, so he stole the school's meager funds and headed west. Fleeing one hanging posse after another, he wound up in San Francisco's Barbary Coast, where as a natural born leader, snake oil salesman, horse thief, crimp, pimp, and murderer, he became a force on the shadier side of the city few could match.

Archibald Pipe never missed an opportunity to line his own pockets. The earthquake and fires devastating San Francisco began to look to him like the opportunity of a lifetime. Travel was so much easier when folks lightened their loads, he laughed, and he was happy to oblige on a grand scale.

The Barbary, one of the most notorious and rundown neighborhoods in the city was a tinder box and it had not taken long for the fires to spread. Drunkenness and civil unrest spread faster than the fire, which gave him the opportunity to become the Grand Duke of criminals, rallying all the criminal elements in pitched running gun battles with both the police and the army. It didn't matter that he hadn't the weapons. He was blinded by greed, drugs, and would not accept surrender. His followers, amateurish and bully cowards mostly, were no match, and he was forced with thirty or so followers to surrender the Barbary to the stronger elements of law and order. There were plenty of spoils to be had elsewhere in the ruins and chaos of a dying city.

Moving on made little difference to Pipe, as he made his way through the ruins towards the waterfront. As he peered out of the still smoking ruins and gazed at the thousands of refugees surrounding the Ferry Terminal, he could not help but run his tongue over his front teeth and out onto his lips. The prize was better than a perfectly grilled steak with all the trimmings. His appetite wet, he looked back at his company of thieves and murders. Hell, these idiots care more for violence and lawlessness than a gold coin. Fine, I'll give them the thrill and keep the coins for myself.

"Well, well . . . Well, what do we have here?" Pipe said to himself with a slight air of bemusement written across his face. Sergeant Frank Darcy was headed his way as if they were long lost best friends. Pipe allowed no one to approach him that way - no one. Darcy stopped two passes short of where he stood. "Half-ass Darcy, how is it that you are alive and still a free man? I was told that you were delivered along with . . . never mind, it has been a most remarkable day."

Darcy figured that he had Pipe in a proverbial hard place, and if he did, he also had Abe Ruef in the same. Sure, he had betrayed his fellow officers for the promise of a sizable cash payoff. He should have demanded the money upfront. In the tunnels, he himself had been betrayed and since his luck had changed one more time, he was going to collect what he was due and then some. Cops had been shanghaied, he had been one of them, and no court was going to take a crimps word over his. If arrests were made, it would all come back to Ruef. How much should he demand? He thought as started to open his mouth.

"Shut your gob, you half-assed, stupid, little man." Pipe interrupted. "You betrayed your fellow officers for a few dollars and had the naivety that you should be paid for that. You should have had your throat slit . . . I'll have to have me a little chat with someone about that." Pipe noticed the fire Captain looking their way. He slid the long lethal blade that was hidden in his walking stick out just enough for Darcy to see. "It is your good fortune that at the moment I am a very busy man. The next time I see your sorry face, I will gut you like a fish and feed your guts to a mongrel dog while you watch with your dying breath." Pipe clicked the metal blade within his stick to let Darcy know that if he did not run now he would use the blade within a blink of an eye.

No one questioned Captain Lafferty's courage. As a fireman in San Francisco he had faced dangers that would make other men of heroic tales cringe. What he saw now, caused him to take pause. He knew of Archibald Pipe by sight and reputation. Pipe was a man for hire when a building needed torching for a price. That women and children might be caught in the blaze, escaped his conscience. Now, he and a gang of ruthless cutthroats were making their way through the rubble. One look told Lafferty that they were not coming for a spring picnic on the waterfront. Pipe was after turf, over which he wanted absolute power and control. It was all or nothing to him and to his men. It was not a fight

Lafferty wanted to take on. Pipe was a force to be reckoned with, but not today, not by him and his men. The fire was Lafferty's biggest adversary. If he lost that battle, and the odds were high that he would, the people that would soon crowd the waterfront would have a lot worse to worry about than a thieving bunch of crimps.

He looked out over the water where more of the tall ships were making weigh, away from the dangerous hot ash carrying winds. It was not the ships that caught his immediate attention. Now that's peculiar, he thought as he noticed officer Darcy walk up to Pipe as if they were old poker adversaries, ready to exchange tall tales over beer, always on the bluff. After exchanging a few words, it was Archibald Pipe who did the threatening, as Darcy kowtowed to his master. The look on Darcy's face said it all. He had not only backed down from Archibald Pipe, he was scared to death. Clearly running away, Darcy gave little, if any, thought to keeping his post, leaving the women and children that had been under his protection, to whatever ends Pipe desired.

The last Lafferty saw of Darcy after he disappeared beneath the wharf, was the coward's back as Darcy rowed the skiff, heavy in the water with the weight of the dead, in the direction of the Long Oakland Pier - a bridge to the mainland. There was no doubt in Lafferty's mind that Darcy had deserted.

With Cornelius otherwise occupied, Captain Lafferty moved his small fire crew a block closer to the fire, and that much distance away from Archibald Pipe's crimps and murderers. Lafferty was a fireman not a cop. He had not the men, time, or energy to face anything more than the fire.

Choice Pickens had gone after Cornelius, at least that was what Lafferty thought. The longshoremen that had remained to guard the wharves melted into the crowd as soon as the crimps moved in. That left the Greek and the boy Sven, which made taking a stand against the crimps pure wishful thinking. Captain Lafferty tried to convince the Greek and the boy to leave. They refused.

Not having time to argue the point, Lafferty wished them god speed and followed the sound of the fire tug that demanded his attention.

CHAPTER 27

THE WALRUS, A MAN WITH WILD HAIR SPROUTING FROM every inch of exposed skin, whose girth equaled, if not bested Achilles', came up behind the big Greek, pressing the point of his buffalo hunter's blade deep enough into Achilles's extended gut to draw a trickle of blood. He slowly edged the knife away as Achilles turned to face him. The two Grizzly sized men stared into each other's eyes, one seeing an evil man who got a kick out of inflicting pain and suffering, the other a timid toothless bear with no stomach for battle.

Achilles shook his head as he raised his hands to show that he had no weapon. "I am cook," he said with a heavy accent and a forced smile, suggesting that he might be a simpleton.

The Walrus smirked, drew back his knife, slicing off a chunk of goat, stuffing his large mouth, grease running from the corner of his mouth onto his beard. Satisfied with the flavorful meat, he nodded his approval, sheaving his hunter's blade. "You are a good cook. Just keep to your cooking and I might let you live."

Archibald Pipe sauntered over as if he were entering a gentlemen's club, gave Achilles a curious eye, suggesting that he might be wondering why he was still breathing. When in doubt the Walrus always opted to eliminate someone in question. Pipe couldn't remember the last time he hadn't.

Not wanting a sudden reversal of his fortune, Achilles turned back to a goat he had just slaughtered, prepping it for the fire.

"Good," the Walrus said with a mouthful of goat, to Pipe.

Sven stood back, scared, not sure what to do. His mother, his two younger brothers, Nils and Patrik clutching her dress, watched with growing apprehension from the wharf.

The wind changed, a thick smothering cloud of smoke settled over them, the air suddenly stilled, tasting of charcoal, heat, and things offensive and corrupt. A breath suddenly became harder to catch, one's eyes stinging, bloodshot and dry.

Pipe, who appreciated the sound of his own voice, was often given to lengthy speeches, regardless of who might be listening, or for that matter, comprehending. He tasted his first breath of hell and knew by its taste where he belonged. "Up North, during the gold rush," he said, not really caring who was listening, "men marked their claims with stacks of stone, and many a good man died daring to move a few stones to claim that land for his own." His breath caught, he had to cough, and he rested his right foot against the low wall of bricks that Sven, Achilles, and others had built. "Those stones became worthless once scattered, and since there was no longer anything to mark the claim, it now belonged to the strongest man willing to call it his own." He pushed a portion of the wall down. The Walrus another, other crimps who had just arrived, pushed the bricks down until there was no wall left standing.

"I say this part of the waterfront is mine," Pipe declared casting his eyes about to see if anyone might dare to object.

The smoke thickened casting everyone in a dark gritty gray fog as the sun, a fading orange globe retreated from the fire demon that devoured the city.

"No." Sven protested.

Archibald Pipe snapped his fingers. He needed something to show that he had the power, and the kid had just given it to him.

Two crimps grabbed the lad, while a third tied his hands behind him. Pipe tossed them a pole. "The boy likes to squeal like a pig, so be it. Lash him to the pole, then toss him on the fire, and we'll see what more he has to say." He turned showing a threatening grin for all to see - his face saying, "who is stupid enough to want to challenge me?"

Achilles, peaceful giant, had had enough. He turned, his skinning knife tight in his hands, still dripping with fresh goat blood. The one he feared the most stood between him and the boy. He had no time to think, only to react, before Sven would be thrown helpless on the fire.

Too late, Walrus turned to confront him, as the full length of Achilles's eight inch knife plowing deep into his huge gut. The fact that he had not seen it coming showed in his anguished bloodshot eyes. The crimps holding the boy were caught totally off guard as Achilles left the Walrus for dead and charged forward like a bull in heat, taking Sven and himself across the fire, sparks exploding, as the remaining red hot brick wall behind the fire collapsed. Bricks sizzled as Achilles, Sven and the two men who had been holding Sven tumbled into the cold bay water below.

A crimp screamed a warning too late, his voice instantly turned into a retching cough as the acrid smoke swirled around the wharf. The steam, smoke, sparks, and surprise masked Achilles' frantic efforts to free Sven from his bonds before they both drowned.

The Walrus pulled the knife out from his own gut, blood spreading quickly, as he stared at it with a look of stupid surprise.

Archibald Pipe clicked his tongue. "Bad luck," he said almost approvingly at the sheer audacity of the Greek cook, as he turned towards the sound of a woman screaming. He could not make out the woman in the dense smoke, but the sound of her fear aroused him.

The Walrus stumbled, waved the knife at invisible foes, then collapsed, dead, his mouth agape, rotting teeth marking the path to a rotten soul.

The remaining crimps who were too close to the fire frantically slapped off red hot sparks from their clothing and hair. The goat that had been grilling now sizzled and popped in the hot coals. The wind shifted, the smoke swirling, lifted, then settled, before rising again. Explosions boomed in the distance, a sea tug sounded from somewhere nearby, the frightened voices of the multitudes incomprehensible in this dark ocean of noise.

"Such a waste," Pipe said as he took one last look at the Walrus. "Well, onward to other prizes." He dabbed a handkerchief at his running eyes, then waved at the nearest cutthroats and hoodlums he considered under his command. "I give you these fair damsels to enjoy, but not at your leisure, for after rape, we have plunder and pillage. Before this city burns we shall take our weight in gold, or die trying. And if that must be, then we will go before the fires of hell for Satan to claim us for his own, as proud bastards who gave it their all." So poetic, he thought as he turned back towards where he had heard the woman scream.

Sven's mother, who had not had the wisdom to be silent, held her two younger sons, as she grieved the loss of her eldest son Sven who she knew could not swim, bound or not.

CHAPTER 28

CHOICE PICKENS RODE BEHIND T.J., HIS ARMS WRAPPED around the cowboy least he be thrown from the horse. He felt like a fool running to put out a house fire with a cup of water. One thing he had learned quickly was that he did not like horses. As they neared the wharf he slipped off his horse awkwardly, pulling out his revolver. The smoke was blowing into the water front, thick, swirling gray, a black cloud rapidly eating the light of day. Sidney rode up to his side in time for them to see Achilles' bold rescue of Sven.

"Damn, where did that come from?" Choice exclaimed, the Greek's courage suddenly drawing out his own.

"Easy, let's do a head count before we go in with guns blazing," Sidney said, his voice firm, but not much louder than a whisper.

Choice knew he was right, there were three of them, and an unknown number of men who would just as likely prefer to kill them than shake hands. Sven's mother's scream drew the crimps in her direction, which brought them out into the open. Through the swirling smoke it was hard to see how many there were, or where they were exactly, which added to their predicament. There was no time to debate strategy, once the crimps reached the wharf, the women and children became perfect hostages. Choice had no idea how the cowboys would measure up, but if they didn't try, those women and children were lost.

The smoke lifted and blew out over the bay to be followed by another cloud just as thick, dark, and cloying. That moment of reprieve had told them what they needed to know. There were eleven following Pipe, eight of them near the collapsed fish market. There were more, but for one reason or another they had chosen to hang back by the ruins that separated them from their old turf on the Barbary. Perhaps they were acting as a rearguard, keeping watch out for any police or army troops who might still be on their trail. A quick count gave Choice, Sidney and T.J. as many as 25 to 30 crimps, few carried guns, most being armed with knives, pikes, and clubs. Most crimps don't carry guns, they weren't much use in close-quarters, and could be turned against them. Men like Archibald Pipe carried a Derringer, perhaps two. Pipe was also known to keep an eight inch stiletto hidden in his cane.

"It looks about even to me," Sidney said as he spat some chewing tobacco. He offered a chaw to Pickens. "It helps make the smoke from the fires taste a bit more tolerable."

Choice shook his head, no, chaw had never been his thing.

"Might be," T.J. nodded, meaning the odds, as both men brought up their rifles. "First thing, we need to keep the crimps away from the women-folk." He coughed, vision blurred by teary eyes and smoke. "Mr. Pickens, your call."

Choice looked behind them, searching the crowds for any sign of Cornelius. The swirling smoke left him with nothing but a gray mass of movement which, given enough time, the smoke would be more dangerous than any of the crimps they were about to take on. Time they did not have, if they were going to do anything that would prevent the women and children from falling into the crimps foul hands. Another minute and Archibald Pipe would have Sven's mother, and god knows how many more hostages.

"OK, Sidney." Choice retched as he tried to speak, "T.J. says that you're the best shot. Why don't you take aim at those boys over by the fish market and keep them pinned down. Inspector McCann may have my ass for this, but take no prisoners . . . take them all out. T.J. and I are going straight at that fella over there with the top hat. We eliminate him, the others just might call it a day. Shoot to kill these bastards." He spat, thinking himself the fool for what he was about to do. He wished he had a cold beer, his mouth and throat were dry. He would settle for water, but that wasn't to be, at least for the time being. "On my count . . ."

Choice Pickens didn't bother to finish the count as he ran towards the cooking fire, jumped over the dead whale once known as the Walrus, taking aim at the last man in the pack following Pipe.

The dense smoke swirled, multiple shades of gray, tinged here and there with the red, orange, and yellow reflections of the flames that produced the suffocating mass. Babies cried, women called out for loved ones lost, separated in the chaos following the quake. Children played while others sobbed, mothers cried out for their children to stay near, while old men demanded order, where none was to be had. No one paid any attention as a single canary in its cage fell silent as the smoke became too much to support its fragile life.

Mounted, T.J. had more speed. He rode fast, coming in on their left, boxing the crimps between himself and Pickens.

Pickens only had his revolver. Between them they only had enough bullets for one pass. The crimps weren't much for guns, preferring to work in packs, a hard blow to the head usually sufficient to bring down their prey. Their long pikes were the most serious threat, and those boys knew how to use them.

The smoke gave Choice and T.J. a brief cloak of surprise.

Choice fired.

A crimp threw up his arms, then dropped dead.

Choice fired twice sending a second man down. A woman ran by holding a small child. Where had the second shot gone? He needed to be more careful.

T.J. dropped two more of the crimps.

Sidney had not taken up a firing position on the fish market. Instead he had ridden to the closest gang of longshoremen. He came at them from behind at a dangerous full gallop, scattering men, women and children as he came about. Out of surprise and self-defense two of the nearest longshoremen grabbed for the reigns of his horse. Sidney cracked his whip, yelling down at the men. "Back off! Inspector McCann," he lied, "needs a dozen or more of you over by the old fish market, pronto. The crimps have come over from the Barbary wanting to take our women and kids into slavery. We don't have enough men to stop them."

The word quickly passed down the line.

"Now you do," one declared. Eighteen prepared to follow.

Sidney brought his rifle to easy use as he galloped back to the smoke covered wharf where the battle was still taking place.

The smoke lifted, their element of surprise lost. The remaining crimps still standing turned on Choice, the easiest target. Just as quickly as the smoke had lifted, it settled in again. A pike whisked through the gray smoke, a tinge of dull orange reflected flame caught in its tarnished metal, missing Choice by inches as he fired at close range. His target died instantly, immediately behind a second man shrieked, the same bullet striking him in the neck, a gusher of blood spouting. Two crimps turned to flee, one taking T.J.'s rifle butt hard to the skull, the other dodged past, fleeing towards the collapsed fish market. The remaining four men backed in close to Archibald Pipe, who now held a Derringer to Sven's mother's head. Her younger sons, terrified, crying, were shoved out of the way by one of the crimps.

T.J. shot two crimps who seemed to come out of nowhere, then wondered if he had just used his last bullet.

The crimp who had been knocked down got to his feet plunging his pike deep into T.J.'s horse, the horse reared as T.J. pulled the trigger fearing that he would come up empty. His fear was well founded, he was now defenseless. The horse, the pike imbedded in its flank causing a long deep wound cutting through the muscle, collapsed, pinning T.J. beneath. Two men, one with a pike, the other with a boat hook came at T.J. who had one leg and his rifle trapped beneath the horse, its last struggle against death mighty but hopeless.

Choice shot the one with the pike.

The boat hook bit deep into T.J,s. shoulder.

Choice fired again and missed.

The crimp with the boat hook put his full weight on the hook driving it deep, hooked a rib, snapping it. T.J. screamed, as the hook dug deep towards his lung.

A leather whip cracked, wrapped around the crimps wrist quickly separating the man from his weapon. Sidney dragged the man several feet before slamming him into a metal cable tie. That done, he took aim at a group of crimps coming from the direction of the collapsed fish market. Three shots. Two down. One struggled to his feet. Sidney sent him back down to his knees.

Women and children ran and screamed around them, making it that much more difficult to find a target. Old men stood their ground, too slow to get out of the way. Choice turned his revolver on Archibald Pipe who still held the Derringer to Sven's mother's head, his finger tight on the trigger. Choice found a split second opportunity and pulled his own gun's trigger.

He came up empty, out of ammo.

The last two crimps went after Sidney as Archibald Pipe turned his Derringer on Choice Pickens, the range close enough to kill. Choice swallowed, dry, sure that within a few seconds he would be dead. He had wondered if his life would pass before his eyes at his moment before death. Time slowed, as his last seconds stretched out before him. He did not know if there was a heaven - hadn't seen the need to concern himself with it. Looking around he found that most assuredly there is a hell and its open gates, raw and enticing, lay open for him now. Fires ravaged the horizon, spinning off dark smoke-driven dragons, both sinister and evil. The roar came from the wail of countless souls calling for him to join them in the unforgiving purgatory waiting below. Around him women screamed, children cried holding onto the rags of their mother's dresses, men fought - slicing and tearing at each other's flesh. The dead lay around him, their silent screams seemingly as loud as those of the living. Madness. His vision blurred, he had trouble catching his breath. If it wasn't Pipe it would be the smoke. He stared at Pipe's trigger finger and into the dark hole at the end of his gun wondering if he would see the bullet.

The crimps who went after Sidney stopped short. The longshoreman had arrived, loud, angry, and more than willing to take on the crimps one on one.

Unseen by Pipe, a large arm dripping with salt water wrapped around his neck just as he fired, the shot missing its target. Surprised, Pipe let loose of the woman as he struggled against a strength he could not overcome. He was drawn backwards towards the edge of the wharf. A double terror to him because he could not swim. Pipe couldn't breathe, his neck twisting, his eyes bulging, catching sight of the big Greek as his neck snapped, his last sight his watery grave.

The remaining crimps fled, their battle would be finished ashore, around the fish market.

Quick to dismount, Sidney tended to T.J.

Exhausted, Choice Pickens was on his knees retching from smoke inhalation and his brush with imminent death.

Achilles pulled Sven up the same rope that August Freeman had earlier pulled him from the cold grip of the San Francisco Bay.

The terror of the women and children drowned out the sound of the surf and the clash of men in hand to hand combat just ashore.

The wind shifted to the South taking with it the thick curtain of smoke. A brilliant sun against a cloudless blue sky immediately above, blinded most everyone, their bloodshot weeping eyes overcome by the sudden brilliant yellowish glare.

The two crimps who had fallen into the bay with Achilles and Sven managed to climb back onto the wharf. Somehow one had managed to recover a pike. The other found one near the body of a dead crimp.

Choice Pickens reached for his revolver, aware that he was out of ammo, but what else could he do. Sven and Achilles came to his side. Weaponless, there was not much they could do either.

Sidney's rifle remained on his mount, out of reach. The crimps were only a couple of yards away. Choice caught the look in Achilles's eyes, it was too late, they were about to be slashed and hacked to death. Sven went to his mother. The women and children fell silent as the crimps, weapons raised, slowed just long enough to get a measure of their prey.

WHOOSH!

A Navy Fire Tug, from Mare Island, had pulled up to the wharf, its high power fire hose, slamming the crimps back, head over heels, in the torrent of water. Captain Ralph Lafferty and two able seamen directed the powerful water stream. The crimps caught in the powerful stream struggled to their feet, failed, and tried again, finally rolling off the wharf back into the bay.

Achilles went to the wharf's edge and pulled up the line he and Sven had come up. It did not much matter, as both the crimps were dragged by the current beneath the wharf. Taking no further chances, Achilles pulled up the last two lines that hung from that side of the wharf.

The tide of battle had shifted providing the remaining crimps with little quarter. Some, but not all of the longshoremen, backed off as Cornelius arrived with a squad of armed soldiers.

The Lieutenant worried little about the 'questionable' shoot to kill order as the crimps were gunned down. The trick was to separate them out from the longshoreman. In history, this would be last day the crimps ruled the Barbary Coast.

Cornelius did not wait to argue the point as he rode out onto the wharf where Choice and Sidney were trying to pull T.J. out from beneath the horse without injuring him further.

Three of the crimps made it back into the ruins of the fish market. Others tried. The army troops hesitating, not sure which were crimps or longshoremen. The returning smoke added to the confusion. "Hold your fire," the Lieutenant ordered, the final volley aimed at the crimps fleeing back through the ruins towards the fires burning in the Barbary. The sounds of the final shots drowned out by the deep whistle of the fire tug, Captain Lafferty on the stern.

Sidney and Choice finally pulled T.J. out from beneath his horse, blood bubbling from his lips, his lungs having been pierced by the snapped rib.

Lafferty held up a small bundle of dynamite.

Seeing the dynamite, McCann worked his horse through the women and children until he was close enough to catch Lafferty's gift. Kicking his horse he rode as hard as he could through the frightened women, hollering for them to get out of the way. As he neared the fish market, he lit the dynamite with his cigar, lobbing it into the partially collapsed building. What remained of the roof, blew off the building, falling back, burying any crimps inside, the building quickly turning into their funeral pyre.

The army took up picket positions just short of the ruins ready to fire on any crimps that had survived the dynamiting.

Cornelius rode back to where Choice and Sidney held T.J. To his immediate sadness, he found the tall, soft spoken man, had died. There was nothing he could do. After a short trot around the perimeters of the battle field, Cornelius added up the hard cost, eighteen, perhaps twenty-two assholes of the world had traded their miserable lives for T.J.'s and a couple of longshoremen. It didn't add up. It wasn't affair trade, no Sir, not a good bargain at all. He had made T.J. an honorary policeman, and T.J had given his life in the line of duty, he thought. "Sidney," he asked, his voice sullen, as he rode back to where the cowboy had fallen. "What is T.J.'s rightful name?"

"I honestly don't know," Marshal. "I've only known him as T.J. It's always been enough."

"No papers, Cornelius," Choice Pickens said, "we've got ourselves a John Doe hero."

Cornelius looked at Sydney, then back at Choice. The D.A. wants me to investigate the brass, he thought, and they're the ones who will decide on my recommendations for awards for heroism. He smiled at the thought. At least he knew the truth about what kind of man T.J. had been. Talking about heroes . . . "Achilles, you all right?"

Achilles sat on a bolted down railway tie, looking with remorse down into his cupped, shaking hands, feeling ashamed for having killed two men with his bare hands. It was something that he had never done before, and he could feel the hurt deep and raw in his heart. The bile, not just from the smoke, soured in his throat. At the moment, it didn't seem to matter that Sven stood alive in front of him hugging his sobbing mom, seaweed and kelp still clinging to him. That either Sven or his mom might not be alive if he hadn't done what he did, had not crossed his mind.

"Damn shame," Cornelius nodded, meaning T.J's. death.

"I barely got to know the man, but what I do know, is that he was a good man to have covering your backside, nor was he afraid to take the front." Speaking of backsides, Cornelius thought as he looked around. "Where's half-ass Darcy?" he asked, his eyes and voice accusatory.

Captain Lafferty jumped off the fire tug. "Your man Darcy, jumped ship, abandoned his post, and was last seen rowing the skiff towards the Oakland Long Wharf. He was one of the five officers who were shanghaied?" This was meant more as a reference than a question. "When Pipe first showed up, they had words. My guess is that they had some type of business deal together that had gone wrong. Pipe didn't seem worried in the least that he was dealing with a policeman. Have you given any thought to the idea that your men were set up from the inside?"

Cornelius' eyes widened, not surprised that Darcy had turned yellow, but treason, that was a whole other kettle of fish. "I'm chewing on that same thought just now."

"Inspector Callahan," his name drawn out, each syllable chewed on before spat out, by the Lieutenant as he called out, as if he were on some parade field. The Lieutenant stood halfway between the ruin where August Summer had died and the fish market where the fire was rapidly spreading. What the hell, does he want now? Darcy will have to wait. "Get back to me on that, will you Captain. You just might have stumbled onto something."

Captain Lafferty rubbed his chin. "Whenever you have a moment. In the meantime I'll have the tug come around and put some water onto what's left of the fish market. I wouldn't want the wharf to catch on fire."

Cornelius raised a hand high, letting the Lieutenant know that he had been heard. "I agree about the wharf, but you might let the market burn. The fish are getting a bit ripe, and as far as these go," he nodded at one of the dead crimps, "you can toss them all on the fire. Not a one of them deserves a good Christian burial, and it don't make sense to keep their stinking hides around to offend the women folk. You do what you've got to do to keep the wharf wetted down until you think that it has burned down far enough to rid ourselves of the garbage. When you see fit, you do what a good fire fighter does and put the damn flames out." He relit his cigar, again. The smoke tasting better than the air around them. "I'll have the Lieutenant detail some men to police the area."

CHAPTER 29

LAVINIA DREW BACK INTO THE DARK SHADOW OF THE doorway as she tried to make herself as small and insignificant as possible. She was lost, scared, and all alone in the world. The worst was being alone. She had twisted her ankle, whether she could walk or not she did not know. She hadn't tried. Instead she hid, much as a six year old might when terrified of things she could not understand. Scared beyond thought, a child waits for her mom or dad to come and save her from the terrifying beasts that lay just on the other side of her imagination.

The air itself shook with the roar of the fire as it drew near consuming everything in its path. The alley had filled with countless people whose fear was palpable. Their language, a high pitched chatter, reminded Lavinia of a chaotic monkey cage she had seen once as a child at a zoo back in Holland. She giggled a sad sob, thinking what a silly thought to have now, of all times. Still, she was mesmerized by the color of their skin, their clothes, their smells, their tight bound ponytails - the way they stared with frightened little animal eyes at her as they passed by. The heat and the smoke caused her vision to waver - a black and white dream with yellowish-orange flickering undertones. She was too scared to move. A flaming ember drifted down into the alley. The Chinese's high pitched chatter rose in intensity as more flaming embers drifted down on them like bright yellow-orange snowflakes, only hungry, and hot. She coughed as the smoke thickened around her.

"Miss? Are you hurt?"

Lavinia did not at first understand the words. All she saw was the face of a white woman, her voice and smile neither kind nor loving, her dark hair pulled back and tied off in a matronly manner. "You can't stay here; the fire is out of control." The touch of the woman's hand on Lavinia's forehead was nevertheless reassuring. Lavinia turned to look up at her stone cold angel in the hot darkness.

"What in Jesus Christ's Holy name are you doing here in one of the darkest alleys of Chinatown?" The woman's lips tightened as she took in Lavinia's strange dress, immediately assuming her to be a working girl, or worst of all a white girl prostituting herself off to a Chinese Tong Chieftain. "Well, we'll leave saving your soul until later. Right now, we need to get you onto your feet and out of here." The woman looked around, getting her out of the alleyway was getting more difficult by the moment. The roof to the building across the alleyway was now aflame. "All right, up we go."

Lavinia tried. She shrieked, the pain on her ankle too much.

Despite her shriek, the woman pulled her up.

"Holy Mother Mary, we're going to need some help here," the woman whispered. "Do you have a name?" she asked.

"Lavinia - Lavinia Loskoor." She answered as she sucked in her breath, hopping a bit on her good foot while being supported by the woman.

Lavinia's accent gave the woman a second thought about her circumstances. Her accent was foreign, but too cultured for a common prostitute. "Lavinia, is it? I'm Miss Camaron." She eyed the fires and smoke rising above Chinatown - the fire was becoming alarmingly close. I'm with the Presbyterian Mission a few blocks from here. Now, hurt ankle or not, we've got to get you out of here. I've got to get back to the Mission before it burns, and I have little enough time to waste. And so my dear, bear your pain the best you can and move on. You have no other choice."

Lavinia tried, her ankle giving her little support.

The woman swatted at a flaming ash as it landed in Lavinia's hair. She then called out in Chinese to a young woman in a black western dress much like her own who hurried through the alley followed by an elderly man and six younger women - girls- all dressed in black - some western, the others Asian in style.

The Chinese woman stopped, turned, and bowed slightly in her direction. "Miss Camaron," she said slowly with carefully pronounced English words, "It's good you are well. How may I and my family assist you?"

Donaldina Cameron[1] was a tough task master, rescuing the souls of the heathen Chinese, she took very seriously. She had little sympathy for those who tried to cling to their Chinese culture and ways. At the Mission, the Chinese were not allowed to speak anything other than English; consequently, most spoke little. Ruth, Chinese, had been given her Christian name after she had been saved by Donaldina from child slavery and prostitution, and converted to Christianity. Ruth worked in the kitchen overseeing all the Chinese kitchen staff. "Ruth," Donaldina said,

---

[1] Donaldina Cameron (July 26, 1869 – January 4, 1968) was a Presbyterian missionary in San Francisco's Chinatown, who rescued more than 3,000 Chinese immigrant girls and women from indentured servitude. She was known as the "Angry Angel of Chinatown." The great San Francisco earthquake and fire forced the evacuation of the Presbyterian Home. Donaldina was able to save records that gave her guardianship over the girls at the home, thus ensuring their safety from being forced back into servitude or prostitution. The Home itself was destroyed in the earthquake; it was rebuilt in 1907 at 920 Sacramento Street, where it still stands today.

directing Lavinia's attention towards the petite Chinese woman, "accepted Our Lord Jesus Christ as her Savior two years ago. She works at the Mission and is a good Christian example to the waifs we are doing our best to save." She looked at the old man, Ruth's father, who she knew to be a heathen unlikely to change in his ways. He did not speak English, nor did he like her, their mutual glares of contempt showed despite the urgency of the situation. "Ruth will help you get to the waterfront where you are more likely to find shelter and medical attention."

"Yes, Lo Mo," Ruth answered. She then dropped her eyes and bowed slightly having forgotten not to address her superior in Chinese. "Yes, mother." She offered her arm to Lavinia as support, speaking to her father in their native tongue, he quickly supported on the other side.

"Off with you now, I have no further time to waste." The stern Christian Missionary known to many of the Chinese as Lo Mo - mother - left without another world as Lavinia was guided out of Chinatown.

Lavinia bore her pain, not wanting to appear weak amongst these strange yellow people her father had often warned her about.

CHAPTER 30

THE LOSS OF T.J. WEIGHED HEAVILY ON CORNELIUS' HEART. He had lost more than one good man this day and the day was far from over. The crimps were finished; nevertheless, he steeled himself for whatever was going to happen next, and rode out to meet with Lieutenant Charter.

"Marshal," again, the word long and annoyingly drawn out, "I'm going to need more troops here." This too was drawn out and exasperating. With your permission I'd like to pull your detail from the Ferry Wharf until they're needed. We don't know how many of the crimps and street ruffians are holed up in the ruins, nor what type of weapons they might be laying their hands on, and if that isn't enough, Sir, we have a situation developing on our left flank."

Cornelius had to think for a moment before he looked back towards the fire line that Lafferty had been building, remembering that it separated them from the fires headed their way from the Financial District and Chinatown. Left flank? Oh yes, I see. A couple of dozen Chinese, old men, women, children, all dressed in soot and ash stained black apparel stood in the middle of the rubble littered street, flames licking high behind them where Chinatown burned. They stared at McCann and the Lieutenant; the two white men in uniform were authority figures. They were afraid to move forward, unable to move back. McCann drew down on his cigar. "It seems that we have ourselves a Mexican stand-off . . . make that Chinese, and it does seem that we have ourselves a situation." He took his time with the word, breaking it down into syllables, mimicking the lieutenant's speech.

"Do you want me to send them back the way they came?"

"No, Lieutenant, I do not want you to send them back the way they came." Cornelius could now see that there were more Chinese hiding in the shadows just beyond this first group. He did not see the tall oddly dressed white woman being supported within their midst.

Cornelius knew that there would be no easy answer. The white folks occupying the water front wouldn't be too happy sharing their space with their yellow brothers and sisters. It didn't matter the emergency, someone was going to make a problem out of it, and that was when someone was going to get hurt. He looked back towards the crowd and the ferry terminal. The army and the longshoremen must be doing their jobs because the crowd is swelling and no one is trying to shoot someone else- he thought. "You wait here," he said to the Lieutenant, as he turned and rode back for a powwow with Captain Lafferty. After a few words were exchanged, Cornelius rode back to the Lieutenant.

"Lieutenant, the more I thought about this, the more questions arose. We let the Chinese onto the waterfront we've got us a whole passel of problems. Looking at that wall of fire behind us, I don't see where we have too many choices." He paused, slowly taking in the chaos that surrounded them. "I tend to think too much. My best decisions come when I stop thinking and simply do what's right. Pull your men off the Ferry Wharf. You are to create a safety corridor that will allow the Chinese to go to that wharf over there." He pointed at the Vallejo Street Wharf just beyond the burning fish market.

The Lieutenant could not see the Vallejo Street Wharf from where he stood. All he could see was the burning market.

Captain Lafferty is going to bring the fire tug around and put that fire out. You and your men are going to put the Chinese to work clearing a path on the left hand side of the market which is the farthest away from my precinct, and the wharf where all the good Christian women, kids, and old folks are gathering. There is a boarding plank connecting the two piers, drop that in the water, and station two guards, one on each wharf, where that boarding plank used to be . . . a friendly reminder to both the white and Chinese alike that they can loathe each other all they want on another day, and another place. No white folks on or near the wharf, and no Chinese beyond your picket line. Is that understood?"

The Lieutenant acknowledged each step of the plan with a curt nod of his head. His troops would be stretched thin, but Marshal McCann was giving the orders, and he was beginning to trust his judgment. What galled him, was letting in the Chinese in the first place.

"The rotting fish, crimps, anything that will burn, are to be drug over to the street car barns and burned there under Captain Lafferty's command. Any questions?" Cornelius asked, not expecting any.

"No, Sir." The Lieutenant saluted.

"One moment, Lieutenant. You look like you have something on your mind? Go ahead and spit it out. Like it or not, we're stuck with each other for the duration."

"If the Marshal insists," the young officer said reluctantly.

He then paused, tight lipped, not sure how far he should go.

"Well, I don't have all day."

"Mad dogs and Ching Chongs, Sir." He practically spat the

words as if they were bitter to the taste. "The yellow peril, it ain't nothing to laugh at, them yellow bastards aren't like the rest of us. White men I mean. They're not quite human beings. You've got to keep them in control, like any other inferior animal. You let a pack of dogs go wild and you've got one hell of a problem. The chinks are a whole other story. You let the slant eyes from Japtown mix with the Ching Chongs and we'll have a fricking Tong war on our hands. Pardon my French, Sir. If the longshoremen want to mix it up with the Ching Chongs and throw them into the bay, don't expect my men to stand in their way."

Cornelius hid his anger. Lieutenant Reaves Charter was a bigot. He was inexperienced, trigger happy, and a bigot, which made for a dangerous combination. He had lost track of the number of times fools like Charter had caused stupid things to happen. The problem was, that the Lieutenant was right. Cornelius had more confidence in the night watchman at the Coroner's Office - at least there his charges were already dead. This was a man-sized crisis and he doubted the Lieutenant was up to the task. Well, it is like he had said they were stuck with each other for the duration.

The Chinese were not the only problem that had just been added to his list. Cornelius had seen the stray dogs coming out of the rubble, house pets, now more likely to bite someone than wag their tails. They were hungry, scared, and with the fire to their backs, and the bay in front, they were cornered with a whole lot of humanity not wanting to share what solid ground there was. If allowed, the Chinese would hunt the dogs, driving them god know where. "I get your point Lieutenant, and being that dog is a delicacy the Ching Chongs . . . the Chinese. . . take a liking to, I'll have a word with Achilles about setting up some kind of kitchen for them."

The Lieutenant gave a frustrated salute. It was not what he was looking for. If he couldn't shoot looters then he had hoped for a little more latitude with the Chinese, or at least mongrel dogs. "Sir, with you permission . . ."

Cornelius did not return the salute as he turned to ride back to where Captain Lafferty waited. "One more thing, Lieutenant, soon as you've cleared out the last of the crimps, I want you to set your command post back up on the Ferry Wharf." Cornelius said.

The Lieutenant scratched his head. "You just ordered me to pull my men from the Ferry Wharf. Now you want me to set up my command post back there. Sir, I . . ."

"For the time being your men are needed here. Those are your orders, the next hot spot will be at the Ferry Wharf. That is where I need you to keep an eye on things, and to tell me when circumstances change. I trust you are capable of doing that Lieutenant," Cornelius answered just loud enough to be heard as he rode away.

CHAPTER 31

A DARK CLOUD OF SMOKE MIXED WITH HOT ASH BEGAN TO settle again on the water front. It had been a long day and it would be one without a 24 hour clock. Cornelius had been on his feet for better than twenty-four hours, smelled worse than a sea lion in heat, and needed to find a moment of privacy to answer nature's call. He had a half formed thought tapping at the back of his mind that wouldn't quite gel as long as he had thirty other things demanding his immediate attention. He looked around. There were thousands of people, not counting the Chinese, no guessing how many of them might show up. He counted a few peons from Mexico and further south, along with a handful of niggers, and not a privy to be had. If there was one, there would be no mixing of the races without a piss pot full of trouble. Damn it, he was a cop, not a sanitation engineer. The people looked hungry and so was he.

"Cornelius." It was Choice Pickens. Cornelius had not even had a chance to figure out where there might be a pot he could piss in before someone else was shoveling crap in his direction.

He had never been one to complain. He hadn't asked for the job - he had it, so whatever cards were dealt him were his to make do with. Shit happens, and experience told him that it usually stunk. Nevertheless, he was annoyed.

"Cornelius, we've got two ferry boats waiting to come in,"

Choice Pickens said as he ran up beside Cornelius' horse.

"Damn it, don't do that." He snapped. "This horse is skittish enough." He reigned it in, feeling more competent handling it as the day wore on. Two ferry boats, that's good news - or is it?

If the army isn't in place, the boats just might be overrun, over loaded, and capsize right there. And damned if the bureaucrats back at City Hall wouldn't try to dock my pay for it."

Choice did not have time to appreciate Cornelius' humor. "The boats can't come in, there's too much debris in the water."

Cornelius had to scratch his head on that one. The smoke settled in dense, temporarily blotting out the sun. From where he sat, a little higher than most, he could see that the area surrounding the ferry wharf was jammed with people. The longshoremen and the army had their hands full just keeping folks from pushing each other into the bay. It won't be long before Chinamen started coming in behind him by the hundreds. Behind the smoke was one hell of a fire, and the hot wind told him that it was burning hot in their direction. Now rescue boats couldn't get in because of debris. First thing first, he thought as he got off his horse handing the reigns to Choice Pickens. "Here, hold this, I'll be right back.

"Inspector McCann." A woman called out.

"Cornelius?" Pickens, again.

It seemed that all of a sudden everyone wanted his attention. "Excuse me, ma'am." Tipping his hat, he fast-stepped through the women and children on the wharf until he reached the fire tug which he could see was named The Active. "Captain, can I have a word?" He called up to the bridge.

The Captain allowed him to board. The two men spoke for a moment, then before getting on to the business at hand, Cornelius disappeared into the ship for a private moment in the

Captain's Quarters, where the door to the only head on the entire water front quickly closed behind him.

When Cornelius returned, feeling a pound or two lighter, he found Ralph Lafferty standing on the bridge with the ship's Captain.

Lafferty spoke first. "Midshipman Pond, the boat's Commanding Officer here, tells me you've got a debris problem."

There it goes again, somehow it's my debris problem. What, I own the water front? A guy's got to laugh sometimes, Cornelius thought.

Pond jumped in. "Pending the size and type of debris we should be able to push much of the smaller stuff out of the way with high pressure hoses. If we can get a line around the larger flotsam, I might be able to pull it out of the way. That is the easy part. The tide will just bring in more debris, which might trap the ferries in port. That, and I'm going to need the boat for firefighting. The fires have to be my priority."

The three men stared through the pall of dense smoke seeing nothing - seeing everything - saying nothing. The boats' engines as loud as the roars of the fires outside.

"Any suggestions?" Captain Pond finally asked.

Their silence was as dense as the smoke.

Sidney rode up onto the wharf and hollered up to where he could see Cornelius on the bridge. "Marshal, I rode over to have a look-see. Debris from the stockyards has washed up. You've got timber, fencing, wire, barrels, dead animals, hides and butcher parts. The largest piece is part of the roof to the tanning shed. The debris is all along the waterfront and until the tide changes it ain't going nowhere. Even then, I doubt it'll move. One of them Chinese junks have capsized; their fishing nets and floats are tangled throughout the whole mess." He paused to catch his breath. "And Marshal, I don't mind telling you that it's beginning to smell a lot worse than it looks." He took off his hat, wiping his soot covered brow with his sleeve, then glanced back over his shoulder at the masses still gathering. "How many more can we take? It ain't looking very good out there, that's all I gotta say."

The truth spoken, simple and true, Cornelius thought as an idea came to him. "I was on the dock this morning, when the sun came up, and the earth turned upside down. Now, I'll give you that things were a bit confused, but one thing I don't recollect is the Japanese fishermen bringing in the morning catch. You usually can set a clock by them."

The ship's Commanding Officer answered. "Coming out from Mare Island, I almost ran over a few of them. It looked to me that they were planning on anchoring off Goat Island. Why?"

"How many boats have they?" Lafferty asked.

No one knew the answer. Cornelius pegged a guess. "Ten, twelve, perhaps?" The air he was breathing smelled of scorched earth, things burned that shouldn't, and unwashed humanity. He lit a cigar. "It was the capsized junk that gave me the idea. Once we pull the first round of shit out of the way, we could bring in the Jap boats with their fishing nets and create a barrier that could keep the ferry basin clear."

"Why would the Japs voluntarily sacrifice their boats and nets they need to earn a living?"

"That's a fair question, one that ought to be asked." He wasn't sure, but thought that he had seen a couple of Japanese earlier in the morning. He looked around, finally spotting two Japanese women, sitting near the edge of the wharf, trying to look invisible, their colorful but now stained kimonos making them stand out like flowers on a cold winter's day. Coincidence, blind luck, or divine grace, he didn't give a damn; he needed something to hedge his bet, and there they were. Now for Christ's sake, let them speak some English. "Why?" he asked the other men back. "Hell if I know. Give me a moment and I'll see if I can find out."

Cornelius left the boat, walking towards but not directly at the women to not frighten them.

"Konnichiwa," He fumbled the simple Japanese greeting, the word sounding more like kon'nachwack. "Do either of you speak American?"

The women were nervous; the white man before them wore a badge which too often meant trouble. They did not raise their eyes to his, keeping a demure, submissive caste on his shadow, which seemed soft and alien because of the smoke and the dark orange colored sun. The mama-san did, and Cornelius quickly learned that they had come ahead of the rest of their clan. There were close to two hundred, mostly women, children, and men too old to fish anymore. Their little Jap neighborhood had burned and they had not wanted to mix with the Chinese as they made their way to the water front. When the women had first arrived, they thought that the Vallejo Street Wharf might be their sanctuary. That had been the one Cornelius had allocated to the Chinese; bad luck and bad timing. The Green Street Wharf was all he had left, the ruins blocking East Street were too close to the next wharf, any one of which would go up like a Roman candle if they caught fire. With no sanctuary, the clan waited in the ruins between Vallejo and Broadway Streets for as long as they could.

Cornelius followed the women to where their clan waited, where he met a clan elder who could speak for them.

On the way back, Cornelius told Choice Pickens what he wanted, adding a few words and a smile to be passed on to Achilles, before he returned to the tugboat. The cigar clinched between his teeth had come unraveled. He tossed it overboard as he reached into his shirt pocket for another. It was his last one. He studied it for a moment, then put it back in his pocket.

"Gentlemen, we've got some work to do."

The Slocum, a navy tugboat, took the clan's elder out to Goat Island where the Japanese fishing fleet had anchored. Meanwhile, Achilles moved his kitchen closer to the Green Street Wharf where the Japanese could help him prep and cook the days catch which Cornelius had guaranteed the city would purchase.

Choice Pickens had been detailed to kept things moving, intact, and orderly at the precinct while Cornelius and Sidney rode over to the Ferry Wharf to see exactly how bad things were. He watched them ride off through the crowd. After what they had been through, he was beginning to almost like Sidney. *Goddamned dwarf.*

CHAPTER 32

"ITS ALL ONE BIG MESS; BAD." SIDNEY SAID AS THEY STARED down at the mess clogging the ferry basin.

"That would be an understatement." Cornelius said. He reached for his last cigar, the stench rising from the mess bobbing in the water offensive. He appreciated the fact that most of the hundreds of people surrounding the wharf liked it even less. The smoke only added to the stench, and it was getting worse.

"How are we going to get all that out of there?" Every sort of debris that could be imagined, including animal parts and carcasses floated and bobbed, completely filling the ferry basin.

The largest chunk, part of the roof of the old tannery, with stinking hides slapping against it with the tide, seemed to make the task damned near impossible. Nothing could be seen of the

Chinese junk, though there were ropes weaving around and caught in the debris. If the junk had sunk and was now trapped beneath the debris island, that would be it. Why bother with the debris on the surface when the damned junk made the ferry berth useless until they got it all cleaned out.

Sidney just shook his head.

"Give me a moment, and if I don't come back, send my dear old mom a nice card." Cornelius went to the edge of the wharf where he had seen a worn and tattered rope hanging over the side. With some hesitation he lowered himself down until he was submerged waist deep and low enough to get a clear view into the darkness below the wharf. He did not waste any time pulling himself back up, the effort causing the wound on his shoulder to bleed again.

Sydney gave him a final hand up.

"The aft section of the Chinese junk is wedged between two wharf pilings. It's jammed tight, not even moving an inch with the current. We could blast it out of there. However, if we do that we're apt to lose the wharf. Any ideas?"

"Come to think of it, I do have a thought." Sidney said.

It took twenty longshoremen about twenty minutes to locate and pull out of the bay another section of the tannery roof. It took every able man and both horses to maneuver the roof section into place back in the bay on the land side of the ferry berth. Three loggers, expert at walking rolling logs on a river, tied the flotsam together using both sections of the roof as a giant scoop. The debris, tied together with ropes and grappling hooks made for a pretty good raft. The big question is 'will it hold?' They waited for the tug to come and pull the stinking raft out.

It would not budge.

"Are you thinking what I'm thinking?" Cornelius asked.

Sidney nodded. "There is a good chance that it's snagged on the stern end of our Chinese junk."

"Ours?"

"You've got a point there. Marshal, since you're the head honcho on the waterfront, I reckon it's yours."

"Thanks, I always wanted a fishing boat- though it seems to me that it's riding a little low in the water."

"You could say that." Sidney replied.

The Japanese fishing fleet came in and made fast work off-loading their catch to Achilles makeshift kitchen before sailing on towards the Ferry Wharf where they had agreed to position themselves and their nets.

After the fishing boats were in place the tugboat reversed engines as she prepared to hook onto the lumbering raft.

"What the hell?" Sidney exclaimed as Cornelius was about to do the same.

Cornelius had never heard so many people scream in terror as he did at that moment. His trained cop's eyes looked first one way then the other, searching the crowd for a gang of crimps that had gotten through, a drunken fool who somehow managed to retain a firearm, a crazed steer, trouble cloaked in its many disguises. The panic seemed wide spread. Most of them, reacted to the terror of those around them, although they didn't know what it was. They were tired and hungry, having lost everything they had in the world, and packed into a sea of sweating, unwashed humanity - few speaking a common language - trapped together on the fringe of hysteria. From his perch high in the saddle he could see people jumping up and down as if their feet had caught on fire. The cause escaped him until a squealing squirming gray wave - a hoard - caused his already high strung horse to rear. He should have been thrown, but when he saw where he would land, he hung on for the ride of his life as tens of thousands of sewer rats swarmed beneath him.

The rats had been driven from their networks of tunnels, burrows, and nests beneath Chinatown and elsewhere beneath the city by the quake, numerous aftershocks, fire and smoke. Provoked by hunger, their own fear of the fires that raged and the fever of the hunt, drove thousands of rats to the waterfront. They ran, stampeded, until there was nowhere else to go but into the bay, where most - not all - tried to climb from the deadly brine, clawing and biting their way over each other, forcing each other down, until the survivors found refuge on the garbage island, the smell and taste of rotting meat taking over as they fought for each bite.

The raft appeared to be a gray quivering mass as the Slocum hooked on, a few of the rats tried to climb the towline as the tug tried to pull the raft free of the ensnared Chinese fishing junk. At first it wouldn't budge, the steam engines of the tug straining against the load. Finally one line under the water, then another snapped until the raft sprung free. The Slocum blew a loud victory whistle as it began to turn the rat-encrusted garbage heap out of the ferry basin.

There were plenty of rats left behind. Many had drowned, some still tried to climb the wharf pillars, or rope lines, only to be torn apart by snarling dogs, or kicked back by human feet. Lieutenant Charter, on the wharf near the water's edge, wasted no time firing at point blank range into the hoard of terrified rats. Bullets from his troops tore into them, round after round sending rats and a few helpless dogs into the bay. Longshoremen's pikes speared fleeing rats, tossing them back into the bay. A few civilians fell over the side to land in the mass of wet quivering terror - two did not come out.

BAMM!

"God damn it!" Caught up in the chaos, Lieutenant Reaves Charter shot himself in his left foot. Unable to stand he fell at the edge of the wharf, his men stopped firing, afraid that they might hit him, or that he might roll over the edge. Then, it was quiet, if one were to call the ear numbing din quiet.

Cornelius had hung on for as long as he could, then with one final hard twist, he was thrown from his horse for his second salt water bath of the day. When he surfaced two rats tried to use his head as a perch, only to be pulled off, squeezed, and drowned for their efforts. One managed to bite his left hand, but that was not something to be worried about now.

Sidney splashed in a few feet away.

The shooting, sharp pikes, terrified rats and dogs made any attempt of climbing out more dangerous than remaining in the water. They shoved vermin out of the way as they swam to the mouth of the ferry berth where the Japanese fishermen were already positioning their nets to keep additional debris from floating into the ferry berth.

Helping hands from one of the Japanese fishing boats pulled Cornelius and Sidney from the water as fishermen held out torches, driving swarms of frantic rats away. Spitting out a little foul water Cornelius looked into a small man's smiling yellow face. "Never have I been happier to see someone in my whole goddamned life," he said. "I'll bet you never heard that from a white man before."

The Japanese fishermen had their hands full keeping the surviving rats from climbing on board. Hand held torches were shoved into their furry faces as they scurried up a net, or along a line. The flame usually enough to convince them that death by drowning was a preferred fate.

The raft was towed out into the bay and cut loose half way between the shore and Alcatraz Island. When the Slocum was clear, the Destroyer Preble from her anchorage just off the Barbary, fired explosive rounds from her three inch guns until the raft and her sharp toothed passengers were no more.

With the debris raft out of the way, part of the wreck of the

Chinese fishing junk could be seen beneath the murky waters of the ferry berth. The stern was wedged beneath the wharf with its nets and lines wrapped around god knows what. The ferry boats would not be able to dock until the sunken craft was removed.

Cornelius reviewed all the options. He came up empty.

The wreck was jammed tight, too tight to be pulled free by the navy ships - not without damaging the wharf. If that happened, that would be the end of any hope for the ferry boats to take some of the masses of refugees off the waterfront and over to the mainland.

With the Lieutenant injured, his troopers became all but useless with more than a few abandoning their posts. The longshoremen, without strong enough leadership to keep them in line, were becoming vigilantes exercising their power of brute force as they saw fit. Without the army, the crowd began to become unhinged, their fear mounting, as civil authority began to vanish from the waterfront. The only authority that remained was back at the wharf where Cornelius had set up the new Waterfront Police Precinct, though in reality there were not enough cops to handle even a stumbling drunk. Choice Pickens, Captain Lafferty, and Achilles had their hands full. If there were any longshoremen left there to lend a hand, that alone would be a miracle. The soldiers who had been stationed at the end of Market Street had been pushed back by the size of the crowd. The fires, now strong enough to create their own weather, gave the soldiers cause to abandon their posts and seek duty elsewhere as they sought out other troops stationed throughout the city.

Inspector Cornelius McCann remained clueless regarding the deterioration of law and order on the wharfs and streets on shore. His shoulder, swollen, both ached and burned. The wound he had received when he had first been thrown beneath the wharf by the earthquake wasn't healing, and the sting from the salt water seemed far worse than right after he had first grazed the barnacle covered pillar. His throat was dry, his mouth tasted like an old ashtray, his eyes were heavy and bloodshot, he was tired, hungry, and the rat bite on his left hand stung like a son-of-a-bitch. How is it that the small things like a rat bite or an ingrown toe nail can hurt so much? For the moment he had only one task - to get the sunken Chinese fishing boat out of the ferry's way. That was the blister on his behind and he hadn't a clue on how to go about it.

Sidney, his mustache drooping oddly after his swim with the rats, felt the same - helpless. No, make that useless.

The Japanese grunted as they talked amongst themselves.

Cornelius couldn't understand a word.

Sidney, mostly silent, was uncomfortable being on the boat with the Japanese. That it was their boat, only added to his angst. He had never considered himself a prejudiced man, however, it was a known fact that the Japs and the Chinks, all the Asian slant-eyes, were an inferior species. Who knew what diseases they carried? Sharing space with them was a foreign experience to Sidney that he couldn't quite wrap his head around.

The man Cornelius guessed to be the senior or elder among the Japanese fishermen approached. "If you please, I am Tanaka Hiroshi." He then executed a full forty-five-degree bow, slow, low and slightly long, with his hands at his sides, so as not to offend.

Cornelius, who bowed before no man, wasn't sure how to respond.

After a moment of awkward silence, the Japanese spokesman straightened and said. "We have an idea." His English was not bad, though spoken with a strong accent, as several consonants are unpronounceable to the Japanese.

"And for the moment, I haven't," Cornelius acknowledged. He paused, carefully choosing his words. "I'm willing to listen. You said that your name is Tanaka. Well, Mr. Tanaka, I'm Inspector Cornelius McCann, San Francisco Police." He thought about that. Most Asians were afraid of the police, not a great way to start a collaborative relationship. "One might say that things have changed a bit since the sun first rose this morning. It seems that down here on the water we are all . . ." He caught sight of a torch, as it dashed another rat off the boat as it tried to climb up a fishing net. "You might say that we are all rats on a sinking ship." His eyes gazed toward the crowded wharf backlit by black turbulent smoke clouds, their undersides reflecting the brilliant red and orange flames beneath. If the Captain saw me shaking a Jap's hand, I'd be drummed out of the department or horse-whipped. Well, hell, he thought, they saved my ass from drowning in a sea of rats. He extended his hand. "My friends call me Cornelius."

"Yes, many things have changed, more than we suspect." He said, as he bowed again, this time more quickly and not as deep. "Please, I am Hiroshi."

Arrogant little son-of-a-bitch, Cornelius thought. Wants me to call him by his last name. The next thing you know, he'll be wanting a white man to be calling him Mister.

Tanaka saw the tightening around Cornelius's eyes and the edges of his mouth. Catching the confusion, he thought, This gaijin is no fool, that he is a police officer may prove favorable for my people. Still, I must be careful for gaijin, especially white ones are not to be trusted. "Please, it is a custom among my people to be called by my family name Tanaka, even among friends. You honor me by allowing me to call you by your first name -

Cornelius. I would be honored if you called me Hiroshi.

Cornelius smiled at the Jap's attempt to pronounce his name. The guy is fairly sharp for a Jap. Well, live and learn.

Sidney watched as Cornelius listened to what the Japanese fisherman had to say. Cornelius looked the Jap straight in the face, as if he were a regular human being. So far, Sidney had not spoken to one, let alone locked eyes with one of them. They were on new territory here and Cornelius was raising the bar a bit too high and too fast for him. Still, what the Jap was suggesting made sense. Finally, with a nod of his head, he turned to Cornelius saying. "I think it will work."

Sidney continued to listen, as Cornelius and Hiroshi hashed out the details into a workable agreement. Who would have thunk the slant-eyed Japs to be that smart. Come the day, I think I've heard and seen it all, along comes something that sets my brain a-spinning. He spat, reached for the hat he no longer had, then chuckled, as he picked a small chunk of green kelp from his mustache. "Well, let's get to work Marshal, times a'wastin," Sidney said.

Cornelius watched the city burn as the small fishing boat set sail. There had never been a day in his life where Cornelius could have imagined himself sailing out to a U.S. warship on a Japanese fishing boat. No Sir, the thought had never crossed his mind, which was another first in a day full of them. He had never thought much about the Japanese. He had dealt with the Chinese before, didn't much care for them one way or the other. Mostly he saw them as hard working strange little yellow dwarfs who spoke a language that sounded like a flock of jungle birds chirping. They smelled funny. The men wore their hair pulled back in pigtails like little girls. Mostly, they kept their distance, just as afraid of the white man as the white man was of them. He thought about that and it occurred to him that afraid wasn't the right word. Most folks that he knew thought of the Chinese as not being human, but dangerous animals that didn't belong anywhere but China. Most of the cops on the Chinatown Squad could tell you that. He, on the other-hand had always adopted a live and let live attitude about them. Now, somehow the

Japanese seemed more human. Maybe it was the way they talked, slower, less bird like, seemed like they might have an intelligent thought in their heads. Quiet spoken people with a touch of dignity. People? He thought, perhaps?

He had to laugh, for he had bought into the Jap's plan to save the ferry berth, and it was his ass on the line if they failed. He looked back at the fire storm that lit up San Francisco beneath a monstrous black cloud of smoke and cinders. It looked like there would be no city left by this time tomorrow. No city, no police department, his badge worthless. So why not shake hands with the Japanese and the Chinese for what it is worth. They might be the last ones willing to stake a claim in what would soon be nothing more than a desert of windblown ashes.

He chuckled. These were thoughts he had best keep to himself, lest they lock him up in the loony bin. For the time being, he needed to concentrate on one goal: to get the ferry berth clear of debris and, in particular, the sunken Chinese fishing boat. Without the ferries, a whole lot of folks were going to perish - and the fire storm didn't give a damn about the color of their skin.

They were on their way to the Destroyer Preble to get enough explosives to blow the sunken fishing junk clean out of the water. He leaned against a low bulkhead, until they reached the Preble. He had a chance to rest. His shoulder hurt, but there was nothing he could do about it. He looked at the rat bite, there was nothing he could do about it, either.

CHAPTER 33

SIDNEY DID NOT MUCH CARE FOR THE TASK CORNELIUS HAD given him. However, he had signed on for the duration, and as a man of his word, he'd do his best. His assignment was to get two of the Japs back over to the wharf where their families were camped out. It wasn't far, but there were a few thousand people who didn't cotton to any slant-eyed Asians walking upright amongst them - not when there were women and children around.

Off the boat, on dry land, Sidney quickly saw that his chance of peacefully guiding the Japs to their encampment was near to impossible without some help. He was a cow poke after all, not a cop.

"Where the hell do you think you are going with them?" *Them* was accented as if he had a sour taste in his mouth. Sidney turned defensively. When someone spoke to him like that, it usually means they are up for a fight. Sidney had lost his rifle, whip, and hat, which showed him to be a short tough man not much bigger than the Japanese. If someone was going to get in his way he might not be able to stop him. Admittedly, he had had his share of fights, won some and lost some. Today, of all days, he did not to need to get his ass whooped. There was too much to lose if the Japs weren't allowed to get the sunken Chinese junk out of the way of the vitally needed ferries. The Japanese were willing to fight if they had to, but if they did, they'd most likely be lynched for trying. Why they were willing to take that kind of chance was beyond him.

The good news was that the loud mouth belonged to the Army Lieutenant. The bad news was that the Lieutenant was on the ground, his back against an old barrel, his leg raised just slightly, resting on his army boot, his bare foot where he had shot himself wrapped in a bloody rag. Sidney digested the fact that the Lieutenant was all but useless, not that he wasn't anyway.

"Where the hell do you think you are going with them?" The Lieutenant repeated a second time. *Them* bitten off and practically spat.

Chapter 34

Lavinia sat out on the Chinese wharf dressed only in the bloody butchers apron and the tuxedo top coat she had been given, a white woman alone in a sea of yellow faces. She was not welcome and she knew it. How far could she get with her ankle swollen, and more importantly, where could she go? With her father missing she had no one. She did not belong anywhere. All she knew was that she did not want to be where she was and that she really didn't know where that was.

At first it had all been too much. The loss of her father and her pending vagrancy, with no family or friends to fall back upon, had at first not seemed real to her. How could this happen to her? Why? Next, she was abruptly ejected from her home in a violent bathtub ride, as the city of San Francisco was stricken by a violent upheaval of the earth. She had truly been thrown naked out into the world with the bath water. She had been stunned beyond thought into the bleakness of despair. *Why?* had been her only thought. *Not what, where, or how* she might climb out of her despair, only, *Why?*

Beyond the wharf, not far from where she sat, the city burned, towering flames danced with joy at its destruction. There were so many people, all lost, asking the same unanswerable question: *Why?*

At first she had been frightened by the Chinese. Now, she realized that they were more afraid of her than she of them. The sound of children laughing brought a drop of hope to her aching heart. Their world besieged by massive misfortune and tragedy, they somehow manage to find a place to play, explore; their innocent laughter, music in the air. Through foggy eyes she watched as the children nearest to her amused themselves, while another one cried, their joy softening the other one's tears. A few steps away, a small boy in a dirt and smoke stained white smock played with sticks, building perhaps an imaginary fort, while two prepubescent girls whispered, giggling in one another's ears. Nearby a hungry baby suckled on her mother's breast. The children laughing are Chinese and the sing-song within their laughter she found to be a pleasant sound.

The people around her chirped and chattered, their voices a sing-song of foreign sounds. Their appearance, smell, everything about them startlingly new. That was when she understood that the Chinese were people, not little yellow devils, but people just as lost and frightened as her. People struggling to survive, all of their lives, in a world that was a bitter disappointment and as far away from heaven as one might find on earth. There, before her were children too young to understand that they laughed, giggled, and cried for all the right reasons. Salty tears drew lines through her soot stained cheeks as she smiled, her lips quivering as she wondered what the two little girls were whispering about.

Beyond these images, there only seemed to be smoke and fire. Deep down within herself she felt something happen, a sense of courage, perhaps usefulness, a reason for being. The question still stood: *Why?* The answer could wait; there were things more important.

Ruth, the Chinese woman the Missionary Donaldina Cameron had entrusted her care to, had gone off to see if she could find some food, leaving Lavinia in the protective care of her family. Weren't the Chinese supposed to be stupid inhuman creatures never to be trusted? It wouldn't be the first time that her father, in his condemning correctness, had been wrong.

Ruth's father sat across from her, his eyes old and weepy.

Although silent he seemed to growl at her with hostility. However, he had given his word to his daughter that the white woman would be treated as an honored guest - and so she was.

One of the girls brought over an old woman with patchy gray-white hair and stained brown teeth. Aged well beyond her years, the old woman neither smiled nor frowned as she immediately knelt and began to examine Lavinia's ankle. "Old mother will make your foot well." The young girl said as she backed away. The old woman twisted and prodded Lavinia's swollen ankle, her touch neither tender nor caring.

Lavinia cast her eyes out towards the roaring flames that devoured the city. The smoke came and went along the waterfront and for the moment the air was reasonable. She coughed as she remembered how hot the air had been, how the smoke had tasted as it roiled through the alleyway in Chinatown where she had fallen. *It must now be like the inside of a coal furnace,* she thought, *where nothing can live, where everything is consumed.* She closed her eyes not seeing or feeling the tiny needles the old woman inserted into her leg and foot.

CHAPTER 35

"Mother, why aren't you on the wharf with my brothers?" Sven asked as he filleted a large salmon preparing it for roasting over the fire.

His mother managed a tired smile. "Your brothers are fine." She looked back toward the wharf where she could see them playing a game of kick the can with a half dozen other boys. "A number of the women have come together," she explained, "to watch over the children, giving each other a little time for rest, to search for other family members, or to just be of help. I came to see if I could be of help.

She could see that not much more help was needed. There were more hands than work. The Chinese had made themselves useful by taking over the fire maintenance, food preparation, and most of the cooking. It was a busy place, the Chinese scurrying around like so many cats, the rich grease from the fish popping and sizzling as they were turned over the fire, while hot baking potatoes were turned and rolled beneath. Like Achilles, Sven mostly watched over the Chinese, he wasn't much good at supervising. Sven wiped his greasy hands on his filthy pant legs. "Achilles, this is my mother."

"Yes . . . We've met." He also wiped his hands on his filthy shirt before extending his ham-hock sized mitt. His sheer size made her appear even more petite than she was. His mind flashed back to the moment where she had been held hostage by Archibald Pipe, and Achilles had no other choice but to kill him.

He withdrew his hand ashamed of his deed, apologizing. "My hands, they are filthy. I am Achilles Leonoudokis, a simple cook as you can see."

She gazed over at the wharf occupied by the Japanese and wondered why the Chinese were doing all the work. *It was none of her business,* she thought as she brought her face back to smile at his. "Yes, we have met, and I am so grateful. Marta Theorin. Please call me Marta." She looked over at her son. "Sven is a good worker, but sometimes he does not listen very well."

Sven gave her his mother a *don't embarrass me* look.

Achilles laughed aloud and unabashed, the roar of a giant but gentle bear. "Sven, a problem? No. No. Sven is a good worker. I could not do this without him."

"Well, I'll be on my way then," Marta said as she hiked her skirt and turned back towards the wharf where her sons played.

"I could not help but overhear, you came to offer your help." Archilles said. "I have no work here, the Chinese are good workers - a big help. But . . ." he paused, "They cannot serve the fish to the people." He looked out over the crowd. "The American people hate the Chinese and the Chinese are afraid of them. Can you help serve? I also need fish taken to the women's wharf, and to that one there." He nodded towards the Japanese.

He scuffed his feet on the rough wood deck nervously as he asked. "Please, I would be grateful."

CHAPTER 36

THE LIEUTENANT MUSTERED WHAT WAS LEFT OF HIS PRIDE, which was greatly diminishing having shot himself in the foot. In pain, neglecting his command, he had allowed most of his men to desert without saying a word. He felt like a fool and a failure. The only good news was that Marshal - Inspector- McCann wasn't around to see him wallow in his own self-pity. Sidney, the little Jew cowboy, had embarrassed him into finally behaving as a United States Army officer should in a time of crisis. The worst part had been the Japs just standing there bowing and smiling, bowing and smiling.

He tried to get to his feet. His wounded foot put up a splendid argument on why he shouldn't. Getting to his feet was one thing, getting anywhere on his wounded foot was another thing altogether. It had swollen to better than twice its normal size and hurt like a son-of-a-bitch, and that was when he put any weight on it. He clenched his teeth so tight to hide the pain he thought they might shatter. He studied the two Japs and the Jew, three small men determined to do what no one else seemed capable of: clearing out the ferry berth so the ferries could come in and get all these people somewhere safer than the waterfront.

A small rolling aftershock reminded him that he was out on the edge of a wharf and he had never learned to swim. *Swell, what next?*

Sidney shook his head. "Well, you are about as useful as a back pocket in a shirt." He exchanged glances with the two

Japanese men. "I guess we'd best be a-gettin on while we still can. Say, come to think of it, I don't even know your names. Hope you didn't take no offense, working with your kind is new to me. When I woke up this morning, I was just another cowhand, now I'm herding people. Listen to me run off at the mouth." He extended his hand. "Sidney, everyone calls me Sid."

Neither of the Japanese fishermen showed any inclination to shake his hand. The closest man bowed, introducing himself as *Katasui*, followed a second later by the other who said that he was *Ichirou*. Sidney got lost between the bowing and the strange pronunciations of their formal names, and which order they ought to fall. "If you don't mind, I think I'll just call you *Kat and Itchy.*"

Kat and Itchy smiled. This was not a time to be offended. Katasui bowed again accepting his new nickname Kat'san. "We are honored Sidney'san," Itchy'san said with an unusual touch of mirth to his voice. His smile hid the blow to his honor that he concealed. *The land may twist and buckle, the sea change the course of its currents in a single day. A great city like this may burn to the ground in a few short hours. But men, with all their pride and arrogance, cannot change the stupidity that he has learned over a thousand life times. We need each other for the moment - nothing more.* He bowed slowly, weighed down by a heavy heart. *And you are a fool,* he thought as he watched the Lieutenant try to rise.

"Most anyone with a foot looking like yours ought to get a shot of whiskey, followed by an equal amount of sympathy. I ain't got no whiskey, and you sure don't warrant no sympathy," Sidney said, giving the Lieutenant a *you are a worthless bastard, aren't you* scowl.

Regardless of the pain, the Lieutenant stood, but only for a moment as his leg failed to support him. He struggled, a little more determined this time, to get up on his one good foot. "For Christ's sake, the next thing I know, you'll be inviting these yellow skin monkeys home for milk and cookies with your Mama."

Without hesitation, Sidney abruptly turned and shoved him back down. "That will be quite enough, Lieutenant, we've got enough problems around here without your mouth adding to it." Sidney grabbed the Lieutenant's single silver bar officer's insignia, ripping it from his raised uniform collar.

"The man has a point there, Sid."

His anger vented, Sidney turned towards the sound of a good friend's voice. "Well I'll be damned. Henry!" Sidney declared, hollering a hoot, a sound the Japanese were not familiar with, bringing astonished expressions to their faces. "I thought you went home to take care of your own, now, here you sit proud as a peacock, and on my horse I might add. Henry, good to see your sorry ass. Get on down here so I can see if the grin you have on your backside is anything like the one you're wearing on your stupid mug."

Sidney gave one last hard look at the cowed Lieutenant. "You don't deserve this," he muttered as he held up the insignia bar and tossed it into the bay.

"When I left this morning," Henry said. I feared for the worst. By the time I got home the fires were licking at our door step. There was no fighting it, so I took my wife to her uncle's place in Daly City." He glanced back at the fires that consumed Rincon Hill. "Nothing could be done, lost it all, so I thought I'd see if I might be able to lend a hand with you fellows. Where's T.J.?"

Like T.J., Henry was not one for small talk. Cut from the same cloth both men were - tall, lean, and sat hickory stick straight in the saddle. Henry's facial hair, mustache, and hair cut always reminded Sidney of a picture he had seen of General Custer. Custard's face was weathered, the skin tight hard leather to protect against blowing sand, hard sun, and cold nights. His eyes, a penetrating purplish hue, with his hard weathered facial features, the eyes stood out sharp and memorable.

Henry scratched his beard thoughtfully as he took in everything around him, including the Japanese and the wounded Army officer. "Where is T.J.?" he asked again. "I was able to latch onto his mount about the same time as I found yours."

Sidney knew that Henry and T. J. were like brothers, and it pained him to be the bearer of bad news. "Henry, there is no easy way to say this. The long and the short of it is that the Marshal, me, and T. J., got into a bit of a fracas with a bunch of crimps over yonder. We were outnumbered six to one. When the dust settled most of those good-for-nothings were dead or had scampered back into the sewers they had crawled out of. Old T.J. gave them quite a show, but one of the bastards got the better of him. He didn't make it."

Henry gazed at the horizon on the far side of the bay as he checked his emotions. Leaning forward on his horse, he spat as he mulled through the news. He took a good look at Sidney, who had no horse, no gun, no whip, no hat, and looked somewhat like a wet dog that had just crawled out of a storm drain. "Well, Sid, you are alive and old T.J. has checked out, and that is the hard truth of it. T.J. never could walk away from a good scrap. I always knew that one day it would catch up with him. When this is all over we'll raise a glass to one of the best men I ever rode with. If there is a drink to be had when this is all over." He nodded at the two Japs. "Sid, what's your excuse for them?"

As time was short, and they couldn't discuss the details,

Sidney quickly explained the best he could, the Jap plan to raise the Chinese junk from the ferry berth. Crazy as it sounded, it almost seemed to make sense. Almost. "Count me in," Henry said. He could see two ferry boats circling off shore. "So all we need to do is escort these Japs through forty-thousand folks who would prefer not to share the same air space with them, pick up their women folk over yonder where they have set up camp, then ride right back through the same folks who are already pissed off at us." He scratched his head as he tried to digest the route, having some trouble wrapping his brain around it. "No, I think I've got it. It ain't the most foolish thing I've done or seen, but damned close." He spat, taking a long hard look at the Japanese. "The Jap women folk, not the men, are going to somehow set off the dynamite under water without blowing themselves into smithereens." *Well, a few less Japs won't hurt anyone except for the Japs*, he thought. "Your women folk up to this?" he asked.

"Yes, for generations our women have been diving for pearls. They have great skill. Here they dive for abalone, which are often deeper and harder to harvest than oysters. Our women can do this," Itchy said, his eyes growing tight and determined. "They will; many lives and our honor is at stake."

"The horses are a godsend." Sidney said.

Henry had a Colt sidearm the Army had ordered him to surrender as he came off of Market Street. Not willing to surrender it, he dropped back and reentered the waterfront closer to where the stockyards had been. No questions were asked, because there was no law or authority there. It was there that he had found the horses which had returned to the stockyards by instinct. Of course, there were no stockyards; the horses nervous and skittish, had come to Henry as a familiar and protective wrangler. Along with the horses, Sidney and Henry had one gun between them and a good leather whip which had belonged to T. J.. Having lost his own Sidney had kept T.J.'s whip. He held onto the whip preferring it to a gun in close quarters.

Sidney wanted Itchy and Kat to ride with them double mounted for speed. Henry put up a quick veto, pointing out that there were more than a few white folks who wouldn't take too kindly to seeing Japs riding with white men as if they were equals.

The Lieutenant convinced them that an Army officer among them might make some trouble makers hesitant to try to stop them. That, and he had a gun, not that he was proud of the last shot he had fired, won the argument. As much as they did not like the Lieutenant, Sidney's argument that he was not able to walk had merit, and won him a saddle. The Lieutenant and Sidney rode with Itchy and Kat boxed in between their mounts. Henry took point, on foot, armed with a pike and his Colt 45. There were tough men on the water front, but not too many who would risk taking Henry on without a second thought.

In the short time Cornelius' attention had been fixed on the problems plaguing the ferry berth, law and order quickly vanished on the water front. It hadn't taken long for the crowd to develop a *me first* and *the hell with you* attitude regarding their mutual survival. The crowd was dense with a few bullies and thieves working the crowd. A cry for help in Polish or Italian met deaf ears with the Portuguese, Irish, or Swedish. Unless the cry for help was in one's own language, it went mostly ignored. The towering flames ate the sky until lost in roiling black smoke, adding a terrifying roar to the din. The waterfront nearest the ferry terminal was thick with people who were scared, and confused, their nerves at the breaking point. It was at this tense maze of humanity that Sidney, Henry, and the Lieutenant had to get the Japanese safely through. An Asian face, any Asian face, was enough to incite the crowd to violence.

Itchy and Kat, proud men, kept pace with the horses, their heads high, eyes alert, aware of the danger and of the shame of losing face if they did not stand up as men. Here on the water front, at this moment, men were equal regardless of who or what they might have been a mere day before. They could see it written on each face, regardless of where they had come from or who they were, they were tired, hungry, confused, afraid for their lives, uncertain of any future, the air choked with smoke as the fires bore down on them. Any weakness shown by Itchy and Kat's determination, or arrogance, would draw the wrath of the crowd down on them as if they were responsible for this terrible calamity, because they were Asian.

CHAPTER 37

ORNELIUS FOUND THE TORPEDO BOAT, DESTROYER USS Preble tied up at Pier 8 next to the Howard Street Wharf. Men from the Preble and the Fire Tug Satomoyo, headed up the waterfront to try to stop the Rincon Hill fires from spreading. The Rincon fire was the biggest threat to the waterfront, as well as the slot south of Market Street. The fires raging on the hill were out of control, streets were blocked by rubble and refugees, and all the water mains were broken. The fire hoses brought in by the San Francisco Fire Department were not adaptable to the navy hoses. The high power pumps on the ships useless except for the high pressure spray coming directly from the ships which fell short of the fires. Too few ships, not enough working hose, and the high pressured spray could only go so far. Gangs of able sailors from the ships moved from building to building, ruin to ruin, tearing down and pulling away awnings, curtains, anything that could easily ignite.

The Great California Wine Company,[1] now in ruins, had spilled millions of gallons of wine, leaving small lakes and a large stream of wine flowing towards the bay. The drunks got in the way of everyone trying to fight the fires. The Navy had its hands full.

Lieutenant Frederick Freeman, Commanding Officer of the Preble had little time and but one answer to give Inspector

---

[1] It is estimated that between The California Wine Company and Swiss Colony, close to four million gallons of wine were lost, along with almost all of the cooperage needed to make wine barrels in the United States.

Cornelius McCann when he came aboard. "I appreciate your plight Inspector, however, I am short of everything needed to fight these fires and have nothing to spare."

Cornelius needed to acquire enough dynamite to blow up the sunken Chinese junk. He boarded the ship confident that he could achieve that goal.

Lieutenant Freeman could read it on his face. "Inspector, don't waste your time or mine. The answer is no, and that is my final answer." He paused. "I might consider your request if you represented the fire department. You don't. We've all got a long day in front of us. I wish you God's speed and good luck. Now, if you will kindly get off my ship, I have work to do. Master at Arms, see that the Inspector finds his way safely ashore."

Escorted off the ship, Cornelius had run out of ideas. Without the dynamite there was no way to get the sunken Chinese Junk out of the way. *Could the ferries dock somewhere else? He doubted it. The boarding planks were specially made. That, and there was too much junk floating around the multiple piers and wharves.*

A sudden explosion jarred him out of his funk.

He couldn't see it but knew that the explosion had come from the direction of Chinatown. "Now why didn't I think of that earlier," he said aloud. After a quick word yelled out to Hiroshi on the Japanese fishing boat, he set off in the direction of Chinatown at a dead run. He could barely maintain breathing in all the smoke.

"Inspector McCann." He heard his name boomed just above the din. He turned towards the sound, grateful for the interruption. This was not a day for running. The ship's Master Chief Boatswain's Mate used a megaphone to call down to him from the bow of the ship. "Mr. McCann, the Captain has changed his mind. Catch." McCann barely caught the brown paper wrapped package. On close inspection he found it to contain four bound sticks of dynamite. "Much obliged," he called back." *Not enough, but at least it's a start* he thought.

"I hope the fuse is long enough," the Master Chief said as he turned back to more pressing business.

Me too, Cornelius thought. He had never seen Japanese women dive and doubted their abilities. However, on this day, logic seemed to have taken a vacation. He had cast his lot with the Japanese and from that roll of the dice, his fate would be drawn; of that he had no doubt.

He held up the dynamite as he turned back towards the Japanese fishing boat where Hiroshi stood. What he saw next nearly gave him instant heartburn. The Japanese fishing boats were pulling up their fishing nets and about to make way. They were abandoning their positions around the ferry berth and appeared to be heading north. "What the hell?" Cornelius swore as he quick stepped to Hiroshi's boat.

Hiroshi offered a hand as the boat pulled away. Juggling the dynamite, his balance off, Cornelius barely made it, Hiroshi's strong grip the only thing that kept him from plunging backwards into the bay.

"Thanks . . . I." Cornelius set his jaw firm, eyes hard, as he tried to restrain an urge to strike the man. "You yellow bastard, you might just as well have let me take a swim with this here dynamite. What good is it if you cut and run?" He opened and closed his mouth a few times, at a loss for words. Finally, with an incredulous laugh he said, "Oh, I see, after all this, you are telling me that your women folk aren't up to it. Hell, I can't find fault if you want to cut and run. Blasting that thing out of there without taking out the wharf is near impossible. Why should you Japanese risk your women folk to save our white asses." He looked out towards the burning city. "San Francisco has always been a white man's city and we've always done everything we could to exclude you Asians. Now we've got our up and comings. The grand old lady will be gone by tomorrow or the day after. You can all go back to Japan where you belong, you've got no stake here, at least not anymore." He held up the dynamite as if to throw it overboard. "Guess we won't be needing this."

Hiroshi's eyes went dark and tight as he reached out taking the dynamite from Cornelius. His first words were angry words, not easily said to a white man without taking great risk. He spoke rapidly, his accent and inability to pronounce the 'r's and the 'w's' making him that more difficult to understand. "No, we Japanese are not afraid of this." He looked out over the same scenes that Cornelius had just seen. "Perhaps it is the white man who should be afraid. This disaster has given us Japanese an opportunity to prove ourselves your equals." He took in the masses of people pouring onto the waterfront with nowhere to go beyond that. "When the ferries pull up your people will leave what has become impossible to save. Perhaps it is destined that the city that will be raised from these ashes will be Asian."

Cornelius looked thoughtful for a moment as he gnawed on the thought. His eyes no longer able to hide his amusement, he slowly nodded his head and said. "That would be something to see."

"Perhaps you will be my guest."

Cornelius chuckled, saying nothing more.

There was a long moment of silence as the boat drifted farther out into the bay.

Reading Cornelius' thoughts, Hiroshi spoke. "You are concerned about the movement of our boats. The fishing nets must be moved before the dynamite can be used." He handed the dynamite to one of the crew saying something to him in their native language. The fisherman responded with a quick bow. The dynamite was taken to the starboard side of the boat where another boat, which had been signaled, pulled up, bouncing and bobbing, as the dynamite was passed on aboard. With a watchful eye on the dynamite Hiroshi continued. "Our women are most capable. However, I have grave reservations that they will be allowed to come." He nodded towards the mass of white humanity clogging the shoreline. "They do not share our vision of the future."

"I see what you mean. What idiot made the decision to send your people through that mob of vigilantes?" Hiroshi acknowledged Cornelius with a low bow. With a chagrined look, Cornelius took responsibility. "How long will it take you to get this here boat over to the wharf where your women folk are?" Why he had not thought of that the first time around made him feel even more the fool.

"Perhaps twenty-minutes. However, the Navy has restricted all movement. Beyond this point we cannot sail." It was a busy waterfront with more Navy ships arriving, rescue vessels attempting to pull people who had fallen into the bay out of the oil slick, trash laden waters. There were a few boats demanding a fare before rescue was offered. In the chaos, it would be easy for the small Japanese fishing craft to be run over and sunk. If they were to sail towards the wharf where their women and families waited it was unlikely any Navy craft would have the time to stop them. Hiroshi nodded. "All is not lost, my friend." He pointed towards a lone fishing vessel that had stayed behind in the ferry berth. "There, on that boat are two brave young men who have volunteered to dive should our women divers not get here in time."

Cornelius could see the boat that carried the dynamite heading their way. "They have experience?"

Hiroshi's voice trembled. "Enough for what they have been asked to do. Sometimes the fishing nets get tangled or caught on something beneath the surface. It is their job to free the nets. They are very brave because there are sharks in these waters. If there is enough air trapped in the wreck to allow them to attach and ignite the dynamite they will do what must be done. It is most unlikely that they will get away in time."

"That's suicide."

"In our culture, the sacrifice of one's life for the benefit of others is considered noble and not a sin, as it is regarded in your Christian world."

Cornelius wished he had a cigar, he did his best thinking when chomping down on one. He found it hard to deal with all these issues without one. He watched the Jap fishing boat that carried the dynamite approach the boat where the two men waited. "No, that won't happen. Take me over to that Navy Tugboat over there. We'll get your people out here one way or another. "Your women folk can out swim those boys . . . you say?"

"Inspector, there is always some risk. I am not asking my own wife, the mother of my two sons, to commit suicide."

CHAPTER 38

"RUTH." AGAINST THE DIN OF THE CROWD, DONALDINA CAMERON could barely hear her own voice. "Ruth!" Her voice went unheard.

She loathed using a heathen Chinese name but she had no choice. Finally she called out: "Quing Zhen Xu". She needed to know if Ruth knew where any of her other students were, if they were safe and where. The young Dutch woman, was she still with Ruth's family?

Stumbling over a brick she dropped the bundle she had put together back at the mission when she had raced against the flames to save what she could. Much of what she carried was meaningless to anyone but her: her only picture of Jonathan, the only man she had ever loved - and lost because she had been too afraid of her own feelings, and believed that lust was an unforgivable sin. An ivory rose pendant, the only keepsake left to her by her mother. She did not wear jewelry and had never worn it. The rest consisted of the Baptism records and any other documents that would separate her girls, young Chinese women, from their ugly past.

They could never be anything but God's second hand creatures, as they were not white and made in God's image. This was God's sad reminder that man was not perfect, that the Chinese were not far removed from the rodents that infested the sewers and the foulest abodes where human beings might dwell. Imperfect as they were, the Chinese were human beings and as such had souls and it was her life's mission to save as many of their souls as Christ would allow. In doing so, she had tried to strip them of everything Chinese. Once they accepted the Lord Jesus Christ as their one and only Savior, they were to forever give up everything Chinese - their names, families, language, culture, clothing, most everything that connected them to their heathen past. Should God allow them to marry, it would only be to a good Christian white man of Donaldina's choosing. Her greatest disappointments were the failure of her girls to forsake everything Chinese. That they had accepted Jesus as the true Son of God was not enough, for come Judgement Day, they would be denied their place in heaven if they had not forsaken all things wicked. Being born Chinese made them unworthy from their first breath. Donaldina prayed and struggled and would not give up, if she could only save one or two souls, her sacrifices and Christian duty would be acknowledged when her own day of judgment came.

The bundle of clothes she had salvaged for the poor Dutch girl, should she find her again, opened as she stumbled, some of the papers hidden within spinning away, stolen by a sneak-thief breeze. *No. No. Please I must not lose these.*

A wooden tray of steaming fish spilt as the woman carrying it reached out to help her recapture some of the papers stolen by the breeze. Three pages twirled and danced away to whatever fate waited them in the fires now only a few blocks away. At first, Donaldina had thought it to be Ruth. It was not. The face behind the helping hand was not Chinese. It was white, small, belonging to a petite woman whose alabaster skin streaked here and there with soot seemed terribly out of place, her eyes a mothers eyes, always loving, always forgiving, her face etched with hard years of always caring for others, smiled at her. "Here, let me help." The accent Donaldina guessed to be European, perhaps Norwegian. The lost papers were thrust gently back into her hands as she rolled her cloth package back into place to protect against anything else from slipping away.

"You speak Chinese," the woman asked? The ask was curious rather than reproaching. Her English was good, the accent clear.

"I teach Christ's love to Chinese girls in hope of salvaging their souls." She answered somewhat curtly. "In English . . ."

"Yes, but you do speak some Chinese? If you do, it would be oh so helpful to Dear Achilles. He tries so hard to understand them." The woman pointed toward a neatly well-managed fire in a makeshift kitchen where a number of Chinese men labored, preparing fire roasted fish under the watchful eye of a hairy, terribly filthy, giant of a man. "There, you see . . ."

Donaldina got to her feet, hugging her cloth bundle protectively. She could see that the dangerous looking giant seemed at ease, comfortable overseeing his flock of little yellow men, who for one reason or another trusted and obeyed him as she had never seen the Chinese do before. "Achilles is his name? What a curious man."

"Yes, Achilles is a gentle Greek fisherman and a wonderful cook." The woman saw her spill fish and sighed. She finished, then turned and introduced herself. "Marta Theorin." She then added proudly "The young man helping Achilles is my son Sven."

Donaldina nodded, grateful for the help. Her lips were tight, she was too busy for small talk. If she did not find her girls they might fall back into their Chinese ways and then she would lose them. She glanced back at the fire storm ravaging the city. *Satan is impatient my children, have faith, I will find you.* Her eyes searched the crowd, the cooking area, the wharf beyond - no Ruth. The next wharf seemed to be occupied only by the

Chinese. Surely, her girls could be found there. There, among the Chinese she saw a solitary white woman - the young Dutch woman she had found in the alleyway.

CHAPTER 39

ABE RUEF SAT ACROSS FROM MAYOR SCHMITZ, HIS SUIT pressed, bow-tie perfectly aligned, mustache trimmed, face clean shaven, seemingly unruffled, considering the state of the city. A snifter of brandy sat between them. Ruef was the brains and the power behind a potent organized crime syndicate that ran the city. There were other men in the room, each listening to Ruef, few adding any thoughts of their own. They were the first to assemble, the committee chairs of the Emergency Committee to Save San Francisco. The fires that devastated the city only seemed to feed Ruef's power and influence over them.

Ruef sipped at his brandy, intently observing each man, as the Mayor laid out Ruef's plan to salvage what would be left of the city. A committee of fifty men was to be formed . . . *A committee of fifty men,* Ruef thought as he looked over the list, most of whom he knew, many who were on his payroll, or could be if he used what he knew about each one; and he knew most of their transgressions. These men held the future, the destiny of San Francisco in their hands. *Since when have fifty men, especially those who are wealthy and influential, agreed about anything.* There were five who he would prefer to have nothing to do with. He could hardly stand to be in the same room with James Phelan, the former mayor of the city. Fifty outstanding and concerned citizens - it would look good to the press and to Washington, from whose coffers huge dollars would be needed. As long as he controlled the committee chairs, it would be a win for him.

"Who authorized the dynamiting of Chinatown?" Ruef asked.

He was now asking as the self-appointed chair for the committee to decide the future of Chinatown and its valuable real estate assets. The dynamiting that had spread the fires in Chinatown had been done by three police officers who were seasoned in doing his dirty work under the cover of a uniform and a badge. This time, it had cost him twelve hundred dollars. Expensive, yes, but worth every penny. Once the fires were set, the three officers had shed their uniforms and fled town with promises to never return.

Schmitz shifted uneasily in his chair. He suspected that the man across from him was responsible for the burning of Chinatown, but those words would never cross his lips. "I'm told, the army," Schmitz answered. "General Funston informed me that they lacked the authority and suggested it was set by members of our own police department. They suggested it was the fire department. Fire Chief Sullivan is critically injured and could not have given the order. I doubt anyone in his command did so; the explosions were poorly placed, spreading the fires rather than hindering them."

"I've heard rumors that it was the Chinese themselves," Ruef added. "They have a long history with explosives. Who is to say that the ignorant heathens didn't blow themselves up?"

The Mayor sat up. "Yes sir, that makes more sense than anything else I've heard so far. Why, if that were to be true, and the good people of San Francisco were to find out that the Chinese had started the fires, they would lynch every one of the slant-eyed devils from each surviving light pole in the city."

"Yes, that would be most unfortunate," Ruef chuckled, "and I might add, could have considerable influence regarding Washington's decision on how much emergency money they might be disposed to send my way - our way."

Schmitz thought about that. As the former President of the San Francisco Musician's Union, he lacked the depth of insight of the man who had put him into office. "I see what you mean." He held one hand out, finger gesturing, as if he were about to make a point.

Abe Ruef knew that Schmitz was posturing to save face. The other men in the room knew the same, that it was Ruef who would make the call, and the Mayor would only rubber stamp it. "At first, I wasn't so sure about your martial law decree, but now that it is in place, might I suggest that you issue orders to the army, and all relevant legal authorities, that the Chinese are to be arrested - no, I don't mean arrested . . . I mean taken into protective custody and escorted out of the city for their own safety and welfare."

Ruef paused for a moment, the room thick with smoke, either from tobacco smoke or the fires rapidly approaching where they were. It was no secret that the District Attorney was working closely with Police Inspector Cornelius McCann to get enough evidence to bring him up before a Grand Jury. McCann had come too close when he had closed down the Municipal Restaurant and bordello the year before. McCann had given Ruef no choice but to put an end to the investigations by getting rid of him; the how in eliminating McCann had proved to be a challenge.

Ruef had plans for the Chinatown property once it was cleared of the Chinese. And, as luck would have it, the earthquake and fire were handing him everything on a silver platter. It would become awkward to have this cop snooping around just as Ruef was about to file the papers. He cleared his throat, careful not to sound too anxious. "I might also suggest that some thought be given to the whereabouts and activities of

Inspector Cornelius McCann. I've heard rumors, rumors mind you, that McCann has acquired land bordering Chinatown, part of which is in Chinatown. That property could become quite valuable should Chinatown cease to exist. If the dynamiting of Chinatown was done by the police, well I'm just saying that it's something that ought to be looked into. There is one other matter that does trouble me." He looked around the room measuring each man for their feelings one way or another regarding Inspector McCann. "Last night seven valiant police officers were shanghaied in the tunnels beneath the Barbary."

A look of surprise swept the room.

"A few days ago a police Sergeant shared with me, in confidence, some very troubling allegations regarding Inspector McCann. The Sergeant was afraid, not just for his job, but for his life, to say anything within the department regarding McCann. While he did not name any of his superiors, he suggested that there might be some highly placed officers above McCann who are taking bribes from McCann, to look the other way."

"Abe, I can't see how investigating a crooked police officer is relevant when the whole city of San Francisco may be nothing more than a pile of ashes come tomorrow morning," Rabbi Jacob Voorsanger said. "I've known Cornelius McCann for a few years now, and if there is a police officer on the force who isn't crooked, it's McCann." Several members of the committee nodded their heads in agreement.

Ruef nodded back.

Bolling, the mayor's confidant and messenger boy jumped in. "Rabbi Voorsanger, we are all busy men here and we've just been handed one mother of a crisis. Do you, for one moment think that Mr. Ruef would have brought this up unless it is damned important? Pardon my language, Rabbi."

"Point is," said Ruef as he leaned forward in his chair, "that this police Sergeant, one Frank Darcy, was one of the officers who was shanghaied. Five of the officers reported directly to McCann. I'll lay this out as straight as I can, it is my contention that Inspector Cornelius McCann is responsible for the dynamiting of Chinatown to cover up his criminal activities in illegal land transactions, orchestrating the shanghaiing of his fellow officers to silence them as they were beginning to uncover that McCann committed federal crimes while smuggling illegal Chinese, forbidden under the Asian Exclusion Act."

Agitated, everyone spoke at once.

The Rabbi sat back in his chair in disbelief.

Abe Ruef's driver appeared at the door with an urgent look on his face. Ruef waved him over, then listened to a discrete whisper in his ear. He nodded, took a gulp of his brandy, and began to rise.

"Gentlemen, please." He repeated this several times loud enough to quiet the room. "Gentlemen, I've just been informed that the fire is now dangerously close to where we are. I would suggest that the Chinese be taken to the Presidio where the army can look after them. The rest to Hunter's point where the ship yard workers, many of whom are in the union, can do the same." *Loyal Union me, will have no qualms about keeping the Chinese under lock and key until they can all be shipped back to China,* he thought as he rose and donned his hat. "Committee Chairs," he nodded to each as he looked around the room, "please contact your people and see if they can, under these difficult circumstances, join us at The Plaza in two hours. As for McCann, violating the Asian Exclusion Act is a federal crime. Judge Harvey, I leave that matter to your good auspices. Might I suggest that a Federal Warrant be sent out for McCann's arrest before he gets lost in all the confusion. I wouldn't be too surprised if we find that those seven police officers were not shanghaied but murdered, their bodies left to rot in a rat infested tunnel, their bodies all but cremated by the hellish heat of these fires."

Ruef then turned with a crisp smile towards the Rabbi who now bore a strong look of shock and dismay across his face. "Rabbi Voorsanger, we need a chairman for the Food Committee. We have a lot of hungry people on our hands, few resources, and it is going to get worse before this whole thing is over."

"The people have got to be fed," the Rabbi said accepting the position.

"This meeting is adjourned," Ruef announced. He was the first one out the door.

CHAPTER 40

DISTRICT ATTORNEY WILLIAM LANGDON READ THE PAPERS in his hands for the third time. Without the signature of the United States District Attorney or a Federal judge, they were worthless. The Mayor had declared Martial Law illegally and he meant to stop it before any more people were shot. The Federal Court House still stood, surrounded by fire. It had been abandoned, and now he was trying his best to track down Marshal Woodworth, the United States District Attorney. He had been told that Woodworth had set up a temporary office at the Bohemia Club. By the time Langdon got there, Woodworth had come and gone. There, he was told that Woodworth could be found at the Mark Hopkins Hotel which was located on top of Nob Hill.

Langdon listened to his driver curse as he shifted gears for the climb up the hill. The fires burned ferociously just a block away and his car hadn't the power to make the hill. He had purchased the 1905 Buffalo Stanhope, an electric car that was supposed to get 50 miles to a battery charge, and 17 miles an hour on a good road. He could walk faster than it was traveling.

It ground to a stop, the grip brakes squeaking into place. His driver, an Italian with poor mastery of English, turned, shrugging his shoulders, with brown puppy dog eyes that said that he was sorry, and they could go no further. Langdon stared through the smoke at the distant summit, a far distance to go, especially since he wasn't sure if Woodworth was even there. He asked the driver to wait, if he could, but not to risk his life in doing so. He tucked the papers into his pocket, knowing that his journey was most likely pointless; nevertheless, he had to try.

His eyes began to water as the smoke swirled around him, the air thick and harsh in his lungs, and hot on his face as the fires jumped from building to building. He turned back to see that his driver had already fled. So be it, he placed one foot in front of the other as he began the long climb. The noise, the death throes of his city deafening, as he climbed that steep hill.

At the top the hill, he found most of the guests and staff of the Mark Hopkins outside watching the fires grow. Woodworth had again eluded him and time had run out. There was nothing left for him to do but return to his own home to see what he could salvage.

On the way down the hill, he heard and saw one of the explosions that lit up Chinatown. There is no way that is an accident, he thought. It also crossed his mind that the fast moving events overtaking the city were ideal for Ruef to make his move against McCann . . . and for that matter against himself.

CHAPTER 41

FRANK DARCY ROWED UNTIL HIS SHOULDERS AND ARMS could row no more. That he was overweight and had never been interested in strenuous exercise showed within his burning muscles. That he was rowing for his life did not seem to count for much. Archibald Pipe had told him that he was a dead man walking because he knew too much. Darcy knew that was not an empty threat. His boat was filled with dead men - only he was the one who did not know it - yet. He looked back towards the burning city and shivered. He wasn't cold, he just had one foot in the grave and with each minute he was getting deeper.

As much as it shamed him, he wept.

He couldn't row. Oakland was too far away even if he could. His feet were wet. The boat was overloaded with the weight of the dead. They had been there long enough to start passing foul gas which he guessed was fair judgement on him. There was a leak in the boat, not a slow one, somewhere beneath the bodies - not that he had a clue about how to stop it. The water slowly and surely rose around him. A series of bubbles gurgled up through the rising salt water filling the bottom of the boat releasing a foul odor as they quickly disappeared.

He wanted to scream out to the nearest of the tall ships to rescue him. But, that would put him into a situation worse than death. He most likely would be shanghaied, then worked to death, his body thrown over the side to feed the sharks.

He laughed hysterically as he tried to row back to the

waterfront - where the city was being ravaged by a firestorm - where Archibald Pipe waited to gut him with a fishing knife - where he was a traitor to his oath as a cop, to his fellow officers, and as a man - to Cornelius McCann. All for a lousy few bucks Archibald Pipe had refused to pay him because the police officers he had betrayed remained free and alive - well most. He hated himself for being a coward, and even more for being scared to death of all the options he had left in his miserable life.

He stripped off his wet uniform to his skivvies and rowed out of sheer terror of dying, alone in a boat full of dead, two who were cops he had betrayed and the equal terror which waited for him on shore. It wasn't Archibald Pipe he really feared - it was McCann.

CHAPTER 42

LAVINIA CLOSED HER EYES AND LET THE OLD WOMAN DO HER work. The needles the old witch stuck in her foot frightened her. That they did not hurt frightened her in a different way. She was being drawn into some dark evil spell the Chinese used to enslave women into becoming depraved creatures of the night. She had seen the women at night while walking with her father. The women with their eyes glazed over, shaking, from whatever form of drug induced abuse. Was she going to wind up like that? She shivered.

"Ouch." A needle hit a nerve.

She tried not to open her eyes.

She did not want to know.

The old woman said something in old raspy sing-song Chinese, her voice admonishing. "Try not to move," said one of the girls. "When they are placed just so, you will not know the needles are even there."

She tried to remain still, but could not help herself as she braced for another sharp sting. She tried letting her mind drift back to some happier place, a happier time. She imagined herself standing by a ship's rail, her father by her side, waving at people she did not know, as the ship set sail for America and, its promise. In the last year, her father had lost his job. Both her mother and sister had fallen ill with influenza and died. Her father, heartbroken, sat for months looking out a corner window at nothing - a proud man trapped in the past by the loss of his work and almost everyone he loved. His pride would not allow him to acknowledge his anguish. He was a failure as a man. He had been helpless to save her mother and sister, and now he could not provide for her. It shamed him. He could not look her in her eyes for the cause of the sadness he found there. He could find no words that would make a difference, so he remained silent and remote. The future had become as elusive as one small moment of happiness.

It had broken her heart to see him that way, and there was nothing she could do to bring back his smile. It seemed like Papa's smile and that marvelous twinkle in his eyes were gone forever. Then, as if God himself intervened, a letter came offering him a job as the Brew Master of a small, but profitable brewery in San Francisco, California, America. She had to look it up on a map. It was so far away, but if they did not go, she knew that she would lose her father, and he was all she had.

"Thank you, God," she had said at that ship's railing, as her homeland receded into the distance. America, with all its promises waited for them. San Francisco, the largest city on the West coast of America was to be their new home. "Thank you, God," her father had said, as he stood alongside her. She had looked up at him vowing that she would never leave his side again.

Lavinia squeezed her eyes tight, fighting off a sob as well as a scream. She was alone. Alone. There was an evil Chinese witch sticking foul needles in her leg and foot. The needles . . . "No. Stop!" Her eyes fluttered open, her pupils wide. "NO!"

"It's all right, dear, you must have had a bad dream. You're exhausted; it's been a long and horrible day." The woman almost smiled. Almost. But, the shorter, slightly older woman next to her did. In contrast to the missionary's thin lipped smile, the second woman's warm motherly smile felt like the first ray of sunshine after a long winter's night.

"Oh, it's you. I . . . I . . ." Lavinia looked down at her foot.

There were no needles. While there was still some swelling, the red puffiness seemed to be shrinking away before her eyes. The pain of her twisted ankle was gone.

"Donaldina Cameron," the woman introduced herself again.

"Yes, of course, you helped me in the alley. The Chinese girl who brought me here, Ruth, where is she?" Still confused, Lavinia couldn't take her eyes off her foot. With caution she straightened it just enough to test her weight. While there was still some discomfort, it was minor; she would be able to walk on it.

Upon seeing Donaldina come onto the wharf, the old Chinese acupuncturist quickly removed the needles and left. The old woman and the missionary were set in their different ways, faith, and customs, neither respecting the other. The old woman hadn't finished, but close enough. She had no stomach today for a tongue-lashing from the Christian crone.

"How?" Lavinia felt relief. The pain was gone. Whatever kind of magic the old woman had used, her foot was much better, and she was not drug enslaved to the Chinese. She looked around. She was on a wharf, the city a raging firestorm for as far as she could see. The bay behind her was filled with tall masted ships setting sail, their images lost within swirls of smoke. Onshore, a sea of desperate people were trapped between the water and the flames. The air was heavy with the stench of humanity at their worst, bay waters fouled by this and that, and the smoke from the raging fires darkened the sky, swirling all around them. Somehow, snaking through all the foul smells and corruption, the aroma of roasting fish from somewhere nearby reminded her that she was hungry.

On the wharf were hundreds of Chinese - men, women, and children – and none of them meant her any harm. Nearby, was Ruth's family, who smiled shyly while keeping a respectful distance from the white women. She looked for, but could not find Ruth.

Donaldina understood her confusion. "Another time, I'll try to explain," she said, "there is too much to do now. Here, I brought these for you." She held out her cloth bundle.

Lavinia had no idea what it was.

"Marta, take these." Donaldina thrust the papers that were hidden within the bundle into Marta's hands. The cloth bundle unraveled to become a set of woman's clothes. As she held them up to Lavinia for size," she said, "Yes, I think this will do.

Lavinia's eyes glistened with gratitude. "Oh . . . I . . ." She remembered her atrocious attire and near nakedness - to her further embarrassment she realized there was no place to change. "Thank you." In the confusion she thought she had heard the woman's name. "Myrtle?"

"Marta," she corrected with a smile.

"Marta, yes. I'm pleased to meet you. Please call me Lavinia."

Donaldina snapped something briefly in Cantonese, clapping, as if a command. The girls of Ruth's family, as well as a number of women in the surrounding area formed a circle around Lavinia, their backs to her. They were short and did not provide much protection, but the circle allowed Lavinia some privacy to change.

The women laughed as the bloody apron and the coat sailed

over their heads. Done, the circle parted revealing Lavinia dressed in a white linen Pouter Pigeon blouse, with a front bodice and high neckline, finished with a black trumpet skirt. It was the same outfit that Donadina Cameron wore, with the exception of the shoes. Lavinia had lost hers. On Donaldina, the attire looked conservative, bordering on the point of being severe. On Lavinia, it seemed to bring out her charms, highlighting a soft sensual face.

Noticeably missing was a hat.

Donaldina's hat, black, not in the least way stylish, was securely pinned to her tightly pulled up hair. Lavinia did not have a hat, her hair was an uncombed tangle having not worn a bath cap when she was thrown naked out into the world in her bathtub. Washing one's hair was not an everyday luxury, but rather a chore. The lye soap, which was all she had, was harsh and dried out the hair. She hadn't even had a chance to use any of the dreaded soap before her abrupt departure.

Marta's hat, filthy, once white, with colorful feathers and dried flowers still managed to look festive, though it had been crushed and almost set afire by flaming ash.

CHAPTER 43

CHOICE PICKENS SENSED AN UNEASY QUIET. THE TYPE OF quiet that precedes an earthquake or a volcanic eruption, or the minute before a former lover storms into a wedding, just as the minister is about to ask if anyone objects. He took in the surroundings he thought he understood ten minutes earlier - something had changed but he couldn't quite put a finger on it.

Let's see, he thought as he ran through a mental check list:

Let's see now . . . the great city of San Francisco and my employer is one big bon fire - check. Captain Lafferty has moved farther down towards the Barbary to work with the Navy fighting the fires there - check. Marshal . . . excuse me . . . Inspector Cornelius McCann, my boss and pal is off playing cowboy, God knows where - check. I've got a wharf with about a couple of dozen Japs, mostly women and kids - check. Another wharf with a hundred or so Chinks - check. The so-called Waterfront Precinct is full of women, children, and old folks - check. I've got a big dumb Greek cook roasting fish and potatoes for the multitudes . . . and the chinks are working with him- check. No, everything seems normal, perhaps I'll go find me a game of cards.

He could see that a long line had formed for the fish. He also could see that more than a few people were venturing into the nearest ruins to relieve themselves. The multitudes had grown into a whole hell of a gathering. *Moses, part these bay waters, and get these people the hell out of here.*

Where was the army? He couldn't see a single uniform in the crowd. From where he stood, he could count just short of a dozen longshoremen. They had been his first line of defense but most had moved on. He slowly turned a full three hundred and sixty degrees in place. 'Check! No one here but one dumb pecker-wood." He felt for his side arm which of course he no longer had. "Check." He said aloud. "And to think that I started this day out on a nice little boat ride. I could have had me a picnic and a pleasant day on the bay. Hah!" His laugh was loud and self-mocking. *Cornelius, I've never let you down one God-damned day in my life and you . . .*

An aftershock rattled the waterfront, followed immediately by the cries of the nervous and terrified crowd.

His mouth dry and tasting of smoke he tried to laugh. *No Sir, and I'm not about to let you down now. OK, what are my resources?* He looked towards Achilles. The man was big and dumb, but he had a heart of gold, and while they had just met he could tell that Achilles would become a remarkable friend, loyal to a fault, fueled with enough energy to drive a six-ox team up a steep mountain pass. He was irreplaceable as the master chef on the Waterfront. He was also indispensable as a cop to cover his backside. Cornelius had deputized him before he had become the cook, so the decision was made. *Time to go to work, big guy - time to go to work.* Choice called out to him as he ran it through his mind one more time - *cook or cop?* How could he best use the only cop left on his team.

CHAPTER 44

D ARCY TRIED TO ROW.

His efforts were becoming futile, he hadn't the strength nor the energy to fight the current as it took him right back to where he had started, back to where he did not want to go. His boat carried too much weight and had begun to sink. He was too afraid of drowning to give up. The rest of the way, he would have to take his chances and swim for the wharf; and he had never been much of a swimmer.

His greatest fear was that the current would drag him beneath the wharf where he would be skinned alive amongst the barnacle covered pilings. Now, it seemed like the least of his worries was Archibald Pipe.

From a distance he heard the gunshots and had seen some of the battle. The Navy ships that were now tied up alongside the wharves told him who had won, and the crimps like Pipe and Walrus, and dozens of others were all part of yesterday's history. Darcy was a coward and a traitor; and he knew it. The smart thing, the easy way out would be to open his mouth and drown himself, but he didn't even have the courage to do that.

The boat filled with water. The bodies of the brave officers who had been betrayed and shanghaied with him, went down with it. He was too afraid of drowning to give up.

The closest wharf was the one occupied by the Chinese. To the North, was the Navy and any crimps that might still be around. Once ashore, if he turned South, he could get lost in the crowd.

A Chinese woman spotted him in the water and began to point and scream in Cantonese. A crowd immediately drew close to the wharf's edge.

CHAPTER 45

Henry Rabbitt set the pace on foot while Sidney and the Lieutenant boxed in the two Japanese seamen between their horses, as they forced their way through the crowd. There were not many horses on the waterfront. Most of the stock yard herd had perished in the quicksink. The Army commandeered all horses anyone tried to bring through to the waterfront anywhere near Market or Mission Streets - there just wasn't room. From where he sat, the Lieutenant could see only two other horses tucked into a sea of hats bobbing this way and that, as people crowded and pushed each other with an urgency waiting to explode. The women's hats, adorned with bright feathers, flowers and bird plumage, seemed like tiny islands of brilliant color adrift in a sea of beaver and leather hats - brown, gray and black - much like the dense clouds of smoke that reflected the fires that bellowed and swirled above them. The crowd gave the Lieutenant some concern regarding the Army's command and control up on Market Street. Mostly, what alarmed him were the hostile looks from almost everyone around them as Henry guided their horses and the Japanese towards the wharves where the Chinks and the Japs were holed up. The crowd was dense and surly. Beneath their hats, their eyes and faces flashed with anger and desperation. At least for the moment, few took notice of the Japs running between them. All it would take is one loud mouth to rile the crowd into an out of control lynch mob.

The closer they reigned in the Japs, the more the Lieutenant's foot was jarred. Sidney's mount crowded against Itchy who then crowded Kat, who then jammed the Lieutenant's foot causing his horse to push back. He glanced down, the hot pain felt like so many sharp needles with a few No #2 penny nails thrown in for good measure. *He was wounded, for God damned sake, and needed to be taken off the front line, Lieutenant* Reeves Charter whined silently. *Now, here he was playing nursemaid to some friggen Japs, who were more than likely to have their ponytails cut off, strung up and hung from the nearest bent street lamp before another hour passed by.*

"Watch it Mac! What the hell? Hey Burl, look at them their Japs . . ." a voice shouted nearby. Hats tilted, revealing hostile eyes. There were more voices rising up around them. The Lieutenant nudged his horse forward with his good foot. "Rabbitt, step it up, folks are beginning to bristle."

"They started out that way," Henry Rabbitt snapped back.

Burl, a thickset, full-bearded man, with lard-matted tangled hair - no hat - reached out to grab Sidney's reigns. His right hand flew back to cover his cheek as Sidney's whip cut an angry blood red stripe through his beard. A tough man, he tried to grasp the whip, but fell beneath the horse as Henry's pike cracked down on the back of his head. Sidney's horse reared and snorted as it tried not to stumble, as the man's body rolled beneath its hooves.

The Lieutenant's horse reared, then tried to back away, revealing the two Japanese fishermen for a critical moment.

"Burl?"

It was too late. The man who had fallen beneath the horses tried to roll out from beneath their flying hooves. Burl was down, the Japanese stumbling over his body. Another man, just as big and burley, perhaps a mule skinner by trade, bellowed as he reached out for the Lieutenant pulling him from his saddle. "Burl, get the hell out of there."

The horse, riderless, panicked.

The Lieutenant's Colt 45 went off as he fell.

A woman nearby screamed as she was struck by the stray bullet.

The Lieutenant landed on his wounded foot, snapping his ankle. One of the horse's hooves came down on his wrist as he tried to reach for his gun.

Alive, conscious and a bloody mess, Sam, the first man who had gone, down saw the gun and rolled for it.

Katasui and Ichirou were out in the open.

Ichirou, closest to the gun, dropped, rolled, and rose back up on his feet with the gun before the bigger white man - Sam - could get to it. He turned, pointing it at Sam, his finger tight enough on the trigger to cause the man to freeze.

"That Jap shot my Emma!"

The crowd parted, allowing everyone to see a fat middle aged man, still in his night clothes, holding a woman's lifeless body, bright red blood soaked her night gown where she had been shot too near the heart to have stood a chance.

The crowd became a lynch mob.

"Trouble . . . Shit!" Henry reigned in his horse, lost his pike as he reached down for Katasui, who grabbed the pike, then quickly mounted the horse behind Henry.

Sidney spun his horse around in a circle snapping his whip in the path of anyone who tried to draw near.

A Jap with a gun was all everyone saw. A white woman was dead, and a Jap had done it. That is all it took. The crowd, swelled by the curious, moved forward ready to tear the smallish

Jap fisherman into wild dog bait.

Sidney drew back his whip. A second later the Colt 45 was stripped from Ichirou's hand along with the nail and the tip of his finger that had been about to close down on the weapon's trigger. The mob stopped, expecting to see the whip strike the small, now helpless Jap until there was no flesh left to cut away.

Ichirou looked up expecting the same.

Sidney screamed. "Get on! You got one chance." His whip snapped slicing a neat tear in the front of the shirt of the nearest man who appeared to threaten them. There were multiple targets all around them. All Sidney needed to do was get their attention - to buy a few seconds.

Ichirou, with no hand reaching out to aid him, practically flew onto the back of Sidney's mount. With little regard for anyone in their path, the cowboys kicked their mounts into a full gallop. Neither felt they had much of a chance.

The Lieutenant, fearful for his own life, lay on the ground, close to passing out from the pain. Through clenched teeth, he called out just barely loud enough to be heard. "Those yellow bastards are my prisoners. Don't let them escape." He passed out as two women came to his aid.

A tall, thin man in a dusty drivers smock, still wearing auto goggles, retrieved the Colt 45, took aim and fired.

Sidney felt, rather than heard Ichirou's gasp. He tightened his grip around Sidney's waist for a second before his body went limp. The brave, smallish Japanese fisherman fell backwards, dead before he hit the ground. The bullet that had killed Ichirou had gone completely through his body and up into Sidney's right shoulder. A nerve severed, his whip fell from his grasp, as he had no choice but to ride on.

Grief tightened Katasui's grip, as he held onto Henry as they rode for their lives. Katasui glanced back as a swarm of blood-lust driven men quickly surrounded Ichirou's body. A dark wave of angry longshoremen, bakers, bartenders, haberdashers, dentists, and drunks grew by the hundreds as they pursued the two cowboys, who they had determined had helped a Jap who had murdered a white woman, get away.

CHAPTER 46

"OH DEAR," EMBARRASSED, LAVINIA TRIED IN VAIN TO UNTANGLE the dried-together knots in her hair. While she was grateful for her clothes, she now felt naked out in public without a proper hat.

"Oh dear," Marta repeated sympathetically.

Donaldina could care less, while she could see that something needed to be done with Lavinia's hair - in time - that she was without a hat on a day like this wasn't the end of the world. After all, she had been all but naked, except for a bloody apron and a musician's top coat only a few moments before. *Perhaps she should get down on her knees and thank The Lord Christ for the bounty she had been given.* Donaldina had always been impatient with people who were not appreciative of Christ's blessings.

"You must be hungry, my dear, and a drink of cool water wouldn't hurt." Marta interrupted.

Until that moment, Lavinia had not realized how hungry she was. "Famished," she answered. The word didn't come out quite right because her mouth was so parched.

"Donaldina, would you be so kind as to take Lavinia over to Achilles and see that she gets some roasted fish and a drink. He has a keg of cider tucked away that he'll share if asked."

Donaldina's eyes went wide.

Marta continued. "The cider, it's not hard, if that is what you are thinking. Now off with you both, I've got to check on my boys and I'll join you in a short while."

"Well, I never . . ." sputtered Donaldina. She had just been told what to do by a woman. She was used to telling people what they should or should not do. She did it with the Chinese and they obeyed. She did it with most white women. They usually batted their eyes, their lips quivering for a moment as they sought words of protest, but, in the end, they did the same as the simple Chinese and obeyed. Men, she had a harder time with. Of course, good Christian men understood that she had a special relationship with God and soon acquiesced, and did as Donaldina asked.

"No, my dear you probably haven't, and for that I'm sorry." She gave Lavinia a knowing wink. "You've missed out on so much." Normally, Marta did not look down on anyone. She had taught Sven, and now taught Nils and Patrik, that none of us are perfect, and not to judge their imperfections too harshly as long as they did no harm to others. That did not work out often; this was San Francisco after all. Her patience was tried when bigots, high and mighty capitalists, and self-serving bureaucrats stepped on the small people to benefit themselves. She had pegged Donaldina as a religious zealot, if not a bully. The Chinese were small people - that Donaldina, in her own way, tried to raise their plight in life to a slightly higher standard, was a good thing. That she was an unforgiving religious bully, was not a good thing, as far as she was concerned.

As Donaldina turned away, Marta giggled, just loud enough for the prim missionary to hear. Marta had never been outspoken, and had always tried to keep herself invisible to those who thought their shadows were mightier than others.

After her husband had passed away from typhoid just after her youngest son, Patrik's birth, life had been hard enough. She had enough to get by, but raising the boys took all of her time, energy, and money. Thank God for Sven. That was until this morning, when her world was turned upside down. She had lost her home, job, and any illusion of safety she had had. She had no man to provide for and protect her and her three sons. Sven did his best.

If they were going to survive, she could no longer remain a quiet little church mouse. Befriending Donaldina Cameron might prove to be beneficial in a world where women were considered to be only a step or two above the Chinese. Donaldina was a power unto herself. However, she was not going to dictate how Marta and her children were to live, and to her own surprise she had just clipped Donaldina's wings.

CHAPTER 47

THE BURNED RUINS OF THE FISH MARKET AND THE SHATTERED brick remains of the trolley and streetcar barns still blocked access to the Barbary Coast and the waterfront that curved around the northwest side of the city until it reached the Presidio. The Navy, with what few ships it had, had a herculean task in trying to keep the fires from burning down to the waterfront, blocking one of the few remaining escape routes. Cornelius had ordered that a path be carved through the mountains of debris, and that had not happened because there were not enough Chinese to do it. Without the ferries running, the fires could burn right down to the water, trapping tens of thousands of people.

Choice Pickens studied Achilles, wondering if he was up to the task. He wasn't a trained police officer, he was a cook. He had showed courage during the fight with the crimps, but was that a one shot thing? He was a big bull with the heart of a lamb. If Choice were to do the job himself, there would be no real police presence left at Cornelius' Waterfront Police Station. If that even mattered any more, was a question he could not ignore. Their hold on the waterfront was precarious at best. Cornelius was somewhere down by the ferry wharf. The Army had all but abandoned their posts, at least here, which as far as Choice was concerned, was the only place that mattered. The waterfront was at a bursting point with too many people, the fires were burning closer by the hour, and there was not enough authority to hold things together. When, not if, the firestorm reached the waterfront, ferries or no ferries, the only way out for god knows how many people, would be a narrow track through those ruins.

The rub was that to get the masses of people out, they would have to go right by the wharf where the Chinese were holding out. He had been a policeman long enough to know that would be like lighting the fuse to some dynamite while holding onto it and not letting go - Boom - mixing that mass of panicky people with the Chinks would become one god-awful blood bath.

"Achilles, are you still a sworn police officer of the City of San Francisco?" Choice asked as he came up to the man. The aroma of the fish whet his appetite. The breeze shifted, Achilles' stench killed his appetite.

Achilles straightened his posture and beamed. "Yes, I am police officer," he pointed, "as are you. You want some fish?" He clapped his hands. A Chinaman brought over a wooden plank with a chunk of sizzling fish.

Choice waved his hands rejecting the fish. "No, perhaps later." He needed to get to the point. "Can Sven manage the cooking station?"

"Yes. Sven is a good worker, a smart boy. The Chinese like him. He is a fast learner. Why do you ask?"

"Because, as you are a fully sworn officer, I have an assignment for you."

Achilles looked puzzled. "Assignment? I do not understand this word."

This is going to be harder than I thought. I need this big galoot to act as my Pied Piper and get these Chinks out of here.

The Japs too. I forgot that his English ain't so good. Choice thought. "I have a job that requires a police officer, and you, Achilles, are my man."

"But I have a job." As Achilles paused, his thick eyebrows

furrowed. "You no like the fish? Ahhh, the goat was better, but as you can see, I have no more goat."

"Sven, I want you to take over here," Choice snapped with frustration. "Achilles, you are a sworn officer and when I give you an order, I expect it to be obeyed."

Achilles remembered having killed Archibald Pipe a few hours earlier. "Perhaps it is not a good thing for Achilles to be a policeman. I am better as a cook. I give you back the oath. The next time I see Inspector McCann, I tell him that he does not have to pay me. OK?" The big man's face behind the filthy beard, dried sweat, and soot became almost childlike. "OK?"

Choice Pickens wanted to say OK, but he couldn't because too much was at stake. "I wish I could, big guy. I wish I could, but I can't. Like it or not, you are a sworn police officer." He had a hard time playing the tough Sergeant. "Failure to follow my orders when Martial Law has been declared is desertion."

Achilles understood the word desertion. In his own country, Greece, to be found a deserter meant that you went before a firing squad, were shot, then buried with no marker. "No, you cannot do this?" Achilles pleaded.

Choice regretted what he had to say. "I can and you will follow your orders or face the consequences."

The energy and strength that made up the huge Greek went out of him with a long sad sigh.

Sven could not believe what he had just witnessed.

The Chinese had all stopped what they were doing, their gaze on Achilles' face. Few understood anything of what had been said, but the sadness overcoming Achilles told them that great tragedy was about to unfold.

Having seen that her two younger boys were safe and playing under the watchful eyes of other mothers, Marta Theorin hurried to the cooking station, concerned that Donaldina would make a scene about the cider. She did not know if the cider was hard or not, though she suspected it was. If Achilles, toiling unselfishly around a hot fire trying his best to feed whoever was hungry needed a drink of hard cider, he deserved it. She hoped that she could beat the two women there before Donaldina started preaching about the evils of alcohol and threatening Achilles with eternal damnation, fire and brimstone. He did not deserve that - there were more than enough fires this day. She could not help but smile, having to stifle a giggle as she thought of Donaldina being picked up, screaming, the threat of a vengeful God, as she is thrown into the bay after pouring poor Achilles' cider into the cooking fire. She quickly glanced around to see if anyone had noticed her behavior - free of that simple guilt, she tightened her hat as she quietly admonished herself for being so spiteful. She couldn't help it, Donaldina reminded her of her Aunt Dora, a strict Christian woman who considered anything fun to be a sin. As a young girl, her worst summers had been those when Auntie Dora came to visit. *Perhaps it was herself,* Marta thought, *who needed to be a little more understanding of Donaldina.*

Alas, Donaldina and Lavinia had beaten her to the cooking site. As she approached, she saw there was a heated discussion going on between Donaldina, the Police Sergeant, and Achilles. She also saw that the Chinese had all given up their duties preparing and cooking the fish and were returning to the wharf where their families waited, while Sven was anxiously running around trying to prevent them from leaving. Lavinia stood quietly back from the argument nibbling on a piece of fish.

Marta grabbed her son's shoulder. "Sven, what is it? Why are they all leaving?" She gestured towards Achilles and the heated discussion around him. "Why is everyone so upset?" Her first inclination was that it was something Donaldina had done. *Had she been right about the cider?* Since the cider jug was nowhere in sight, it did not appear to be the cause, unless Donaldina had already thrown it into the bay. *Had Donaldina said something to offend the Chinese, driving them all away, leaving poor Achilles and Sven alone to do all the work?*

Sven answered with tears building in his eyes. "Sergeant Pickens says that Achilles is a deserter and is to be arrested and shot."

"A deserter? From what?" Marta demanded, aghast at the idea.

"Mother, I don't know. All I know is that Sergeant Pickens is going to take Achilles away. He has put me in charge of the kitchen." Sven pointed towards the Chinese, his gestures exaggerated. "Stop, don't leave." He pulled away from his mother's grasp, started after the Chinese, abruptly stopped and turned back to her. "Mother, what am I to do," he begged with wild eyes, "I can't do all this by myself. We're running low on fire wood. What am I to do with the fish if the fire goes out? Are they really going to shoot Achilles?" His words were rushed, all jammed together in one breath.

Marta could see that her son was overwhelmed and frightened. "Shoot Achilles, most certainly not. You must have heard wrong." She raised her hands as only a mother can, to calm him. "I'll have a word or two with Sergeant Pickens and we'll straighten this out. Right now, you need to go out onto the wharf where the Chinese are and find the young Chinese woman named Ruth. She speaks English and seems to have the respect of her people. If you ask nicely she may be able to persuade the workers to come back." She paused. "It will be all right, son. I'm very proud of everything you've done. Sven, you are right, there is still a lot to do so we had best get about doing it."

Sven saw in his mother's eyes and smile that she understood and loved him. "Ruth, I think I know the one you mean."

He's becoming a man in his own right, she thought as she watched her son walk a little more confidently towards the Chinese wharf. She put her hand to her cheek as she shook her head. *Shoot Achilles, what on earth is that all about?* She had always been one to avoid confrontation and here she was walking willy-nilly straight into one. *Oh my, but she was becoming the brave one. If only her husband could see her now. Alas, he wouldn't have liked it, not proper for a woman.*

A pile of luggage had been left near the field kitchen when the site was thought to be a police station and Sergeant Darcy had been around to guard it. *One police officer,* she thought, *trying to wrestle a dozen problems at the same time does not make a police station. It pushes an officer to the edge of a nervous breakdown. It leaves a field kitchen,* she further observed, *that happens to have a policeman running around in circles herding chickens barely able to accomplish anything.* That the luggage was still there was a fluke unto itself. Raising three boys by herself had prepared Marta to have an eye for a dime saved or an opportunity to earn an extra quarter.

Attached to a steamer trunk by a flowing scarf was a small brimmed hat finished with a black silk band and contrasting stitching. She had been admiring one just like it in a store window a few weeks back, but could not afford it. Now there it was. She adjusted her own hat as she discreetly glanced around to see if anyone was watching. *No, oh you wicked girl.* It did not take but a second and the hat was free from the trunk and in Marta's hands. *What a brave and foolish girl you have become,* she thought as she fondled the hat. It was so much nicer than her own.

She was about to pin her newly acquired hat in place when she remembered that Sergeant Pickens was a policeman and that she was in possession of a stolen hat. "Here my dear," she said to Lavinia with a whisper, "I found this on the street. It doesn't quite suit me, but I think on you it will do just fine." It did complement Lavinia's youthful face and eager doe eyes, while softening the conservative outfit Donaldina had given her.

While helping Lavinia with her new hat, Marta listened to the argument taking place: "No, no . . . no, I'm not arresting Achilles, and I have no intention of doing so. It's just that . . ." Sergeant Choice Pickens sputtered, feeling berated, if not helpless, under the withering verbal deluge spat at him by Donaldina Cameron. *Sven is right,* his mother thought, *Achilles is in trouble, but not as serious as she had been led to believe.*

To Donaldina, Achilles was a filthy Greek immigrant in desperate need of a bath. The Chinese respected him so she was confident that somewhere buried deep within the hairy beast was a good Christian soul - or at least there would be once she was done with him. In the short term, she had her sights set on Sergeant Pickens, who was, after all, a Police Officer in a city where the police were notorious for abusing her Chinese.

The argument was at a standoff. Baffled, Achilles feared he was to be shot for desertion and did not understand why. Perhaps, he should run away?

Donaldina, who cared less whether Achilles was guilty or not, focused her wrath on Sergeant Pickens, charging that he was abusing his authority. The city was burning to the ground and hundreds of thousands of people were homeless and caught in unimaginably desperate straits. In her eyes, he was neglecting his sworn duty to protect and serve the people, while he focused his limited attention on one poor Greek cook.

It annoyed the hell out of Sergeant Pickens that the holier than thou missionary was right. There were far too many things that demanded his immediate attention and here he was caught in this inane argument that had blown the situation regarding Achilles completely out of control.

Achilles stood, trembling, tightening his ham-hock sized fists repeatedly, and wanting to run, but afraid that the policeman would pull out his gun and shoot him if he did. Neither Sergeant Pickens or Donadinia would give ground, each was right, the other wrong, and neither heard the heated words the other said; the issue of Achilles' so called desertion, forgotten in the storm of verbal abuse each threw at the other.

Marta had heard and seen enough. Without the Chinese workers, the cooking fire was dying and with it, the field kitchen. While the police station was now nothing more than wishful thinking, the field kitchen had been an oasis of civility, where generosity and hope stood alone against the hopeless chaos threatening everyone. Now, as the fire died, one person followed by another, each desperate for a few extra feet they could call their own, filled the space. It wouldn't be long until there were so many people they couldn't rebuild the kitchen even if they wanted to. She went over to the two sanctimonious bellowing idiots. "Excuse me." Her words went unheard. She tried again, this time a little more forcefully. It was as if she were invisible to them. *OK, I'm going to have to treat them like quarreling children.* She stepped between them and looked directly at Donaldina, who continued her barrage of words uninterrupted. Without a word of warning, Marta reached up and pulled Donaldina's hat down over her eyes, tearing the front brim in the process. Then without any wasted motion, she turned to Sergeant Pickens, put her finger to her lips and said, "Not one word." She then commanded that he step back two paces, as she pushed him back with the firm tapping of her index finger on the center of his chest. That done, she beckoned Achilles to come to her and positioned the big Greek between the police Sergeant and the overwrought missionary.

Hissing like a cat whose tail had been stepped on, Donaldina pulled her hat up then off to examine the damage. "How dare you!" She really had not seen Marta and assumed that Sergeant Pickens had done it. Dropping her damaged hat to the ground she raised her hand to slap him. She could not, for she now faced Achilles' huge back, his shirt torn and filthy, blocking her access to her intended target. She tried to step around him only to find her way blocked by Marta and a moment later by Lavinia on the other side. "Well, I never . . ."

"Donaldina, we addressed that issue earlier, and I told you then that I was sorry that you have never . . " she let whatever last word might follow fall silent. "Now, Sergeant Pickens," Marta continued, shifting her attention, "please explain in as few words as possible what you need Achilles to do." She held Achilles' tightened fist until she felt it loosen. "Achilles, you are now a Police Officer; the kitchen work is finished. Do you understand?"

Chapter 48

NO SOONER HAD SVEN FOUND THE CHINESE WOMAN CALLED Ruth, he found himself caught in another dilemma. Ruth was trying to negotiate the rescue of a white man who was clinging to one of the exterior pilings of the wharf. The Chinese men gathered around the edge of the wharf, did not want to rescue him. Had it not been for Ruth, they would have thrown enough debris down on him to either drown him or cause him to be drawn by the undertow beneath the wharf, where he would be battered to death amongst the pilings and razor sharp barnacles.

Ruth recognized Sven as the young man who worked with the Greek at the cooking station. She had seen that he was gentle and different from most white men as he worked alongside the Chinese. As a white man, she did not fear him, though trust was a complicated thing. She had to trust someone before the white man clinging for his life below drowned. One of the Chinese men had told her that the white man was a police officer who served with the Chinatown Squad and had beaten many Chinese just for the fun of it. The Chinaman held up his own left hand showing three useless crooked fingers where the bones had been broken multiple times. He spoke rapidly; there was great anger in his eyes and desire for revenge. Ruth translated this information to Sven saying that the Chinese will never let him up and wish him only great misfortune.

Sven had heard of Sergeant Darcy's betrayal of his fellow officers and his association with the crimps. His mother and he had almost been murdered by them had it not been for Achilles.

His first inclination was to let Darcy drown. However, his conscience strengthened by his mother's teachings would not allow him to do that. He asked Ruth to try to keep the Chinamen from dumping any more debris down on Darcy while he ran to fetch Sergeant Pickens.

219

Chapter 49

S ERGEANT PICKENS HAD TO ADMIT THAT HE WAS A LITTLE more than jealous of Cornelius. Cornelius was out there in the thick of things, where the action was, riding high on a God-damned horse. A hero for all to see. *Goddamned dwarf cowboy. I could learn to ride me a horse if given a chance,* he thought as he readied himself to lead Achilles into the ruins. The orders he had given were quite simple. Someone needed to break trail through the mountain of debris that blocked this end of the waterfront from the Barbary Coast and Little Italy. If Cornelius did not get the ferries working, this might very well be the only way out should the fires burn all the way to the wharfs. Deep down in his gut Choice knew that if they tried to run forty thousand people directly by the wharves where the Chinese and Japanese had taken refuge, a blood bath was sure to occur. Priority one was to find a way through the rubble suitable for the women, children, and old folks, and to make sure that there were no armed crimps left lurking there. Second, he needed to have a chat with the military on the other side to make sure he wouldn't be sending folks through to a dead end blocked by fire. Last, he needed to get the Chinks and the Japs off the wharves and on their way to the Presidio. The nearest and most dangerous fires were in Chinatown and he had already heard rumblings that the Chinese had started them as well as other fires throughout the city. Those were the type of wild rumors that gave lynch mobs their self-imposed authority.

He wished he had a chance to run all this by Cornelius, but he didn't, and that was that. Cornelius had left him in charge and by gum, he was going to do what needed to be done. There was one more thing that was nagging at his craw - Achilles. Right or wrong, he had scared the bejesus out of the big guy, and he hadn't deserved it. Now, in his state of mind, why wouldn't he cut and run? Choice couldn't blame him if he did. That being said Choice needed him; Achilles was the last card he had in his deck.

The final decision was that he was going to have to take the initiative and do the job himself. Odds were good that at least one or two crimps were holed up in the ruins. In the smoky, twisted, confines, they had the edge. He and Achilles would make a two-man reconnaissance patrol, that was the best he could do. He knew that by leaving his post he would be leaving this end of the water front without any legal authority. He had to laugh at that. What the hell could one man do? If the situation worsened and, sure as this day was one bad day for the record book, it was going to, and he was willing to bet a month's pay on it - if he ever got paid again. If he stayed, he would just be playing nursemaid to mostly women, kids, Japs and Chinks. *What a glorious end to my career as a cop. I've never been much of a gambling man because I usually lose. Well, I'm about to roll the god-damned dice and just for once it would be nice if a little luck might come my way.*

Marta Theorin had shown herself to be one tough old gal. Choice had asked her to round up her son Sven and tell him that he was hereby deputized and in charge of the police station - kitchen - whatever it was, until he got back. If the kid couldn't do it, then his mom just might. He had no other choice, Sven would have to do . . . after all, he couldn't appoint a woman, could he?

"Achilles, you ready?"

Achilles nodded. He wasn't happy about it, but things were sure looking up from a few minutes ago when he expected to be shot for desertion. Desert his post? He had thought about it. Now, he was about to follow this hard headed cop into some smoking ruins looking for a bunch of cut-throats who lurked with pikes, knives, and anything else they might use to rob and murder him. Rob? He didn't have nothing worth anything, not even the shirt on his back.

"Sergeant Pickens, hold on one moment. I've got something for you." Choice turned to find Sven approaching from the direction of the Chinese wharf. He was followed by a jabbering mob of Chinks, mostly men, and Ruth, the Chinese girl. His first thought was that the Chinks were angry with Sven. *Crap, don't tell me I've got to bring the kid along with me and the Greek. I ordered him to take charge here.* He had picked up a pike for their trek through the ruins and held it up ready. "Achilles, hold up, let's see what the kid wants."

"Sergeant Pickens, you'll never guess what crawled up onto the Chinese Wharf." Sven announced proudly as he turned, bowed as if on stage, tipping a derby hat he had found somewhere along the way. The Chinese behind him raised clubs and stones shouting angrily as they parted, shoving their hog-tied prisoner to the ground in front of them. The pike in Choice's hand felt suddenly as hot as the macabre blood red image of hatred and revenge that crossed his mind. It took every ounce of will he had not to bash in the traitor's head. "Darcy, you traitorous snake, I've got a mind to . . . to . . . ." He brought the pike slowly back down to his side as he stared at the figure wavering on his knees in front of him. "By all rights I ought to give you to the Chinks and let them have at you." Choice looked at the Chinese, tempted to do just that. Something in Ruth's eyes kept him from it. "But I ain't ah going to do it, because I'd much rather see you shit your pants as the hangman drops you dead on a rope."

Darcy shook like a beaten dog, whimpered, unable to say anything. A stone thrown by one of the Chinese hit him in the back of the neck knocking him face down onto the street's cracked and buckled brick surface.

"Enough," Choice roared at the Chinese, waving his hands, pike raise, as if to chase off so many black ravens. "Achilles," he snapped, not meaning to sound as if he were angry at the man, "get this pitiful excuse for a human being onto his feet. You hold onto him. I don't want to see for one solitary second, your hands anywhere but on the back of his neck. If he so much as sneezes, you have my permission to break his frigging neck. This is the type of scum we hang for desertion, treason, and murder. When we get through these ruins we will turn him over to the military authorities."

Achilles raised Frank Darcy to his feet with one strong arm. Darcy's eyes bulging from the pressure on his neck, his feet kicking as if he were already at the wrong end of the hangman's noose. Achilles shook him just long enough to terrify his prisoner before plopping him roughly back down to cower on the ground.

At Ruth's urgings, and satisfied that justice would be done, the Chinese returned to their wharf.

Sven told Achilles that Sergeant Pickens had put him in charge of the kitchen while he and the Sergeant explored the ruins, only there wasn't much of a kitchen now with the fire burning down to nothing more than hot embers.

"I stay, and you go with the Sergeant. I will get the fire going again." Achilles said with a hopeful expression.

"No, you are coming with me, and the kid stays." His temper

still not in check, Sergeant Pickens slapped the pike hard against his thigh causing him to grimace at the impact. "All right, let's get this here parade ah going," he said as he stepped over some fallen bricks into the smoky dark shadows of the ruined street car barns. Still holding a tight grip on Darcy's neck, Achilles gave him a shove as they followed the Sergeant.

Proud of his part in the capture of Frank Darcy, Sven stood tall, his chest puffed out, as he surveyed his surroundings. He was in charge of all this, and it scared him to death. He had started the day out as an apprentice cook, now he was a police officer. While the position was honorary, he was for the moment the ranking policeman in the area and responsible for the safety of all these people. Over by the once-upon-a-time kitchen he could see his mother in animated discussion with two other women she had for some reason bonded with. The Chinese stayed to their wharf, the Japs to theirs, and the women and children to theirs. The fire fighters were having some success keeping the fires at bay, and were now working a good block out from the waterfront. There wasn't much room left down by the ferry terminal, the mass of humanity now pressing in from all directions. Considering the chaos, everything seemed relatively calm. There was nothing for him to do, and after the excitement of capturing Frank Darcy, he was prime for adventure. That and the tremendous responsibility he felt, was unnerving. *What if someone actually needed help?*

"Sergeant Pickens wait for me." Sven said aloud as he made the decision to follow Sergeant Pickens and Achilles into the smoking ruins. While Achilles had his hands full with a traitorous and dangerous criminal, the Sergeant could use an extra set of eyes and ears. His mother's back was to him when he tried to wave. He called out, his cry going unheard as he turned and stepped into the ruins hoping that the Sergeant's trail would be easy to follow.

CHAPTER 50

IT IS DAMNED HARD TO RIDE TWO TO A SADDLE AT FULL gallop. It is even harder to keep the horse from throwing you when riding through a crowd as thick and as angry as the one they were in. At times it seemed impossible to move forward without running someone down. Henry felt his horse shift its weight to its rear quarter. Two riders on a rearing horse is suicide. As a lone outrider, Henry had had plenty of experience with this working cattle. If the horse reared with two riders it was pretty much a forgone conclusion that they would be eating some dirt. When he felt the horse's weight shift he leaned forward, arms extended, giving his horse loose reigns, while at the same time making sure that Katasui moved with him in a rider's dance. The moment his horse's feet were almost back on the ground, he kicked hard urging his horse forward, letting the horse know, with no doubt whatsoever, that it had to go forward regardless of the crowd of human beings boxing it in. When the horse went forward a little ways, Henry would then rein him in, then suddenly drive him forward again. The trick here was to double him the other way, then drive him forward from it giving the horse no chance to rear. The horse had to be brought to a stop, when again it wanted to panic as the crowd pressed forward, it had only one place to go - as it tried to rear, Henry had to repeat the process while doing his best not to lose Katasui.

Angry hands were all around them as he used his feet and the horse's bulk to push away strong men who wanted to pull them out of the saddle. They veered to the left, then to the right, no matter how they turned they were knocking folks over, running over some, and pissing everyone off. The horse's eyes bulged with terror, a terror even the most experienced rider could not keep in check much longer.

Sidney had to do the same, but couldn't. He knew that he had been shot. The pain wasn't bad yet. He could feel his shirt, front and back, grow wet, warm, and sticky as the hard riding helped pump blood out of the bullet wound. Because of the bleeding on both sides the bullet had most likely gone all the way through - that was the good news, the bleeding the bad. The edge of dizziness began to fog his thinking as he kicked his horse commanding it forward, aware that it wouldn't be long before he slipped from the saddle.

"Can you ride?" Henry called back to Katasui who clung tightly to his waist. "Yes," Katasui shouted back too loudly in his ear. The truth was that Katasui had never ridden before. He had good sea legs and could keep his balance in rough seas.

A quick learner, he had watched how the cowboys commanded their horses. He had also seen the brutal murder of Ichirou by the blood thirsty mob which gave him plenty of motivation to hang on. Given the choice, he would rather be the one in the saddle in charge of his own fate. "Yes, I can ride." He answered again.

Henry knew that Sidney was in trouble. Hell, they were all going to buy it if a little luck didn't come their way. If he were going to take on the final scrap of his life, he'd rather do it with Sidney, a man he'd long called a friend and brother, than with a Jap. He had never cottoned to the Chinks, neither had he given much thought to the Japs. This one seemed to be all right, but when the cards are laid out, he had no choice but to choose

Sidney. He coaxed his horse as close to Sidney as he could. Sidney tried to wave him off but was too weak to argue; seeing what Henry was about to attempt, he slowed his mount just enough to make the transfer possible. It was a risky move, the odds were lousy to change riders at this pace, even without the wild eyes and grabbing hands that wanted to yank them and their horses down.

"Take the reins," Henry shouted.

Soon as he felt Katasui's hands take hold of the leather reins, he leaned out to his right, forcing himself from his stirrup with a solid kick. He propelled himself onto the back of Sidney's horse, wrapped himself around Sidney while grabbing for the saddle horn to steady his seat, lest he go over the side taking Sidney with him. A quick glance to Katasui told him that the jump had been successful, however, the few seconds it took allowed the crowd to get dangerously close.

Sidney had almost fallen too weak to hold on. Grateful for Henry's embrace he allowed Henry to take the reins and command of the horse and their lives. "There," he said, his mouth as dry as pitch. He pointed over the heads of the crowd they had to ride through towards the makeshift kitchen and where he thought the waterfront police station to be - and help.

Rumors flew as fast as the cowboys drove their horses, each worse than the other, all feeding the lynch mob mentality: There was a gang of Japs, six or eight of them, riding on stolen horses, looking for white babies to steal right from their mama's grasps. Many a tall tale had been told over a beer in a saloon about Chinks who stole white babies so they could grind their tiny bones into a powder they thought to be an aphrodisiac. The Japs were no better, the slant of their eyes, different than the Chinks, suggesting a blacker more evil cunning.

The mob was led by a self-appointed vigilante, a tall thin man in a dusty driver's cloak with black rimmed auto goggles perched on his head rather than a cap. "One of the Jap bastards," the tall thin man announced for all to hear, "somehow got himself a gun and shot a white woman so he could steal her baby. I winged the yellow son-of-a-bitch just as he was about to snatch the babe from his dear mama's dying arms." His voice took on hellfire preacher's authority as he gave witness a second time, just as if it were God's truth as he waved the 45 and took a pot shot at the fleeing riders. Most had not seen or heard a thing, few knew that it was two white men riding with a lone Jap, the only thing they needed to know was what the man in the dusty driver cloak said was the truth.

A dozen longshoremen, a few who had earlier stood on the picket line established by Inspector McCann, now paid little heed to the former police station. They stood idly by, telling tall tales while sipping whiskey from several bottles that had been lifted from a collapsed saloon. Tired, drunk, hungry, and bored, they quickly fell behind the tall man and his cries to drive all the Chinks and Asiatics into the bay. "Let them drown or swim back to where they came from. God brought this calamity to cleanse the city of its sins and debauchery. It's time to rid it of plague ridden-rats and the yellow heathen that have plagued us all for too long. Drown them all, I say." The longshoremen with their pikes, clubs and lynching ropes gave the tall man the power and authority he needed to do just that. More than once in San Francisco's racist history, mobs like this had taken it upon themselves to remove the filthy plague-ridden Chinks, Filipino tree monkeys, and Japs from the city. This time there were no police or military to stop them, not that they would.

The jump Henry had made saved Sidney but had cost them the scant few seconds lead they had. They rode hard. Weak from blood loss, Sidney barely held on to consciousness as Henry held him as firm to the horse as he could.

Katasui was the first to run his horse directly through the hot ash remains of the cooking fire. He had been told that if they made it this far there would be police to protect them. He saw no police. All he saw were scores of refugees, mostly women as he drove his horse towards the Japanese wharf screaming in his native language a warning to alert his people.

Henry's courage faltered when he saw what remained of the police and cooking station. Sidney had said that once they got this far there would be plenty of help. He hadn't known what to expect, and had not hoped for much, but nothing came as a jarring disappointment. He reined his horse in as he felt Sidney begin to slip from his grasp.

Dizzy and barely holding on, Sidney leaned down towards a woman who seemed to know him. There were three women who came to his aid. "Where is everyone? What has . . . ?" He did not recognize any of them. He fell silent, too weak to find the next word.

"He was shot in the back," Henry said as he pointed towards the fast approaching mob. "by them."

"Take him over there," Donadina ordered as she pointed towards the wharf occupied by the Chinese.

"If it's all the same to you, I'll follow Katasui." Henry said. "You had best come with me, ladies, the Chink wharf should hold the attention of these bastards for a while. Sidney, if you can stand, Kat and me will get you there." He glanced around to see that Katasui had already ridden to the wharf.

Sidney made a small effort to stand then fell still.

It galled him to leave Sidney, though his odds were likely better in these women's care than with him. On horseback Henry remained a Jap loving traitor. On the ground he would soon become a dead man. He cursed his own stupidity in leaving his family in Daly City and coming back to lend a hand. He clicked at his horse telling it to get going as Sidney tried to rise but failed again. There was nothing else Henry could do; his presence would only incite the crowd. "You take care of him," he said as he coached his horse towards the Japanese. "Now, if you will excuse me."

Donaldina called out in Chinese to three Chinamen for help with carrying Sidney to the women's and children's wharf. They shook their heads in terror and ran back to their wharf as a pack of menacing white men came within a few yards of the still smoking cooking fire. "Come on ladies, help me with this poor man, we've got to get him somewhere safe," Donaldina demanded as if she were the leader God had chosen to rally His children on this bleak day.

Marta took Sidney's feet and lifted as Donaldina tried to lift him from the other end. Weak, fighting to stay conscious, not sure who held him, Sidney struggled to pull free. "Come on, if we stay here, we will be beaten to death." Marta's stern words were far from reassuring.

"Leave me," Sidney said wanting to be anything but a useless dying man who put others in needless danger. Odd, he thought, as he saw her pale face turn three shades paler. He closed his eyes as he faded into a swirling, meaningless fog.

Donaldina had never been one to cower before brutish men. This was different, there were so many of them. She had not felt as helpless as she did now since she was a small child fearing the wrath of her father. She felt a little giddy as her blood seemed to rush from her face as she tried to rise.

Marta set the man's feet down as she turned in a slow circle.

They were surrounded by a hundred hate-filled, ugly men, who demanded a sacrifice for their blood lust. Their eyes were on this small man who now lay unconscious at her feet. She remembered that the man had been with Inspector McCann. Police? Where were the others? Sven? *Sven, oh please, God, where ever you are do not come here. You are so young and they are so many. I love you son. Please remember that I love you and take care of your brothers.*

Lavinia slowly turned the same circle seeing what Marta had seen - the blood lust and anger written on the faces of so many men. *Are all men like these? Would my papa have sought to murder other men as these men do?* She looked at Marta and thought, *She stays by the side of this helpless man knowing that she may be murdered because she has stayed - Dear Lord, her children?* With that thought she set her eyes on the tall man. She took one step at a time forward until she was close enough to smell him, close enough to hear his breathing, close enough as a woman to challenge his space.

"Rufus Crowley, is it now?" Her Dutch accent was strong, but so were her words. She knew who this man was. Crowley owned one of the larger saloons on the Barbary and had come one night with money in hand to offer her father a job. The quality of the beer her father made was stealing business from Crowley's saloon and so he offered her father double his wages to come and work for him. The money had been tempting, but in the end, her father would have nothing to do with him, not even at three times the pay. Crowley had his hand in every vice that gave the Barbary Coast its wicked reputation. The thought came to her that Crowley had come to their home just before her father disappeared.

Crowley recognized her, but couldn't quite place from where.

Perhaps it was her black missionary clothes that befuddled him. In other attire, she could easily pass for a saloon girl, a dancer, a higher class working girl that can only be found at a fine French restaurant. He slowly smiled. Yes, it had been at the Bistro La Promenade where he had enjoyed her - still, he wasn't quite sure. Looking down, he was a good two feet taller, he could see when she tilted her head just right that beneath her hat she had an alluring, sexy face with strikingly beautiful eyes made all that more attractive without any makeup. A beautiful young rose ready to be plucked. The little flower had stopped him, had stopped his posse dead in their tracks only a few yards short from one of the riders he intended to hang. "Give me that rope," he demanded from a man who stood nearby leering at her. Taking the rope, he reached out to push her away. "We'll hang the son-of-a-bitch right now. Someone get some water; I want him awake so he can feel his own neck snap."

Lavinia took two quick steps backwards to avoid his touch.

"You will not."

It was her voice that was formidable, and the way that she stood up to the tall man who just as easily could take the Colt 45 from where he had it tucked in his belt and shut her up with one quick clinch on the trigger. A few in the crowd knew that it was not beneath Crowley to shoot a woman. Their angry self-important roar quieted as they waited to see what would come of this little woman's impertinence.

"You stand there a mighty man, with a hundred or more good citizens from what is left of this fair city, ready to commit murder of the foulest kind, that of an innocent man." Lavinia said as she struggled to keep shaking legs from collapsing beneath her.

"The Japs shot and killed a white woman while trying to steal her baby to use in their filthy heathen practices. That man helped the Japs get away. I shot one dead, and we'll bring the rest to justice." Crowley said. "That man helped the Japs get away and for that, we'll be sending him to the same place we are going to send every yellow skinned monkey we find this day - straight to hell."

Many of the men around her roared their approval, with a few taking a step forward. Lavinia took another step back to where Marta knelt next to the unconscious man they were about to murder.

Donaldina was stopped just short of the wharf by three rough looking stevedores who would let her go no further.

The Chinese were gathered just beyond her reach. Silent. Trapped. They watched with an understanding of what was about to happen. As soon as they had hung one of their own, the white men would come for them. The dark brooding smoke throughout the city foreshadowed the bleakness that awaited them.

Donaldina could see there was nothing she could do to stop it. The mob, led by the tall, thin, devil himself, would murder the fallen cowhand, then Lavinia and Marta too - or worse. *You will answer to God for this on Judgment Day and it will be you who will suffer the agonies of hell.* She ached to scream this aloud for all to hear. The men who stood between her and the wharf frightened her. She remained silent. She turned, her eyes demanding that the quay of men who stood between her and the Chinese step aside. No one wanted to take on this holier-than-thou matron, and let her through. Without looking back, she went directly to the wharf, wondering with each step how she could have turned her back on Marta and Lavinia. Her most urgent need was to find a way to save her Chinese.

"This man is a police officer." Marta screamed as she rose to stand beside Lavinia.

Sidney heard distant voices but could not find his way out of his mind's fog. He remained unaware that the only things keeping him alive were these two women's skirts which he lay behind.

"He's no cop. Where's his badge?" One man asked, now slightly hesitant about moving in for the kill. "He's too much a runt to be a cop."

"He rode with Inspector Cornelius McCann only a few hours ago, driving the crimps from the waterfront." Marta knelt back down taking Sidney's hand in hers.

"This man saved my life." Lavinia raised her arm pointing toward the women and children's wharf where many had gathered to watch. When the crimps came, we thought we were all lost. Hope never seemed so distant, so fragile, until Inspector McCann and a few brave men rode in against staggering odds." Many of the men mumbled and muttered amongst themselves as their thoughts moved from the yellow heathens to the dreaded crimps. There were some who had been shanghaied in the past who swore aloud. Lavinia's words seemed to drain the blind hatred right out of them.

The tall man sensed that he was losing control.

"There is not one man amongst you who does not fear the crimps." This time Lavinia pointed at the tall man. "Isn't that right, Mr. Rufus Crowley, owner of Crowley's Saloon, and three or is it four boarding houses that cater to sailors and long-shoremen, many of whom are robbed, murdered or shanghaied. How many crimps on your payroll, Mr. Rufus Crowley? How many here have had the pleasure of Mr. Rufus Crowley's hospitality, taken from your boarding rooms after drinking liquor spiked with laudanum. It has been said that you do business with the Chinese Tongs in smuggling Chinese girls to serve as prostitutes." Her father had told her much about Rufus Crowley but never anything about doing business with the Chinese. Her lie turned the mob instantly against Crowley, not because they had any sympathy for the Chinese girls, but because smuggling more Chinese into the country only made it more difficult to get rid of them all.

"I say we hang Crowley with his own rope," one man shouted as three others moved towards Crowley. A second later, the man who shouted died with a bullet through his heart.

The eight men immediately behind Crowley stepped up to protect their boss. The two men who remained were beaten to the ground with clubs. Rufus Crowley fired a shot into the wave of men who now came at him. What started with a dozen men wanting Crowley, turned quickly into a melee, a free-for-all, where a couple of hundred men fought, some not knowing whose side they were on or what had started it.

Marta shielded Sidney as the melee raged out of control.

Lavinia stood alone for a moment then lowered herself placing her arms around Marta as they prayed to survive the storm around them.

Cracking the nearest man who seemed a threat over the head with his pistol, Crowley reached into his coat pocket for more bullets. "Bill," he called out to one of his body guards," find me that little flower and bring the bitch to me. Now!"

CHAPTER 51

All but one of the Japanese fishing boats had returned to the wharf where their family's anxiously waited.

Cornelius stood transfixed at the view from the lead boat as it made its way from the Ferry Terminal back to the wharf where the Japanese were encamped. This was the first time in a long day that he had more than two minutes to catch his breath and to reflect; to sweat over what could possibly happen next. He was not the worrying kind, usually letting things happen as they may. Today was different, it had seemed that when something bad came, it was followed by something worse, and then worse again. He thought of his close escape from beneath the wharf, their betrayal by a fellow officer, the stupid army Lieutenant, the battle with the crimps, then the rats, the death of August and T. J. - it had been one thing after another. He was tired, but knew that somehow he had to steel himself, for the worst was yet to come. Worst? No matter what he imagined might come next, he would underestimate its ferocity. He looked at the smoke sodden sky wondering what time it might be. He wondered how much time had passed. An hour seemed like a day, a day a week, and he was feeling every bit of it. His shoulder hurt, but so did every muscle in his body, every inch of skin covering his flesh. Hell, even his eye lids ached. He was thirsty, bone tired, and had a headache, a pounding drum behind his exhausted blood shot eyes that reminded him with each beat of that drum that this day was far from over.

He caught a glimpse of the sun and guessed it to be around

four in the afternoon. The massive smoke cyclone that bellowed above the flame engorged city blotted out most of the sun so he really couldn't tell. *The fires will light the night,* he thought, *in some places it will be brighter than it had been during the day.* He looked at the gently rolling bay knowing that below the surface it will grow dark early, the water reflecting no stars, no moon, only the brilliant orange, red, yellow, and deep hued blue of the flames reflected on the surface, leaving the water below as dark as dark can be. This worried him, because if they did not get the divers back to the ferry berth in time, they wouldn't be able to plant the dynamite in the sunken Chinese junk until morning. "Can't you make this thing go any faster?" he muttered to Hiroshi who stood beside him. He did not mean to sound angry, but he was. He was, in truth, helpless and vulnerable against everything that raged against him. He was subservient to the generosity of the Japanese in saving the lives of thousands - if they could.

Hiroshi held his hand up to test the wind, gauged the sails, and grunted - saying nothing more. They were at the mercy of the winds. The fires created their own winds making it difficult for the best of sailors to make any headway. Both men watched with dread and amazement the huge throng of people filling the waterfront. They searched for but could not find anyone on horseback. All they could do is hope that Sidney and the others had gotten through. If so, could they get there before Sidney and the Japanese divers tried to return overland, the return trip by boat not only quicker but much safer?

Cornelius' head turned sharply, every instinct he had testing the wind for a gunshot, a shift in the raw noise that sounded most unfriendly towards his riders. His gut told him that on shore things were not going well - that he should not be out here - that he should be with them - but there was nothing for him to do but stare at the mass of humanity where trouble brewed. The wind shifted, the crew reacting immediately bringing the craft back onto due course for the Japanese wharf.

Chapter 52

HENRY HAD NO CHOICE BUT TO LEAVE SIDNEY BEHIND AND it brought bitter acid to his stomach. He had made the right decision, to stay would have would have accomplished nothing. That he was the only white man on the Japanese wharf only added to his guilt and confusion. His horse, exhausted, breathing heavily, remained otherwise quiet, while he paced an angry man's path ten steps forward, then ten steps back; and back again. This wasn't anything like being caught between a rock and a hard place. He was looking at a landslide of killer boulders thundering down a steep mountain slope. He was out of time and all the choices led to either heartbreak or an early grave.

Katasui spoke quickly to his people.

Henry paced.

The Japanese nodded to each other, their decision made. They would not stay. They had nothing to defend themselves with besides the meaningless sacrifice of their lives. A wasted life does not mean an honorable death. To take a stand here, against these white men would be suicide. A few of the old men spoke amongst themselves about a noble death. Their clan were fishermen, not warriors and here, there was no shame in fleeing to the safety of the sea.

Henry could feel the eyes of the Japanese on him, curious and mistrusting. He grabbed the reigns of his horse, his feet positioned for him to mount, his weight shifting with his uncertainty.

"Is your life that meaningless?" Katasui asked the man he had just ridden through hell with. "Ichirou, my friend and brother is dead. There is no honor in his death, nothing can change that. If I were to ride back to seek revenge, my death would be just as meaningless and my ancestors would turn their eyes away in shame. I know little about the white man's ways, but I have heard that suicide is an unforgivable sin. What good will it do for you to seek death in this way?"

Henry's feet settled flat on the ground as his shoulders fell in defeat. The look in his eyes said more than words could ever convey.

"Mr. Sidney will live, it is not his time. Nor is it yours.

Nor is it my peoples'. We will seek safety at sea and I would be honored if you would join us as a friend; a man I have learned to respect."

Henry followed Katasui's arm as he pointed out over the water to where the first of the Japanese fishing boats could be seen coming for them.

I'll be damned. Henry thought, *I will not flee like a coward, under the protection of these . . . these yellow monkeys.* He corrected himself with that last thought, having learned to his surprise a little respect for the Japanese. Chuckling at himself internally he admitted that he was a bigot, always had been; this day the old cowboy who was set pretty much in his ways had learned a thing or two.

In one practiced movement, he mounted his horse, prepared to ride towards whatever fate awaited him.

Katasui was just as quick in grabbing the reins. "No. I cannot let you do this."

Henry didn't much care for a Jap holding him back, even if he was right. If it had been anything but a Jap boat, he might have considered it. He also knew that Katasui was right in trying to keep him from riding head-strong and foolishly into the melee, where he would more than likely get his head bashed in. He had to trust that the three women they had run across would find a way to care for Sidney until he found help. "Katasui, I appreciate the offer, but I can't go sailing off to no sunset when a pal of mine is down. And, I ain't stupid, if that is what you're thinking. I won't be riding into that ruckus like some drunk cowboy whoopin' it up on the first payday after riding herd for six weeks without a drop of whiskey or a woman. Sorry about the loss of your pal. Ichirou," Henry said, mispronouncing the name. "Right now, I've gotta ride out and see where the army is holed up and get their sorry asses down here where they can do us some good."

Katasui let go of the reins.

Henry clicked his tongue twice as he kicked his horse forward. He doubted his horse could make it through the ruins around the collapsed trolley barns, so he rode straight toward the fire engulfed financial district where he hoped he'd be able to swing to the left and find a safe route to Market Street where he had last seen the army. As he left, a large fire erupted just in front of the Chinese Wharf startling both he and his horse. Distracted, he was off course from the first moment he tried to ride for help.

CHAPTER 53

DONALDINA'S HEART RACED AS SHE REACHED THE EDGE OF the wharf. She had been chosen to bring the Chinese under God's care. Had she failed God somehow and is He now punishing the Chinese for her sins? She had converted so few, too few, and now the fires and the legends of hell were drawing near. She stopped at the edge of the wharf where she could see two or three hundred Chinese, most of them women, children, and the elderly. There were not enough men to make a stand, and if they did, their efforts would only further light the fuse of violence and hatred.

Donaldina turned and stared at the mob now surrounding Lavinia and Marta, regretting that she had not demanded that they come with her. She paused, for the first time not sure of herself. "Please, Holy Mother, give me the strength and the wisdom to save these children of God." Oh, how she wished these violent men would just go away. *Why today, why now?* Hadn't the Chinese suffered enough? Her children, the ones who had chosen Christ as their Savior, will find joy and peace in heaven. But the others, the ones she had not yet been able to convert, would surely go from this hell on earth to an even greater one where their heathen souls would feed the fires that are never quenched.

What is this? What she saw both surprised and angered her. Lavinia, a small, quiet spoken woman, had somehow brought the lynch mob to a standstill. There she stood, a helpless pixie, standing up to one hundred, no hundreds of enraged men who could rape and murder her without blinking an eye. They had stopped their bloodthirsty march and were listening to her words. It looked as if she was directly challenging the tall menacing man who had been leading them. *What is happening here?* She thought. *First, it's Marta, a mother who should be thinking of the safety of her children, who instead thought for some reason that she could challenge my every move. Has God abandoned me? And now Lavinia, Lord, have mercy on my poor tired soul.* With these thoughts she knew that she had only one choice: to save the Chinese, even if it cost her own life. She looked around frantically. *What? How? Please, Lord, give me something.* The Chinese were trapped on a wharf and she doubted if any of them could swim. If she tried to bring them off, the devil's legion would seize them and they would be murdered right down to the last child.

Wait, what is this? She stopped, waiting for her thought to mature. A few of the Chinese women had built cooking fires using small ceramic containers filled with oil or grease to heat tea and to make soups that stretched the fish they had been given by Achilles. Not far away, she saw that Ruth was pouring tea that had been heated on a similar fire. *Bless you child.*

The women had found cooking oil, as well as coal oil, in barrels in the back of the fish market that somehow had survived when the market had burned - that the barrels, most dented and crushed, had not caught fire had been luck.

Donaldina had her miracle.

At Donaldina's urging, it did not take long for a crew of quick Chinese men to discreetly make their way back to the ruined fish market and return with as many pieces of the crushed oil barrels as they could. The oil soaked wood from the barrels ignited with a sudden thump, soon burning hot enough to ignite the tar resins that were used to coat and protect the wooden wharf from the ravages of time and weather. The fire produced a thick acrid plume of smoke obscuring the view of anyone looking towards them.

Donaldina hoped the flames and dense smoke was enough to give the vigilantes cause to think twice before coming after the Chinese. Now the greater threat was the fire itself. If it spread to the rest of the wharf, it would finish the Chinese just the same. The fire had to be fed and burn as long as the threat from the vigilantes remained; its spread carefully managed. In a continual chain, buckets, teapots, anything that could hold water was filled with sea water, then dumped on the wooden planks nearest the fire to keep it from spreading farther out onto the wharf.

The black cloying smoke prevented Donaldina and everyone else on the wharf from seeing what was happening onshore. If the vigilantes decided to challenge the smoke screen they would be trapped. Donaldina called Ruth and her Christian Chinese to her as they all knelt and prayed.

CHAPTER 54

THE FLAMES AND SMOKE THAT ENGULFED THE CITY MADE IT impossible for Cornelius to distinguish one or two mounted riders surrounded by tens of thousands of people as the boat angled in towards the wharf. *Well, it can't get much worse than this.* He thought. So far, he had refused to accept the thought that they might not be able to clear the ferry berth in time. Time was something they did not have. If he was a betting man, and he wasn't, he'd have already bet all he had on the Japanese saving this day. He smiled at that. He did not smile at much, but now and then, one snuck up to the surface. He was just beginning to recognize what a remarkable people the Japanese are.

"What the hell!" Cornelius exclaimed.

The entire Japanese crew turned as one, surprised at the suddenness of an explosive fire. A short, squat, fisherman, on the bow, called back in Japanese to Hiroshi pointing ashore where a sudden dense black column of smoke and flame had erupted from the land's end of the wharf, which sheltered the Chinese. The fire was dangerously close to the Japanese wharf, but it was not what the man was pointing to. Just to the left, where Cornelius thought his police station and field kitchen ought to be, there appeared to be a large skirmish. From where he stood, Cornelius guessed there were several hundred involved. *That is no skirmish. That is a full blown, god-damned riot.* He thought as he cursed himself for allowing the Chinese to stay. *Hindsight is a bitch. I should have kept them moving off and away from the waterfront.* He had thought that something like this might happen, and damned if it hadn't. *Folks down on their luck, caught between a rock and a hard place, are apt to look for someone else to blame. Well, there you have it, and there isn't much I can do about it without some sizable help, and the army has so far proved to be all but useless.* The longshoremen he had recruited earlier were probably knee deep into the fight . . . but whose side were they taking? What are they fighting for? Cornelius scratched the back of his head. *They've just plumb gone nuts.*

"We must get our people off." Hiroshi said, his fists clenching with tension. Orders were shouted, the crew already doing everything that could be done to get their boats beside the Japanese Wharf as fast as humanly possible.

"You won't get any argument from me," Cornelius answered, as he studied the riot ashore. Sure enough, he could just make out a few of the longshoremen. It was white man against white man, no sign of the army, no sign of any lawful authority. The riot was spreading in every direction except towards the three wharves which he had assigned to women and kids, the Chinese, and finally the Japanese.

Cornelius chuckled to himself. Smart. Sidney must have gotten through. The smoke from the fire masks both the Chinese and the Japanese wharves. He checked that thought. Hold on, Sidney is a good man but I doubt he is that sharp. But, of course it's got to be Choice. Choice Pickens, you clever bastard. While I've been off playing Sheriff and cowboy, you have been the one good cop left standing.

Puzzled, Hiroshi looked at Cornelius. It was then that he felt a knowing sadness and began to understand Cornelius' dilemma. White men have always been prone to violence; ego driven, they are often blind to common sense and honor. It did not matter what the cause of the riot ashore was. With this great calamity turning this once great city into nothing but ashes, it is more important to come together rather than destroy what little is left. When he thought of his people, he felt pride in how they had all stepped forward to help in a place where they were not wanted.

The shadow of ignorance and prejudice had always darkened their lives at times, lowering their spirits to no better than that of a caged bird. Frightened of what might lay outside its cage, its bittersweet song lifting just enough above its imprisonment to understand the music of its own heart. He knew that it had been difficult for Cornelius McCann to cross the bitter line of race and take his hand in friendship as two men on equal standing. Hiroshi shook his head sadly at the riot ashore and then brought his gaze back to this one brave white man, the first he could honestly say was his friend.

The bow bumped against the wharf as the sails were brought in, and ropes tossed ashore. There was room for only two boats alongside the wharf, so no lines were tied off as the waiting family members quickly boarded.

The Japanese had every right to take their families to the mainland or to just anchor somewhere out in the bay to wait and watch the city burn. He thought as he looked at the late afternoon sun. He doubted there was enough time to get back to the Ferry Terminal and do what had to be done. He could not fault the Japanese if they turned their backs and simply sailed away. What had the white man ever done for them besides spit on their race and tell them to go somewhere else. His back-up plan . . . Hell, he did not have one. This was where it ended. He just hoped that he could find Choice, Sidney, and Henry and get the hell off the waterfront themselves before it was too late.

He jumped ashore while there was still a good foot between the bobbing boat and the wharf. Ashore, he turned and bowed towards Hiroshi showing his respect. "Thank you, and good luck."

Hiroshi noted Cornelius' effort, appreciated it, and bowed to him, his eyes never leaving Cornelius. Respect was not something the Japanese often got from a white man. He saw the exhaustion beginning to consume the man, the look of defeat beginning to mask Cornelius' face. He grabbed a line and swung ashore.

"This is not done." Hiroshi admonished as Cornelius started to turn away. "There is still enough daylight left to do what must be done." He put his hand on Cornelius's shoulder, a gesture that carried great meaning. "We both made an oath to do everything within our power to open the way for the ferries to come in. There are many people who will be hurt if we do not do this. I still plan to honor my oath." He paused. "And you, Inspector McCann, will you honor yours?"

Cornelius looked around, stone silent, as he measured himself against the task one last time. He was bone tired, physically ached 'most everywhere, his mind as fuzzy as his spirit. There was nothing to be done here, but much to be done if they could clear the way for the ferry boats. His eyes gazed back towards the Ferry Terminal whose building appeared remarkably intact. The truth he feared was that the building might collapse at any time. "I guess I've got nothing better to do at the moment. How much time do you figure we have?"

"Too little, but enough, if we hurry. Soon as my people are aboard we will make sail to the Ferry Terminal. Please come aboard and we will make our plans as we sail back together."

Cornelius nodded as he held up five fingers. "Give me a moment to find Sidney, Sergeant Pickens, and Henry. We can use all the help we can get."

"The boats will set sail when everyone is on board. We cannot risk a confrontation with the vigilantes, there are the women and children to think of," Hiroshi said. If you are not aboard, I will have no choice but to sail without you."

Cornelius hesitated, unable to decide if he should board or not.

Hiroshi understood. "We thank you for providing us this wharf as a temporary shelter against this bitter day." He bowed again. "Your heart says that you must at least try to save these men who are your brothers." We will go directly to the Ferry Terminal. Our divers must get into the water while there is still enough light. Please, where is the dynamite?"

Cornelius knew that he was right. There was not a moment to lose. If he found Choice and the others, they could make a run to the Ferry Terminal and be there about the same time as the boats. It made no sense to hold the boats any longer than necessary. The big *IF* was getting into and out of the riot with his crew intact - that is if Pickens, Sydney, and Henry were still standing. He told Hiroshi where he had stored the dynamite on the boat, then waved one last time as Hiroshi cast-off to make room for the next fishing boat to come in.

This time Cornelius did make a personal oath: With or without his team, he would meet Hiroshi at the Ferry Terminal within the hour, or die trying.

Salt water had rendered Cornelius' side arm most likely inoperable. If he got into a no-win pissing contest, he might get a shot off, more likely it would blow up in his face. He took thirty-seconds to study the melee that now surrounded Achilles' former outdoor kitchen. He knew himself to be a fool for staying ashore when he should have gone with Hiroshi. Now, he was one big stupid damned fool to think that he could find any of his men in the mayhem and extract them without getting himself or them killed. *Well, I've been knee deep in shit more than once in my day, but today I've managed to go in head first.*

Cornelius did not often wear his badge, sometimes the shiny metal shield made it more difficult to get the job done. His tendency had always been to show it when and where needed. This time he pinned it on what was left of his raggedy shirt for all to see. Eyes narrow, fists ready, the crick in his neck telling him to turn around and walk away. Inspector Cornelius McCann went where duty dictated he had to go, wishing like hell he had a good cigar.

CHAPTER 55

THE HAPHAZARD TRAIL THROUGH THE RUBBLE HADN'T BEEN that difficult or taken long, and their luck had been good as they found no crimps lurking in the shadows. Choice Pickens and Achilles could hear voices ahead which sounded as if they might be firefighters or the military. Relieved, he started to quicken their steps. "Come on, the sooner we turn this rotten traitor over to the military, the sooner he'll find the hangman's noose." With that thought, he hesitated. There was no guarantee that Frank Darcy would ever be tried and hung. Still, once they crossed back out into the light of day he would have no choice but to turn him over. Here in the shadows he could make sure that Darcy got the justice he deserved. *Damned if that weren't tempting. He could almost taste the satisfaction. No bullet, just slit his throat and let him choke on his own blood. No . . . No, Achilles would never go for that. The gentle giant has too much heart and not enough hatred for the son-of-a-bitch.*

He heard a few bricks fall and the sound of someone running hard through the rubble behind them. His decision was made for him, better to push on through than risk a fight with who knows how many. This was a stupid place to die, after all he had been through today. Darcy will only slow them down. He took out his gun, counted the few bullets he had left, took aim at Darcy's right knee. *If the shot didn't give them away, Darcy's scream would.* Choice thought as he hesitated. The paralyzing fear in Darcy's eyes was a wonderful thing to see.

"Sergeant Pickens, it's me, Sven."

"Sven?" Choice turned as Sven came over a small pile of rubble. He listened as the breathless youth tried to explain why he had abandoned his post to join them. It all made sense, the kid had never gotten the order, and lacked the experience to do the job if he had stayed.

He ordered Achilles to go back to the wharves to protect the women and children the best he could, and see if he could get the cooking fires going again. Sven could watch his backside as Choice dragged Darcy out to the authorities and arranged for an escape route for all the folks trapped back on the waterfront.

"Were you really going to shoot him?" Sven asked.

Choice pulled the trigger. BLAM!

Darcy shrieked as the bullet shattered his knee as he was thrown down onto a haphazard pile of bricks.

"Thanks for reminding me." Choice said.

Achilles couldn't believe what he had just seen.

"Sven, you and me have some work to do and can't be slowed down any longer by this slime-ball. Damn fool tried to escape, so I shot him. Cornelius said he didn't want any more killing so I shot him in the knee."

BLAM.

"I just shot him in the other knee because he wouldn't stop squawking. The first time I only nicked him. Now he's got both knees busted. There will be no running away for him, that's for damn sure."

Achilles almost laughed, shook his big shaggy head, and turned back towards the waterfront.

A moment later three soldiers appeared in the path leading

towards the Barbary, their rifles aimed square on Choice's chest. Choice held his gun hand high, not dropping the weapon, spinning it slightly on an extended finger. "Sergeant Choice Pickens, San Francisco Police Department, glad you gentlemen could make it. I've got a wounded prisoner who tried to escape. I'm here to turn him over to the Army on charges of manslaughter, shanghaiing, treason, and a few more charges, soon as I can figure them out."

CHAPTER 56

CORNELIUS CAME WITHIN SPITTING DISTANCE OF THE donnybrook. *Two women down,* he thought as he approached the edge of the skirmish reluctantly. *Wait, there's something else awry here. Man down, the two women are protecting him.* By God, its

Sidney . . . And he don't look too good. I know one of those women, small, petite, good looking. Where have I seen her before? Down boy, now is not the time to invite her to a Sunday picnic overlooking the goddamned Golden Gate.

"Damn!" He saw and heard a club come down, crushing the skull of a heavy bearded man who slumped dead from the blow almost on top of the women. One of the women had covered Sidney's body with her own, hiding him. The younger one, as pretty as any gal he had even seen, rose from her knees to stand, eyes full of spitfire and damnation to challenge a man with ox-like forearms and a battle scarred face who had just bludgeoned to death the other. Through the roar, Cornelius could hear her defiant words.

"It's over, do you hear me, it's over! Look around you, this city is dying and too many good people with it. There will be no more blood spilled here this day. What kind of mad animals are you?" She was so small and frail addressing this carnivorous grizzly bear.

The crowd quieted to her plea.

"Over, not yet little flower, not until the boss has had his way with you." His laughter rolled like bad thunder.

Cornelius read the man's intentions. He wanted to pluck her petals for his own pleasure before passing on any remains to his boss. He also recognized the boss. Rufus Crowley was as dangerous as he was tall. For the moment, Cornelius forgot that he was human and as vulnerable as any man. He forgot about Sidney who lay perhaps mortally wounded only a few feet away. He knew that a second woman was there, just as vulnerable, but saving this beautiful young woman from these murderous apes became the single overpowering event, a catharsis for everything that had driven the day . . . or for that matter his life up to this moment. He sized up the man he faced, found himself to be lacking, and charged ahead anyway, knowing he hadn't much of a chance.

Lavinia knew exactly who Cornelius was the moment she saw him. Her heart wept as she watched her knight charge forward. The grizzly sized man dropped him cold with one blow from his steel like arm and right fist. Cornelius had never been flattened like that by any man - yet alone with one blow. His sight blurry, the violent chaos around him swimming in a gray fog, he tried, but failed to rise.

Crowley stepped forward kicking a fallen club from out of Cornelius' reach. While Crowley had a gun and easily could have used it, he restrained himself. He had had altercations with Inspector McCann before, and watching McCann being beaten beyond recognition might prove to be more entertaining.

The donnybrook around them quieted as each man, regardless of side, saw that the game was up for McCann. A few knew him, others wondering if the tall man was going to sanction the murder of a police officer with this many witnesses. A few started wagering bets as McCann, Crowley, the grizzly -

the man the crowd knew as Brubeck, and the brave little flower of a woman, became the center of it all, the lynch-mob soon forgetting the Japanese.

"I got two bits that the cop can last three blows from Brubeck."

"Two bits more, Brubeck finishes him in two," another answered.

Cornelius heard ringing in his ears. He barely could make out the voices, but nevertheless heard the bets and doubted that he could take another blow. He had seen some of Brubeck's handy-work in the morgue. Brubeck was a heavy weight bare-knuckled fighter who had never lost a match. Cornelius tasted blood, knowing that his nose was busted without having to touch it, not that it mattered. He looked at the young woman, who had stood so remarkably brave, and saw the tears as they formed in her eyes. It was then that he knew where he had seen her before, in the window in the apartment house just at the edge of the Barbary. *How had such a beautiful and refined woman come to live in a neighborhood like this,* he remembered thinking. Now, here she was, which left him with no choice. Stretching his bruised jaw, trying to clear his vision, and the ringing in his ears, he tried to rise.

Crowley scooped up the club and tossed it to Brubeck.

"Finish him!" He ordered. "Any other wagers, gentlemen? I'm offering four to one this poor excuse for an officer of the law can even rise to defend himself." His laughing bark was quickly followed by a few guffaws from the crowd.

"I've got ten cents he gets to his feet." Another bet. He fell back, his coin went flying through the air as he was nearly bowled over. "Look out!" someone cried, as an equally-sized bear of a man plowed into Brubeck.

As surprised as everyone else, Cornelius stared as Achilles met Brubeck blow for blow, his strength overpowering and defeating the street fighter in four powerful punches.

Crowley withdrew his gun from inside his coat, bringing it immediately to bear on Achilles.

"No!" Lavinia put herself immediately between Crowley and Achilles, the gun a mere foot from her heart.

Crowley turned his sight on Cornelius, still unable to rise. That left the big Greek. Crowley brought the gun back leveling it first at Achilles face then back at the little woman who stood between them. "Too bad," he said as he pulled the trigger."

"No," Marta screamed.

"You miserable bastard." Cornelius swore as he struggled to rise.

The shot was deafening as it echoed across the waterfront. The bullet missed as the gun was knocked from Crowley's grasp as two men seized him from behind. The gun had been close enough to leave a flash burn on Lavinia's cheek. A third man picked up the club that lay nearby and drove it forcefully into Crowley stomach, quickly pulling it back before striking Crowley's left knee shattering it.

The suddenness and shock of the tremendous bang told Lavinia that she had just died, and she couldn't quite grasp that she had not. Her right eye temporarily blinded by the flash and powder residue, hearing only a piercing shrill, she slumped to the ground.

Thinking that she had been shot, the two men holding the anguished bully pulled him upright, as the man with the club brought the club around with righteous anger shattering his other knee.

Shocked, not shot, aware that they were all still caught up in a violent dangerous moment, Lavinia grabbed the gun, and held it close to her chest as she crawled backwards to Cornelius thrusting it into his hand.

Crowley, once the tall man, now beaten and small, howled with agony and helplessness as he was released to drop to the ground a legless scarecrow no longer menacing to anyone.

Cornelius used his loose shirt sleeve to dab at the gun powder stain that stung and partially closed one of Lavinia's eyes.

To a man, those nearest fell silent, the only sounds that of the fire raging around them, the lap-lap-lap of the waves as they rolled beneath the nearby wharves, an enraged flock of gulls, and Crowley's last whimpers.

Achilles helped Lavinia and Cornelius to their feet. He could not help but notice the way Lavinia looked at Cornelius, as if he was the hero she had longed for all her life.

"Damn, now I have done seen it all," whispered Sidney to the woman who held him close. Marta had not noticed that he had come to, in time to witness Lavinia's courageous moment. "That there gal has more guts than I've seen in any man," he whispered, as he tried to work his words through his dusty dry mouth.

Cornelius heard Sidney and smiled. Sidney was alive and that was a good thing. This courageous and beautiful woman, looked up at him with her one good eye as no woman had ever looked at him before. He wondered what she looked like beneath all the grim and bruises. Nevertheless, his closeness to her was the sweetest, sharpest thing he had ever experienced in his life. That she had just saved his life was something that he was very much aware of and grateful for.

"Sidney, are you all right?" Cornelius asked as he searched the crowd for any further threats, the gun pointed down but ready at his side.

"I've had better days." Sidney answered as he looked at the woman holding him and winked. "At least it ain't raining."

"Sidney is it?" Marta asked.

"Yes, Ma' am."

"I'm Marta." Her smile was warm and reassuring.

Achilles gave out a deep rolling laugh, which was part relief and part confusion, because buried beneath it lay an uncomfortable feeling caused by the way Marta looked at Sidney.

Things being what they were, Cornelius blanched at his lack of manners. Before he could introduce himself, Lavinia put a finger to his lip. "Inspector Cornelius McCann," she said. "I know who you are. You have stood outside my window under the gas street light many a night." Her smile melted his heart as he heard her name for the first time. "Lavinia."

Lavinia.

Her name was whispered from ear to ear throughout the waterfront and with each whisper the story of her bravery grew.

"Lavinia. I don't think I've ever heard a prettier name," Cornelius said, as he spotted Hiroshi's boat turning towards the women and children's wharf and a point closest to them. No one gave a damn about the Japanese or the Chinese as word spread across the waterfront of the heroic young Dutch woman who stopped the riot, brought down the malicious tyrant Rufus Crowley, as well as the monster Brubeck, while saving Inspector Cornelius McCann's life. Those closest had seen and knew of

Achilles' death match with Brubeck, but the magic of the story belonged to the beautiful Dutch girl. This was the moment the legend of the *Angel of the Waterfront* was born.

Cornelius motioned that it was okay for Hiroshi to come into the wharf.

Achilles helped Sidney to his feet. He was weak and shaky, and it would be some time before he would be able to stand on his own. The men surrounding them, who only a few moments before, were tearing at each other's throats, stood quiet, humbled, as they watched Lavinia and Marta help Cornelius and Sidney aboard the waiting fishing boat.

Watchful, Achilles stayed ashore keeping an eye out for anyone to make the slightest wrong move as Marta ran back onto the wharf to collect her two youngest sons.

All aboard, Hiroshi set sail for the Ferry Terminal.

Holding Lavinia close to his side, Cornelius looked back at his San Francisco, still ablaze, as it would be for some time to come. He looked at her, both her eyes now seeing him clearly, and understood that this special woman had just brought the first majestic breath of life . . . hope . . . back to his golden city.

CHAPTER 57

ORNELIUS WATCHED AS THE JAPANESE DIVERS PROVED TO
be more confident and skilled than Hiroshi had promised.
With the light fading, the shadows already deep, the three
women, Kameyo, Norika, and Yoshie, did not hesitate to drop
into the murky water that slapped back and forth within the ferry
basin. It was dangerous work; each slap of the tide brought in
more debris, and there was plenty more trapped within the
treacherous undercurrent. The stern of the Chinese junk was
completely submerged, wedged between two mussel-covered
pillars. The aft section of the boat was beginning to break apart
and it was not easily approachable because of the debris tangled
with the numerous ropes and mast lines that whipped around in
the current, like hungry eels. Under these conditions, two of the
divers had to enter the submerged cabin and hopefully find a
trapped pocket of air large enough to refill their lungs while they
unwrap and plant the dynamite.

No one knew much about fuses. Cornelius and Hiroshi had
cut and tested two fuses and now the women's lives were
dependent on a fuse that would burn long enough for them to
get out of the submerged wreck and back to the surface where
their husbands waited with lines to pull them out of the water
before the explosion.

Kameyo, was the first to enter the cabin. Inside, she found the
darkness she had expected, bleaker and more disturbing than
anything she had imagined. Now, she swam and felt her way
around the cabin until finally her hand broke the surface into a

black void still filled with enough air to feed her starving lungs. It was too dark to tell how big the air pocket was; it just needed to be large enough for the fuse to be lit.

Norika waited at the cabin's open portal with the carefully wrapped parcel of dynamite, enough sticky tar to attach it to wet wood, and five matches. Yoshie swam just outside, making sure none of the ropes and debris blocked their exit. To each of the women, the seconds seemed both eternal and brutally short, as it grew darker by the moment.

On the stern of the fishing boat Hiroshi held his own breath as he watched the divers air bubbles rise deceptively to the surface. He could not show it, but he was very much afraid that they had waited until it was too late. The two men next to him watched anxiously for their wives to surface, their arms reaching out anxiously for their life lines. To each man, the seconds seemed brutally short.

As they watched from midship, Lavinia held Cornelius, his strength still waning from his beating. Sidney lay nearby with his back and head supported by the mast beam and Marta, her two sons, young and excited, were held in check by Achilles. It was only the two boys who breathed while everyone else held tight in fear for the divers.

Kameyo gave three quick tugs on the fishing line she had tied around her wrist. It was the signal for Norika to follow the line and bring in the dynamite. Another few seconds and Norika would have had to break for the surface for air. Now, she swam forward, her skilled diver's lungs painfully close to depletion of life-giving oxygen.

In the dark it would take the two of them to plant the dynamite and light the fuse. There was no time for a mistake and no one had thought about fixing a second fishing line to help guide them out.

Hiroshi had been quietly counting the seconds since the women had first dropped into the water. He knew how many seconds Kameyo could stay under. She had not surfaced gasping for air so he concluded that she must be inside the sunken wreck. He closed his eyes and tried to imagine what she was doing, to encourage her to hurry but above all else to be careful. Had she found the air pocket, if there was one? Is the fuse long enough? His lips parted as he started to call out to her.

At first he thought it was another aftershock. The explosion seemed to happen in slow motion. First there was a giant bubble on the surface of the water. From its center rose a mighty geyser that exploded thirty feet into the air, followed by a thunderous boom that seemed to compress, then warp the air around them. One of the pillars supporting the wharf shattered. The bristling splinters incapable of supporting any weight, a large section of the wharf dropped towards the water only to be pushed up by a fountain of debris that had once been the sunken Chinese junk. The roar of the explosion echoed across the city, and then just as quickly, disappeared.

Debris rained down on the wharf, the crowd that had pushed right to the water's edge to watch, and the Japanese fishing boats that had been waiting for their divers to surface. A limp, lifeless rag doll, landed with the debris on the damaged wharf. Yoshie. Her husband closed his eyes, thanking her for her sacrifice as he bowed in farewell. Of the hundreds of people who had crowded the wharf to watch, nine lost their balance and fell into the basin. Their rescue became paramount; the loss of the Japanese women soon forgotten.

Hiroshi mourned for the loss of his wife quietly. She had been courageous and given her life for the greater good. Yes, he would miss her, but she was now with her honorable ancestors who would be proud of her bravery and self-sacrifice. He bowed slightly towards the water, then ordered the ship's crew to take the boat around the wharf to a place where Yoshie's husband could go ashore and claim his wife's body.

The other boats caste their nets into the basin to rescue those who had fallen in, and to pull the debris out of the way of the incoming ferry boat. Seeing that this was being done, Hiroshi turned and walked over to where Cornelius and Lavinia stood.

Lavinia's first instinct was to somehow comfort Hiroshi, his wife's loss so sudden and violent. Cornelius squeezed her hand giving her a quiet shush. Hiroshi bowed slow and formally as he stood before them. His eyes were moist, but he was a man in total control of his grief. Cornelius started to say how sorry he was but was interrupted before the words reached his lips as Hiroshi said, "No words, my friend, not here and not now. We Japanese have our own way of dealing with a loss such as this. Kameyo was very brave and will be missed. Now is not the time to grieve, for we must finish what she gave her life for. The ferry basin must be cleared of everything that can interfere with the ferry boats landing here. They must be allowed to come in and take all these people to a safer place. You are tired and have done much. It is time for you and your people to go ashore and to claim your rightful place on the first ferry boat that waits just over there."

"I . . ." Cornelius needed to speak.

Lavinia squeezed his hand.

Cornelius bowed saying, "It is our destiny that we will meet again."

CHAPTER 58

THOUGH THE BULLET HAD PASSED STRAIGHT THROUGH Sidney's shoulder he was still going to need a doctor's care. Everyone was exhausted; the shock of the divers' deaths still raw in the memories, balanced with the knowledge that they had cleared the ferry basin, allowing for tens of thousands to flee the raging fires. Cornelius said little as they waited for the ferry to take them to Berkeley, where Marta had told them that she had a cousin and a place for all of them to stay. That was all Cornelius needed, a place to lie down, to sleep as he had never slept before, and to wake up knowing that Lavinia was not a passing dream. He did not believe in angels and here he was falling for one.

"My Sven?" Marta asked. A mother's look of fear and worry for a lost child written across her face. She would not board the ferry without knowing that Sven is safe. She also could not stay because she had her younger sons to think about. It had been a very hard day and no one knew what other disasters might occur if they stayed any longer. How could she ask her cousin to take these people in if she was not with them? She looked at Sidney with tears building in her eyes. *What a wonderful man,* she thought. *It would be good for the boys to have a man about the house. Marta, what are you thinking?* She laughed. *What house?*

"Please," said Achilles, as he felt her concern. "I know where to find Sven. He is with Sergeant Pickens. They have arrested Sergeant Darcy and taken him to the nearest military authorities in what you call the Barbary Coast. I will find them and bring Sven to you. You give me address in Berplet. I will find you." He looked at Sidney for just a moment thinking: *this, I can do and you cannot. Marta needs a strong man, big like me. You get well, my friend and go tend to your horses.*

"It's Berkeley, Achilles . . . Berkeley." Cornelius pronounced the name of the city slow.

"Yes, Berkeley," Achilles answered. "The ferry boat is almost here, you must get onboard before someone else takes your place. I will go and find Sven and bring him to you, Marta."

CHAPTER 59

CHOICE PICKENS TURNED FRANK DARCY OVER TO THE ARMY, asking them to hold him on charges of conspiracy to kidnap five police officers and murder. Shanghaiing was a federal, as well as a maritime crime, over which the Navy had legal jurisdiction. Under Martial Law, the army had the authority. Choice did not care who hung Frank Darcy, just as long as he got hung.

The fire fighters around them had been staring at Frank Darcy. It is not that often you see a man with both knees shot out dragged towards a Navy ship. Their attention turned back toward the fire, but it was not the fire that had them all mouth agape. A man, his hair smoldering, his clothes more cinders than cloth had just walked out of the towering flames.

"What the hell, Henry?"

Henry Rabbitt walked straight out of a block of burning buildings. The tall cowboy, clearly suffering from burns, walked towards Pickens as if he hadn't a care in the world. That he was alive was no small miracle.

"You have no idea how good it is to see you." Henry said, his lips chapped raw from the heat, his left cheek an angry blister, its center black char, his eyebrows frizzled, the remains of his hair smoldering, his left ear looking much like a black shriveled apple core. What remained of his clothes still smoldering around his angry burns. "You wouldn't happen to have anything to drink, would you? Whisky would be my first preference, but I'll settle for water."

Captain Ralph Lafferty, who was now the ranking fire fighter after he had crossed through the ruins, rushed over to where Rabbitt, Sven, and Pickens were standing. "Get me a stretcher, now!" He bellowed. Two fire fighters with buckets of water followed close behind. Dowsing his smoldering clothes there was just enough water left in one of the buckets for Henry to drink; his blistered lips raw making it difficult.

"Sergeant, me and Sidney were ordered by Cornelius to bring two Jap fishermen from the ferry basin to the wharf where the rest of the Japs were camped out. The crowd turned ugly, one of the Japs was killed." Henry's speech grew slurred and hard to understand. "Sidney was shot. A lynch mob was about to go after the Chinese and the Japs so I rode out to get Marshal McCann. I couldn't ride through the mob so I rode in towards the fires hoping to circle around. I got caught in a box canyon of flaming buildings. I didn't see it coming, a goddamned building collapsed on me. My horse didn't make it. I couldn't do nothing to end its suffering. I walked out through blocks of fire, everything was burning but me. Now, that there is a story that will buy me a few free drinks in almost any bar." Henry's knees gave out on him at the same time his eyes rolled back.

Lafferty had two fire fighters carry Henry to the nearest Navy ship that had a dispensary. "I don't know how he came out of there alive," he said.

Sergeant Choice Pickens watched as Henry was carried away, thinking that for him to be alive was a sad thing; the pain must be unbearable.

Lafferty was glad to see Sergeant Pickens, but there was no time for small talk. At the moment, they were losing the battle against the fires and might have to pull the fire fighters and the Army out of the Barbary. That meant for the time being that there was no escape route from the ferry blocks through the Barbary.

His job done, Choice Pickens was anxious about what Henry had told them about the lynch mob. While he didn't much like Sidney he was now worried about the man. Sven was worried to a breaking point about his mom and little brothers. "Well, we had best be getting back. It sounds like all hell has broken loose back there.

"Wait, perhaps you should see this." Captain Lafferty pulled some folded papers from his breast pocket handing them to Choice.

Unfolding the documents Choice began to read. The bad news reflected in his eyes. "Is this true?"

"The first is a Federal Warrant for Cornelius McCann's arrest for conspiracy, racketeering, and breaking the Alien Exclusion Act. The second warrant charges him with first degree arson. The last two are for murder. It seems that someone has suggested that Cornelius started the fires in Chinatown. With these charges he has officially been released as a police officer and is to be arrested on sight. I doubt that Cornelius knows any of this." Lafferty cleared his throat. "Since Marshal Law has been declared, you might say that whether-or-not he is brought in alive or dead is optional."

Choice knew that all the charges were fabricated. Cornelius had made more than a few enemies over the years, some within the department, and quite a few at City Hall. He needed to get this to Cornelius before someone tried to take him in with a bullet through his back. "Mind if I keep these?" he asked, as he folded the papers, pocketing them.

The last words Lafferty heard as he watched Sergeant Pickens and Sven head back towards the path through the ruins were: "God damn, what next?"

CHAPTER 60

ACHILLES HAD JUST PASSED THROUGH THE RUINS OF THE OLD streetcar barns into the Barbary when an aftershock brought what was left of the brick ruins down in a loud dusty roar. There was now no safe passage left back to the waterfront surrounding the ferry basin. The truth was, that he did not know if there was a way around the fires that was scorching the Barbary Coast block by block. His mission was to find Sergeant Choice Pickens and Sven. He had promised Sven's mother, Marta, that he would find Sven and bring him safety to her. "Sven," he called out at the first sight of the men as he stumbled out of the ruins.

As the dust and ash cloud settled Sergeant Choice Pickens thought he saw an aberration, a wild bear, a monster that had crawled out of one of Hell's grottoes. "Achilles, you big stupid Greek, I thought I told you to . . ." Laughter overwhelmed the Sergeant before he could ream Achilles out for dereliction of duty. "Achilles, if there were a contest to find the dirtiest, ugliest, woe-begotten poor soul in this whole stricken city, I think you've just won it hands-down."

Sergeant Pickens swore that he could smell Achilles soon as he stepped out of the dust cloud. The first time he had met Achilles, the man had stunk of months at sea and poor hygiene. He knew that Achilles was ripe, something that couldn't be helped in these conditions, but this was beyond anything he could imagine.

Sven smelled it too, and knew that it had to be Achilles before he turned to greet him. He was glad to see the big man who he had come to think of like a father since they first met earlier in the day. True, it had been one long hard day, but no matter what was thrown at them, Achilles wore his heart on his sleeve and that had made an indelible impression on Sven, whose father had passed on two years prior.

Achilles' offensive odor was off the scale and potent enough to scare off a starving family of skunks. "Hold it right there, Achilles. You stay right where you are, while there is still a little breathable air between us," Choice ordered. "Achilles, I've got to tell you that I have never smelled anything as bad as you do right now."

Achilles stopped, held up in arms and sniffed. "Hee, Hee! I no smell very good." He looked around at all the men who had stopped what they were doing to gape at him. Those closest were laughing, but they were laughing at him not with him. He dropped his grin feeling very much the fool."

"What the hell happened?" Choice asked.

With his strong Greek accent, the information that flooded out of Achilles' mouth was not easy to understand. "Inspector McCann, he and the Japanese got the ferries running. He and the women folk have gone to a place called Berkeley. Mr. Sidney, he was shot, but he be okay. There were many angry men who wanted to murder all the Chinese . . . Japanese too. Inspector McCann was beaten to the ground and could not get up. I fought man big as me before he kill McCann. It was not me but a beautiful woman whose words brought peace that saved Inspector McCann's life."

"Whoa, slow down Achilles," pleaded Pickens.

"Sven, your mama wants you to go to Berkeley where you find her at her cousin's house. I come to take you back." Achilles glanced back at the collapsed streetcar barn. "Sergeant Pickens, you know another way to this Berkeley?"

That was a lot to take in and Choice had more than a few questions. Getting intelligent answers out of Achilles was all together another thing. It wasn't that the big Greek was country stupid, he was bright and a quick learner, but he lacked street smarts and a decent handle on the English language. Choice crossed his arms ands said, "I'm still waiting . . . How did you become the filthiest, worse smelling excuse for a human being that ever crossed the Barbary Coast?"

"On the way here, I took a short cut behind the field kitchen. Too many people, I go around. I found where the Chinese had dumped all the fish guts, the goat and steer hides. I think every fly in the city meet and party there. I slipped and fell into this.

I tried to jump off the wharf to wash but I would not have been able to climb out. It getting dark so I hurry here to find you."

Captain Ralph Lafferty, San Francisco Fire department, who had been talking with Sergeant Perkins, nearly keeled over laughing.

"It not so bad, I get used to it. I will wash when we get to this Berkeley," Achilles said, thoroughly embarrassed.

Choice understood that the big Greek was humiliated, and it was time to do something about that. "Captain Lafferty, how far will that high pressure water gun on that ship shoot?"

Lafferty looked up at the water stream that was trained on a roof fire across the street. The fire captain walked out to the middle of the street and said, "Right about here."

"Achilles, you go and stand right where the Captain is. When I tell you to, you close your eyes and hold your arms up high over your head."

Achilles did as he was told.

While he stood there waiting, Captain Lafferty called up to the ship's bow and the men operating the water gun. They dialed down the pressure the best they could. A moment later a stream of water hit Achilles head on, and if he hadn't weighed nearly three hundred pounds, he would have been knocked to the ground and spun away like soggy tumbleweed. Achilles appeared in his own comical ballet as he was blasted and spun around in the powerful torrent of water until most if not all the fish guts, ash, and mud and his suit of rags had been stripped clean. The water stream was turned back to the roof fire as Achilles shook his head as a mangy dog might after having been caught in a torrential rainstorm. The firefighters, Navy, Army, and civilian volunteers had hooted and catcalled all the time Achilles had been under the current of water. The laughter that had begun to fall away, returned at higher level. The pressurized water had stripped away everything, leaving Achilles standing alone in the middle of the street, the fires that lit the night revealing a wet, hairy, naked albino gorilla. Albino? In time his skin would go back to its pale origin, for now he was a raw pink.

There were no spare clothes to be had, and if any were to be found none Achilles' size. There were still a few women around, many who were listed in the cities records as seamstresses - a polite term used to give a working girl a legitimate sounding job. It was amazing how many seamstresses found their way to the Barbary Coast.

Bettina B, a large flamboyant redhead, a good twenty years too old to find work as a seamstress, although she had been there and done that, came to Achilles' rescue. "Hold on there, big man, this is no time to be swinging your glory while Rome is burning in all hers." Bettina carried with her two white table cloths she had taken from a shattered window of a neighboring hippodrome and a sewing kit. "My, my, just look at you, it's not that often I get to see a man as big as you in his birthday suit." Bettina laughed as she wrapped a table cloth around him. "I think I underestimated, you're a three table cloth man aren't you."

Choice Pickens recognized Bettina B as the backstage costume designer for the Bella Union. She was a real seamstress who designed, pulled together, and patched up the many theatrical costumes the girls wore in the popular stage shows that had made the Bella Union and other hippodromes famous. The Bella Union was on Kearny, not quite on the Barbary Coast, and Choice could see by the fires that it was already history. The Bella Union's last poorly done show had been back in 1893. Since then, a penny arcade had occupied the front; a waxworks in the rear. Bettina B, stayed on as a live-in caretaker, earning a meager living patching costumes for other stage and burlesque shows. It occurred to Choice that Bettina B's last production might be Achilles' comic opera.

The fires consuming Chinatown, the Financial District, and Little Italy were pressing in on the Barbary, giving the Navy little choice but to begin the evacuation of all civilian firefighters and refugees. A rough count suggested that there were between four to five hundred people that needed to get out - and this had to be by land - and soon, before the fires took away their last escape route.

"Sergeant Pickens," Captain Lafferty said, "first I'm going to apologize unreservedly for what I'm about to ask you to do. We need someone with authority to take the evacuation column out of here. As far as I know, you are the last and only policeman left in the Barbary. The column is yours, and for that I'm sorry.

You're sorry, my aching ass is sorry. It did not matter how much he bitched and moaned he was a sworn officer of the law. "Do I have a choice?"

"No, you don't," Lafferty said, "and neither do I. The Navy is in charge. My orders are to stay here with the Navy and what few firemen I have and try to save this little part of paradise. I've always thought that if the world needed an enema, the Barbary Coast would be a good place to start. I wish I could just let her burn, but I'm a fireman . . . and you, sir, are an officer of the law. Congratulations, like the Pied Piper, you get to lead the rats out of hell."

"How many, and where to?" Choice studied the ruined streetcar barns. "We sure as hell are not going to go back through there."

Lafferty nodded towards the opposite direction. "The only way left out, is along the wharfs until you reach Van Ness. There are places the fire is burning dangerously close to the water's edge. If one of the wharves goes up that will be it, it will burn hot as Haiti until the bay waters have their final say. That said, time is something you don't have much of. One more thing I think you ought to know. The area is built up over unstable landfill. Back in the gold rush, ships were abandoned, sunk, and buried in place. There are dozens of ships buried all along the waterfront. How stable that whole area is after the quake, I can't tell you. I'll put it this way, I'm glad it's you going and not me leading this band of fools and seamstresses." Seamstress was a polite term for whores of all classes.

"Thanks. Remind me to have you buy a few rounds of drinks when this is all over." For the first time, Choice was glad to have

Achilles back and close at his side. For the moment, Bettina B had Achilles tucked away in some corner as she outfitted him in table cloths. Then there was Sven. All Choice had was a big dumb Greek and a kid, to herd drunks, dancehall girls, seamstresses, cutthroats and card sharks, stevedores, musicians, cooks, able seamen trapped ashore, and a few crimps who had been too chicken to get out with the other shanghaiers when they had the chance. "How many?" he asked again.

"It's not that bad, last count I had was sixty-three. By now, you might have seventy-five to eighty. Oh, and that is including a handful of criminals we've got chained up back there." Lafferty knew exactly what Pickens was thinking. "And that includes Frank Darcy."

Choice cracked a knuckle as he thought about having to carry Darcy out. His mind flashed over a dozen ways to drown, shoot, or let the fires have him, but in the end, he knew that with six or seven dozen witnesses that was not in the cards.

Lafferty could guess what he was thinking.

"From what you tell me, things are too risky to try to carry someone out. I'll not have my column put in danger by someone who can't stand on his own two feet. Darcy stays here, the Navy can take him out, or you can feed him to the sharks."

"None of the ships have much of a dispensary," Lafferty said. "The truth is that word's gotten out about Darcy and frankly, the Navy does not want him either. I wouldn't be surprised if there isn't a betting pool already in the works regarding how long Darcy will last under your tender care."

Choice considered it. "Did you bet? I might be able to help you make an easy buck." Lafferty did not answer, nor did Choice expect him to. "How many on the chain-gang?"

"Nine" Lafferty answered. "Last I heard we had five looters, one for attempted rape, one for arson, if you can believe that, one crimp, and then there's Darcy. All of them were arrested under the Martial Law order, so you can turn them over to the Army if or when you get to the Presidio."

There was one man Pickens couldn't leave behind. "Henry?"

"Henry? Oh, you mean the cowboy who walked in out of the fires. From what I saw, he is too badly burned to be taken out with you. He would never make it. How he walked out of those burning buildings alive, I don't know. While he stood tall and delivered his report he was nevertheless in shock. I've seen burn victims, and I'm not giving Henry very good odds. When we delivered him to the Pharmacist Mate on the ship he took one look and said that if Henry can survive until morning they'll try to get him out on the first ship headed back to the Vallejo Shipyard where they have a hospital. For right now, all they can do is keep him cool and hydrated. They don't have any ointments for the burns. There is nothing more they can do for him.

Bettina B was still tucking and pinning as Achilles stepped out of his make shift dressing room in the corner of a partially collapsed bar. His image bordered on theatrical, which Bettina B's work usually did. She had dressed him in white cotton cut from common table cloths. He wore a long loose fitting tunic with a slit on both sides at waist level, and a sleeveless cloak. This fell, over loose white cotton pants that tapered just an inch above his ankles. This was finished with a wide red cloth belt that had come from the bar's curtain. A white skull cap perched on top of his full head of thick black hair brought Choice Pickens' attention to his broad full face with the black caterpillar eyebrows, brown puppy dog eyes, and a full beard that Bettina B had somehow been able to trim into a respectable cut. Achilles might have been able to pass for a Moroccan Sheik, if he had not insisted on keeping his well-worn and soggy deck boots. Tucked between the belt and the cloak on his right side was a 27 inch iron lanced whaling harpoon.

Choice gave an incredulous laugh.

Captain Lafferty swallowed his laugh, finishing it with a big grin. "I suggest you put our Arab Sheik at the end of your column. I'm sure he will be able to prod any slackers into a quicker step with that harpoon. Where the hell did you get that Achilles?"

"It was hanging on a wall in the saloon," answered Bettina B as she finished her last tuck and stepped back to admire her work.

"I no stink so much now do I, Sergeant?" Achilles asked as he stepped up to the police and fire officers and saluted with the wrong hand. "We go to Berkeley now? Sven's mama is waiting." The look in Achilles eyes suggested that returning a lost son to his mother was not his only motive.

"Why, Achilles, if I didn't know better, I'd think that you might just have a hankering for the woman. What is her name again?"

Sven started to answer.

Achilles beat him to it. "Marta. She very good woman. I think she has eyes for Mr. Sidney - but he is wounded and her nurse's heart worries about him too much. I go to Berkeley soon to show her that I am better man. Ahh, that I bring Sven to her as promised."

"Attention everyone who can hear my voice, everyone still remaining in the area known as the Barbary Coast. This is

Lieutenant Frederick Freeman, United States Navy. The city of San Francisco is now under Martial Law and I am the Senior Commanding Officer of the waterfront. All civilians are to be evacuated immediately. Your destination is the United States Army Base at the Presidio. You will be guided there by a San Francisco Police Officer. You are to follow his instructions to the letter. Anyone disrupting the safe passage of this column will be shot." The Lieutenant looked down from the bow of his ship where he stood with a bullhorn in hand. "Captain Lafferty, San Francisco Fire department will be looking for volunteers to stay and man the fire lines. If Captain Lafferty selects you to volunteer, you will volunteer. Any questions?" He did not wait for an answer. "Good. Everyone will form up in the street in columns of four, women first. Now, not five minutes from now. As for luggage, if you cannot carry it you cannot bring it. No rolling trunks, carts, carriages, or items that cannot be carried by one person. You are going out along the waterfront docks and we do not know what hazards may be in the way. A Navy fireboat will be following your progress from just off shore and will target high pressure sea water as needed. Captain Lafferty select your volunteers; this fire waits for no one.

CHAPTER 61

SERGEANT CHOICE PICKENS LOOKED BACK AT HIS RAG-TAILED column of refugees, bums, and criminals. A sorrier lot he couldn't remember. He fought back the urge to laugh at the thought that he had just become the Pied Piper to the worst flock of rats the Barbary Coast could offer. The chuckle died in his throat with the further thought that this very well might be his last official act as a police offer for the once great city of San Francisco, which, based on the fires baring down on them would cease to exist in a matter of hours, one or two days at best.

Captain Lafferty shook his hand and wished Sergeant Pickens well, then waved to a Navy fireboat just off shore, that the column was ready. The powerful water guns on the boat were cranked up as the boat prepared to add a water screen wherever possible as they attempted to beat the fires that were threatening to burn right down to the water's edge.

Pickens waved at Sven who guarded the middle of the column. Sven turned and waved to Achilles who held up the rear of the column. Seeing that the column was about to move out, he yanked the chain-gang of criminals they were forced to take along, to their feet. They were rough and uncooperative, nothing that Achilles, with his size and strength, couldn't handle. There was one man missing. Sergeant Pickens had refused to take charge of the column if Frank Darcy was aboard. The navy doctor, having done his best to stop Darcy's bleeding, refused to keep him aboard ship. Frank Darcy was to be left behind. On a makeshift stretcher, Darcy was placed at the land's end of a fishing pier, where he could watch the column and his last chance for escape march by. The Navy was fighting a losing battle with the fires, it was understood that once the refugee column was out, the navy's commanding officer could order the ships withdrawn to fight the fires somewhere they might do some good.

Pickens eyed Darcy one last time as he fingered his sidearm.

If there was a chance that Darcy could live to see another day he was prepared to finish him right now regardless of the witnesses.

Darcy was a pitiful sight, both knees shattered and wrapped in bandages that showed his bleeding had not entirely stopped. He was pale from the loss of blood, and despite the pain he returned a look of pure hatred through his dark shadowed, red-rimmed eyes. Pickens spat at Darcy, then turned away. He was not going to lower himself to Darcy's level. "Okay, Bettina B, let's get this show on the road."

Bettina had wanted to stay with Achilles at the end of the column. She was a big woman who needed a big man, and despite an age difference, she was determined to test her womanly wiles on her well-costumed Greek. She, of course, did not know that Achilles had his eyes set on another woman, who waited for him in a place called Berkeley. Sergeant Pickens argued that Achilles needed his full attention on the prisoners and the rear of the column. Finally, to his own embarrassment, Pickens had to sweet talk Bettina B to get her to come with him to the front of the column under his personal protective custody.

The powerful streams of water from the fireboat went into action cooling the air and dousing any flaming embers that rained down on them as they began their trek towards Van Ness Avenue and perhaps the Army Presidio.

A small aftershock reminded Pickens that this was not going to be a simple walk in the park. A strong southwestern gale pushed at them as they moved out of sight of the firefighters. The wind was hot, laden with red and white hot cinders that caught easily wherever they landed, which included hats, clothing, and hair. The curve of the shoreline drew them farther away from the fire boat's spray. Thick cloying smoke choked their lungs, stinging and watering their eyes, as the column struggled to stay together. The wind, heat borne, created by the massive force of the fires, pushed back the streams of water sprayed at them from the fireboat. What water reached them, felt like a hot tropical squall, steaming, cutting off their breath. The desire to turn and run was evident in every cough and set of bloodshot eyes.

The shoreline consisted of a narrow cobblestone street that ran between menacing wooden warehouses ready to burst into flame, and rickety old fishing piers, many of which had not fared well during the great quake. The cobblestone street was crisscrossed with multiple fractures and sinkholes that gave them reason for caution with each step.

The shadows grew deep as the sunset died in a plume of death-black smoke. A waning crescent moon played a feeble game of hide-and-seek, providing little light for the rapidly darkening night that cloaked the bay. It would be the fires that would light their way.

How am I supposed to get eighty panicky people through this? Choice muttered beneath his breath, as he slapped at his left cheek where a hot ember had landed leaving an angry red singe.

Bettina B went into a sudden crazed dance as a flurry of growing red embers flittered and darted around her, as if they were an angry flock of fireflies, with the sting of yellow jackets. Her hat caught fire. She shrieked. Additional shrieks rose from the crowd as the red hot embers and gray ash began to resemble a mid-winter snow squall only with no danger of frost bite. The air, hot, thick with smoke, became hard to breath.

Sergeant Pickens remembered reading about Pompeii and how the people had died there. While there was no volcano, the building firestorm was becoming just as deadly. Just as quick as the spark had caught and landed he unpinned Bettina B's burning hat and flung it in to the bay, Pickens examined their options. There were few. They could not outrun the fire and equally deadly smoke. And even if they could, where? They could not turn back because the wind driven storm of sparks and glowing ashes was worse behind them. The roofs of several warehouses were already aflame.

Pickens stopped dead in his tracks. Just ahead was the large Tubbs Cordage Company warehouse. Tubbs was a major manufacturer of industrial and nautical rope. The company's name was painted in large blue letters facing the waterfront, and a wharf where the raw hemp and abaca fiber was brought in from the Philippines and the Yucatan, for sorting and cleaning. The huge warehouse was made of weather-worn wood. Once caught, there was nothing that would keep the fire from spreading throughout the building. When it went up, it would explode, burn hot and fast, searing and sucking the very air from their lungs. Pickens knew that if they stayed where they were now they were good as dead.

He looked through tearing bloodshot eyes at the fireboat just off shore. The boat had come in as close as it could, its plume of water falling short, dousing the wharf, offering little protection to Pickens' pitiful column of refugees - eighty people under his protection that would die in the next few minutes if he didn't recognize and grab ahold of a miracle when he needed one.

He slapped at a hot ember that landed in his hair, scorching a patch just above his right ear. He thought about herding his people out onto the wharf beneath the fireboats spray. It wouldn't be enough, when the warehouse went up, either the explosion would get them, or they would suffocate as the fire drew all the good air. If only the fireboat could put out more water and reach the warehouse. *Water? That's it*, he thought, *we need to get into the water beneath the wharf. The tide is low, it will be some hours before it gets high enough to drown anyone. The fireboat can get closer with the tide. If it can keep the wharf from catching fire and burning over our heads, we might just might make it.*

Pickens cupped his hands over his mouth and yelled as loud as he could. "Sven, Achilles, get everyone beneath the wharf. The tide is low, you won't drown. If we stay here, we will fry." He pointed at the warehouse.

Sven did not need to be told twice, the option had already crossed his mind. He did not waste time waving back or getting a consensus from his brood of mostly dancing girls and younger working women - seamstresses, an odd name for the work they did. The muck was thick, but the dancing girls had strong legs; they waded in with the fire reinforcing their determination. As they crowded under the wharf, Sven could see that Sergeant Pickens was having trouble moving his flock through the muck.

"This way ladies, we'll bypass this lot and find our own place a little deeper in the water farther from the fire." They worked their way just outside the shadow of the wharf until the water was almost too deep for some of the smaller girls, where Sven brought them all beneath the wharf telling them to all hold hands to keep each other on their feet. The women held each other close with Sven in the middle.

WHOOSH! The cordage warehouse caught, a swirling devilish funnel of flame erupted through its roof rising hundreds of feet above them. Even those who could not swim did not hesitate to follow Sergeant Pickens deeper into the gloomy protective water beneath the wharf.

The fireboat blew a long whistle acknowledging their plight.

There wasn't much else they could do but stand by until the tide could bring them in closer. At the moment, their spray barely reached the wharf and there was serious concern that the wharf would burn leaving those beneath in dire straits.

The first unexpected obstacle was the muck. The wharf was built over landfill not sand. The moment they waded into the water the black gooey sludge drew their feet deeper relieving many of their shoes. One amply endowed, petite woman, panicked, tried to turn back to shore, fell, taking the woman behind her down into the muck with her. It took Choice Pickens, Bettina B, and four others to wrestle them from the muck. At another time, their tar-baby appearances might have bought some serious laughs - nothing was funny as eighty scared, if not terrified, people were driven by the horrific firestorm growing around them, into the sucking muck beneath the dark wharf. The mussel and shell covered wharf pilings added additional danger as people reached out for them for support, cuttings hands, shoulders, anything that brushed against them in the gloom.

Finally, Sergeant Pickens bellowed that everyone was to take each other's hands, firmly using their combined strength to overcome the muck that had all but stopped them in their tracks. One slow excruciating step at a time he guided them deeper into the gloom where the smell of salt and foul sea debris mixed with the smoke and human odor that came with exhaustion and fear;

the strength, heat, and stress enough to cause more than one to vomit. The water was cold, the muck beneath unrelenting, as they forced themselves deeper beneath the wharf until they reached water deep enough to protect them from the rising heat coming from the inferno ashore.

Achilles had no choice but to unlock the leg shackles on the prisoners before they dropped into the muck. Once beneath the wharf, it was too dark and chaotic to tell who was who. Achilles and his prisoners were the last in, the heat scorching their backs as they tried to force their way through the prostitutes and working girls who made up much of the tail end of the column. Many of the women were in a panic. Some of the girls knew the men and told them to bugger-off. And bugger-off they did. While Achilles tried to calm and move them deeper beneath the wharf, the prisoners disappeared. It wasn't until they were all packed tightly in the slowly rising water, as deep as they could go, that Achilles realized that his prisoners had taken flight.

The heat rose, the smoke thickened.

The flickering yellow-white light cast from the burning warehouse was too frightening to look at, or to look away. The cold bay water rose and fell, gently pushing, and pulling, their feet unsteady in the sucking bay bottom. It rose just above their knees - for now; for some crowded deepest beneath the wharf the water was up to their waists, the water bone shivering cold, the air hot and foul. Most were thirsty without a drop to drink.

Sergeant Choice Pickens held on to Bettina B as she cried on his shoulder, while he quietly tried to counsel his own fears. The fire raged so close it felt like the vibrating rumblings of an old steam boiler.

SsssBlamm!" The warehouse exploded.

The wharf above them groaned pitifully.

MOOoob! The towering flames drew back as the building collapsed in on itself.

The planks nearest landfall tore free, rising with the nearby blast as the end of the wharf closest to shore collapsed. Three of the women nearest Achilles were crushed before a single scream could be uttered. Achilles shoved one woman and a skinny bartender out of the way as a large wooden crossbeam smashed down just an arm's length from them. Had they not fallen into the black tar-like muck a blast of superheated air would have killed them just as easy as the massive beams and hardwood decking that crashed down around them. Fourteen, men and women alike, were not so lucky as the broiling blast of air blistered their faces, scorched their hair, and cooked their lungs, to die the next moment, as their lungs filled with cold muck and their last scream fell silent; the last horrible two seconds of life. A second massive section of the wharf collapsed, deflecting the deadly heated air from killing them all. Ten died beneath the debris.

"Cover your ears," Pickens screamed, as he dropped Bettina B's hands and covered his ears. "Hold on!"

Yoooeeess! The shrill wind being drawn into the vortex of the explosion penetrated their brains, overwhelming all other sounds, including their screams, as they fought the excruciating pain that erupted in their heads, quickly seizing control of their lungs as their life's breath was sucked from them becoming part of the screeching wind being drawn into the maelstrom.

The wharf behind them collapsed, its impact throwing out a three to four foot wave of cold water, muck, and debris which swamped them. Chunks of the wharf carried by the wave struck some, the wave taking others, leaving the rest floundering. It had only taken seconds, no one having a chance to react other than to the excruciating pain in their heads and lungs emptied of life giving oxygen.

YOOEEI…ieee . . . ssssh! Supppp.

Silence. The silence that can only exist within a vacuum.

Sergeant Pickens could see Bettina B's face as she floundered in the rapidly retreating surf. He could not hear her scream, nor the screams of those around him. Nor the bay as the water drew away from them. Nor the groaning remains of the wharf as it threatened to collapse entirely. Time stopped, not one breath could be taken. Death reached out to them with an unfathomable silent vibration. There was a blinding flash as one last explosion erased the remains of the warehouse, the blast so powerful it extinguished itself.

A surreal darkness wrapped itself around the silence, as the underside of what remained of the wharf above them rose, then fell haphazardly back on its remaining pillars leaving the survivors in almost coal mine darkness.

Choice felt the pain lift from him as he rose from the depths of the stillness, the muck releasing him, his head breaking its surface with a mighty gasp. He felt rather than saw Bettina B's hand as it surfaced, waving frantically for help. His hand grasped hers, pulling her free, the white of her eyes barely visible in the gloom were wide with fear and gratitude in being alive. She vomited a second before she could gasp in her first breath.

Sven and the women who held onto him, or he them, heard and felt the same mind numbing shrill, only the collapse of the wharf behind them acted as a buffer for most of it. It was too dark to see the wave coming. It took them, spinning and clinging to each other, out through the last dark ruins of what remained of the wharf - the mussel-covered pilings shaving off some of the women who were unfortunate enough to be on the outside of their spiraling human ring. The wave carried them out into the bay where clouds of dense smoke hung close to the surface. No one could tell where they were, where they were going, where land was, or what threats lay ahead of them. The wave carried them further out into the bay, the body fat of the women helping to keep them afloat.

It was their screams that told the crew of the fireboat that they were perilously close to running them over.

That they had somehow survived, was not the first thing Achilles thought about. Few of the people in his care survived the superheated airburst and the collapse of the wharf. He was surrounded with death and debris, with a small window of flickering light showing him a way. When he had first brought his head out of the muck, he struggled to catch a breath, finding more air being driven from his lungs than coming in. Nearly blinded by a shrill wave of pain in his head, he used his massive reserve of strength to lift himself from the muck, pulling first the young woman and the skinny bartender from where they struggled next to him towards the window of flickering light. It was only when they emerged from beneath the ruins and caught their first breaths, did Achilles realize that they had survived.

The fireboat maneuvered through the burning debris looking for survivors.

The ferry boat docked in Berkeley releasing their first load of exhausted, frazzled, refugees, most who had no idea where they were to go from here. Most had lost everything. There were to be many more ferries to come.

Once ashore, supported by Lavinia, Cornelius took a moment to look back towards the still visible flames that consumed San Francisco. "Choice, old buddy," he said as if the wind itself would carry his message, "soon as I catch my breath I'll be back for you."

Marta tearfully held onto her two remaining sons, fearing that she had lost Sven.

Lavinia heard Cornelius's words, and knew that he would go back. If she truly wanted to keep her man, she would go with him.

The end of a very long day